...IT HAPPENS!

To Good Friends
Jane & Bob
Hope you get a
few laughs

Ed

...IT HAPPENS!

A novel by

Edward A. Zanchi

Writers Club Press
New York Lincoln Shanghai

...IT HAPPENS!

Writers Club Press
an imprint of iUniverse, Inc.

For information address:
iUniverse, Inc.
2021 Pine Lake Road, Suite 100
Lincoln, NE 68512
www.iuniverse.com

ISBN: 0-595-25924-3

Printed in the United States of America

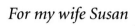
For my wife Susan

MAN PLANS,
GOD LAUGHS,
…IT HAPPENS!

CHAPTER 1

A stiff breeze blew across the Atlantic and the mighty ocean kissed the luxury liner, rolling it gently, while three decks below Bruno was in a fight for his life. It was the last night of the fateful cruise and, at the celebration in the main banquet room, Al sipped his twelve-year-old scotch and watched the scantily clad young ladies perform their Las Vegas review. Unaware that his oldest son was locked in mortal combat, accompanied by his youngest son and lovely wife, all was right with the world. Well, almost all. His tranquility was in sharp contrast to Mary's dark mood as she clutched her double Chivas, straight up, until her knuckles turned white. From the strangely unfamiliar, almost desperate, look in her eyes, she was obviously fighting the urge to devour her drink, as she had done with the first.

A casual observer might think she had a severe drinking problem or was suffering from extreme shock. The first was a conclusion that could not be further from the truth. In reality, she was the next thing to a teetotaler and normally strained to finish one, relatively weak, pina collada. Up to this moment, she could not stand the taste, or even the smell, of scotch and not more than a few lonely drops had ever made their way past her lovely lips. However, the latter conclusion was a definite possibility; this had been an exciting cruise to say the least. The strain of the last few days had apparently taken its toll on an otherwise mild mannered, gentle woman. A woman who possessed an inner strength that had allowed her to weather her share of storms with a quiet composure that provided a bedrock for the rest of the family.

Concerned by his wife's abnormal behavior, Al asked, "Are you all right, Mary?"

"Oh, I'm just great considering my youngest son got mugged by those brutes today, Jennifer has wandered off again—God only knows what close calls our innocent young daughter has had on this cruise from the netherworld, and Bruno promised he would be back a half-hour ago. So you can see that I am just ducky—you putz!" Mary fired back as she took another gulp of her drink. It was not at all like her to be this short with Al or to use such language.

"Careful, Mary, we aren't alone. Besides, except for a few bumps on B.J., we are all none the worse for wear. Right Ace?" Al tried the best he could to lighten the mood by bringing their youngest son, Brandon Joseph, alias B.J., into the conversation.

"Ya, Ma! Those guys didn't hurt me and, besides, this is the best vacation I have ever had." Then B.J. added with enthusiasm, "Ma, what's a putz?"

Al then realized he should have left his son out of it. "Never mind, B.J., just drink your beer and watch the show."

"That's great, Al! Teach our son to drink beer and become a womanizer. What's next, a 'cat house'?" Mary growled.

"Now, Mary, you know that it is non-alcoholic beer and this is just a little song and dance show," Al said calmly.

"The only thing little about this show is the outfits that those beautiful young tarts are almost wearing."

"Ya!" B.J. sighed as he gaped at the exposed derrieres of the dancing girls. "But Ma, don't worry, I don't like cats. What's a tart?"

"See what I mean," Mary retorted.

Al knew when he was beat. "Yes, dear."

"Don't give me that condescending attitude. You have to admit that this was an extremely trying experience for a mother," Mary's voice was softening. "And I am still worried about our other two; I wish they were here with us."

"Yes, I understand." Al was all too aware of the potential problems that their two other children could be getting into.

First, there was the matter of their fifteen-year-old daughter, Jennifer, who was out there somewhere having fun. That's right having fun, much too much fun to suit Al or any other respectable, responsible father. She had fallen in with a group of other young teenagers who had taken over control of the ship. Well, if not the entire ship, at least the best lounge and the only pool on board, and it took them less than two days to accomplish this. Which is all the more amazing when you realize that the ring leaders are cute little fourteen and fifteen year-old girls with sweet, innocent, names like Melissa, Nicole, Julie, Tina, and Jennifer. Take their daughter Jennifer, for example, she is a good student, a ballet dancer, a cheerleader, and a soccer player. She has a vibrant, open personality, but she's not wild, not normally anyway, though you would never know it by her conduct on this cruise. Since boarding ship, six days ago, she has gone through some form of metamorphosis, a Dr. Jekyll and Mr. Hyde transformation.

There are a total of seventy-five of these teenagers on the ship which, considering there are over fourteen hundred passengers, clearly puts them in the minority. However, they are a well-organized, finely tuned machine, with the stamina that goes with their age and makes them a formidable force. Because of their natural bond, it took them less than two days to seek each other out, become acquainted, and plan their method of attack. By the second evening, their strategic plan was complete; they had their operation in full swing and were ready to move in. Mary and Al were having a drink in the relatively upbeat lounge when it happened.

They had been sitting in the large lounge area in the front of the ship having a drink, getting bored. Although there were a considerable number of people there, it was not very lively. In fact, it was a morgue.

Mary gave Al a sarcastic look, "Most of the people here seem to be enjoying this music. Of course most of them are a bit older than we are; their favorite entertainers being Fred and Ginger."

"You can be a tough woman, Mary, but you're right. I expect to see Lawrence Welk come out and start counting; I swear, if I see bubbles in the background I'm jumping ship."

Mary now gave Al her pleading look, "If we stay here any longer I'm going to fall to sleep or kill myself, I'm not sure which."

"Again, you're right. It's time to leave this to the Ballroom Set. I think that we should try the lounge in the back of the ship. Finish your drink and we'll follow the standard directions of one down, one over, and one up or one up, one over, and one down."

This drew a dirty look from Mary, she was getting tired of hearing: "one up, one over, and one down or one down, one over, and one up" from every Master of Ceremonies, comedian, and speaker on the ship, including the Captain. You see the ship had been enlarged a few years ago by cutting it in half, sticking a piece in the middle and welding the new middle together with the original ship ends. This was done in such a way that you could not go from one end of the ship to the other on the middle deck, thus giving rise to this rather annoying little comment that seemed to be repeated ad nauseam. What concerned Al about this little engineering feat was how safe it would be in rough weather. In fact, he believed that this was one of the main reasons for the establishment of the special crew designated as the "Portly Humans Allocation Team", alias PHAT squad. As Al learned from his oldest son, the purpose of this special detail was to make sure all the really heavy individuals were properly distributed throughout the ship at all times. This was a very important function since a cruise attracts people who love to eat and proper weight distribution was critical on a ship that had been cut in two and then glued back together.

As they walked into the new lounge, they were greeted by the sounds of 'Midnight Hour' and knew they were in the right place.

"Now this is more like it," Mary said as they found a table a little out of the way.

"This music is right up your alley, you're still a dyed in the wool rocker at heart," Al responded.

"I know, but you have to admit it's a lot better than that other lounge," Mary replied, "and you're right, unlike you, I haven't graduated to John Denver and Neil Diamond yet and, heaven help me, I hope I never will."

"Let's not get nasty now, I like this music, too. At least we fit into the average age of this group."

Al and Mary settled in to what had the possibilities of a romantic evening and ordered their usual drinks; a pina collada for Mary and Chivas on the rocks for Al.

As Al sipped his drink and listened to the music, he couldn't help but notice how attractive Mary looked and began to feel this cruise did have romantic possibilities after all. Although rapidly approaching forty, an age well beyond what American advertisers would have us believe a person is capable of looking and feeling good, Mary was a vibrant and attractive woman who was fully capable of being very sensuous and exciting. Sitting there looking at her now, Al realized that one characteristic that he appreciated most was her sophistication.

It was while he was letting his mind wander, getting lost in what might be, when he noticed it. At first, it looked very innocent; a few of the young girls came in and took up a position in a booth near the far entrance. Then another group came in through the entrance next to Mary and Al and seated themselves on the bar stools, ordering cokes all around. Simultaneously, from the back portion of the lounge, shrouded in darkness, a number of boys in groups of two, three, and four simply materialized. It was like having a fifth column quietly planted inside the lounge that was now fanning out and occupying the best tables around the dance floor, mixing with the girls.

Al observed the infiltration of the lounge by the young people with growing apprehension. He commented to Mary, "I'm beginning to feel the average age getting younger and younger."

Having established a beachhead, other groups of teenagers began pouring in through both entrances and taking over the dance floor with a ferocity that would have made Attila the Hun proud. Al half expected to see a group of them plant a flag reminiscent of Iwo Jima.

Then he felt a chill go up his spine, and the hairs on the back of his neck began to prickle, as he heard the words that finished this as a romantic setting for good. "Hi Mom! Hi Dad!" Jennifer bubbled as she came by their table with three of her friends, all of them overflowing with enthusiasm.

"I thought you were going to the 'Moon Deck' room that was reserved for you teenagers," Al said as he took a long sip of his drink. A very long sip—make that a gulp!

"Oh, that was too small and too dull for us," she quickly replied, with the obvious consensus of her friends.

You could see the adults start to feel uncomfortable, realizing they had rapidly become the minority, so they started to filter out as unobtrusively as possible. The walls were closing in and the window of time for escape was rapidly approaching. It was an awesome display of coordinated teamwork, combined with tremendous psychological warfare, intended to make the adults feel out of place. It worked magnificently, making them feel very old and just wanting to pick up their canes and hobble out as inconspicuously as possible.

"All of a sudden I feel older! Much older! And grayer! I think I'm getting arthritis or something. Is this what it's like to turn forty-five?" Mary said.

"I'll ignore that sarcastic remark wise guy," Al responded. "I think this is more like you would feel just before open heart surgery. Or maybe after it."

"We should finish our drinks and then go in search of some Geritol. We can go back up to the forward lounge, I'm sure someone in the Ballroom Set must have some."

"This takeover was even more impressive than the one we experienced at the pool today; we had better get back to our room before we lose that, too. By the way, you didn't see B.A.D. here did you?"

"No, I don't think so."

"Good, for a moment I thought we were really in trouble. Are you sure that you didn't see him in the back? This was too organized, too insidious, not to have his hand in it. It's just like today at the pool, I know he was behind it."

Al was referring to earlier in the day, when the pool area had been another battleground lost to the teen terrors. They literally came in waves, first forcing the adults against the side of the pool and eventually to the outer edges of the ship. You wouldn't want to have to beat these young kids to a lifeboat or, worse yet, share one with them. They would make you feel like you didn't belong and that you should jump overboard and tread water. Come to think of it, you probably would rather; more about this later.

"Let's stroll out on the deck where we can be alone," Al suggested, trying to rekindle the spark that had begun in the lounge before it had been so cruelly snuffed out.

Mary gave Al that seductive smile she saves for those special times, "That sounds good to me."

Al's hopes soared as he opened the door for her to go out, but, before Mary could take a step, she was almost blown past him. Instinctively, he reached out and caught her arm, using all of his strength to keep her from slamming against the far wall. Simultaneously, Al grabbed the railing with his other hand and held on for dear life. Slowly they made progress towards the door, eventually managing to get it closed.

Just then, a crewmember walked by and Mary shouted that there must be a hurricane outside. He just laughed and said that it was merely an evening breeze on the Atlantic.

At this remark, Mary whipped her head around and gave him a look that would have melted an iceberg and mumbled something under her breath. She never swears in public, but Al could tell that she was really teed off and silently giving him a nasty piece of her mind. The crewmember decided that discretion was the better part of valor, did an about face, and got the hell out of there as quickly as possible before he got reamed a new one by this crazy lady.

"Not exactly the Love Boat," Al remarked, trying to lighten the atmosphere and to regain the romantic moment.

Mary turned her icy stare on him as she tried to straighten her hair and dress, "Very funny, Al. This place is so G.D. far from the Love Boat it isn't funny. If I could get off I would do it right now."

Al decided not to respond. Although she was normally mild mannered, when Mary came this close to swearing in public it wasn't wise to say anything that could fuel the flames. Better to let her calm down on her own and then maybe some wine, soft music, and low lights would change the mood. You have to admit that, if nothing else, Al was persistent and ever hopeful.

As they hobbled back to their cabin, Al at least knew where Jennifer, his first problem was, but Al couldn't help but wonder what his second and bigger problem, B.A.D., was up to.

Yes, although sometimes reluctantly so, Al had to admit that Bruno Alphonso DeGregorio II, alias B.A.D., was his nineteen-year old son. Although there have been times when Al brought into question the fact that there really was no proof that he bore any direct biological responsibility for this, since he refused to take a DNA test. Mary hated it when he talked like this and he knew it sounded like a terrible thing for a parent to say; and it was, or would be under normal circumstances. However, 'Bruno The Terrible' was anything but a normal circumstance.

Al knew at the time that they never should have named him after his grandfather, Bruno Alphonso DeGregorio the first. Deep down he sensed they would be punished for this, but little did he know how much.

As the first generation born in America, it was impossible to name their first-born son anything but after Al's father. After all, he was named after his grandfather, Alphonso Nunzio DeGregorio, and he took it like a man, without seeking revenge on his family. Although there were times that he did want to seek some form of satisfaction for ruining his life. However, his father had a very convincing manner when dealing with his pathetic attempts at rebellion.

Bruno often cursed his parents for this and demanded to know why his younger brother got such a "normal" name. This was a valid question and the answer that, by then, they realized it was time to change didn't help much. Besides, his brother Brandon would have had to be named after his great grandfather, Nunzio Guisseppe DeGregorio, and they just couldn't bring themselves to do it. Actually, Al was prepared to carry on the tradition but Mary made it perfectly clear that if they had another son he would have a normal, American name. She said it with that look on her face that told Al that was the end of the discussion. Of course, in order to save face, Al continued the charade right up to the end when he said that he would relent and "allow" their son to be named Brandon Joseph, a name ostensibly picked by Mary out of one of those name books. It wasn't until much later, after Al's jealous nature had mellowed a great deal with age, that Mary admitted she really got the name from some 'real hunk' on her favorite TV soap opera. Al protested that it wasn't very motherly to name their son after some stranger just because he aroused some deep seeded sensual feelings. Whenever Al mentioned this, she just smiled and gave him that devilish little look that made him wonder what was going on in her mind; and always made him wish that they were alone.

From the day that Bruno II was born, Al knew that they were in for trouble. The doctor had to slap his rear repeatedly to get him to cry, which he never did. Instead, he just urinated on him. It hasn't gotten any better since.

They still contend that they switched babies at the hospital on them. Bruno doesn't look anything like either of them, or their other two children. For instance, Jennifer, has blonde hair, is about five feet five inches tall, medium build with a very outgoing personality. Actually, they didn't know where she got such an outgoing personality, either. Since she was four years old she would open up to anyone she met and start telling them their life story, and she hasn't changed any as she has grown up. It has been predicted that she would be the next Elsa Maxwell and they could believe it.

She is very energetic, as well as sociable, and, as a freshman in high school, she was a cheerleader, made the honor roll while taking a full load of college level courses, took ballet lessons twice a week, and had a weekend job in a little gift store in town.

Jennifer has always had adults think very highly of her, and rightfully so; although after this trip they might change their minds.

As for Brandon Joseph, he could be described as the typical all-American boy. First, he is very smart and, like his sister, does very well in school. He is his own taskmaster and pushes himself to excel.

He is a very even-tempered, good-natured young man who loves sports and is a pretty-good athlete, as well as a very good student.

So when Al thought how great his middle and youngest children were he couldn't help but wonder—what the hell happened to the oldest one!

It would seem that it was his sole purpose in life to give them trouble. As good as the other children are, he is bad. Al realized that his son had a cross to bear with a name like Bruno Alphonso, but how much does this justify.

Bruno has long black hair, a thin black mustache, a stupid earring, and specializes in creating as much havoc in school as possible. He is good at it! Very good! It's not that he's not smart enough to do the work. If he channeled his energies into schoolwork, he would have no problem being the equal of his siblings. Unfortunately, this is not the case as he channels his energies into creating chaos for the rest of the family. For example, by the time that he was two years old he had already broken five windows in the house. Since there were six French doors he had plenty of opportunity, and Bruno never lets a good opportunity pass him by. He was also very creative in what methods he employed; no two windows were ever broken in the same way.

The first one was the result of using a wooden spoon as a drumstick and the window as the drum. They chalked this one up to just one of those things that little boys do; even getting a little chuckle out of it. They didn't laugh so hard when he threw a baseball through the second one.

The third window was the victim of a well-placed slap shot that sent a hockey puck sailing through the family room window; this was becoming decidedly less cute.

The worst one occurred as Mary and Al were getting ready to go out for the evening. Mary was upstairs dressing and Al was in the family room watching Bruno and waiting for his grandmother, who was coming to take care of him for the evening.

Al was sitting in his easy chair, with one eye on a football game and one eye on Bruno, when it happened. Bruno was sitting in his little rocking chair, also watching the game, when he put on a move that would have made Michael Jordan drool with envy. In one fluid motion he stood up, pivoted, and grabbed the back of the chair, then he looked at Al with the devil in his eye, smiled, and began to rock.

Al yelled at him to stop as he leapt from his chair. Unfortunately, his moves resembled those of Rosie Grier rather than Lynn Swann. Which is to say that he was only about halfway out of his chair as

Bruno propelled himself backward, smashing the back of the chair and his right hand through the glass in the French door. Mary and Al then spent the next two hours at the emergency room while Bruno received six stitches in his hand. Of course, that was the end of their going out that evening.

As he grew, the inside windows became somewhat less vulnerable. However, this was at the expense of the windows in the garage. What's worse is that, as he grew older, he acquired accomplices. One of his friends hit a tennis ball through the second floor window of the garage and another broke the window in the garage door simply because he was tossing a baseball into his glove and missed. It has gone downhill ever since!

Finally, Mary and Al were back at their cabin and his thoughts returned to romance and the hope that there still might be a chance for them to get together.

As Al poured each of them a glass of wine, Mary changed into something more comfortable and much sexier. Al handed her the wine and, as she sipped it, he began to kiss the nape of her neck and nibble at her ear.

"Did you hear something?" Mary asked.

"I think it's just the waves lapping against the ship," Al replied while kissing her shoulder.

Then they heard the noise again, followed by a muffled, "Hey Dad!" It was Al's worst fear come true. B.J. was knocking at the adjoining door while Mary was quickly putting on a terrycloth bath-robe and crawling into bed.

Al opened the door to find out what he wanted, hoping to quickly satisfy him and get him back to bed.

He stood there and looked up at Al with that look that makes it impossible to say no. "Hey Dad! Do you wanna play Mario Bros. with me?" B.J. pleaded. "I'm bored and there's nothing else to do."

"It's late. Why don't you go to bed so you can get up early?"

"I'm not tired. Besides I already get up before anyone else and eat breakfast alone," he answered—a touch of sarcasm in his voice.

That was it. What could Al do but agree to at least one game.

"OK, B.J., I'll play. But just one game, because I'm getting tired myself."

"You can go first, Dad," he offered. His generosity was rather hollow knowing that Al's games usually last less than a minute.

True to form, Al's effort took about forty-five seconds. Al wished he could say it was just because he had other things on his mind, but he never could quite get the knack of these damn video games.

As B.J. took the controls, he tried to hide his contempt for this pathetic display of his father's lack of eye hand coordination. However, he couldn't conceal the look of superiority he gets in his eyes as he begins to concentrate and go into a trance like state. It is as if his hand and the controls are one as he effortlessly moves through the different levels of complexity with a smoothness and grace that made his father think that he had learned under a great Zen master, rather than one of the older neighborhood urchins.

A full twenty-five minutes later he had reached a level of complexity that Al couldn't even dream of. He didn't even know it existed; and just watched in awe as B.J.'s total concentration centered on that game as if he were at one with it.

Al looked over at Mary who was sound asleep, having given up on any romantic feelings and letting the sleep fairy take over.

Al sighed, breathed deeply, gave up on the last vestiges of his romantic ideas, and agreed to another game; what the hell, maybe he would finally get lucky and get to level two.

CHAPTER 2

*A*lmost before it began, the next number instinctively brought Al out of his trance. It was a dance performed by the chorus line, consisting of a dozen attractive, shapely, young women.

These young ladies were dressed, so to speak, in skimpy outfits that plunged to their navels in front and were, for all practical purposes, non-existent in back. Their firm, young breasts were sufficiently revealed to allow appreciation of their soft, supple nature—yet covered enough to stimulate the imagination. The back of these costumes was simply a string all but lost between their firm, full buttocks.

It was not very many years ago that you would only see this much of a woman's derriere in semi-public from an exotic dancer, but please understand that Al was not complaining. It was definitely progress at its best since these young ladies were not only very attractive, they were also excellent dancers.

Of course, Al wasn't really interested in their physical appearance, it's just that he had to make sure that this was something appropriate for B.J. to watch. It was hard to tell if he enjoyed it or not; boys of his age try to make it look like they are not interested when they are actually a combination of curious and embarrassed.

It would be different with B.A.D., he would not only be interested but probably would be back stage trying to get a closer look, maybe even a date. In fact, earlier in the week Al had seen him talking with some of the chorus line girls; he had a gleam in his eye ever since. At nineteen years old, he was young for them and Al knew he shouldn't be worried. However, he can be quite charming, mature, and resourceful when he puts his mind to it. Al wouldn't be surprised if he had had some form of 'interaction' since he has been acting like he has a case of puppy love for the last few days. Earlier in the week, at another show, Al thought that he saw one of the girls give B.A.D. the eye as he sat in the audience with his friends. Al guessed that he should have a talk with him.

Al was not ready to deal with his number two problem at the moment, but that was nothing new. He rarely looked forward to dealing with B.A.D and his antics. But it was particularly so now since he was currently pre-occupied with his third problem, which was the fact that he didn't have a job at present; for the first time since he graduated from college, twenty-two years ago, he was unemployed.

He had thought about this while sitting in the bus station on the first leg of their cruise. In retrospect, he should have taken this experience as a precursor of things to come. There has to be something wrong with a luxury cruise that begins in a bus station that was as barren and run down as the one in Boston. How can such a beautiful city have such a dumpy bus station?

The only thing that the place looked good for was to meet derelicts. There certainly were enough of them around and Al began to wonder where these poor 'rummies' came from. Were they poor when they were young? Maybe they once had a good job and then lost it? Then it hit Al that some of these men may have even been 'successful' before they lost their jobs and were unable to find another one. Eventually their lives begin to deteriorate until as crushed, broken men they ended up here. Al started to break out into a cold sweat.

In one corner, there was a man that was propped up against the wall wearing a filthy, greasy dunk'n donuts T-shirt. He certainly looked like he ate the whole thing, grease and all. Only it didn't all make it into his mouth from the looks of his clothing; he could have another meal if he scrapped the food off. He probably did.

Even though it was in the middle of the summer and ninety degrees, there was another man up against the wall wearing a dirty, threadbare, wool sport coat and had what looked like all of his belongings in three shopping bags that he guarded zealously.

Al couldn't help it, but his attention kept wandering back to this man—there was something about him that made him think he had a significant past. Al's mind began to wander; he had a certain air about him that made Al think he probably was a very successful businessman with a prestigious position, a lot of responsibility, money and, most of all, power. A successful man with a good family, a big house, expensive cars (BMer's, Land Rovers), multiple gold cards, power lunches, Perrier water (benzene and all), a different red power tie for every day of the month, six sets of braces (alias suspenders), and, of course, country club and health club memberships (complete with designer sweat suits).

Al wondered what happened to him, how did he end up here in this place, in this condition—with drool hanging from the dirty gray stubble on his chin—begging for change so that he could buy a cheap bottle of wine, having given up his beloved Dom Perion long ago. Maybe he got caught in an economic downturn, or the big deal that went sour. For the first time in his life, he has failed in a major way and he has to face his family, friends, and himself as a 'failure'!

"Al! Al!" What was that? He could faintly hear his name. Was he calling him? Did he know Al? Did Al know him? Was Al one of the people that had ignored him in his time of need? The cold sweat came back, complete with clammy hands and bristling hairs on the back of his neck.

"Earth to Al, Earth to Al." Finally, Al realized, with great relief, that it was Mary calling his name.

"Yes, yes what is it," he responded; the color starting to come back to his face.

"You certainly were out in space somewhere, again. I think the bus is here".

"O.K. I'll go check." As he got up to go, he took out a few dollars to give to the man he had been studying. As he approached him, the man had a look in his eyes as if to ask him what went wrong. Al searched his mind to come up with some great words of wisdom that would turn this poor soul's life around. With intense thought, Al recounted many of the problems that he had to face. In his infinite wisdom he remembered the only thing that ever really made sense consistently and particularly in the most incomprehensible of situations. So, as he reached him, he bent down to give him the money, looked him in the eyes, shrugged his shoulders and repeated the deep philosophy that gets him through many a day: "HEY, SHIT HAPPENS!"

As Al handed him the money, and began to walk away, a look came across his face that told Al he understood. You see, you can either believe deeply in fate or not at all; that everything that happens is pre-ordained or is totally at random. You can believe in 'Divine Providence' or in total chaos, but if you have experienced some of the real difficulties of life, and have spent anytime wondering why some things happen, then you may conclude that there is but one answer that has universal truth, it is simply one of the few truths of life that—shit can just happen of its own accord. It doesn't need any particular reason or any outside help—it just happens.

The bus was there, so Al went back to get his family and their belongings. As they gathered up everything and made their way to the gate, pushing and dragging and lugging suitcases, Al couldn't help but feel like they were a group of vagabonds—catching a bus to head out for a chance at a job and a better life in the land of opportunity somewhere out west—wagons ho!

Struggling in line, pushing their bags along, being jostled by the sea of humanity, clutching at what represented all of their worldly possessions and trying to keep their place in line. Al has to keep telling himself that they aren't destitute or anything like that. After all, they are about to go on a luxury cruise and they do have some money in the bank. It is just that this bus station is a dump and offers many examples of individuals who have not been able to deal with their problems and are struggling daily to barely survive. One can't help but wonder if—'but there for the grace of God'. "Oh shit!"

A concerned Mary asked, "Al, is something wrong?"

"No. I was just thinking out loud."

"Well, please watch your language."

"Yes, dear."

They finally got to the front of the line and prepared to get on the bus. That's when Al first saw their bus driver. It was a young woman, a very young woman, and she looked confused, very confused. She was struggling so hard to get the luggage stowed in the compartments under the bus that the bags were piling up beside the door and the passengers could no longer get on.

Al turned to Mary and grunted, "Are you sure that this is the right trip. I suppose that, when we get to New York, we'll find we're booked on a banana boat bound for Guatemala instead of a luxury liner headed for Bermuda."

"Oh, quit complaining and help her put the baggage away so that we can get going," Mary instructed.

So, with the help of a few of the other male passengers, they loaded up the rest of the luggage, but not without their fair share of grumbling, groaning, and, of course, grunting.

All the while the young woman was telling them that she was a new driver and that this was her first solo trip. She kept repeating that—"she was a new driver, but that she was good, and would get them there by the one o'clock departure, she hoped." Al thought that she was trying to convince herself more than them. Of course she was getting a lot of support from the female passengers while the men grunted that they could have stayed at home and worked this hard, and saved a lot of money in the process.

When they finally got on the bus to leave, Nadine, their driver, indicated that there was suppose to be thirty passengers in all. Al really knew they were in trouble when she announced that the head count was only twenty-eight, but that was close enough, and they were on their way.

As Nadine backed the bus out of its berth, Al could feel a bump. He thought they had crushed an old Volkswagen bug, but this didn't deter Nadine one bit. Actually, Al thought that she was totally oblivious to it, but it was none of his business. He began to change his mind when she started to turn left onto the one-way street, going the wrong way.

Al couldn't help but bellow out, "your going the wrong damn way you…"

"Cool it, Al, you're not driving this bus. Let her do her job," was Mary's command.

"I would if she knew what the hell she was doing," Al snapped back, feeling his blood pressure rising all the time.

"Oh, you wouldn't say that if she were a man."

"If she were a man I wouldn't have to say anything, she'd know how to drive the damn thing."

While they mumbled back and forth, the bus pulled out into traffic—going the right way this time—heading for the Massachusetts Turnpike.

As the bus approached the entrance to the Turnpike, Nadine over steered and was in the process of missing the entrance completely when she came to a dead stop in the middle of the road.

Then some damn fool got out of the bus to stop the traffic and allow her to back up and make another attempt at the entrance. Getting out into traffic like that was a very dangerous thing to do; Boston cab drivers are noted for ramming anything that gets in their way and that includes damn fools that are trying to direct traffic in the middle of a busy intersection. Fortunately, one of the few things that they have some respect for is a twenty-ton bus. Al thought that this was a good idea, since he wanted to get going before the driver rammed the Prudential building, until he realized that the damn fool out there was his son. There he was, like a jerk, standing in the middle of this busy intersection, risking life and limb, to halt the traffic.

An excited Al shouted, "What the hell are you doing out there, get back in this bus right this minute."

"You can't talk to other people like that, it's not your responsibility."

"It damn well is when it's Junior out there about to get run over by some crazed Boston driver."

"What the hell do you mean it's Junior out there? Junior you get your ass in here right now," Mary screamed out the window.

"Mary please, I thought that it wasn't any of our business."

"Will you knock it off and get Junior into this bus before he gets hurt and I have a nervous breakdown."

Al was already up and out of his seat, heading toward the front of the bus, when he saw Junior getting back on.

"Hey B.A.D., that was awesome," applauded an impressed B.J..

B.A.D. took his seat near the driver and was giving her the eye and a big smile.

Al was going to give him something to smile about when he got up to him. Unfortunately, he never got the chance. The driver, with B.A.D.'s assistance, had been able to back up just enough to make the entrance to the Pike and now she just put it into first gear and floored it. Al went flying against one of the seats and hit his head on the overhead compartment.

"Damn it, Junior, I could kick your butt sometimes," Al grumbled under his breath.

"Come on pal, why don't you lighten up and have a seat." The words came from the man in the seat that Al had practically fallen over.

His temper was about to get the better of him, what with Junior almost getting run over, him bumping his head, and now being lectured by a stranger. Al was about to give him a piece of his mind, and maybe more, when he caught Mary's eye. She had that look that told him she meant business and Al knew he had better get control of himself or he would be in real trouble.

The driver just managed to make the turn to enter the Mass. Pike, barely missing the wall as they descended into the underground entrance.

Al stumbled back to his seat, cursing under his breath all the way, as the other passengers were cheering Nadine and Junior, which only added insult to injury. Al promised himself that, if he survived this bus trip from hell, he would fix B.A.D.'s ass good. By now his blood pressure was sky high, as evidenced by his bright red face.

"You have to learn to take it easy, your on vacation and your suppose to relax," Mary said.

His blood pressure went up a few more notches, as his normal teddy bear look turned into his grizzly bear look. This time Mary determined that discretion was the better part of valor and went back to reading her book.

Al sat back and made a conscious effort to regain his composure and let his blood pressure return to normal. As he did, he began to look around the inside of the bus for the first time and noticed that it was not the newest nor in the best of shape. It was definitely something less than plush and Al was beginning to have serious doubts about this trip. This was the first time that 'IT' came to his mind.

'IT'—was the 'Bermuda Triangle'. Al never believed in this kind of crap. However, the way that this trip was going could just change his mind

Of course, Junior first brought the subject up. He was having a good time getting his siblings all worked up about the danger involved in this trip and was the cause of the first argument concerning their cruise. After hearing Junior's tales of all the ships and planes that had disappeared without a trace in this area, B.J. didn't want any part of it—some crap about not wanting to drown or disappear in the mist or some other damn fool thing.

Al remembered that the discussion wasn't one of their better family conversations and went something like this:

"C'mon, B.J., you don't believe in that stuff, do you? You know that your brother likes to exaggerate and get you worked up."

"But, Dad, he showed me a book on it. There are a lot of missing ships around there and I don't want to go on this trip anyway."

Great, Al thought! That little shit never reads the books he's suppose to, but goes out of his way to use one on his brother knowing that he will accept it as fact.

"Junior get your butt over here this minute! Junior!"

"What is it?"

"Did you tell your brother that we were going to drown or disappear on this trip?"

"No. I just showed him a book I was reading; I can't help it if he's a little wimp."

"And I suppose that you just happened to be reading a book on the Bermuda Triangle when we are about to take a trip there?"

"Well, Dad, you're always telling us to learn more about other parts of the world and you said yourself that this trip would be a good learning experience for us. So I was just trying to follow your advice and look what happens."

"Oh, don't give me that 'poor you' crap. I know that you were just trying to get your brother all bent out of shape."

"No, I wasn't. He's just a little creep that always tries to get me in trouble."

"Don't try to turn it on him now. You…."

"What are you boys fighting about now?" Came the exasperated query from Mary, as she entered the room.

"Junior here is trying to sabotage your long planned vacation by introducing B.J. to the saga of the Bermuda Triangle. And, as usual, he has been quite persuasive."

"Junior and B.J. get over here. Now!"—Mary said. "Listen to me! And listen good! I have been planning this vacation for a very long time and if you two spoil it you'll be eating hash for the next year. Is that understood? Well, is it?"

"Yes, Mom"—came the reply in unison.

Mary had always known how to handle the children; knowing just when to be forceful and when tears are called for. However, a few months ago she found a new weapon for her already considerable arsenal. She was reading a book that described how a wife who, when she got mad at him, would fix her husband his favorite hash. What he didn't know was that the hash was made out of Alpo dog food. Well this made quite an impression on Mary, a fact that was not lost on the rest of the family. And since eating is the most important thing in these boys' lives, and the thought of eating dog food really grosses them out, this has been a very effective threat.

This confrontation hadn't come to his mind since that discussion and he surely hoped that this bus ride was not a precursor of things to come because, the more he looked around, the more he realized that this was really a crappy bus. Especially when he realized how much they were paying for this trip and that the newest information was that the bathroom facility was out of order. Since it was a four or five hour bus ride to New York, this was a serious situation and Al wished that he hadn't had that last cup of coffee.

Fortunately, the driver indicated that they were scheduled to stop in Stamford to pick up two more passengers and they could use the bathroom there. Finally, a long three hours later, they pulled into the Stamford terminal without further incident, unless you call the woman wetting her pants in the back of the bus an incident.

All of them, except for the one woman, couldn't get out of the bus fast enough to use the terminal rest rooms. As one might expect from this bus company, the terminal had only one small bathroom and they had to line up to use it. Little did Al realize that this was just the beginning of many lines that they would be waiting in during this trip.

This wasn't the type of line that you might have expected from a group of well-dressed, well-mannered, adults who were at least familiar with one another after having spent the last three hours on a bus together. No indeed, this was a line that was getting increasingly impatient and aggressive, with the urge to relieve oneself becoming a primal need. Al leaned forward and half jokingly mentioned to Mary that this line was getting out of control and that if trouble broke out he would cover for her while she made a break for the bathroom door when it opened. He would then knock three times and whisper that it was Jake, at which time she was to let him in. This was funny until they laughed and their bladders reminded them that, if they didn't get into the bathroom fast, they would end up wetting their pants, too.

Al noticed that some of the men left and, he believed, went out behind the building to answer the call of nature. Things were really starting to go down hill when a husband and wife went into the bathroom together. No one dared ask how they were going to accomplish this, but it didn't matter, as long as they managed to take care of their business in short order, which they did. Al really believed that it was getting out of control when one very attractive woman, at the end of the line, openly offered herself to an elderly gentleman at the head of the line, if he would trade places with her.

You could see the look in this old man's eyes as he was seriously considering giving up his place. Sometimes you have to wonder about men. He would risk an exploding bladder, and the wrath of his wife, for the chance to be with this beautiful woman and, from the look in their eyes, there were other men in line that envied his position.

At this point, the elderly man's wife turned on the woman—"listen sweetie, you can have him if you want him, but if you take one step towards his place in line your dead meat."

The situation was getting out of control until one of the children came in and announced there was a McDonald's across the street that had sufficient bathrooms available. This broke the tension, as two-thirds of the line left and went over there. Al still doesn't know where Junior and B.J. went and he was damned if he was going to ask; some things are better left alone.

Finally, they were back on the bus and on their way. They were all more at ease and a lot friendlier. Of course, Nadine never did pick up those two missing passengers, but something told Al that they were the lucky ones.

As they were driving down Rt. 95, Al was beginning to start to sit back and relax. It looked as if they would make it to the docks on time. As is usually the case, Al spoke too soon because they were becoming snarled in bumper-to-bumper traffic. As they edged forward, they could see that the traffic was stalled ahead of them for miles, while Nadine kept mumbling that she would get them there on time, everyone was getting increasingly nervous about missing the boat. Frankly, Al thought that most of them had missed the boat a long time ago.

This was when one of the passengers suggested an alternate route, using the Triborough Bridge or something like that. Al thought he didn't know the way then, he doesn't know the way now, and he doesn't expect that he will ever know the way or give a damn, either. Nadine said that she didn't know the way, but that she was game for it if the other passengers were.

By now the rest of the passengers were losing confidence in her and were ready to follow anyone. Al was just glad this guy took over before Junior did; God only knows where they would have ended up then. He just knew that it would not be a place fit for adults.

At least the traffic was lighter on this route. When they came to a tollbooth, however, the bus ride really became a joke. The toll was only two dollars but, incredibly, the bus driver didn't have any money at all. It was hard to believe that anyone would drive a bus from Boston to New York without having a penny in her pocket, but she did.

Of course, Al was quick to point this out to Mary. There wasn't much that she could say. She just gave him a look that told him she didn't appreciate his 'I told you so attitude' and that she would get even when she got the chance.

The passenger who suggested the route gave the bus driver her tip in advance so that she could pay the toll.

As they proceeded on their way, Al began to wonder what would go wrong next. It wasn't long before he found out. As they drove into New York City, it soon became painfully obvious that they were hopelessly lost.

Al was not about to let this opportunity get away and, with the trace of a smile, solemnly announced, "We're lost in New York City Mary! I told you that this bus driver would get us lost or killed. She has already gotten us lost and, given the area of New York that we are lost in, death is probably imminent."

"Oh stop exaggerating! At least we are in the city and can't be too far from the pier."

"Take a good look around! This is not Park Avenue, I think it is a foreign country by the look of the writing on the buildings, and I don't like the way some of these people are looking at us. We must make quite a sight, a bus full of HICKS dressed to kill. Sorry, bad choice of words, but I can see the headlines now, 'Burned out bus found in streets of New York—no trace of twenty-eight cruise line vacationers. Police are baffled as to what they were doing so far from the pier.'"

"Your imagination is working overtime again."

"Oh ya! Well look at that kid who has his eye on the hub caps."

"Okay! Okay! But why aren't we moving?"

"Because she has it wedged under this overhead trolley and can't complete the right hand turn that she was trying to make and, unlike in Boston, no one is volunteering to get out of the bus to hold up the traffic so she can back up,"

"C'mon Nadine! Put this G.D. bus into reverse and let's get the hell out of here," Mary shouted.

"Please, Mary! Get a hold of yourself! After all, she's the one who is driving the bus."

Mary was about to really let Al have it when they were both thrown back in their seats; Nadine took Mary's suggestion to heart and threw the bus into reverse and floored it. The horns started blasting and people were screaming obscenities in languages that none of them could understand. To her ever lasting credit, Nadine was not deterred by this and shoved the gear shift into first, flooring it again and the bus leaped forward, narrowly missing one of the abutments and four pedestrians, and hurtled down the street ahead of some very angry people.

They were on the fly now, with a maddened cab driver chasing them yelling what they assumed were obscenities in what was probably Pakistani. Within minutes, they came to an intersection with a police officer directing traffic. Nadine pulled to a screeching halt in front of the officer and asked him if she was going in the right direction to get to the pier. Unfortunately, the officer indicated that they were going the wrong way and that, if they turned around and headed back, they would reach the pier in thirty to forty minutes, if they were lucky. On hearing this, one woman sobbed that she was going to miss the first cruise of her life and that she would never get another chance. It was at this point that a transformation came over Nadine. There was a fire in her eyes and a look of determination on her face.

"Stop this traffic and let me turn this bus around right now!" Nadine demanded.

"You don't have enough room to turn the bus around in this intersection, and don't tell me what to do," was the reply of the stern faced officer.

"Listen to me bud. You had damn well better stop this friggin traffic right now so that I can turn this thing around. I promised to get these people to their cruise on time, dead or alive, and I'm damn well going to do it! I'm a woman with a 'MISSION"!

With that she pulled her cap on tight, revved the engine, yelled for everyone to hold on, spit on the floor, and gunned it. The bus leaped forward, shooting across the intersection. When she was three quarters of the way across, she slammed on the breaks and turned hard to the left, putting the huge bus into a power slide that would have impressed even Joey Chitwood's stunt drivers. The bus then shot forward going in the other direction, leaving the officer standing there with his mouth open and his shorts wet. The bus was hurtling forward and Nadine was going through the gears like Sterling Moss at the Monte Carlo Grand Prix.

The bathroom had been hastily repaired in Stamford and, unfortunately, it was in use at the time. There was a somewhat large woman occupying it when Nadine forced the bus into the power slide. This maneuver threw the passengers against their seats, forcing them to hold on for dear life or risk being catapulted from the bus via one of its closed windows. Unfortunately, there was nothing for the woman in the bathroom to hold on to, so when the bus swung around so did she. Her bulk crashing against the door forced it open and she came halfway out before she was able to stop herself.

It was not a pretty sight to see this three hundred pound plus, half-naked woman, clawing at the doorframe with one hand and trying to pull her pants up with the other. At the same time this was happening the woman's husband gallantly attempted to come to her aid. He threw his whole body behind his shoulder as he buried it into her side and started driving his legs, as hard as he could, in an effort to get her back into the bathroom. Unfortunately, he was a slightly built man and was losing ground in his efforts to save his wife's dignity, and there was concern that he might be crushed against one of the seats. All this time the woman was screaming hysterically that she was going to sue the bus company and kill Nadine.

Fortunately, as they careened down the street, the bus swung back in the other direction and, just as quickly as she had appeared, the woman disappeared back into the bathroom. Only this time her husband was sucked in with her as the door slammed shut. They could hear his cries for help, his pitiful gasping for air, and thought that they heard him plea for someone to call 911 and get him some oxygen.

As the bus barrel assed down the street, Junior was hanging out the window next to Nadine yelling 'HANTA YO', 'HANTA YO' at the top of his lungs and alternating this with his version of an Indian war cry.

Through gritted teeth Mary managed to ask Al what the hell he was yelling. Al replied it was from that damn Indian book he had been glued to about a month ago. He thought it meant 'clear the way' in Sioux. The strangest part is that it appeared some of the people on the street understood him.

"Well, you had better get up there and get him back in the bus before he gets killed".

"Bullshit! The last guy who got up almost got crushed by a three hundred pound projectile that shot out from the bathroom, the guy in the next seat is strangling his wife, the woman in front of us could have used the bathroom, and there is a cruiser and three cabs chasing us. It's each man for himself and I'm staying right where I am. That's if I can manage to hang on tight enough."

Al could hear the woman in the next seat whining at her husband that they were not going to make their first ever cruise. They were sure to be killed by a crazed bus driver who was speeding down a congested city street, totally defying the entire population of New York City cabbies, which is something just short of being a kamikaze pilot.

However, even though New York City cab drivers may be crazy and the area was a very tough one, everyone got the hell out of the way of the twenty ton bus hurtling down the street with a driver blasting the horn, a crazed look in her eyes and an eerie smile on her face, and a long haired, wild looking teenager hanging out yelling something in Sioux Indian. To add to this, one woman was leaning out the window screaming for someone to call 911 because a mad bus driver and her wild teenage accomplice were kidnapping them.

Another woman kept saying that they were all going to die and she thought that they should jump for it. Her husband had had enough of this wimpy attitude and told her in no uncertain terms that if she didn't get a hold on herself that he would make her fears come true—because he was going to strangle her himself.

She was moaning that her premonition was going to come true, as she did a few laps around her rosary beads. At this point, she was almost incoherent, but she had been having a recurring dream that she would die on a bus in a foreign country. Then Al realized this was the woman nipping on Bloody Marys all morning long. It turns out that she was deathly afraid of buses and now she was getting totally out of control and rambled on about Nadine being too young and inexperienced to be driving a bus in a wild, uncontrolled, place like this.

"We are going to die here, Harold. I know it!" The woman moaned as she tried to climb out the window.

CHAPTER 3

The half-drunk woman and her frustrated husband, who was trying to restrain her, seemed eerily familiar and reminded Al of the
first time that Mary and he traveled to the Caribbean. In all, they had
a wonderful time, but it did have its moments. The first thing that
anyone who is visiting the islands has to learn is 'island time'. Call it
quarter time because if you take the pace of life in a city like Boston
and slow it down to about one quarter of its normal pace—then you
have 'island time'. Stated another way, it takes the islanders about
four times longer to do anything, if it gets done at all.

Once you get accustomed to this pace, it can be wonderfully relaxing and enjoyable, for a vacation anyway. When they first arrived,
they were ready to go out of their mind in a very short time; the service was so slow that it sometimes appeared to be non-existent.

However, once into 'island time', a week of it will leave you very,
very mellow. The long, leisurely days on the beach, wonderful
romantic dinners and a little bit of fun gambling in the casinos can
leave you ready to deal calmly with the most difficult of situations.

Unfortunately, the problem that resulted at the end of the week
would certainly test this. Al and Mary had booked the vacation with
a tour group and had had a very enjoyable week. The flight down
was on a new and comfortable L1011 and, since they had spent a little more for an upgrade, the room was very large and comfortable,

by Caribbean standards anyway. When the end of the week came, everyone packed up, got on the bus, and headed for the airport, and that's when it started to hit the fan. They were supposed to leave at noon and at one they were finally told there had been a mix up. Because the tour scheduled after them was under booked it had been cancelled, and the plane that was to take the next tour down was the same plane that was suppose to take them back, but, when they cancelled it, they forgot that they still had to send a plane for them.

So there they were, about a hundred of them all packed ready to go home and no way to get there. They were rounded up and taken back to the hotel. The tour company found a large function room for them to stay in until they could locate a flight crew and get a plane down there to take them back.

Mary and Al took all of this with a mellowness that Al wouldn't have believed possible prior to this vacation. Most of the others in the group also took this in stride. However, others apparently did not have as good or as relaxing of a time since they were doing a lot of complaining about the situation. A surprisingly large number of the couples were short of, or completely out of, funds. For one middle aged couple this was their first vacation outside of the states, they had been given it by their children, and they were very upset when things did not go as planned.

The tour company provided everyone with sandwiches and an unlimited supply of alcoholic beverages in the hope of keeping them from rioting. Unfortunately, a number of people took full advantage of the drinks and drank too much, especially the middle aged woman whose children had given her and her husband the trip for their thirty-fifth wedding anniversary. It turned out that this woman, whose name was Madeline, was deathly afraid of flying and had had a premonition that she would be on an old broken down plane, flown by an old man, and a young boy. Her husband, Harold, was getting very frustrated with her and had thrown up his hands and walked away in disgust.

Fortunately, Mary and Al had enough money left so that they could go next door to the casino to kill a few hours while most of the others stayed there and drank. Finally, at seven o'clock, after six hours, they were taken back to the airport and provided with a decent dinner in the airport restaurant. Of course, they had to eat in three shifts because the restaurant was too small to accommodate all of them at one time. Amazingly, Mary and Al just kept taking everything in stride with their same newfound mellowness. If one could bottle this mellow attitude tranquilizers would become obsolete.

After dinner, they had another few hours to kill and everyone was getting pretty bedraggled. Some of them were beginning to believe they would be spending the night in the airport. People were flopped out uncomfortably in chairs and others had just given up and spread out on the floor. Over in one corner, Madeline was wringing her hands and moaning about how she was never going to see her family again and Harold was trying to convince her that this was not some dastardly plot thought up by her less than favorite daughter-in-law, whose idea it was to give them the trip.

Finally, at eleven o'clock, a full half-day after they were suppose to leave, the plane arrived and they were starting to filter out to board it. In the islands, the passengers don't get on the plane directly from the gate but, instead, have to walk across the tarmac to the plane and then up a long flight of stairs.

As Mary and Al slowly walked toward the plane, there was a full moon and they could see the different groups of people heading for the plane. Many of these people were in a hurry; as if there was limited space and some of them wouldn't make it.

You could make out the silhouette of the plane in the distance and the people scurrying up the stairs. Except for the tour group and a skeleton airport staff, the airport was deserted and possessed an eerie feeling. In the distance, the buzz of a large crowd could be heard. It was coming from a nearby casino, but their imaginations started to get the better of them and they imagined it was a crowd coming to take their place on the plane.

Al couldn't help but remark—"Mary this feels like the last plane out of Saigon." Although she hadn't been there, either, she gave him a knowing look.

When they finally reached the plane and began to ascend the stairs, they turned to each other with the same worried look. It was an old plane, a very old plane. A DC9 that looked like it was one of the first ever built. When they got inside, it went from bad to worse. Madeline was beside herself with fear and her husband, Harold, had all he could do to keep her from opening the emergency exit door. She was babbling on about flying in an old plane that had engine problems. Harold then gave her another drink that quieted her down, at least temporarily.

Mary and Al just looked at each other and took the mellowness thing to its extreme, shrugged their shoulders, and went to take their seats. Along the way, they noticed a lot of nervous people with blank stares.

As they took their seats, the plane started to vibrate when the engines were revved up to begin taxiing to the end of the runway. While they vibrated in their seats the mellowness crap began to fade and they were turning somewhat pale, along with a hundred other passengers.

The bucket of bolts rumbled down to the end of the runway and made its turn to prepare to take-off. Now Al was not usually a white knuckled flier, but when the stewardesses were saying their prayers, lighting candles, and spreading holy water around the cabin, Al did begin to get a tad bit nervous.

As they sat there waiting to take-off, the plane began to shake even more and one of the overhead doors opened spilling its contents onto the floor. This was the last straw for 'Mad' Madeline and she struggled even harder with Harold to reach the safety of an exit door, but, by now, he had enlisted the aid of another middle-aged couple seated next to them. The other woman was holding Madeline's right hand, at once both twisting it and patting it, while she attempted to whisper soothing words of comfort to her. Madeline's husband made no pretense of attempting to calm her down. He took the firm approach of applying a half-nelson, while biting one of her fingers, as she tried to tear his face off. Obviously he had had enough of this day, this island, and, most of all, this woman, and he wasn't going to let anything or anyone keep him from getting out of there.

In the rear of the plane was a would be priest taking confessions, giving benediction, and the last rites to some of the older passengers preparing to meet their maker. However, as Al looked around the plane most of the people were relatively calm, if somewhat paler. Scanning the plane, his eye caught that of another passenger about his age, and then another, and another, and it appeared to him that they all had the same calmness that comes from knowing one of the few great truths of life. At this point Al knew what he had to do, so he got up and went over to where Madeline was struggling with her captors. She looked up at him and pleaded that she was afraid that they were going to die. He answered that he understood as he put his hand on her shoulder, looked her in the eye and, in his most Moses like voice, stated "but Madeline you have to understand that regardless how much we try to fight it we have to accept one of the true facts of life. Yes, Madeline, that's right…'Shit Happens'". Suddenly Madeline became very calm as she absorbed the truth of these words. She stopped struggling and quietly took her seat; prepared to stoically endure whatever was to come, having no rebuttal for one of the constants of the universe.

Al took his seat as the plane began to roar, well semi-roar anyway, down the runway. Frankly, Al felt like he was going faster in the sluggish little four cylinder Toyota he had been wrestling with all week; the planes engines had that same whiny, eggbeater like sound. He was really going to appreciate the quality, comfort, and power of his Pontiac Bonneville when he got home.

As they proceeded down the runway they picked up speed slowly, too damned slowly for comfort. Al knew they were getting close to the end of the airstrip when Mary remarked, "I know I said that I wanted to take another dip in the ocean, but I didn't want to do it while sitting in a plane."

"Well, if this plane can't fly, I sure hope it's a good skimmer and floats well," was Al's response.

Just then, the plane reached the end of the runway and the head stewardess shouted, "lift", as if they were one, everyone stood up, and the plane lurched upwards, the engines screeching and the metal creaking. Now they knew why they had been told not to buckle their seat belts.

As he looked out the window, reflected in the moonlight, Al saw a nude couple making love on the beach. It appeared that they were just culminating their lovemaking session as the plane boomed low overhead. It must have been one helluva climax, as they must have felt the earth move. It's certainly going to be a hard act to follow.

The plane continued to slowly gain altitude and, fortunately, there weren't any large waves to have to get over.

It was only after they had gained sufficient height, to handle the passengers jumping up and down in a temper tantrum, that the Captain announced that they would have to make a stop in Puerto Rico. Upon this announcement, Madeline started sobbing again, the would be priest went into the rest room to get some more holy water—from the toilet bowl—and one guy said that he thought that they should take control of the plane and force them to take it to Boston.

The Captain explained the runway was too short and the plane too old to take off with any more fuel than necessary to get to Puerto Rico. This made the would-be hijacker give up his aspirations of taking over control; he just went to the back of the plane to listen to the 'priest' and sob along with Madeline.

Contented they were finally in the air, they sat back and tried to relax. It would take an hour, or longer on this plane, to reach Puerto Rico and it was all they could do. Even after their long, terrible day, this was still not very difficult. The two nudes on the beach reminded Al of how laid back and uninhibited the island was.

He didn't think he would ever forget the first time that they were lying on the beach and a nude couple came strolling by. Both Mary and he were somewhat dumbfounded and didn't quite know where to look. Mary didn't know whether to look at the sky or the ground and Al didn't know whether to look at the woman's face, her breasts or well, you know. Eventually Mary had to slap Al to get his eyes to pop back into his head.

What they hadn't realized was that a number of beaches on the island, although not officially sanctioned, were clothing optional. They had started their vacation by going to the beach at the hotel, which was nice but very commercialized. So they had spent the next few days sampling beaches when they came upon one called 'Baie Paradis'. This beach was one of the most remote on the island, which made it all the more attractive. While it was quite long, it was enclosed at either end by mountains giving it an isolated, cove effect. Some small islands and a reef protected it, providing a very calm, tranquil bay, ideal for swimming and sailing. These islands also served to further shelter this spot from the rest of the world and added to the atmosphere of isolation, of a total escape from reality. As soon as they stepped onto the beach they both felt it immediately; it was Mary who spoke first.

"This place is wonderful. It has an atmosphere all it's own."

"I know what you mean. There is a serene, tranquil feeling that permeates the air."

They were lying on the beach, soaking up some rays, when they noticed a small plane flying low, back and forth, over the beach. They wondered what this was all about when, shortly thereafter, they were approached by a strikingly sensual looking young woman; Goddess was more accurate.

"Bonjour," came the melodic greeting. Immediately the hairs over Al's entire body were alive with feeling.

Both Mary and Al looked up, but it was Mary who replied with a friendly "Hi!" Al managed a barely audible gasp as he observed this tall, slender, French nymph with sandy blonde hair. She was deeply tanned with steel blue eyes, high cheekbones, and pouty, sensual lips. She was 'dressed,' you have to stretch your imagination to call it that, in a mini-halter top and short shorts, a combination which covered only enough to increase one's interest.

First of all, it appeared that she had just come out of the water so that you could see through her clothing. The low cut halter top, which was open down to a knot loosely tied under her breasts, revealed a pair of breasts that were small but firm, with nipples enlarged by the cool breeze, that were straining against the wet fabric and flowed to her flat stomach and then to her very short, very tight light tan shorts. She was obviously not wearing any underwear, as the shorts were molded to her buttocks and appeared to have shrunk onto her. They had to have, or else she would have had to butter her butt to get them on.

"My name is Monique," she purred.

That's it Al thought, 'I'll never pass the stand-up test now.' Mary just looked at him with the devil in her eyes. She obviously could see that any man would enjoy the view presented by this nubile, young nymph. But she new that the added combination of the seductive French name and the French accent would make a complete bowl of Jell-O out of her husband, and she was right.

"Would either of you be interested in taking a plane ride over the beach?"

If Al could have spoken, he would have gone anywhere and spent anything; but, of course, he just kind of gasped, stared, and drooled a little.

Mary, the wonderful woman that she is, understood perfectly and came to his rescue.

"No, I don't think so. I'm not interested and my husband can't get up right now."

"Oh! Are you injured? You look fine," she cooed as she came closer and bent over to see what was the matter.

Mary was uncharacteristically devilish, as she commented, "Oh, it's just a little problem that comes up now and then when he gets overly excited. It's no big thing, hardly noticeable at all. A little rest and he'll be back to normal in no time."

"Well, Messier, I am sorry that you're not feeling up to it today. I was going to fly this one myself, but it is very close in the cockpit and not a place to be if you are not feeling yourself."

Al finally managed to blurt out, "Perhaps tomorrow."

"Ah, perhaps Messier. I hope that you are back to normal soon," she said as she stood up and turned to continue down the beach.

She moved with such a feline lightness that Al couldn't help but observe the sway of her hips and tightness of her buns as they alternated between hard and round, and soft and fleshy, with each step that this nubile nymph took.

"Oooooofff!" Al let out a gasp as Mary hit him in the stomach with a powerful left hook.

"What was that for?"

"That was for what I know you were thinking and as a cure for your condition. You should be ashamed of yourself, Al. She's almost young enough to be your daughter."

That did it, as the combination of a shot to the solar plexus and a reminder of his advancing age were enough to deflate his ego, and everything else.

"I was just being sociable and, besides, you know how much I like to fly. And you should talk, I saw you checking out those young Australian hunks."

"Don't change the subject. Here use this to de-fog your glasses and to wipe the drool off your chin. Then lay back and relax before you hyper-ventilate," Mary said handing him a tissue.

Mary's ability to cut to the chase and grasp control of a situation had had its affect, again. Al soon lay back to soak up the sun's rays and retrieve his mind from its trip down fantasy lane, for now anyway.

"Earth to Al! Earth to Al!" Mary attempted to bring him back to this world.

"Yes! What? What is it?" Al blurted out as he fought to bring himself back to reality.

"We are about to land and I think that prayers are in order. Besides, I know what that smile was all about."

It was about an hour and a half after they had taken off and they were now making their descent into San Juan, Puerto Rico. And a rapid descent it was.

"I'll say one thing for this old DC9, it doesn't have any trouble losing altitude. We are only going to have one pass at this, this old crate wouldn't have the power to abort the landing and be able to stay in the air."

"You are full of encouragement aren't you, Al."

By the time that they landed and taxied to the refueling area it was almost one a.m. and the airport was totally closed, save for the refueling tanker truck.

The refueling only took about half an hour and they were ready to take-off again. There was only one problem. One of the engines wouldn't start. The Captain announced they would be delayed indefinitely and they would roll out a stairway to let the passengers out to stretch their legs if they wanted to.

Some of them decided to take advantage of this and were just outside of the cockpit when the door opened and the co-pilot came out. Unfortunately 'Mad'Madeline was there, still pretty high, when he came out; she took one look at him and screeched, "Who the hell are you?"

The young man sheepishly replied, "I'm the co-pilot."

"You can't be the co-pilot, you're only twelve years old for Christ sake," Madeline blurted out. "What the hell are you doing in there? You shouldn't be in there! You can't play with this plane; it's not a toy! Get out of there you…"

"C'mon Madeline let's get some fresh air." A not so happy, 'Happy' Harold said as he dragged her kicking and screaming down the stairs.

The embarrassed young co-pilot turned beet-red as he followed Mad Madeline down the stairs and disappeared into a service hangar, only to re-appear a short time later with a tall stepladder. He then placed the ladder up to the disabled engine and climbed it with his manual in one hand and a flashlight and Swiss Army knife in his back pocket.

Al was standing on the tarmac talking with a couple of other guys. One was Mickey O'Rourke, a young computer programmer from South Boston, who was in his early twenties, of average height, about five nine, broad shouldered, and powerfully built. He was a jovial sort of a fellow with carrot red hair and the map of Ireland for a face. The other was about thirty and, at five eleven, was tall for someone of Asian descent. He had lived in America for the last ten years, spoke perfect English, was a U.S. citizen, and the owner of a Cambodian restaurant in downtown Boston. His name was Johnny Ho Yo.

"I have this gut feeling that we shouldn't be getting on this plane," Johnny said.

"I know what you mean," Mickey agreed. "I didn't want to get on this flight in the first place, and that was before we had that take-off that damn near wasn't. Did you see that couple on the beach? Christ! I could count the hairs on his arse! I'm beginning to think that I'm pushing my Irish luck too far this time."

"I'm just glad that everyone had the presence of mind to stand up on queue. Especially since we hadn't even rehearsed it and we weren't going to get any second chances," Al said, trying to lighten the mood.

"I'll probably get back on anyway, but I don't know why. With everything that has happened today, I still feel very mellow," Mickey said.

"I know exactly what you mean," added Johnny.

The three of them looked at each other, smiled and in unison announced—'Baie Paradis'. They laughed and felt the tension ease.

"I had the most incredible plane ride along the beach with this vixen named…"

"Monique!" Johnny and Al gasped at once, their envy obvious.

As they stood there, intently listening to the details of his flight, the co-pilot came down the ladder, walked around the end of the wing carrying his do-it yourself instruction manual, and, as he came past them, he smiled, very proud of himself, and announced—"I think it's fixed."

Al gasped.

Mickey turned white, red hair and all.

In addition, Johnny Ho Yo, well, he lost it completely and started jumping up and down like a Yo-Yo, shouting, "You think it's fixed You think it's fixed? You can THINK that a car is fixed, but for Christ sake you have to KNOW that an airplane is fixed! You can't pull over and get out at thirty thousand feet to have another look at it! Oh no! Oh no! How could Buddha abandon me this way!? *#&@^%$#+!)@(#*@()…….!" Johnny's perfect English had reverted to his native Cambodian and, of course, was incomprehensible to Al and Mickey.

"There! There! Now, Johnny, it will be alright." Both Mickey and Al were concerned that he was going to lose it all together and have a stroke. Even thoughts of 'Baie Paradis' and the beautiful Monique weren't going to help him now.

Unfortunately, Mad Madeline had also heard this and broke free of Happy Harold, temporarily frozen with fear, and was now making a mad dash for the gate and freedom. Nearby, the would be priest had dropped to his knees and was praying with great sincerity.

Mad Madeline had a ten yard head start before Happy Harold could contain his own fear and come out of his daze long enough to notice that she was attempting an escape. When he did, he saw her pumping her arms and legs fiercely as she was rapidly closing the distance between her and the gate. Harold had no idea that his wife could haul ass like that, he couldn't help thinking that she would have given Wilma Rudolph a run for her money. It was amazing what a good shot of adrenaline could do.

However, once he got his senses back he was off like a greyhound after a jackrabbit. He was determined that he was getting on that plane tonight, for better or for worse and he was getting on with his wife, whether she liked it or not. He was not about to have to face his children and try to explain that their mother was a bag lady living somewhere on the streets of San Juan

It wasn't long before Mickey and Al noticed this real life drama unfolding and joined in the chase, knowing that Happy Harold would need all the help that he could get to subdue Mad Madeline, given her current state of mind. So they started sprinting for all they were worth, leaving Johnny Ho Yo jabbering in Cambodian and jumping up and down like an out of control Yo-Yo.

Madeline had kicked off her shoes to gain more speed, but was losing ground to Harold as she began to tire.

Since he was the youngest, and in the best shape, Mickey was rapidly gaining on them both. Al was also gaining, but more slowly and was beginning to question the wisdom of participating in this chase, as his side was killing him and he was quickly running out of breath. Al thought if he was going to have a heart attack and die, from over excitement, that he would have preferred that it had happened on 'Baie Paradis'. At least he would have gone with a smile on his face.

Harold was now just a few yards behind Madeline as she reached the gate and, to her horror, found it locked. Her head was racing and her heart was pounding as, with a mighty effort that was quite impressive, she leaped halfway up the fence. Happy Harold was just as determined and he sprang after her, grabbing one of her ankles and hanging on, like a bulldog, in spite of Madeline's kicking him. One kick caught him square in the face, giving him a bloody nose and temporarily dazing him, but he doggedly held on and begged her to return to her senses and give in—"Madeline, please! How will I ever explain to the children that I lost you on vacation and that I left you to wander around the streets of San Juan for the rest of your days?"

"I don't give a rat's ass about the kids! They're the ones that got us into this trip from hell in the first place. I know it was that scrawny little bitch of a daughter-in-law of ours who planned all of this. She has wanted my son to herself ever since she met him and now she's going to have her way. She probably has taken out disaster insurance on us, too."

"Come on, calm down, and stop being so damn paranoid. Get off the fence!" Harold begged her as he grabbed for her other foot in an attempt to stop the pummeling that he was receiving.

"I swear, Harold, you had better let me go NOW or you are going to be singing soprano," Madeline warned in a tone of voice that made a believer out of all of them.

Fortunately, just as Harold had reached the point where he was going to have to let go or risk the family jewels, Mickey reached the fence, leaped up, and grabbed her free leg.

"No! No! Please let me go! I don't want to get on that plane. It's going to crash in the ocean and we are all going to die!" Madeline's pleading was pitiful.

"Now, now, Madeline, you know how life works," Al managed to gasp in an effort to soothe her. She continued to struggle against both Harold and Mickey, with each of them holding on tightly to a leg and pulling it out straight, her hands were clasped tightly onto the fence—knuckles turning white and finger-tips bleeding.

"Don't give me any of that—'Shit Happens'—crap Al! I understand all about that, but that's for little baby turds, not for this flight from hell. This is more like diarrhea! No, it's PIG SHIT AL! And, if it crashes, it will turn into ELEPHANT SHIT! And you damn well know it, too!"

Al hated to admit it, but she did have a point—even if somewhat less than eloquently expressed. The truth is that there are varying degrees of—'Shit Happening', although not many people are very well versed in this phase of the philosophy.

As Madeline pointed out the first level is 'New Born Baby Turds'. This level barely even qualifies since it is the equivalent of having—'sort of a bad day', breaking a fingernail or being late for an important meeting. Then there's 'Dog Shit', which is something like having a bad case of hemorrhoids or having open-heart surgery.

The next level of 'Shit Happening' is 'Diarrhea', which is like having a bad case of hemorrhoids and a bad case of Montezuma's revenge at the same time. From there it does drop down to 'Pig Shit', which is equivalent to experiencing the previous levels successively or what the day had been so far. And, Madeline was absolutely correct, if the plane crashed it would turn into an 'Elephant Shit Happening' event, as losing one's life definitely qualifies. Fortunately, this level of 'Shit Happening' is rare and can only be experienced once in a lifetime—usually. Needless to say, this is a very significant event and one to be avoided, if at all possible.

However, there is one level even lower than 'Elephant Shit' and is represented by a 'Whale Shit Happening'. This is illustrated by the proverbial—'a fate worse than death' and is unique to each and every individual. Remember, to truly understand the philosophy of 'Shit Happening', you must never forget that the lowest thing on this earth is Whale's shit on the bottom of the ocean.

Al realized now that Mad Madeline had a keen understanding of the 'Shit Happening' philosophy and, therefore, he was going to have to deal with her differently. He would be forced to deceive her. Yes, that is correct, when all else fails then you must—lie!

"Madeline, please calm down," he pleaded with her. "I had a discussion with the pilot about the co-pilot and have found out that he is to the airline industry what Doogie Hauser is to the medical profession. He is an absolute boy wonder, having flown solo across the country at the age of five and around the world at the age of eight. He could have been the youngest astronaut in NASA's history but he chose to be a pilot for Gull Air instead; he found flying these old DC9's more challenging than the space program."

"Is that, is that really true Al?" She asked with a touch of hope in her voice, after all she didn't really want to be a bag lady roaming the streets.

"Does a cat have an ass?"

"Well, yyyes. But are you really sure?" Madeline said.

"Do bears shit in the woods?"

"Yes, yes they do. You're not just giving me a load of crap are you Al"? Madeline said. "I don't want to get my ass blown off when this thing crashes and disintegrates!"

"Of course you don't, Madeline, but remember I'm getting on this plane with my wife and we both like our asses on just the way they are, thank you." Adding in a very serious and convincing voice, "He is rated a first class pilot and a mechanic also. He is very versatile, a renaissance man."

What a bunch of bullshit, the co-pilot probably got his flying license at the local Sears store; the same place the pilot got his. These guys probably failed to get approved to be Alaskan bush pilots and this bucket of bolts should have been mothballed years ago—especially after the top came off one just like it in Hawaii at thirty thousand feet.

For a second, or two, Al felt a twinge of guilt for lying to this pitiful, frightened, shell of a woman, but, what the hell, it was for her
own good anyway. If they left her here without any money she would
have had to live on the streets like a bag lady or try to sell herself.
Either way Al didn't think that she would have eaten very well. She
would never have made it as a bag lady on the streets because she
would have pissed off too many people with her constant whining
and Happy Harold had just about had enough of her anyway and
was either going to break her legs or leave her here, or both. Better
that she attempt to go home with him and take her revenge on her
daughter-in-law.

Finally, a combination of exhaustion from her struggles and a
desire to believe Al caused her to give up the ghost and let go of the
fence.

Of course, having let go without warning caused the three of them
to go sprawling to the pavement. Harold got up cursing and brush-
ing himself off, Mickey extricated Madeline's foot from his mouth
and spit out, "This woman's crazy and dangerous. I'm taking my
chances on the plane." He then stomped off cursing under his breath
with Harold following him.

Al helped Madeline up while she continued to whimper and beg
for divine mercy. As they reached the plane, Mickey and Harold had
already gone up the stairs and were totally prepared, even anxious, to
meet whatever lay ahead. Poor Johnny Ho Yo was still standing there
mumbling incoherently with a glazed look in his eyes. Al thought
about telling him the same story about the co-pilot but said screw it,
since he probably wouldn't understand or believe him anyway. So he
just grabbed his hand and pulled him up the stairs behind him while
pushing Madeline up in front of him. She stumbled along with her
straw hat scrunched down on her head, the brim was torn on the
right side and hung down over her right eye and ear, her dress was
dirty and torn, she was totally disheveled and was whimpering as she

limped to her seat. She looked like she had been attacked by a pack of wild dogs.

Al deposited them in their seats and took his own beside Mary.

"Where have you been? You look like you've been through hell!"

"Oh, nothing really. Just a friendly little discussion on the merits of continuing this flight."

"Well, I'm glad that you all agreed to go on. I'm getting anxious to get home and see the kids."

"Just keep your fingers crossed. By the way, have you seen that priest?"

"Al! Al! For Christ sakes do something! Will you!" Mary's shrieking brought him out of his reverie and he realized that they were still on the runaway bus hurtling through New York City, being driven by a crazed woman. Junior was still up front shouting out the window, one woman was hunched down in her seat saying her rosary and there were strange gagging sounds coming from the bathroom.

"I'm hanging on for my life! Besides, I think that we are almost there," Al managed to blurt out.

"I sure hope that you are right because I'm about to get sick!"

Nadine was just as determined as ever to get them to the pier on time. She missed her true calling—that of a tank commander. Fortunately, she laid on the horn all the way and even New Yorkers have respect for a bus going sixty-five miles an hour through the city streets.

Just then the bus broke out of the congested streets, bolted across a divided highway, did a power slide to the right, and came to a screeching stop in front of the entrance to the cruise ship. It was twelve fifty-nine; she made it with a minute to spare.

Nadine opened the door shouting—"hold that ship!"

The power slide had forced the bathroom door open and a slip of a man, as white as a ghost, was thrown out and splattered against the opposite window. Then a very large woman forced herself through the doorway, with a look of hatred on her flushed face, as she bellowed "you skinny little stupid shit, if I get my hands on you I'm going to sit on you and flatten you like a pancake!"

Fortunately, there were twenty-six other passengers in the aisle between this obsessed woman and Nadine, who was now surrounded by various police and cruise officials.

"What will happen to Nadine? Will she get into trouble?" Junior asked with uncharacteristic concern.

"I doubt it. They will probably give her some kind of medal for getting us here on time and providing the added entertainment to boot," Al reassured him, secretly hoping that they would lock her up so that she couldn't drive the bus at the end of the trip.

CHAPTER 4

*I*t was a mad scramble for the luggage; Nadine and the other representatives of the cruise line were pre-occupied with the New York City Police Department and the passengers were on their own. After a half-hour of hot, sweaty work, the male passengers managed to get everything off the bus and sorted out to the rightful owners. What the hell, they packed it so they were one step ahead of the game when they had to unpack it. Of course, they did their share of moaning, groaning, and grunting just as they had done back in Boston. However, they did still have some mercy left in them as they allowed Slim, the man who was nearly crushed in the lavatory by his wife, Big Bertha, to sit and watch as he tried to recover from his ordeal and was slowly getting his color back. His breathing was becoming more regular and was no longer like that of a man trying to suck in air through a bent straw.

Now that they had the luggage sorted out, all they needed were some baggage handlers to get it inside the building, where they would board the ship. Of course there were many other people arriving at the same time so that there were not enough baggage handlers around. Al would have carried them himself except that they had everything but the kitchen sink with them.

If that sounds like an exaggeration, it's not! When Al's family goes on vacation they like to be prepared for every possible contingency and are deathly afraid they may have to go without some of life's creature comforts, that had become absolute necessities. One thing was for certain, outdoor campers they definitely were not.

Since they were on a cruise, they would have to bring dressy clothes for the evening and casual clothes for the daytime and warm clothes for the nights on the ocean and cool clothes for the warm days in Bermuda. By the time they were done, there wasn't much left in their closets unless they were considered too old or not in style. Of course this meant that they nearly broke the bank to buy everyone a new wardrobe for the trip. Even Al had to get new duds, over his vehement protest as to the lack of need for all these new things. Those old jerseys of his would do just fine, they were just getting broken in and the stains were in just the right places.

Of course, even with as much luggage as they had, it was nothing like what they took with them when the children were younger and they used to vacation for two weeks every summer at Goose Rocks Beach in Kennebunkport, Maine. At one point, they had gone there ten years in a row and had it down to such a science that the pioneers moving west, in their covered wagons, would have been proud of them.

They had purchased a utility trailer just for this purpose, after having gotten tired of trying to get everything in the car for the first few years. Of course this was the ultimate answer because now they didn't have to leave one damn thing behind.

Although it was a good size trailer, at five feet wide and seven feet long, they still used to manage to get it full to overflowing. And this was after already loading the trunk to the point that Al would have to use a rubber strap to hold the lid down, had already piled as much as he dared on the roof racks, and spread out as much as possible between, under, and around bodies inside the car.

They used to take so much shit it was unbelievable: from the electric frying pan to the Weber kettle, from the portable stereo to the portable TV, and from the lawn chairs to the electric fan. Can you believe that, an electric fan on the coast of Maine? When the kids were younger they had the playpen, the stroller, the high chair, and about fifty boxes of pampers. When they got older these were replaced by baseball gloves, bats, footballs, volleyballs, soccer balls, beach balls, whiffle balls, frisbees, fishing poles, air mattresses, kites, monopoly, sorry, checkers, yahtzee, scrabble, cards, toy cars, boats, planes, hair dryers, popcorn poppers, individual stereos, friends, dogs, bicycles, and, of course, the four man rubber raft. The raft was Al's.

Al used to have to start packing three hours before they wanted to leave in order to give him enough time to get everything in and to maximize the utilization of the space available. Al also needed this time to calculate the proper weight distribution of the load so that he would not have an accident as a result of the inability to steer or brake properly. He used to need a half-hour just to secure the load so that he wouldn't lose anything on the road or risk having the load shift, sending them out of control or even flipping them over. This always used to be a source of aggravation between Mary and Al.

She always thought that he went overboard in securing the load and, of course, by the time that he got finished with this everyone was getting testy and wanted to be on their way. By the time that Al got the canvas cover in place, and was in the process of securing it with a third length of rope, Mary would have had enough.

"For the love of God, Al, how many ropes are you going to use on this thing?"

"You know you can't be too careful when traveling on the highway dear," Al would calmly reply, as he was winding another length of rope over, around, and through the bicycles that were placed on top of the canvas.

"Al, hell will freeze over before anything falls out of this thing."

"I suppose that means the chain and padlocks are out," was Al's reply. This never pleased Mary and Al would give in and concede that it was secure enough and they could finally be on their way.

They would all squeeze into the car and begin their trip, the car straining forward under its heavy load. Before they were out of the driveway one of the kids would invariably ask the question that, at that particular point in time, would really piss Al off—"Are we there yet?" By the time they were a mile down the road Al would have heard this same question fifteen times and would have to threaten them to stop asking or they would turn right around and go home. Then they would continue on like a band of gypsies and Al was thankful that it was a three hour ride; he needed that much time to recover before he had to unpack all the crap.

"Maybe we can get a baggage handler over here some day," Mary questioned, bringing Al back to the pier and their current load of luggage.

"I would, if I could get the attention of any of them, but they are very good at ignoring you when they want to. Hello! Hey! Baggage handler, sir, could we get some service over here when you get a chance, please?" Al was hoping that a little politeness, said with just a touch of pleading, might be the right approach.

"Don't worry buddy, I see ya! We'll get there when your turn comes pal!" He managed to grunt with the proper lack of civility in his voice. Al thought that they have to take classes to make sure they have developed just the right amount of rudeness to put you in your place and remind you that you are in New York City, at their mercy, and yet not anger you so much that you will not give them a good tip. In fact, the best ones have an ability to insult you in such a way that you give them a larger tip for fear that, if they are not satisfied, they will really rip you apart and make you feel small and cheap in front of half the world.

Eventually, a big burly guy came over and grunted, "are these yours pal?"

"Yes they are," Al replied pleasantly.

"Do you want them inside?" He grunted again, with a look on his face that said he would just as soon piss on them as pick them up.

By this time Al was about ready to reply, "No, I want you to take them and stick them up your ass," when he caught Mary's eye and realized he would be in big trouble, so he meekly said—"Yes, would you please."

The baggage handler just grunted a few more times and began to load the luggage onto his cart. None of the women or children could understand these grunts, and it's a good thing. Of course being a man, Al could understand perfectly what he meant, even if he did grunt with a New York accent, since it is not unusual at all for men to communicate in this manner. It goes back to the days of cave dwelling and Cro-Magnon man. Even though anthropologists would tell us that Cro-Magnon man has long since been gone, they are really alive and well and living among us. Just look at the NFL if you don't believe it.

Al learned this art from his father who was extremely adept at it. In fact, he can only remember one conversation with him that wasn't related to sports that lasted for more than five minutes and wasn't punctuated with frequent grunts. They were in a room that was fairly large but still felt very close. He could hear Big Bru droning on in the background, even though he had agreed to what he was saying some twenty minutes ago. The significance of this long conversation cannot be understated. Big Bru had never been noted for his long, eloquent speeches—to say the least.

To the contrary, his father usually communicated with a series of grunts and hand gestures, but of course, it was a very complex series of grunts. The scariest part was that Al had learned to understand him quite well. They were always at their best in the morning. His father used to wake him up with a loud wrap at the door and a deep guttural grunt that said 'get your ass out of bed now or you're in deep shit'. Of course, Al's feet hit the floor before the grunt was completed and responded with two quick shallow grunts of his own that said—'I was already awake and getting up'.

They would then meet downstairs and exchange grunts—which stood for good morning. While eating breakfast, they rarely grunted with each other at all; grunting is a very simple and concise form of communication and is not conducive to small talk. When they worked together in the summer, their longest gruntversations were it's—'time for lunch' and it's—'time to go home'.

So this conversation, which used actual words and lasted for over an hour, was of monumental significance. Big Bru had actually opened up and shared his philosophy of life, which was—"you don't want to freeze your ass off do you?".

Truthfully, the main tenant of—'Philosophy by Bruno'—was that one's goal in life should be to get an education so that you would not have to freeze, sweat, or work your ass off.

This may sound funny, but it can actually be quite a serious situation. Think about it for a minute. If you lose your ass then how can you—hold your pants up, or sit down? You couldn't bet it anymore, football players wouldn't have anything to pat each other on, baseball players wouldn't have anything to scratch on national TV, you couldn't moon anyone, and you couldn't tell someone to go kiss it.

Unfortunately, this does actually happen. Surely you've seen guys that have no ass—the back of their pants are flat and baggy and always falling down. This has nothing to do with whether the man is fat or skinny. There are many men that have large beer bellies that hang out over their belts while the back of their pants just hang there drooping. The worst part is that the butt crack at the top of their ass is always showing. Certainly, this is why suspenders were invented. Why else would any man wear something that you have to attach in the back, pull up and over your shoulders, and attach in the front just to hold your pants up when a belt works perfectly well and looks so much better.

It must have been a very cold winter in 1985 judging by the popularity of suspenders in 1986. Al wondered if it were possible to be fitted with a prosthesis to replace an ass that had been frozen, sweated, or worked off.

"Listen to me kid," Bruno continued, "you don't want to go to work in gray work clothes, bust your ass all day, and come home tired and dirty."

Al guessed that busting your ass was the first stage of working it off.

"Ya wanna wear a white shirt and tie, go to a nice office and do easy, clean work, and make lotsa money. Whata ya wanna bust your ass and make peanuts for?"

'Beats the shit out of me,' Al thought.

"In the winter you freeze your ass off, and in the summer you sweat your..."

"O.K., O.K., I've heard enough! I wasn't prepared to risk my ass; I'm certainly not prepared to risk that part of my anatomy! Dad, listen please! You're right, you've talked me into it, I'll go to college."

Tell me? Who could have ignored such a convincing argument, so eloquently presented. Of course, if he had asked Al in the first place he would have told him that he already wanted to go to college. After all Al didn't want to work at a job where you break, freeze, or sweat off various parts of your anatomy. Especially since it doesn't even pay well.

While speaking of Cro-Magnon men you can add New York City baggage handlers to the list, which was quite obvious watching this one load the luggage onto his cart; a pissed off gorilla would have been gentler.

Having completed throwing the luggage onto his cart, he grunted and proceeded towards the elevator, expecting them to follow along like little ducklings. However, Al felt more like sheep being led to slaughter as they entered a large freight elevator, that smelled like it had been used for a herd of sheep, with two or three other groups, also on their way to be fleeced.

The elevator took them up two flights and then opened on the other side so that they were still following the gorillas and, in unison, the three handlers grunted at them and they all dutifully followed them off. They led them to a large open area, deposited them there, and began to unload their luggage.

"Why are you unloading our luggage here?" Al dared to ask. "It looks as if it needs to be down there at the far end of the building."

"It does," he grunted.

"Then why are you unloading it here?" Al asked again, in a somewhat perplexed but civil tone.

"'Cause I'm the outside baggage handler and ya gotta get an inside baggage handler to take them the rest of the way," he grunted in reply, with a mystified look in his eye because Al didn't already know this.

"What is the difference between an inside baggage handler and an outside baggage handler, may I ask?" Al was beginning to realize that this was some chickenshit setup to extract more money from unwary travelers and thus employ more baggage handlers.

"An outside baggage handler takes your luggage from the street to here and an inside baggage handler takes it from here to there," he grunted with a look on his face that said—'what friggin cabbage patch did you just come outta, ya dumb shit'.

As Al's blood pressure rose another twenty points, he wanted to tell him that he knew where all the unemployed lawyers were working and to kiss his ass. But, instead, like a good little country bumpkin, he thanked him for educating him in the ways of the world and proceeded to dig into his wallet to pay him.

Al gave him a ten-dollar tip anyway because he knew the SOB would make him feel like two cents if he didn't.

Now he had to wait in line for another gorilla to come along and give him a ration of shit before finally doing him the extreme favor of moving his luggage one hundred and fifty feet for another ten dollars.

Finally, after another humiliating experience inflicted upon him by the inside porter and after a total of three hours of standing in lines, their luggage was on board somewhere and they were in the process of being herded on board, along with some fifteen hundred other passengers. They were swept along the corridors and down a flight of stairs until, after about twenty minutes, found themselves standing in front of their cabins.

"Thank God we are finally here!" Mary said.

"Ya! I'm starving. I need something to eat," B.A.D. said.

"Me, too!" B.J. chipped in.

"I need to take a shower," Jennifer added.

"No kidding," wise cracked B.A.D..

"Yes, well I want a double, no make it a triple scotch—straight up, so that I can erase the memory of this first day," Al grunted.

Then they opened the doors and stood there with their mouths hanging open. The rooms were like closets, even though they had gotten the best rooms short of the suites.

"What's this shit?" B.A.D. was the first to respond.

"Hey! Watch it!" Mary warned.

"Ya, watch it, but he has a point, these are not what I expected," Al said.

The cabin meant for Mary and Al had two small twin beds, each no wider than a baby's crib, separated by just enough room for one person to walk down. There was a small dressing table that totally blocked the passage to the beds when anyone was sitting at it and there was a closet that didn't stand a snowball's chance in hell of holding all of their clothes.

Then Al opened the door to what he thought was a broom closet and, much to his distress, he was staring at the bathroom. This bathroom was not to be believed it was so small; there was hardly enough room to step inside and then close the door. The commode was in a corner and placed in such a way that, when you sat at it, your knees would be pointed in the opposite corner and the sink would be hitting your right shoulder, while your left shoulder was pressed against the shower stall. This made taking care of personal hygiene quite an acrobatic feat, requiring a great deal of agility and determination.

The shower was another interesting piece of work. It was round, with a door that slid around inside the shower when open, and created a solid, capsule like, enclosure when closed. To say that space within this shower was minimal was a gross understatement.

The children's room was worse because they had bunk beds on one wall to accommodate the three of them. In all other respects, it was just like their parents.

"Are you sure that these are the right rooms?" Mary asked.

"The keys fit don't they," Al answered, more abruptly than he had intended.

"What I meant was that maybe they gave us the wrong room assignments," Mary shot back, with justifiable indignation.

"I'm not staying in this closet with these two creeps," Jennifer said. "It's bad enough to have to stay with them at all, but I at least thought that I would have a little room to get away from the smell of them."

The them rolled off of her tongue with a stinging sarcasm so natural to teenage girls. Of course, this was like pushing the starter button for her two brothers to kick into action and, when these two team up and put it into high gear, you do not want to be the target of their attack.

"Listen dog breath, I don't like having to be this close to you either! In fact it makes me want to throw up!" B.A.D. said.

"Ya, puke face!!" Was B.J.'s vile contribution.

"You shut up, you little dip!" Jennifer sniped.

"Al, please get them to stop," Mary said. "I hate it when they talk to each other like that."

"All right, that's enough you guys. You're not helping the situation any," Al said. "I'll go and try to find someone to see if we have the right rooms."

Just then one of the ships staff came by and Al stopped him to ask about the rooms.

"Yes sir, these are the best cabins next to the suites."

"But these are so small."

"You should see the cheapest ones, if you think these are small."

"No thanks! These are bad enough."

"This doesn't look anything like the brochure I saw," Mary questioned.

"It certainly doesn't," Jennifer felt compelled to add.

"Please let us handle this Jennifer," Al said.

"Well, they do take the picture from a very favorable angle," the staff member responded.

"I guess so," Al said.

"Excuse me sir, but it is almost time to go on deck for the lifeboat drill," the staff member said, hoping to extricate himself from this uncomfortable situation.

"Yes, well thank you," Al said, realizing that he had no control over this.

"He's right, we should be getting on deck. We can put our clothes away later," Mary added.

"I think that we should go and complain to the Captain," Jennifer said.

"That will do a lot of good, you dork," B.A.D. said.

"At least I have an idea, you moron," Jennifer shot back. "You haven't had an idea in your life. At least not one that you could share with us."

"Damn it! Will you two put a lid on it before I really get mad," Al said. "Get your butts in gear and get up on deck."

They all trudged out of the cabin and headed for the outside deck. When they arrived on deck, most of the other passengers were already there and the Captain and crew were preparing to give them the lifeboat and safety instructions. Al didn't quite know what to expect, since this was his first time on this size ship, but he thought that this would at least make some sense, unlike the safety instructions you receive on airplane flights.

The airlines are required to provide these instructions on each flight, but it is really a waste of time, if not an asinine thing to do. They go through these elaborate instructions of what doors to get out of, how to use the oxygen masks, where to find the flotation devices, and how to use them. The only thing that they accomplish is to scare the shit out of people who are already nervous about flying. If they feel that it is mandatory to give some instructions they should give something that is worthwhile.

The flight attendants should come on and announce sweetly, "In the event of an impending disaster would everyone please unfasten their seat belts, lean forward in your seats, bend over as far as possible, grab your ankles, stick your head between your legs, and kiss your ass good-bye. In the event that you are not limber enough to kiss your own ass good-bye, it is perfectly acceptable to kiss the ass of the person next to you. Should the person next to you be hesitant or unwilling to give your ass its final good-bye kiss then please ring for an attendant and we will do our best to accommodate you in the limited time available. Since things will be happening at a very rapid pace, we do request that you refrain from any lingering embraces. At this time the overhead nitrous oxide masks will drop down, taking yours and holding it to your mouth, take two deep breaths and then we'll laugh our freshly kissed asses off all the way down."

Now, as the staff was showing everyone how to put on their life jackets, the woman next to Al was getting increasingly nervous. This was the same woman who had been screaming uncontrollably on the bus earlier in the day. Again, Al thought that she looked familiar, but just couldn't place her. Apparently, after she had left off with the Bloody Mary's, she picked up with the champagne her children had sent her and her husband as a bon voyage gift and she was pretty tipsy.

"In the event of an imminent sinking you will be instructed to take your place on deck, the same location as you have now," the Captain announced over the ship's public address system.

"Oh my God we're sinking? I didn't even know we were out to sea yet! All our clothes are in the cabin! What….."

Her husband interrupted in exasperation, "For Christ sakes will you put a lid on it and stay away from the damn champagne—you dip shit."

"Then put on your life jackets and get into the lifeboat as instructed by the crew member assigned to your station," the Captain continued.

"C'mon Harold we have to get into our lifeboat," she muttered as she bolted for the boat with her life jacket on backwards.

Her husband grabbed her by the scruff of her neck and pulled her back growling through gritted teeth, "Son of a bitch, Madeline, will you get your fat ass back here before I throw you overboard."

Harold? Madeline? Holy shit that is who they were, the same couple from Al's abortion of a plane trip to the Caribbean a few years ago.

"Madeline, get a hold of yourself, this is just a drill and anyway, even if it were for real, remember—'shit happens'," Al said.

"What the hell, it's not, no it can't be! Is it really you? Is it really 'shit happening' Al?" Madeline groaned. "My God we really are in deep shit now, this must be the Titanic."

"Nice seeing you, too, Madeline."

"And that concludes our lifeboat safety drill, you may return to your cabins and we all hope that you will have a very pleasant trip," the Captain concluded.

CHAPTER 5

Finally, the DeGregorios were sitting at their dining table, preparing to have their first shipboard meal, at the end of a very, very long day. After the lifeboat drill, they had returned to their cabin and spent the next two hours struggling to get all of their clothing into the limited space available, which was like trying to put ten pounds of shit into a five pound bag. Then they had to stand in line for another hour for the privilege of getting a table assignment so that they could dine for the next seven days with six, not so perfect, strangers. Apparently someone or thing, a misguided computer program probably, made a rather pathetic attempt to match table companions. There was the Carr family of four to compliment the DeGregorio family. Then there was Sally Roberts and Harry Holt to round out the table. They were not together, but apparently the computer plays matchmaker, too.

The L. Terrence Carr family was noticeably stiff and reserved, as evidenced by the formality of their introduction.

"Hello, I'm L. Terrence Carr and this is my wife—Margaret Elizabeth, my son—Jonathan Francis and my daughter—Alison Marie," he announced. The DeGregorio's received weak handshakes, like holding a dead fish, from the two males and cordial, but cool, hellos from the two women.

"Hi, I'm Al DeGregorio and this is my wife—Mary, my oldest son—Bruno, my daughter—Jennifer, and my youngest son—B.J.," Al said. Immediately thinking he was not going to like this man or his family. Somewhat of a snap judgment possibly, but the one thing Al had always been good at was the ability to immediately spot a real dick-head when he met one and he had a feeling that L. Terrence, alias 'Terry', was going to prove to be a major leaguer.

"I'm a partner in a major Wall Street law firm. What are you into?" Terry asked.

'Shit up to my eyeballs, you friggin turd', Al wanted to shout. Instead he meekly responded—"well I'm in business and currently between positions." Al had felt that he wasn't going to like this shit-head the minute he laid eyes on him, but now he knew that he hated the son-of-a-bitch.

"Hello mates, I'm Harry, Harry Holt," he said in a heavy Australian accent. He was in his mid to late thirties, six feet one or two, blonde, handsome, and arrogant. "I believe that I am going to be your dinner companion during the cruise."

"Hello, Harry, I'm L. Terrence Carr," shit-head Terry pompously announced as he extended his hand.

"Hi, I'm Al DeGregorio," Al said shaking Harry's hand.

Both Terrence and Al then proceeded to introduce him to the rest of their families. He definitely was a very charming man with the ladies and was very free with his compliments, which were well received by them. Al immediately realized that 'Handsome Harry' was, in reality 'Horseshit Harry'. Yes, another one of Al's instant analysis, but he had developed a philosophy over the years that if it looks like horseshit and it smells like horseshit then it probably is horseshit.

While Harry was still busy entertaining the women, the last table companion came in.

"Hello, I'm Sally Roberts." She spoke in a soft and tentative voice. Though somewhat shy, she was friendly as she was being introduced around.

Sally was a pretty, if somewhat plain looking, woman with mid-length brown hair and brown eyes, tallish at about five foot seven, with a medium build at about one hundred and thirty pounds, round pert breasts, a firm derriere and full, inviting lips. As Al watched her being introduced, he thought the smile on her face belied the sadness in her eyes. It seemed to him that life had not always been kind to 'Sally Sad Eyes'. She looked like she was in her early to mid-forties, an age when one often comes to the realization that hopes and dreams are a thing of the past. That they are for younger people who haven't yet experienced the many humiliations and defeats that life has to offer, time after time after time, until you are completely worn down and just simply give up and quit. It may well be this realization that defines mid-life crisis. Sally's sad eyes suggested that she might have reached this point in her life; another of Al's instant analyses.

Just as Sally completed her hellos, the dining room staff, that was to serve them for the week, came to introduce themselves.

"Bonjour, I am Jean Paul Aumond and I will be your Maitre'd for this voyage," came the French accented introduction of a very hand-some man in his mid-thirties. "This is Antonio Zabelli who will be your wine steward."

Antonio was a suave, handsome Italian, also in his early to mid-thirties, who carried himself with a certain arrogance that said he understood these facts. He was about five foot nine, dark skinned, with jet-black hair and of medium build.

"Bonjorno," he said, with an infectious smile, as he bowed from the waist.

"This is Fernando Dallesandro, your waiter," Jean Paul continued. Fernando was in his late twenties, with dark hair and dark complexion and, of course, good looking.

"And, finally, this is Roberto Accosta who will be your bus boy." Roberto was the youngest, in his early twenties, with a twinkle in his eyes and a big smile who, according to the ladies, was more cute and cuddly than rugged and handsome.

"Ola!" Roberto beamed with a smile that went from ear to ear.

Jean Paul continued, "It will be our pleasure and duty to serve you during the voyage. We want to make sure that you get everything that you desire. If there is anything at all that you want, please just ask us, we will do our best to provide it for you."

At this point Al didn't want to know what was going through the minds of the women. He thought he even caught a twinkle in Mary's eye and he knew that Jennifer was about to lose control, like a dog in a meat market. Margaret Elizabeth was breathing heavy and, for just an instant, there was a gleam in the eye of Sally 'sad eyes'. It was obvious there was a standard to be met in order to get one of these staff positions. The criteria has to include the ability to spark a woman's fantasies. This group represented a floating United Nations of female fantasy producing hunks. It's no wonder that women, particularly single women, enjoy cruises so much more than men do. That's why Al questioned what 'Handsome Harry' was doing on a cruise all by himself. Al was going to have to keep an eye on him to see if he was here alone because he expected that there would be many single women available, or if he liked the staff himself.

"Ola, Senor! How are you?" cooed Jennifer sweetly addressing Fernando, as her eyes were bulging from her head.

"You speak Spanish very well, Senorita," Fernando replied a little too attentively for Al's taste.

'Get your eyes the hell off of my daughter and any ideas out of your head,' Al thought. He knew he shouldn't have let Mary talk him out of bringing that chastity belt. He thought about locking her up in the cabin for the rest of the cruise and taking turns guarding the door with B.A.D. and B.J.

"Well, I've been in my school's Spanish immersion program since I was a little girl," Jennifer continued.

Al wanted to scream that she was still a little girl and not to forget it while bounding out of his chair, leaping across the table, putting his salad fork to the would be child molester's throat, grabbing him by his testicles until he was singing soprano, and explaining the facts of life to him and his cohorts about messing with 'Big Al's' daughter.

"Whatta ya mean since you were a little girl, your still only fifteen," B.A.D. sneered.

That's a good boy Junior, Al thought, cut her legs out from under her and make sure that these vultures know that she *is jail bait*.

"I'm almost sixteen and I'm a lot more grown up for my age than you are, puke face," Jennifer retorted, unable to prevent herself from sinking to his level and proving his point, to Al's extreme pleasure.

"All right that's enough you two," Mary said sternly.

"I'd love to be able to practice my Spanish with a real Spaniard," Jennifer continued.

"I would be happy to speak Spanish with you during the meals, Senorita," Fernando replied very diplomatically.

"Perhaps we can also teach you to speak Italian, Senorina?" Antonio added.

Back off paisan!

"Parle vous Francais, mademoiselle?" The words flowed like velvet from Jean Paul.

Sweet Jesus, Al thought, we're surrounded.

Jennifer was certainly enjoying herself, eating up all of the attention. But Al could see that Alison Marie did not like taking a back seat and L. Terrence certainly did not appreciate the fact that he and his family were not the center of attention.

L. Terrence Carr was in his late forties, black hair speckled with gray, medium built with the beginnings of a paunch, average good looks, and obviously someone who was used to being in control and at the center of things. A graduate of Cornell and of Harvard Law School, he was now a partner in a prestigious Wall Street law firm.

His wife, Margaret Elizabeth, was also in her late forties, a woman of average good looks, dark hair, with traces of gray, a little over weight and about five foot five. She was very conservatively, but expensively, dressed. Margaret Elizabeth seemed to be one of those people that almost always have a scowl on their face. It was obvious that she was not a happy woman. She had the appearance of a woman who had long ago settled for having the trappings of the good life—furs, expensive jewelry, an expensive house, many nice clothes, a summer home, and everything else that goes along with a husband who has a big, 'important' job with an income to match. She obviously possessed the loneliness that accompanies marriage to a man who puts his position and career above all else, including his family. She would have preferred to have a close, loving, nurturing relationship with her husband. To have a true friend instead of a man that was driven to 'succeed' and unfortunately measured success by the amount of material possessions that he could accumulate and the power that he could wield. So she has had to content herself with a more distant and material relationship, a relationship that has left her a cold and lonely woman, the type of woman who could only be described as a real tight ass. She has attempted to fill the void created by this relationship by totally devoting herself to her children. This has only been partially successful at best and, now that they were getting older, it was becoming less and less fulfilling, as she was becoming less and less needed, everyday.

Their son, Jonathan Francis, was a rather non-descript young man of average height, with a slight, even somewhat frail, build who, at eighteen, was starting college in the fall. He was going to the college of his father's choice because he had to if he expected him to pay for it. He was also in pre-law, another requirement. It didn't take long to see that Jonathan was wound as tight as a drum and could unravel at any time. He was an unhappy, grouchy, whinny young man who was struggling against the bonds that confined him. His family called him Jonathan Francis most often and, occasionally, Jonathan for short. Al had the feeling that he wanted to be more of a Frank or even a Frankie than a Jonathan Francis. Maybe this cruise could help him accomplish this; after all, he was going to have an 'opportunity' to spend the next week with B.A.D.. Heaven help the Carr's, Al had a gut feeling that their life might never be the same again. Whether it would be for the better or for the worse he wasn't at all sure.

Alison Marie was a cute girl, with short brown hair, an attractive but girlish figure, consistent with someone who had just turned fifteen, the same age as Jennifer. She had a gleam in her eye and a smile on her face that said she was a happy person, certainly happier than her brother. Perhaps, as is often the case, she was Daddy's little girl and had escaped the harsh and demanding manner that her father was so adept at administering to Jonathan Francis, the heir apparent. Al was afraid that Alison and Jennifer were going to get along very well, which could mean real trouble. It was always more difficult when children had cohorts in crime.

"May I suggest the swordfish or the tenderloin of beef, both are excellent this evening," announced Jean Paul as he handed out menus. "Fernando will take your order whenever you are ready."

Fernando was standing dutifully behind and one step to the right of Jean Paul. One thing was apparent very quickly, there existed a definite pecking order among the ships crew.

True to its reputation, the menu offered a wide variety of appetizers and entrees. If you ordered one entree and didn't like it you could order another with no problem at all. The dining staff would do anything they possibly could to keep the guests happy. This was because they would be evaluated at the end of the cruise and, if they got bad comments, they would lose some of the perks they were accustomed to and eventually could even lose their positions altogether. For example, there were a number of waiters called floaters who would fill in to give the regular staff time off or fill in if they were sick. As floaters they were considered back-up and received fewer privileges than the regular staff. This meant instead of having a room to themselves they would have to share facilities with three other floaters or with the busboys. Given the fact these waiters often entertained female guests in their rooms, making considerable extra money doing so, the loss of privacy could be devastating.

"Messieurs Carr and DeGregorio, you both have a selection of wine for two evenings compliments of your travel agents," Antonio said as Fernando finished taking the food orders. "Would you care to order something this evening?"

"Yea Dad! Let's order some white zinfandel," B.J. chimed in.

"What do you know about white zinfandel?.

"Remember I had some at my cousin Judy's wedding and I liked it."

"Yes, I remember that you had a sip and now I suppose that you are an expert and can give Antonio some pointers."

"No, but I do know what I like."

One thing Al could always count on was B.J.'s self-confidence. He was never lacking for any and he had to admire him for it.

"Okay, Antonio! We'll have some white zinfandel with our meal."

"And we will have a bottle of the chardonnay with our meals," said L. Terrence, indicating a French selection that Al didn't recognize. Not surprisingly.

When Antonio brought out the wine he opened Al's first and began to go through the typical ceremony of handing him the cork, to test that it was moist, and then, of course, he would pour a small amount of wine for him to taste to see if he approved of it. Al recognized this was traditional and even necessary when one is dealing with fine wines that can go bad rather easily. However, for someone who considers Gallo Premium a fine wine, Al usually considered this procedure to be unnecessary, if not even a bit ridiculous.

As Antonio was about to pour his sample, B.J. spoke up, "Dad! Let me sample it!"

"What do you know about sampling wine?" B.A.D. and Jennifer snapped in unison. Older siblings can be very tough.

"I've tasted wine before," he replied in as controlled and mature a voice as he could muster. Al always allowed the children to have small tastes of wine and beer because he felt it didn't hurt them and it took some of the mystery and allure out of it. And, since he didn't hold this ceremony in very high regard anyway, he was happy to let him do it.

"Sure! Go ahead Ace. Enjoy yourself."

As Antonio poured a small amount of wine into B.J.'s glass Al could feel the contempt boiling up in L. Terrence. He was probably asking himself how he, a prominent Wall Street lawyer, the son of a judge, could have been placed with such a peasant with an obvious disregard for the finer things in life. But that was all right, Al never did care much what a numb nuts like Terry thought anyway. He always disliked people who put on airs, nor was he ever very politically astute; he would prefer to cut through all the crap and call it the way he saw it.

However, B.J. was eating it up as he sniffed the wine and then took a small sip and rolled it around in his mouth.

"This is an excellent vintage Antonio, you may pour now," B.J. said.

This amused Al's family, the staff and possibly even Jonathan Francis.

"It's Mr. Zabelli to you Ace, and don't forget it," Al reminded him gently.

When it came time for L. Terrence to receive his wine he played it to the hilt. After his first sip he made a little face and Antonio tensed. L. Terrence definitely tuned into this; a predator sensing fear in its prey. Then he did what Al had never actually seen before—he sent the wine back.

"I think that this bottle has begun to turn. What do you think Antonio?"

Antonio dutifully poured himself a sample and tasted it slowly. Telling from his expression, he thought it was perfectly fine but, not wanting to displease his customer in any way, he agreed that it was beginning to turn. "Senor Carr you indeed have a sensitive and well trained palate as this wine is just beginning to turn, ever so slightly. I commend you on your ability, as most people would never have detected this. I had great difficulty myself and might have missed it had you not discovered it and brought it to my attention."

Okay Antonio you're laying it on a little thick; Al thought he might have to roll up his pant legs since it was already too late to save his shoes. He was beginning to understand just how far the staff would go to please the passengers in order to maintain their positions.

The look of disgust on Margaret Elizabeth's face made it obvious this had happened many times before and was getting very old with her. From the way Jonathan's eyes rolled in his head it was obvious he would have been happy to hold his father while his mother kicked him in the ass for being such a turd, as usual.

Antonio was already back with another bottle of chardonnay and a worried look on his face. He must have run all the way. He was probably afraid that L. Terrence would hold this against him and include it in his evaluation at the end of the week.

"Senor Carr, please try this bottle and let me know if it meets with your approval."

Well, L. Terrence played it to the hilt again. Slowly rolling the cork in his fingers, sniffing the wine and then finally tasting it, and swishing it in his mouth. It seemed as if he were making a special point to show Al how it was supposed to be done.

"Oh yes, Antonio, this is much better. The way it should be."

"Thank you senor, I hope that you will enjoy the rest of your meal."

He was probably also hoping that he would fall overboard before the cruise was over. Guys like him were always trying to establish their superior position in life and, in the process, made his life difficult and unpleasant.

By this time the first course was being served and the rest of the meal progressed without further incident. While not the most fabulous food, there certainly was plenty of it. Since they are preparing food for some fifteen hundred passengers you can't expect it to be a gourmet meal. However, they make up for this by making sure that you have all you want to eat. The problem is that, if Al kept eating like this, he was going to put on five to ten pounds and never fit into the ridiculous little broom closets that they try to pass off as showers.

As it was, his shower that afternoon was an adventure in and of itself. He wasn't sure he was going to be able to fit at first and then, as he began to squeeze in, he wasn't sure he wanted to. He managed to get his fat ass into the tube they called a shower then slid the door, which slides around from the inside of the shower itself, closed and immediately felt like he was in an upright coffin. There was no way to turn around in this enclosed space. He could barely move his arms as they rubbed against the sides of the shower and stood there trying to figure out how he was going to wash himself while the water beat on his face, as it poured out of the shower head just six inches away. He slowly managed to reach the soap dish and grab the bar. It was one of those little shitty bars of soap they give you in hotels and motels. He always hated washing with a bar of soap the size of which he usually threw away as used up. He then was able to slowly lather his chest and stomach and let the soapy water roll down the rest of the front of his body, cleaning as it went. Fortunately he had no ground in dirt that required any elbow grease to eliminate.

Al could forget about washing his feet, and that was okay, but he had to wash his back and butt, which wasn't going to be easy. He had to think about this and plan his moves very carefully. He moved his head slightly to the left and then managed to reach his right shoulder with his left hand. Then he reversed the process in order to get to his left shoulder and this is when he got into real trouble as the soap slipped out of his hand and slid down his back.

If he lost the soap he would never be able to retrieve it and there wasn't another bar in the shower. Sure he could have called out to Mary, but how would he explain what happened to the previous one. If the kids ever found out that he dropped the soap and then was too fat to move in the shower he would be ridiculed relentlessly and wouldn't be able to eat a damned celery stick without hearing a cascade of verbal barbs the likes of which few people have ever had to endure. He knew when B.A.D. was given such opportunities he went straight for the jugular with the skill of a brain surgeon and the ruthlessness of a Wall Street lawyer.

So he did the only thing possible to save his dignity. Just as the bar hit the top of his ass and began its inevitable slide down the crack of his butt, towards the floor and his eternal damnation, he simultaneously squeezed the cheeks of his ass and pressed backwards against the shower wall. With this skillful move he was able to stop its slide, albeit leaving him in a very precarious position.

He didn't know how he was going to reach it or how long he was going to be able to keep it from continuing its journey downward, but knew he wouldn't have much time to act. He reached his hand back towards the soap but his arms were getting increasingly tighter against the walls of the shower as he tried to do so. He was now becoming concerned that his arms might get pinned behind him, putting him in an impossible position, and he might not be able to get the door open, then Mary would have to call for help to get him out of there. To his horror, they might have to send the ships emergency safety crew down with the jaws of life to extricate him from his steel prison.

He thought they should put a warning on the outside of these showers that people of certain combinations of weight and height should proceed with extreme caution as they may be hazardous to their health. He didn't see how anyone from the 'fat family' could safely use these facilities. And now he was beginning to believe the story that Bruno had told earlier—when Mrs. Fat wanted to take a shower and, being very determined and not wanting to admit that she was too rotund to be able to use it, somehow managed to force herself into the too small compartment.

The story has it she used a large shoehorn or covered her body with Wesson Oil and slid it in stages. First slipping her right leg and right arm inside, she then forced her large right breast into the shower. As she did this, her nipple rubbed brusquely against the cold steel of the shower entrance and actually felt kind of good. Then, by grabbing onto the cold water handle with her right hand and pushing fiercely against the bathroom wall with her left, she managed to coerce her right buttocks inside the shower. Her asscheek was also rubbed very roughly against the shower door jam but, unlike her breast, this didn't feel good. It hurt! But now she was half-way in and past the point of no return even though she felt quite awkward with her right breast and right cheek inside the shower already getting wet and her left breast and cheek on the outside.

Now that she had half of her body inside the shower, with the water hitting it and washing off the Wesson Oil, she really was beyond the point of no return and, for the first time, panic was beginning to set in. What would happen if she were caught here with the shower door jammed halfway into the crack of her ass on one side and between her two ponderous breasts on the other. The possibilities didn't seem pleasant at all.

So she grabbed the bottle of Wesson Oil in her left hand, held it over her head and left shoulder, and let the remaining contents, over half a bottle, pour out over her and run down her body. With renewed vigor and determination she pushed off with her left foot and hand and simultaneously pulled herself in with her right hand and sucked in her stomach and ass as much as she could while shifting all of her weight to the right with one great lunge of her body.

The combination of all these efforts created a tremendous force that, for an instant, overcame the laws of physics, or at least the relationship of content and space, and the left side of her body was sucked violently into the small confines of the shower. As this happened she was turned around so that her face was pressed against the rear of the shower with the water hitting on her back. The motion caused the shower door to slam shut with a whooshing sound, like air being sucked into a vacuum; it also caused the ship to roll slightly.

Bertha could sense that she was in an unusual and dangerous situation. The net effect of what happened was like somehow managing to stuff one or even two extra sardines into a can just as it was being pressure sealed. There was no way in hell that she was going to be able to get out of this by herself, she couldn't move anything except her head. She was squeezed in so tightly that she was sure that she was at least three inches taller. It was all too apparent to her that she had become hermetically sealed in this would be coffin and that oxygen, or more precisely the lack of it, would soon become a problem.

As if this wasn't enough, she had one more problem—when she was being violently sucked into the shower, she had knocked the face cloth off the small rack it was hanging on and it had fallen on top of the water drain. She was now standing on it and keeping the water from exiting the shower. Try as she might, she could not move either of her feet in an attempt to free the drain. The water was beginning to build up in the shower and wouldn't take very long to fill the entire enclosure since her body took up so much of the area.

She was beginning to panic and started to hyperventilate as she attempted to push the door open. This wasn't going to work because she could hardly reach the handle and, more importantly, her bulk was so compacted into this small area that the door couldn't be budged with a crowbar. Panicking ever further, she attempted to force the door outward through its sealed housing. The door strained under the weight of Big Bertha's huge bulk, but would not move. She gathered all of her strength for one last effort and pushed with all of her might against the door causing the metal to creek loudly, and even buckle slightly, but it would not break.

This was too much for Bertha as she began to cry and then her cries turned into screams. She screamed very loudly, but outside of the shower her screams were only little muffled cries. She kept screaming and screaming for what seemed an eternity, but was in fact only a few minutes.

Fortunately her husband, Willy, was getting up to get another beer and decided that he would relieve himself at the same time. When he opened the bathroom door and stepped in he could hear her and thought that she was singing her damn opera in the shower again until he listened more carefully and then wasn't sure. He knocked on the shower door and asked, "Bertha, honey, are you all right in there?"

"No! You stupid little shit! I'm not alright, I'm stuck in this damned shower!"

"What do you mean, 'your stuck in the shower'?"

"What the hell do you think I mean? I'm stuck in here and can't move."

"Well, then open the door and come on out."

"Listen you dumb shit! I wouldn't be stuck in here if I could open the friggin door. You try to open it from out there."

"There's nothing for me to grab onto. I'll have to get something to pry it open with."

"Well, hurry up! I'm running out of air and the water is up to my waist already."

"The only thing I can find is this butter knife from the snack that we had."

"I don't care what you use, just get me out of here."

Willy managed to get the blade of the knife in between the door casing and the door but, when he applied pressure to it, it broke. "Oh shit!"

"What happened? What's the matter?"

"The damn knife broke."

"Then get something else for Christ sakes!"

"What the hell? Do you think that I brought my tool box with me?"

"Don't get nasty with me you skinny little shit or I'll kick your ass when I get out of here."

"Don't get upset with me. I'm not the one that got stuck in the shower. I told you to pay attention to what the P.H.A.T. squad said. You could have used the special showers, the ones near the kitchen, for those people who might require a somewhat larger shower than was provided in the cabins."

"I'm warning you, Willy! Don't lecture me and you'd better not take advantage of this situation, you little bastard, or I'll fix your skinny little ass good when I get out of here!"

"I'm doing the best I can, but we're going to need help to get this door open."

"Help! What the hell do you mean help? I'm in here bare ass for Christ sakes! What do you want to do, call out the friggin National Guard so that they can parade the naked fat lady around the deck afterwards? Why the fuck don't you just get CNN down here so that we can get the most embarrassing day of my life on the six o'clock news, you putz."

"I know you're frustrated, and you swear a lot when you get frustrated, but I think you should be nicer to me…. sweetheart! I didn't mean I needed to call in the army, but I do think that we need to call in the P.H.A.T. squad because there is no way in hell that I'm going to be able to open this door without some tools and probably additional muscle."

"Can't you just go borrow some tools, please?"

"Sure, I'll just walk up to one of the crew and tell him I have a jar I can't open and ask him if I can borrow a crowbar, or perhaps a blow torch would be better. Besides, even if I could eventually find the right tools it would take too long."

"O.K.! O.K.! You're right, but at least be discrete about it."

"Yes, of course dear," he said, not able to contain his grin as he picked up the phone to dial the P.H.A.T. squad.

"Hello, can I help you," came the voice on the other end of the line.

"Yes, I need some assistance in cabin A266," replied Willy.

"What kind of assistance do you need," Jake, the man who had answered for the P.H.A.T. squad, asked patiently.

"Well, that's kind of hard to say. You see my wife was trying to take a shower and got her fat ass stuck in there. I tried to tell her she wasn't going to fit."

"Just what do you mean by stuck?"

"What I mean is that she is stuffed in there like meat in a sausage and it's impossible to get the door open. It's closed tighter than a gnats ass."

"You can't even get the door open a little. How big is your wife, anyway?" Jake asked incredulously.

"She is about five foot two and was about three hundred pounds before she broke the bathroom scale! I don't know what the hell she is up to by now, but I do know that by the end of this trip she is going to set a new record."

"How the f...excuse me, how did she ever manage to get all the way into one of those showers in the first place."

"Beats the hell out of me, but Bertha can be a very determined person when she wants to be. I also see an empty bottle of Wesson Oil on the floor and I've got a feeling that has something to do with it."

"All right, we'll get a crew down there as quickly as we can."

"I think you'd better hurry before she drowns or runs out of air, and I think you better bring some heavy equipment," Willy responded as he hung up the phone and went back to his wife. "Help is on the way dear."

"Oh, thank God! I assume a woman is coming with some tools that you can get me out with?"

"I'm not sure dear, I left that up to their discretion. After all, they are the professionals and they know how best to handle these situations. I'm sure that this has happened before."

Bertha would have been bullshit if she could have heard Willy snickering and seen the shit-eating grin on his face. He had suffered a lot of abuse from the mouth of Big Bertha and was enjoying her predicament and, besides, he had nearly gotten killed when he tried to help her save her dignity on the bus ride getting to the cruise so he was going to stay clear of this situation. Her dignity be damned, he was going to protect his ass this time.

Within a few minutes there was a loud banging on the door. When Willy opened it the P.H.A.T. squad poured in, all seven of them. All but one of them were men.

Charlie, the one in charge, barked out orders like a drill sergeant. "Fred, you and Sam secure the outside wall and window. Ralph drill some holes in the top of the door for air. Pete, get the water shut-off to this side of the ship and Maxine you drill some holes in the bottom of the door to drain out the water from in there and relieve some of the pressure."

Willy was in awe at their organization and efficiency, but he couldn't help notice that one man stood silently off to the side and just watched the others perform their duties. He was the oldest of the group, probably in his early fifties. As he stood there his face was void of any expression and he had a far away look in his eyes as he held a large tool case in his hands. Hands that were gnarled and missing the ring and little finger on his right one. He was also wearing a flak jacket and a helmet with a shield on top that could slide down to protect his face.

"O.K., Mr. Cochran, this is what we are going to have to do," Charlie broke in on Willy's thoughts. "We've put up a flak blanket on the outside wall to protect it in case any of the rivets holding the shower together should pop loose."

"You need to have a flak blanket for that," Willy asked.

"Oh, yes! This is quite a serious situation! The pressure the door is under now is enough to pop a rivet and send it flying like a bullet in any direction. Once we start to pry open the door the pressure increases tenfold and, if we were below the water line, we could be in danger of sinking the ship. We must be very careful or else someone could get seriously injured. That's why we all wear helmets and flak jackets and we must also be cognizant of the rare occasion when we can have a situation when implosion occurs."

"O.K. I'll play this silly ass little game," Willy responded. "What the hell is an implosion?"

"That's when all the forces that are building up suddenly turn inward and crushes everything in the area that we are trying to relieve."

"Oh my God! What would happen to Bertha?" For the first time Willy was really concerned.

"I have to be honest with you, it wouldn't be a pretty sight. Sort of like when Gallagher smashes a watermelon with his mallet. That's why we required you to sign the release form, but don't worry! We know what we're doing and the implosion phenomena happens very rarely. As I was saying, now that we have the area secured, what we will do is use the jaws of life to peel back a small section of the door so that we can gain access to Mrs. Cochran and attach a rope to her wrist."

"Why do you have to attach a rope to her wrist?" Willy asked, somewhat dumbfounded, not quite sure he believed this implosion bullshit but not wanting to take any chances.

"You can see Fred and Sam hanging the mattress on the bathroom wall opposite the shower. This is so that when Bertha is jettisoned from the shower she will hit the padded wall and not hurt herself; we must make sure that she doesn't bounce off of that wall and ricochet back into the shower, which is not what we want to have happen. So we will attach this rope to her arm and, when she is forced out of the shower, we will pull her towards the cabin, not allowing her go back towards the shower where she could be hurt and become stuck again."

"I see." He did not really, but he was ready to believe anything at this point.

"We're about ready to begin the opening so you'll have to go out into the hall Mr. Cochran," Charlie instructed. "O.K. Cecil we're ready for you now."

Cecil, the man who had been standing quietly to the side, moved with the precision and air of a man who was very good at his job and knew it. He methodically placed his tool case on the bed, opening it with loving care, and carefully removing the instrument inside. The instrument was the Jaws of Life and it gleamed like well-polished silverware; obviously, Cecil took good care of his equipment. Although it was heavy, he handled it with the ease and efficiency of a drum major with his baton.

In an instant, he had started jaws and, as it roared loudly, he was at the shower door prying open a small piece in the upper right hand corner. This would allow Maxine a little access and the ability to talk with Bertha more easily.

"What the hell was that noise," Bertha gasped.

"It's O.K., Bertha," Maxine tried to soothe her.

"Who the hell are you," Bertha had gotten lightheaded from the lack of oxygen and was groggy as she began to remember the predicament that she was in and was very close to total panic.

"My name is Maxine and I am with the P.H.A.T. squad," Maxine said calmly.

"I'm relieved to see that they sent a woman," Bertha confided. "It's bad enough to be in this position at all, but I would be mortified if I ended up naked in front of a bunch of strange men."

"You needn't be concerned about that Bertha. We're all professionals and this is just another day's work," Maxine said, rather matter-of-factly.

"What the hell do you mean—'We're' all professionals! Who the hell are WE! I'm not a God damn professional and surer an shit Willy's not a God damn professional. So that leaves you and whatever friggin troop of boy scouts you brought with you."

"They're not boy scouts, Mrs. Cochrane," Maxine replied. "They're dedicated professionals risking their lives to save yours." Maxine was not the type of person to see the humorous side of things and took her job very seriously.

"Just how the hell many of you are there?" Bertha was getting very nervous.

"There are seven of us in total," Maxine said.

"And how many of you are women?"

"I'm it."

"Willy, you little bastard, I'm going to kick your ass when I get out of here and if you've got that damn video camera running you and it are going overboard."

"He can't hear you. We've evacuated him to the hall. Now please pay attention, our time is running out," Maxine spoke seriously as she inserted the rope into the small opening.

"What the hell is this rope for?" Bertha was both puzzled and scared.

"Just put the loop around your wrist and don't ask any questions." Maxine was using her most authoritative voice. "This is absolutely necessary and will all happen very fast, so all you have to do is relax and go with it. We will do the rest."

"I can't loop it around my wrist you dumb shit. I can't move anything but my friggin head for Christ sakes."

"It's not necessary to use profanity, Mrs. Cochrane. We didn't get you into this situation, we are only here to get you out of it."

"I know, I'm sorry. But I can't move my arms so I don't know how I'm going to loop the rope around my wrist."

"That's O.K. If we work together, we can do it. Now I'll snake the rope through the hole and lower it down towards your hand. Here goes."

"I see it coming in, but it isn't going anywhere."

"I'm still feeding it through. What do you mean it isn't going anywhere?"

"I mean that it is just piling up on me and not lowering towards my hand."

"Piling up on you? What part of your body is it piling up on?"

"If you must know, it is piling up on my breast."

"Oh, I see. I'll pull the rope back out and then let it swing away from your breast and let it drop down towards your hand. Let me know when the rope has cleared your breast and I can let it drop down."

"Listen Maxine! The way that my teats are plastered against this shower wall it is going to be like threading the eye of a needle."

"Then that's what we will have to do. Now you direct me."

"A little to the right. Now a little to the left. That's too far, go back again. No! That's too far the other way! We're never going to get it!"

"For Christ sakes, how the hell big are those teats anyway lady?" Cecil was getting very impatient and could hardly wait to use his power tool.

"Well, they are big enough to hide a couple of six packs in with room to spare!" Willy said.

"I heard that Willy, you little bastard. You promised that if I let you do that you would never tell anyone. I'm going to kick your ass up one side of the ship and down the other."

"All right! All right! Can we get back to the matter at hand before the damn rivets start popping like bullets?" Maxine attempted to take control.

The attempts went on for another full five minutes before they had some luck and managed to get the rope around Bertha's wrist.

"O.K. We finally have it ready now so just relax and leave the rest up to us," Maxine said.

"I guess I don't have very much choice. Do I?" Bertha was becoming resigned to putting her fate in their hands.

"In a moment you are going to hear the roar of the Jaws of Life and, just before Cecil begins to pry the door open, I am going to spray you with this liquid silicon so that you will slide out more easily. This silicon has ten times the lubricating properties of the Wesson Oil that you used, so just close your eyes and relax; it will be over in an instant."

"O.K. O.K. I'll do as you say."

"All right guys we're ready now!" Maxine informed the others.

The rest of the crew bolted into action. Cecil fired up 'jaws' and Fred, Sam, Ralph, and Pete grabbed the other end of the rope, as if they were in a tug of war, and positioned themselves against the wall opposite the bathroom, where they had previously put up another mattress.

On the signal from Charlie that everyone was in place, Maxine put the hose into the opening and then released a spray of silicon under pressure that quickly covered Bertha. Within seconds, she was done and removed the hose and bolted for the door and the relative safety of the hallway. This was the signal for Cecil to move into action and move into action he did, revving the engine and inserting it into the small opening in one swift motion. Then just as quickly, and in one fluid motion, he peeled back the door, turned off jaws and dove for cover.

In the same instant, the pressure that had built up inside expelled Bertha from the shower, and into the mattress on the opposite wall, like she had been shot out of a cannon. The rest of the crew had also sprung into action and pulled with all their might forcing Bertha out of the bathroom and against the mattress on the far wall and, as she hit the wall, the crew made their move towards the safety of the hall. Fred and Sam were the two on the furthest end of the rope and easily made it to safety. Unfortunately, Ralph and Pete were not so lucky; they could not get out in time and were pinned under Bertha's full weight. Both had the wind knocked out of them, but neither was seriously hurt, although Ralph did suffer two cracked ribs and Pete had a sprained wrist and a black eye.

It could have been worse but, fortunately for the men, Bertha lay there stunned from hitting the two walls. If she had been aware of the fact that she lay sprawled naked across two men and in full view of all the others she could have gone berserk and hurt many more people, but Maxine and Willy managed to cover her with a tarpaulin before she regained all of her senses.

Al hadn't really believed B.A.D. when he first told them this story, but now he wasn't so sure at all, given the situation he found himself in. He didn't know how long he could keep the soap from falling to the floor. He was considering his options and there weren't many—he could let the soap fall to the floor and end his shower now or he could try to recover the soap. Since he needed to complete his shower, and hated to give up on anything, he decided to go for it.

The only way he was going to be able to get the soap was to reach in between his legs and grab it before it fell to the floor. This was not going to be a simple procedure, however, since he would have to be very quick in reaching between his legs to be able to get the soap. At the same time, he would have to be very careful or he could hurt the family jewels and be singing soprano for the rest of his life; but he was determined to get himself out of this situation. Therefore, like a karate expert about to break a series of bricks, he brought his entire concentration to bear on what he had to do. Then, with the speed of a jaguar and the coordination of a brain surgeon, he simultaneously relaxed the cheeks of his ass, thereby releasing the soap, shot his hand between his legs, narrowly missing 'Big Jim and the twins', and barely caught the soap as it exited from his butt.

With this crisis past, he managed to complete his shower without any further incidents; he knew that he had better not gain any weight during this trip or he was going to be in deep shit.

"Al! Al! Are you with us." Mary finally managed to get his attention.

"Excuse me. What was that you said?" Al came out of his trance as everyone was getting up and preparing to leave.

"Margaret Elizabeth was telling me that they were going to the show in the forward lounge, to have a few drinks, and then take in the midnight buffet. I told her that we were going to do the same, especially the midnight buffet, since I know you can't resist all those gorgeous desserts."

Al thought, 'Oh shit! I'm doomed'!

CHAPTER 6

"Dad, I'm going to go to the Quarterdeck lounge to see if I can meet some people in the section reserved for young adults," B.A.D. said as he was turning to go.

"O.K. Behave yourself, watch out for your sister, and your brother and don't be too late." Years of practice produced this stream of instructions without giving it a second thought.

"Sure, Dad! Sure!" B.A.D. said, also without giving it a second thought.

"Can I come with you Bruno?" Jonathan Francis asked, as he moved quickly to catch up.

"First of all, don't call me Bruno; I much prefer to be called B.A.D. My name is Bruno Alphonso DeGregorio—alias B.A.D. Second of all I'm not exactly sure what I am going to do," B.A.D. said as he continued on his way.

"What do you mean? I thought you told your Dad you were going to the Quarterdeck lounge," Jonathan asked, somewhat puzzled.

"I did and I am, at least for a while, but I'm not sure what I am going to do afterwards—Jonathan Francis."

"Now it is my turn—please don't call me that. That's what my parents call me, but I hate it." Jonathan was emphatic.

"O.K. What would you like me to call you—Jonathan or Jon? Please don't say Francis."

"I'm not sure." No one had ever asked him that before.

"What do you mean you're not sure, what the hell do your friends call you?" B.A.D. was getting a little testy.

"I don't have that many friends and they all call me Jonathan Francis because my father would kill them if he heard them call me anything else," Jonathan admitted.

"Well, you look like a Frankie to me; so I'm going to call you Frankie. O.K., Frankie?" B.A.D. had said this with such authority and conviction that he had not left much room for discussion.

"Yes, that sounds good, I like the sounds of that. Besides it would really upset my father." Jonathan Francis, alias Frankie, was happy to accept whatever his new friend had decided.

They stopped outside, near a lifeboat.

"Listen Frankie, if you are going to hang around with me, you are going to have to learn how to express yourself properly. For example, when your dad hears you called Frankie it is not going to upset him, it is going to frost his ass. Got it?"

"Yes, I mean yea! It's really going to frost his fat ass." Frankie thought it would be good to add a little of his own touch.

"You catch on quick, Frankie. O.K., you can come along if you want. Maybe we can meet some good-looking girls. You do like girls don't you?" B.A.D. wanted to make sure that he was not going to be handicapped in his quest to meet girls.

"Yea, I like girls. I like them a lot; they just don't like me very much. I haven't had very much experience because I get a little nervous around them. I think that I'm starting to make my father nervous, too. Which gives me a perverse sense of pleasure." Frankie was already feeling comfortable enough to confide in B.A.D.

"Don't worry you'll be all right, just act natural and let me do most of the talking. Maybe we'll get lucky and meet some of those chorus girls I've heard about."

"Don't you think that they would be a little old for us?"

"Listen, Frankie, you've got to get your act together. Older women like to take young guys like us under their wings and take care of us, I hope. Are you sure that you like girls?"

"Believe me, B.A.D., I like girls! I like girls a lot." Frankie was convincing.

"That's good Frankie, that's real good. By the way Frankie, what do you think of Harry Holt?" B.A.D. was probing.

"I don't know he seems o.k., I guess. He certainly knows how to appeal to women; I thought he was going to start putting the make on Sally Roberts right at the dinner table."

"Ya, he certainly is smooth. A little too smooth I think. Did you see how he looked at her jewelry and your mothers, too?" B.A.D. was continuing cautiously.

"No, I didn't. What are you getting at, B.A.D.?"

"I think that he was staring at the jewels a little too much. I've been reading up on cruises and they are one of the favorite targets for jewel thieves? They are like floating candy stores, providing a lot of easy targets in a concentrated and not very secure area."

"I think you are letting your imagination get the better of you, B.A.D." Frankie's imagination was definitely not in the same class as B.A.D.'s.

"Shit, Frankie, you sound just like my mother, but I'm a pretty good judge of people. It's one of the few things that I have in common with my father and I'm usually right about my initial feelings." This was a sensitive area with B.A.D. and he was somewhat defensive. "Except for that unfortunate time with the Pope."

"What the hell did you do to the Pope?"

"I don't want to talk about it, but I do think that we should keep our eye on this Harry, maybe even do some investigating." B.A.D. was getting a gleam in his eyes.

"I don't know B.A.D., what if we are wrong and we get into trouble because of it?"

"We won't get into trouble and, anyway Frankie, you have to be prepared to take risks in your life if you are ever going to realize your full potential." B.A.D. had no reservations in imparting his philosophies of life to Frankie, or anyone else for that matter.

"I didn't know that you were interested in attaining such lofty goals." Frankie was surprised by B.A.D.'s sudden serious tone. "What is it that your parents have in mind for you?"

"My parents definitely want me to go to college and prepare myself for some kind of good career, but they don't push me towards any particular field. Oh they emphasize that I should major in something that is very practical and can lead to a good paying job when I graduate, but, other than that, they want me to study something that I am interested in and don't pressure me towards anything in particular." For the first time B.A.D. appreciated his parents for this.

"My father has determined that I am best suited to be a lawyer, like him, and that there is no question about it."

"What is it that you want to do? What do you think you would be best at and enjoy doing the most?"

"What difference would that make? My father believes he knows what's best for me, and he probably does." Frankie was not used to questioning his father's decisions.

"Only you can really know what is right for you. As Thoreau said: 'What a man thinks of himself, that is which determines, or rather indicates, his fate.' Your father can have input but you have to take control of what you are going to be." B.A.D. was in one of his very serious moods.

"I wouldn't have guessed that you were so philosophical, B.A.D." Frankie was impressed.

"I like you Frankie so I'm going to help you, but I'm also putting my trust in you that you'll keep this to yourself. I can count on you to keep this to yourself, can't I Frankie?"

"Of course you can B.A.D., but I get the impression that your parents would be surprised to hear you quoting Thoreau."

"Surprised? They would crap in their pants if they ever heard me. They are still trying to figure out how I managed to get a combined score of twelve-fifty on my S.A.T.'s, even though they have constantly been on me during high school that I wasn't working up to my potential and could do better than my B average. Of course, they were right, but I would never admit it to them and, besides, I wasn't any different than they were.

"My father thinks that my philosophy of life is rather weird and certainly not based on Henry David Thoreau. Of course, I can't blame him because I feed him some real crap. For instance, the time that my father was trying to be so serious and have that father and son talk with me. You know the one," B.A.D. said.

"Ya, my father was pretty pathetic, too," Frankie added.

"He was trying his best, but it wasn't an easy thing for him to talk about. Unfortunately for both of us, he went on and on trying to explain things to me that, of course, I already knew. Hell, for a while I even thought that he was going to put on a video of some birds and bees.

"I waited very patiently for him to finish; and when he did he asked me if I had any questions, to his chagrin, I said 'yes'. Then I proceeded very slowly with my philosophical question—'Dad, if a young man has a wet dream is he still a virgin or has he crossed over into manhood?' He took a long time to answer, but finally said that he would still be a virgin and then he tried to leave. I wasn't going to let him off that easy since I had to sit there for over an hour as he went around the bush. 'Is virginity a physical thing or a state of mind? I think that it might be just a state of mind and if you have a dream of making love to a woman and then climax, how is that different from having actually made love to a woman? What do you think, Dad?' By this time he was already up and heading for the door mumbling that I could come to him any time that I had any questions."

"That's fantastic, I wish I had something like that to lay on my father," Frankie said.

"I can help you with that."

"Could you, would you?" Frankie was excited at the possibility and the sincere offer of help from someone that he had barely just met.

"Ya! I can and I will. What you need to do is to start messing with your father's head. You really have to screw up his mind. The first thing to do is to appeal to his ego by asking him for his advice. Let's see, he's a lawyer and he wants you to be a lawyer so we should come up with something to do with a legal question. Give me a minute and I'll come up with an idea." The intense look on his face showed his mind was working overtime now.

"I have it. See what you think of this, Frankie. Now you have to approach your father very carefully and, in your most serious tone, ask him if he has a moment to give you his opinion on a legal question that has been bothering you for quite some time. From what I saw of your father, this will really appeal to that fat ego he has. So very seriously ask him: 'Dad, if a bear is in the woods and cuts a wicked fart and a squirrel in a tree branch directly above the bear is engulfed by the fowl odor, passes out and falls to the ground striking his head and killing him, what is it? Is it murder, negligent homicide, manslaughter or just an unfortunate accident?'"

"That's great, B.A.D.! I love it!" Frankie was impressed.

"Believe me, Frankie, that will plant the seed in his mind of just what kind of freaky son he has. C'mon, lets go." B.A.D. was feeling good about himself.

They continued their walk towards the lounge.

"Do you always walk like that?" B.A.D. asked.

"Like what?" Frankie said.

"Like you have a broom handle so far up your ass I expect to see it coming out of your mouth. You walk so damned stiff you could pass for a robot for Christ sakes," B.A.D. said. "Where the hell did you ever learn to walk like that anyway?"

"I don't know. I guess it's something that has developed over the years," Frankie replied defensively.

"It may be appropriate for a sophisticated law firm but it's bullshit for a cool dude like you, Frankie."

"I don't think it's so bad. It seems to have been perfectly acceptable until now."

"Take it easy Frankie, it's nothing personal. It's not your fault you've suffered through years of indoctrination. It may help you to get where your father wants you to go, but it won't get you where I think you want to be."

"How should I be walking?"

"You have to loosen up and put a little skip into your step. Like this." B.A.D. walked a half dozen steps to demonstrate, somewhat over emphasizing what he meant. "You try it."

So, Frankie gave it a shot. It turned out to be a pretty pathetic attempt at trying to be cool and B.A.D. couldn't help but laugh a little.

"Ha! Ha! That's a little too loose I think, Frankie. Try it again, but, this time, try thinking more smooth than loose."

Undaunted, Frankie tried it and was much better.

"That's it! You catch on very quickly, Frankie, and that's good because you have a lot to learn and I don't have much time to teach you."

That made Frankie feel good, very good. He hadn't received very much praise in his lifetime and was more accustomed to being criticized, criticized a lot, mostly by his father. He liked the feeling of being praised better than being picked on and he liked B.A.D.

They began their walk towards the lounge again when Frankie suddenly stopped dead in his tracks.

"That no good son-of-a-bitch!"

"Gees, what's the matter Frankie? You look really pissed off."

"Do you see that couple up their by the pool?"

"Ya, kind of."

"That's my father and he is not with my mother."

"How can you tell that from here? Its dark and they are kind of far away."

"Believe me I can recognize my father from a long way off and I am sure that was him."

"Take it easy Frankie, it may not be him. Let's get up closer and we can see for sure," B.A.D. said. He was very sympathetic because he couldn't imagine seeing his father with another woman.

"I don't want the bastard to see me."

"Don't worry, Frankie, I can be very discrete and very secretive when necessary." B.A.D.'s tone of voice was so calm and controlled that it made it very difficult not to take him seriously.

"Okay, but I don't want him to see me; he can't know that I found out about his girl friend." Frankie was nervous as he followed B.A.D. toward the pool area where he had seen the couple. He admired the way that B.A.D. made his way forward with a combination of grace and stealth that he never would have attributed to him. He led him to a spot where they could see the couple quite clearly, but were adequately concealed, and far enough away, so as not to be heard or seen.

"I don't fuck'n believe it," Frankie was close to losing control.

"Shhh! Be careful for Christ sakes or we will get caught." B.A.D. couldn't believe he was leading a neophyte into such a delicate situation. "Christ you were right, it is him. You have to admit that he is a fast worker. We haven't even been on the cruise one full day and he has already found himself a woman. A foxy one at that," B.A.D. whispered.

"Let me get over there so I can get a better view of her." As they switched places Frankie understood how his father had moved so fast. "That miserable bastard. That's no lady, that's his little bitch of a girlfriend, Charlotte."

"Boy, Frankie, you do learn fast. Your talking just like one of the guys now." B.A.D. was beginning to think that Jonathan Francis might turn out all right after all. "Who the hell is Charlotte anyway?"

"It's his shit head mistress from New York. He doesn't know that I am aware of his infidelity, but I know all about it. I know all about the apartment that he keeps for her in Manhattan, I know how many times he sees her in a week, I can even tell from his mood when he gets home from 'working late' whether he got laid or not and how good it was." Frankie was getting worked up.

"Gees, Frankie, how the hell do you know all of that?" Now B.A.D. was impressed. "By the way, don't use terms like infidelity. That's how your mother would describe it. For you, it's fuck'n around." B.A.D. felt compelled to correct him, realizing that his tutelage was still very much needed.

"Ya, right! Sorry! I know all of this because I was suspicious when he started coming home late from work in much better moods than he normally did and he started to have a lot more business trips out of town over the weekends. So one night I followed him from his office. He met Charlotte for dinner in a fancy restaurant and then they went back to her apartment. That's when I found out her apartment number and her name and I've been checking up on them ever since."

"How did you manage to get that information and what do you mean by checking up on them?" B.A.D. was beginning to realize that there was another dimension to Frankie that he hadn't seen before.

"I used some of the things that my father had taught me against him, and one of those is that money talks. So, I bribed the doorman at their apartment. He was a fountain of knowledge and has been ever since. I suspect that he did it as much to get back at my father, for being the arrogant son-of-a-bitch that he is, as he did for the money."

"I'm impressed Frankie. That showed real initiative, I mean balls. So your dad brought 'Charlotte the Harlot' along on the family cruise because he didn't want to be away from her for a whole week. That either takes a lot of brass, no brains, or both."

They watched as L. Terrence and Charlotte embraced each other quite passionately. It was obvious that they were hot for each other as L. Terrence's hand found its way to 'Charlotte the Harlot's' round, firm derriere, and he squeezed and rubbed it aggressively. For a moment, it looked as if he would strip off her clothes and take her right there, on one of the tables in the far corner of the pool area. Then they managed to control themselves and head for the rear stairway.

"Christ, he is a horny bastard isn't he?" B.A.D. blurted out, the scene he had just observed allowed his emotions to get the better of him. He was glad for the relative darkness.

"We need to see where they're going. Do you think that we can follow them without being seen?" Frankie asked.

"Sure we can, just let me lead the way and don't say anything." B.A.D. was back in control and he liked that.

They managed to follow them down to the third level of the ship without being discovered; although they narrowly escaped being detected a couple of times. Once, when L. Terrence turned abruptly to look behind him, they had to dive into an open room. The startled occupants had just come back to get something they had forgotten and hadn't bothered to close the door. They were quite surprised to see B.A.D. diving head long into their room and his buddy coming a split second behind and landing unceremoniously on top of him.

"Please excuse us, but I lost my pet rat, Ben, and I thought I saw him run in here." B.A.D. did the best he could under the circumstances. Unfortunately this wasn't what the woman wanted to hear as she screamed and jumped on top of the bed to avoid any possible contact with the disgusting rodent.

"Do ya mind getting off of me Frankie so that we can get out of here and leave these nice people alone." Both B.A.D. and Frankie had all they could do to keep from laughing as they scrambled out of the room on their hands and knees—calling for Ben as they went.

Shortly afterward they saw L. Terrence and Charlotte disappear into cabin number 342.

"Okay, now that we know what room she is in we should get out of here before we get caught," B.A.D. whispered as he led a distressed Frankie away.

They quickly made their way to the Quarterdeck lounge and found an empty table in a corner of the reserved area. B.A.D. chose this one because it was out of the way and he felt that Frankie might need a little time to compose himself before meeting new people.

"I can't believe what we just witnessed," B.A.D. was energized by the events.

"I can. My father is so damn arrogant he thinks he can get away with anything that he wants. What really pisses me off is the fact that he will get away with it," Frankie said.

"I don't understand how he can get away to see his girl friend. Where is your mother during all of this?"

"She probably went back to the room with a headache. It seems that she has a lot of those lately. I can't figure out whether she knows about Charlotte and has just given up or if she just can't stand being with the son-of-a-bitch. The part that bothers me the most is that my mother use to be fun to be around. She couldn't do enough for us and she enjoyed her life. Now she has turned into an unhappy, bitchy woman." Frankie was very serious, a fact that was not lost on B.A.D.

"How would you like to fix his ass good? I mean to really put his nuts in a vice," B.A.D. said firmly.

"What do you mean? I don't see how we can get him without getting me in trouble." Frankie was interested but nervous.

"I don't know yet, but I am certain that I will be able to come up with something that can accomplish our goal." This wasn't said as boasting but as fact and with such an overwhelming sense of calm that Frankie didn't even think to question him.

"If we could come up with something that would get my mother to smile again and knock some of the arrogance out of my father it would make my life," Frankie said.

"Trust me Frankie," B.A.D. was resolved, "we will."

CHAPTER 7

"Al! How are you enjoying the show so far?" Mary asked somewhat louder than normal, aware that part of his mind was
probably off somewhere else. "You had that distant look in your eyes
again."

"Oh, it's very good. I'm enjoying it a lot. I think that the young
lady third from the left is particularly talented. What do you think
B.J.?" This was true even though Al was thinking about something
else totally different. A long time ago he realized he had the ability, or
curse, to watch something or even carry on a conversation and be
thinking in depth about a totally unrelated subject. Unfortunately,
this was also a bad habit as it often gave the impression that he was
not entirely interested in the person or persons with whom he was
engaged in conversation. This was sometimes, but not always, true.

"You are incorrigible, Al, and don't answer that young man."
Mary was quite used to him after almost twenty-five years of marriage and they often teased each other.

"What planet was your mind on this time?" Mary had become
quite used to his mental wanderings and could usually spot it when
his mind was on a trip somewhere. Al thought that sometimes she
envied this trait of his as it allowed him to travel about in his fantasies, no matter where he was or what he was doing. He found this
was particularly useful at weddings. Without this ability to allow one

portion of his mind to pursue other thoughts, he did believe that he would become a raving lunatic at having to sit through such affairs.

"Don't tell me that you weren't on one of your little memory trips. What was it this time?" Mary was good-natured about this, but at times he thought that she felt somewhat left out.

"I was just thinking about the incident of Big Bertha's intimate encounter with the shower and how we didn't really believe the story until we heard it directly from a member of the P.H.A.T. squad. It reminded me of the story that I was told about 'Mad Dog Pepe' that summer I worked for him."

"Oh, poor baby, that's a terrible thought. I'm glad that I was not on that trip." Mary was legitimately sympathetic, Al thought.

When Al was going to college he worked summers on construction. One summer he got a job helping to erect a new building at a nearby state mental hospital. He was a laborer, which is at the bottom of the construction hierarchy, and, as the new kid on the block, he was at the low end of the low end of the hierarchy. As a result of his being the youngest and newest guy on the sight, he got the dirtiest of the dirty jobs.

After a little while, he had gotten to know the carpenter shop steward fairly well, a man named Gus and, since he was young and strong and willing to work hard, making the carpenters job that much easier, they liked him. One day, while waiting for him to finish assembling a panel that he was to carry up to the deck of the new buildings first floor, Gus told him a story about the on sight manager, Pepe. He told him, obviously enjoying himself, that Pepe had spent five years in prison for manslaughter and had been released on parole about a year ago.

"Okay, Gus, I'll play your silly ass little game. What happened, did he have an accident while driving drunk or something like that?"

"No, he beat a man to death in a barroom brawl. It took five policemen to pull him off of the other guy, but, by then, it was too late." Gus now appeared to be as serious as he could be.

Al just nodded and let it pass, he didn't want to tell him he thought he was full of shit and just pulling his leg; he was a nice guy and Al didn't mind him putting him on. He also didn't mind working with the carpenters, although some were jerks and could be overly demanding, most of them were descent guys and treated him fine. They were particularly accommodating if you were a good worker because a laborer can make or break a carpenter, physically if not mentally. It didn't take Al long to learn how to handle the jerks.

The first thing to do was to work hard and establish yourself as a good worker, paying special attention to the carpenter foreman, the carpenter shop steward, and the labor foreman.

After you having accomplished this, you can then start to train those carpenters who think that you are their personal slave because you are a rung lower on the hierarchical ladder than they are and, therefore, they can shit all over you and you have to take it. These are the kind of guys that probably go home at night and beat their wife and kids or, at least, their dogs. They are obviously dissatisfied with their lot in life and are going to take it out on whomever they can.

Naturally there was one of these guys on this job. His name was Clyde and he was one of the worst Al had run into. Fortunately Al was working closely with another laborer named Frenchie. His real name was Ron or something like that but, being of French ancestry, he was called Frenchie.

It was very common in the construction trades to label individuals with nicknames like this. For example, because Al was the youngest on the job he was called 'the kid', even though he was also the biggest.

"Hey Frenchie! Get me some more eight-penny nails will ya for Christ sakes. I asked you for them an hour ago. How the hell am I suppose to do my job with a fuck'n lazy shit like you." Clyde was even nastier than usual. Obviously, Frenchie's tactic of semi-neglect was taking its toll on him. Besides it was a particularly hot July day and everyone's tempers were getting a little short.

"If you weren't so friggin blind, and spending so much time thinking about getting laid tonight, you'd have seen them over there where I put them an hour ago." Frenchie was within his rights to blast him because Clyde had crossed the line and opened the door when he called Frenchie a lazy shit. You could swear at someone all that you wanted because this was second nature on construction, but using a term such as lazy was a direct affront and not to be tolerated.

Of course, beneath his outward anger, Frenchie was very pleased with himself. This was exactly what he wanted to happen. By bringing the nails to a spot close to Clyde he had technically done his job. However, this required Clyde to hop up to the deck from his scaffolding on the side of the building and walk a half dozen paces to where Frenchie had left the supply of nails for him and the other carpenters. Of course, when the other carpenters needed nails Frenchie or Al would take them some. The effect of this over a ten-hour day, five days a week, can be devastating, both physically and mentally.

"I've fuck'n had enough of you, you're nothing but a lazy, good for nothing frog. I'm reporting your fuck'n ass to the shop steward." Clyde was mad as hell.

A hush fell over the immediate work area and everyone was focused on Frenchie. When Al looked at him, he could see a look of cold steel in his eyes and his face had turned red with fury as he backed Clyde up against a pole. Al didn't understand then but, it was later explained to him that, the term frog was very offensive to a Frenchman and particularly so to Frenchie.

"Listen, dickhead, you can report me to the friggin Pope for all I give a shit! Everyone knows that you're the biggest fuck off going!" Frenchie shouted at Clyde loud enough for everyone to hear. Then his voice lowered and, in a tone that sent shivers up Al's spine, he continued, "But if you ever call me a Frog again I'll cut off your fuck'n balls and nail them to your fuck'n forehead. Do you understand me, you turd? Well do you?"

"Ya, I understand you, but I'm still reporting you." Clyde had turned white as the blood drained from his face, this last statement meekly forced out as an attempt to save face. Although Frenchie was slightly built, he was sinewy and deceptively strong, without an ounce of fat on him, making him more than a match for Clyde who was somewhat pudgy and soft by construction standards.

Clyde did take his protest to the shop steward and the carpenter foreman but was not pleased with the reaction that he got, which was that Frenchie was doing his job and that there was nothing that they could do. The overall boss was Pepe and he liked Frenchie. In fact, he said that he would like to see Clyde call him a Frog again because he had never seen anyone with their balls nailed to their forehead and was curious as to how that would look. The advice to Clyde was to stop being such a hard ass to the laborers and maybe he would be treated better.

The truth of the matter was that not even the other carpenters liked Clyde and his ass would be canned if it weren't for the union. Apparently Clyde got the message because he made a reasonable effort to curb his assholishness and even learned to say 'please' and 'thank you', occasionally.

Fred, another college student working summers, and Al had been working on the job for about two weeks before Pepe had arrived and assumed the position as overall boss of the job. This was fortunate for them because it gave them a chance to get into shape, as Pepe turned out to be a very hard taskmaster.

At first they didn't have very much contact with him, which was fine with them. This was probably because he dealt more with the guys he already knew and because they were young and inexperienced.

The week that he arrived was also when they were ready to pour the first section of decking. Fred and Al were not to be on the concrete crew and were assigned to work in the basement below the area where they were pouring. This was perfectly fine with Fred and should have been with Al. After all, they were working at their own pace, with very little supervision, and they were in the shade rather than in the direct sun on this very hot, ninety-five degree day. But, for some strange reason, Al felt left out. The real action was taking place above them and he wanted to be part of it. He didn't know if this was either some flaw in his character or just too high of a level of testosterone in his system. It wasn't because he was just plain stupid because he knew, from a comfort point of view, that he was better off down below.

Anyway, their job took them up out of the basement and in full view of the pouring area frequently during the early part of the day. It was on the first one of these appearances out of their hole when they noticed that the concrete trucks were just beginning to arrive and that, just as they did so, Pepe began to bark out orders wildly and that he actually began to foam at the mouth.

Needless to say that this, coupled with the story of his manslaughter conviction, scared the shit out of them and they practically fell over each other getting back down into the cellar hole.

"Did you see that crazy look in his eyes and hear the way that he was screaming at no one in particular?" Fred was near panic as he attempted to become as inconspicuous as possible. Al thought that he was going to hide in a corner and ask him to cover him over with dirt.

"Never mind that, did you see the way he was foaming at the mouth like a mad dog! Just think Fred, someday we'll be able to tell our kids we worked for 'Mad Dog' Pepe, the scourge of Medfield State Mental Hospital," Al said in awe, that friggin testosterone showing up again.

"Ya, great! If we live to tell about it." Fred responded in a tone that left no question that he wanted to stay as far away from the 'Mad Dog' as possible.

The irony of a crazy son-of-a-bitch like 'Mad Dog' Pepe in a state mental hospital was not lost on them, either. They had asked themselves more than once, when they were leaving the job for the day all dirty, sweaty, and tired and some of the residents would be sitting in the shade watching them and smiling, just who were the crazy ones?

"Hey, Big Al!" Tony, the labor foreman who reported to Pepe and was Al's immediate supervisor, hollered down in the hole.

"What?" Al blurted out as he jumped on hearing his name. 'Oh shit, what the hell does he want from me,' Al thought.

"Come on up top, Pepe wants to break you in with the concrete crew," Tony said.

"Oh shit, you're dead." Fred was actually quite sympathetic, even if his choice of words sucked.

"It won't be that bad. I never believed that bullshit about his committing manslaughter anyway. And I'm sure that his bark is a lot worse than his bite." Al was preparing himself for what he was going to have to face up above. It would be necessary to get the adrenalin pumping to get the full benefit of all that testosterone. He was going to need it.

"My prayers will go with you Al." Fred was being a real wise ass now.

"That's okay, Fred, I'll ask Pepe if you can come up, too." Two could play at this game.

"No, that's okay really, Al." Fred was pleading now, as he turned ghostly white, but still managed a wise remark. "Are there any last messages for your family?"

When Al got on top they had finished about a quarter of the area to be poured that day and the men already looked very hot and tired. Al had begun to perspire almost immediately on getting up into the sun and knew it was going to be a long day.

"Ah good, Al boy, come'r. Ya ever pour a fuck'n deck like this before?" 'Mad Dog' was foaming even more than when Al had first seen him and he said this with a gleam in his eyes and in a voice that seemed like he was about to present him with his first real woman.

"No, I can't say as I have had the pleasure." Al wanted to act non-chalant, even though he had a sneaking suspicion that by the end of the day he would have wished that he had dropped to his knees and begged to be put back in the cellar hole with Fred.

"You stick with me and I'll show you the ropes." Pepe was being very friendly, which was of no little concern to Al. He would come to learn that Pepe admired big, strong guys and if you worked hard and didn't give him any shit he would treat you okay. Not to say that you wouldn't work hard, but he wouldn't give you any undo shit, and he would treat you with respect, in his own fashion.

"Ya see those big buckets down there?" He was pointing to two big iron buckets that were used to carry the concrete up to the deck. One had just come down from the deck and was suspended from a cable operated by a large crane.

"Watch how Big John handles the hook and how fast he gets it onto the other bucket so that it can get back up here." As soon as the empty bucket was on the ground, and there was a little slack on the cable, Al saw Big John, a six foot two hundred and thirty pounder, about twenty years old, reach up and unhook the cable, he then, with all his strength, swung it over to hook up the full bucket and jump out of the way as he signaled the crane operator to take it up, which he immediately did. Then, almost before the full bucket was clear of the area, Big John swung the chute from the concrete truck to the empty bucket and began to fill it. It was obvious that speed and strength were of the essence and Big John possessed both.

"Look at that. Good hey?" Pepe said. Al would find out later that they had worked with each other for about two years.

"Yes, he obviously knows what he is doing." What else could he say?

"Pay close attention and maybe I can train you to be a back-up to Big John." Pepe was very sincere.

"Okay, thanks." Ya that would be a real pisser please don't do me any favors Al wanted to say.

"Now watch as the bucket comes up. Billy will jump and grab the handle and pull it down to release the concrete. Then the other guys will get in there with their shovels and spread the concrete around." Pepe went on like he was imparting the secrets of the universe to Al.

As the bucket came up over the deck one man at the edge would direct the crane operator with a series of hand signals. Al was wondering what you had to do to get that job. As the bucket came within range of the desired area he saw Billy jump as high as he could, grab the handle, and, as he swung with both feet off of the ground, dump the entire load in one pile on the deck. He then let go of the handle and dropped to the deck, barely managing to maintain his balance. As he did so, the bucket was immediately pulled clear of the deck and lowered to the waiting hands of Big John. Al thought that Billy was afraid if he didn't let go quickly enough that he would end up being whisked away with the bucket. Al believed that he had something to be concerned about.

He wanted to ask Pepe why they didn't lower the bucket a little more and release the concrete more slowly and evenly, which would create less work for the shoveling crew. He quickly realized that making things easier for the shoveling crew was the furthest thing from 'Mad Dog's' mind and he was much too aggressive to stand there and watch the contents of the bucket being slowly released onto the deck.

"Cut it down! Cut it down! Jesus fuck'n Christ cut the fuck'n shit down you dumb sons-of-bitches!" Pepe was screaming at the top of his lungs and was clearly losing control. He was shouting at a second crew of shovelers that had been brought onto the job for the first time that day. This was done so that while one crew was finishing spreading a bucket the other crew would be beginning to spread the next.

Unfortunately this new crew was made up of all Portuguese who couldn't or wouldn't understand that Pepe was trying to lower the pile by spreading it around. Pepe was getting so wild that the drool from his mouth was flying everywhere as he ran, still screaming at them, and jumped into the pile of concrete on his hands and knees and he started to dig at the concrete with his bare hands and throwing it threw his legs just like a dog digging a hole and yelling: "Cut it down! Cut it down!"

Then he got up, covered in concrete, wild eyed, with drool hanging from the corner of his mouth and down the front of his shirt. As he walked up to Al he looked straight at him and said—"Al boy, I was fucking better off in prison!" Then he continued past him and signaled Al to join the English speaking concrete crew.

Al thought to himself, 'Holy shit the story is true, he is crazy and did kill a guy in a barroom brawl'. You can bet that he did double time in getting his butt over to the next pile of concrete and busted his ass, without relief, for the entire miserably hot day.

This wasn't the only incident that happened that day, either. At about four in the afternoon, after almost eight hours of working their asses off in ninety-five degree heat, one of the guys passed out from heat exhaustion and fell face down into a pile of concrete. This was a guy that, it was rumored, was going to be made a foreman on another job that the company had going. When this happened a couple of the other guys stopped shoveling to pick him up and help him to the shade and some water.

"Fuck it! Leave him there! He's no friggin good to me if he can't take a little heat." 'Mad Dog's' eyes were glazed over, his nostrils were flaring, and the drool was flowing freely.

Fortunately one of the guys knew the right thing to say, "Ya gotta let us move him. He's in our fucking way."

"All right, all right just drag the candy ass bastard over there and get the hell back here and cut this pile down." Then he stomped off to go scream at someone else.

One thing that Al learned from these summer jobs was that he was going to continue to go to college so that he wouldn't have to do this for the rest of his life. It was hard enough to do this for the summer time, but he couldn't imagine having nothing to look forward to but this kind of work for the rest of your life. Not only was it physically demanding, it was dangerous and you were never going to get anywhere financially, especially since you couldn't even be sure of having the pleasure of busting your ass year round. You could be laid off at any time. It could be as a result of the conclusion of the job, a downturn in the economy, or for a hundred other reasons that were out of your control.

Thus Al learned to have respect for the people who go to difficult and unrewarding jobs day in and day out, year in and year out, struggling daily just so that their families can have food on the table and a roof over their head. Unfortunately this was getting harder and harder to do and more and more families were failing in these efforts. There must be an admiration for these individuals, and, even beyond this, they can be looked upon as heroic; rather than looked down upon and their needs ignored.

Al couldn't help but wonder what Harry Holt did for a living. He was very elusive about his occupation and it was certain, from the looks of his hands, that he didn't do menial labor for a living. Al thought that he spent his whole life aboard these cruise ships making moves on the female passengers. He certainly put the moves on Sally Roberts in such a way that she didn't have a chance. Al had spent a lot of time observing him and how he handled her.

Al watched as Harry played Sally like a violin master plays a rare Stradivarius. He paid particular attention to her at dinner, making sure that everyone knew that he found her interesting and, by making her the center of his attention, giving her a feeling of importance in front of the rest of them that she had obviously not felt for a long time, if ever.

They had come to learn that Sally had been divorced a few years earlier by a husband who left her for a young model in her early twenties, making her the victim of an all too familiar story. She had met her husband while they were both in college and they married upon graduation. He then went on to medical school and Sally went

to work as a teacher and supported them while he obtained his medical degree. Once he graduated, he went on to become a successful
surgeon as he totally devoted himself to his profession. So much so
that he had continually managed to postpone their having children
until it had become too late and had ceased to be a consideration.
They were married for almost twenty years when her husband
dropped the bomb that shattered her life. She was aware that they
were not as close as she would have liked, but she had no idea that he
had been having an affair, possibly affairs, and that he wanted to
leave her. The fact that her friends had told her that he was going
through a mid-life crisis, and went for a young woman to try to
regain his youth, didn't ease her pain or improve her self-esteem,
which was about as low as whale's shit.

During the past two years, Sally struggled to try to put her life
back together. She had received a very favorable settlement from her
ex-husband so she continued to teach more as an anchor, and as a
means to put some meaning in her life, as for the money. She had
had a few unsuccessful dates that had been pushed on her by some of
her well-meaning friends. One of these same friends managed to get
her to take this cruise with her. Then, at the last minute, the friend
had a medical emergency and couldn't go with her. Sally wasn't quite
sure why but she had become somewhat excited about going and
decided to go by herself anyway.

This emotional baggage was effective fodder for a man like Harry
Holt. He knew just how to play on her pain and fears. His major
weapon, besides his good looks, was that he listened and spent time
with her before he got aggressive. The first two days on board ship he
took her to the shows and the gambling casino in the evenings and
spent time by the pool. They even played shuffleboard during the
days. But what really sunk the hook was the fact that he didn't even
expect a good night kiss during this time. Al believed that this acted
to heighten the air of mystery that already surrounded him and com-

bined with his rugged good looks to intensify her interest, no desire, for him.

It was on the third evening that he made his move. Al actually had the pleasure of personally observing the initial moves that he used on Sally. It was innocent enough on Al's part, he was out taking a walk up in the forward part of the ship, where he had found a comfortable seat under a stairway, and was looking at a gorgeous moon when he first heard them. Sally and Harry had strolled up to the most forward part of the ship and stopped in a very secluded spot; not twenty feet from where he was sitting. He was in a quandary, he didn't want to disturb them nor did he want them to wonder what the hell he was doing 'hiding' in the shadows. Before he could decide what to do it was too late. Harry had started to make his move on her and there was no way that Al could let his presence be known now.

"You look wonderful tonight, Sally!" Harry whispered softly in her ear as he stood behind her, putting his arms firmly around her waist, and slowly pulled her close to him.

"And I feel wonderful tonight, Harry! How could I help it on such a romantic evening and with such a handsome and charming man like you?" Sally was really getting caught up in the atmosphere of the cruise and the moves that Harry was putting on her.

The moon shining on the ocean was enchanting and did cast a spell over the ship. Al wanted to jump out from his perch and rescue Sally from this Casanova, but he knew that she was a grown woman and it was none of his business, besides how would he explain what he was doing there.

"Do you know that you are a beautiful and very sensual woman, and I don't think that I can control myself any longer?" Harry whispered to her as he gently kissed along the nape of her neck, and started to move his hand in circular motions along her stomach, making slow but steady progress toward her waiting breasts.

"I don't know what's come over me, but I think that I'm about to lose control and the last thing that I want you to do is to control yourself." Sally was definitely becoming overheated.

"If you let your passions flow, and allow yourself to follow your desires, I can help take you to a place you have never been and experience an ecstasy that few women ever allow themselves to feel." Harry managed to say this with such sincerity, and lack of boasting, that the effect was overwhelming on Sally. He even had Al believing him. He was going to have to remember this line, although Al was sure he would not be able to deliver it like Harry did. He had obviously had a lot of experience at this.

"I've never done anything like this before, especially with someone I just met." Sally's breathing was heavy as she responded to his touch.

"I know, that's why it is going to be so good. Don't fight it, go with it, and savor it." Harry was convincing, as he moved his hand inside her bra and felt her bare breast for the first time. "You have a very lovely body. One, which, I must admit, I feel compelled to explore." Harry was getting into high gear now.

"Not as lovely as a young girl in her twenties, I'm sure."

"Oh, but you are wrong Sally love. A woman like you is so much more sensual than younger women. I have known both and I believe what I am saying. As a slightly older woman you have experienced more of life than they have and, thus, can feel more deeply and give of yourself more fully. All that you have to do is let yourself go, release yourself from your inhibitions and you will be able to know the full joy of being a woman."

Sally couldn't believe that she was standing there with her breasts nearly exposed. She felt strange, not fully comprehending what was happening to her, almost like she was another person, standing there with the warm night air caressing her body. Unbelievably, she wanted him to continue. She had already experienced feelings that she had never known before. He had awoken desires that came from deep within her, completely dissolving all of her inhibitions.

"Come to my cabin now, please!" Harry was in complete control and becoming increasingly more forceful.

"I'll go anywhere you say! Take me there now!" Sally could wait no longer.

He quickly buttoned her blouse as they hurried towards the stairway on the way to his cabin, laughing as they went.

As soon as they were out of sight, Al got up and headed back to his cabin, thankful for the darkness to conceal his emotions. He hoped that the children were in bed, fast asleep, and that Mary was not. He couldn't get to the cabin fast enough. It was only eleven o'clock and he remembered that B.A.D. and Jennifer would still be out. They had worked on Al and Mary until they had relented and allowed them a mid-night curfew. A curfew that Al was now thankful for, because, not only would they still be out, but Mary would be up waiting for them. That left only B.J. and Al prayed that he would be in his room, fast asleep, now that he couldn't find his Mario Bros. electronic game anymore.

"Hi hon., did you have a nice walk in the fresh air?" Mary's greeting was warm and inviting, Al hoped.

"Yes, it was very interesting." He couldn't wait to tell her about it. Hoping it would have the same effect on her as it did on him.

Then he heard the fateful words—"Hi, Dad! That was a long walk. I've been waiting for you. I found Mario Bros. It was way up on the top shelf of the closet under the spare blanket. I can't figure how it got up there. Wanna play?" B.J. was wide-awake and ready to go.

"No, I don't think so. Do you want to play the slots? Here's a hundred dollars, go ahead up to the casino." Al was desperate.

"Gee thanks, Dad!" B.J. loved the slots.

"Al! What are you doing? He can't go up there by himself and he certainly can't have a hundred dollars." Mary didn't know what the hell was going on.

"Okay, you're right. Sorry, B.J., we'll go to the casino tomorrow. Get Mario Bros. out and we'll play a game, but first I need to take a shower." A damn cold one Al wanted to add.

"Be careful, Al. Remember Big Bertha." Mary's good-natured remark had the same effect that the cold shower would have provided and in only a fraction of the time. Big Jim and the twins were at ease and would see no action this night.

CHAPTER 8

"*I* don't know, B.A.D. I don't think that there is anything that we can do to stop my father. He always gets what he wants. He always wins." Frankie said, getting nervous and reverting to his previous wimpishness, as he and B.A.D. sat in the lounge discussing their plans.

"Cut the shit, Frankie! We can and will bring him to his knees. Trust me we can do it." B.A.D. was serious and his mind was working overtime. "We have to cut him off from 'Charlotte the Harlot', which we hope will cause problems between them. This will put them both on edge and open them up to make mistakes. We also must accomplish this without letting your mother or your sister become aware of your father's affair. There's no sense in letting them get hurt by this. In the process we will get him to have some respect for you and understand you for what you are."

"Gees, B.A.D., that sounds great, but how the hell are we going to do all of that? He's too smart and too powerful for us." Frankie wanted to believe B.A.D., but was having great difficulty in doing so.

"We are going to have to set up some surveillance on L.T."

"L.T.?"

"Don't get stupid on me now, Frankie. You know your father, alias L. Terrence, alias L.T." B.A.D. was beginning to wonder what he had gotten himself into. "I think that we are going to need to recruit some additional help, too."

"I'm not sure who we can get, especially since we will have to tell whoever we get what we are trying to do and why. Won't we?" Frankie said.

"Of course we are going to have to tell them what we are doing. How the hell are they going to help us if they don't know what they are suppose to be doing. C'mon Frankie get with the program will you." B.A.D. said.

Just then, right on queue, another teenager that Francis had met earlier in the day came over to their booth.

"Hi, Jonathan Francis, can I sit with you guys?" He asked.

B.A.D. looked up to see this very large young man standing there with a big shit-eating grin on his face.

"Hello, Louis. How are you?" Frankie said. "Sure you can sit with us. This is my friend B.A.D."

"Hi, Louis," B.A.D. said as he offered him his hand. As they shook, B.A.D. couldn't help but think—'first Francis and now Louis, what the hell is this bullshit, I'm almost beginning to like Bruno a little'.

"Hi! B.A.D. is it?" Louis answered back. "What kind of name is that?"

"It stands for a name that I don't like very much. I don't like Louis very much either. I like Louie better, yes 'Big Louie', that's much better." B.A.D. was at it again.

"What's wrong with my name, I like Louis."

"Don't get all bent out of shape now, Big Louie. With a name like Bruno Alphonso DeGregorio I have a God given right to comment on other peoples names," B.A.D. said. "Besides, what's wrong with 'Big Louie'?"

"Nothing, I guess. Bruno Alphonso huh, boy that is a tough one. I guess you're right; Big Louie is not so bad. Actually I kind of like it. What do you think Francis?" Big Louie was a happy go lucky person and it didn't take him long to adjust to B.A.D. and his opinions.

"I like it Big Louie, but I'm not Francis anymore, I'm Frankie. How do you like that?"

"Ya, Frankie, that's good, I like it. It is much better than Francis and the more I think about it the more I like Big Louie, too."

"Okay, guys don't the two of you turn into the friggin bobsie twins on me. Just how big are you anyway, Big Louie?" B.A.D. was beginning to like him and realize that he might be very useful in their campaign against L.T..

"I'm six foot two inches tall, two hundred and fifty pounds and I love to eat. I'll eat anything. By the way is there something to eat around here?" Big Louie responded.

"Ya, Louie, I've got a two foot kielbasa and a loaf of pumpernickel right here," B.A.D quipped.

"Great, I love kielbasa. Can I have some?" Big Louie really did love to eat.

"Well, Big Louie, I really don't have any food here, but I know where we can get plenty." B.A.D. quickly realized that joking about food with Big Louie was not a particularly smart thing to do. "We'll go to the midnight buffet and you can have all you want to eat there. But first we have something to discuss."

"Awe gee, B.A.D., that's a whole hour away and I don't think I can wait that long. I haven't had anything to eat for an hour or two."

"Look Big Louie just listen to what I have to say and then we will go and get some food for you. Okay?" B.A.D. was fearful that if he didn't get his mind off of food, and quickly, that Big Louie would continue to fixate on eating until he worked himself into a panic state and then anything might be fair game for him

"Okay, if you promise." Big Louie was regaining some control.

"That's better, Louie. The situation is that we have to monitor the activities of some people."

"Who? Why?" Big Louie was beginning to take interest.

"Easy, Louie, I'm getting to it. There are at least two individuals, one of them is Frankie's father, L. Terrence alias L.T., and the other one is a young woman named Charlotte. Now we think that this woman, alias 'Charlotte the Harlot', is attempting to seduce L.T. and then blackmail him or something like that." B.A.D. thought up this little twist to the story to help protect Frankie and the rest of his family. He felt it was a little white lie that was for the best and from the relieved look on Frankie's face he knew he was right.

"What makes you think that?" Louie asked.

"We don't have any hard evidence, but we have observed her trying to come on to him," Frankie interjected.

"What we need to do is be able to monitor her activities, and keep her from getting to him and getting any evidence to use against him. We may also have to monitor L.T. to make sure we don't miss anything," B.A.D. continued. "We are going to have to set up surveillance and some means of communication."

"I can help with the communications. I have a set, actually two sets, of walkie talkies that will be perfect for this. They are small and powerful," Frankie enthused.

"Where the hell did you get those?" B.A.D. was impressed.

"My father bought them for me as a present. Both he and I like electronic toys and he is not stingy about things he likes and understands."

"That will work great. Ya need to have the proper tools to do a job right," B.A.D. responded.

"That's not all. I also have a 35mm camera with a telephoto lens and a pair of high powered binoculars." Frankie was happy there was more he could contribute to the plan.

"Well, that's good but I'm afraid that they won't do us much good at night. And that's when we could really use them." B.A.D. hated to burst his bubble.

"Oh yes they will, they're both infrared," Frankie beamed.

"No shit, Frankie! What the hell are you doing with an infrared camera and binoculars?" B.A.D. was really surprised now.

"I told you that we love electronic toys and these are some of the best," Frankie continued.

"This is going to be a lot more fun than I thought." B.A.D. had his imagination into overdrive now.

"Good! Can we get something to eat now?" Big Louie pleaded.

"Soon, but not just yet, Big Louie. We need at least one more individual so that we can work in two man teams."

"If I get someone else to join us, then can we go get something to eat?" Louie was getting desperate.

"Sure, Louie, I promise. You get us another team member and our first assignment will be to get food, lots of food."

"I'll be back in a minute!" Louie said, as he left in a hurry.

"Do you really think that we can accomplish this?" Frankie's insecurity was showing again.

"More than ever after hearing about the great equipment that you have. I can't wait to find out what else you have in your arsenal. And I think that Big Louie might be quite an asset, especially since it is so easy to motivate him. I just hope that the ship is as well stocked as I've heard and seen so far." B.A.D. was beginning to understand just how much reassurance Frankie was going to need. He was really beginning to wonder what that son-of-a-bitch Frankie called a father did to him. He couldn't understand a father treating his son like an object to be used in an attempt to enhance his own image. Yes, he made a big deal out of being stuck with a name like Bruno Alphonso, and he played it for all it was worth, but deep down he understood that his father didn't have any choice. He was forced by custom to do it; after all he had to suffer with a name like Alphonso Nunzio, alias Al the Nun, himself.

What he really couldn't understand is how Frankie's father could treat him so callously and only be concerned with having Frankie accomplish the 'right things' in order to enhance his own image. After all, if a father uses a child for his own benefit how could he love him? And, if he didn't love his own child, how could he like himself?

It was no wonder that L. Terrence was so uptight and seemed to be searching for something. Perhaps that was what Charlotte was all about, as he looked outward for fulfillment rather than focusing inward to himself and his family. He was obviously an unhappy man and, thus, had fostered an unhappy, dysfunctional family.

How could a father treat his son like this? B.A.D. had read about child abuse, both physical and mental, but had a great deal of difficulty understanding how parents could do this to their own children. He couldn't remember ever having been hit himself and couldn't understand how a parent could look into the eyes of their little child, eyes pleading for forgiveness for whatever it was they did to make their parent that mad at them, and then actually striking them. How does a parent face them afterward, when they have had a chance to realize what they had done? Surely this must pain them deeply. He knew how he felt even when he would get into an argument with Jennifer or B.J. and give them a whack that they definitely deserved. He would always feel badly afterward, and they were only his pain in the ass siblings.

He wondered if other people saw or felt things the way that he did. For instance, when he walks down the street and sees a middle-aged woman of obvious modest means, who may be struggling with a heavy bundle, he feels a sadness that he can't explain. Once, when he was sixteen, Bruno had seen an older woman, in her sixties, walking along the street, struggling with just such a heavy load. It was very cold and she wore an old cloth coat to protect her against the weather. It was not torn, but it was tattered, well worn, and, in any event, in its best day it could not claim to be anything more than an inexpensive cloth coat and to see her all alone, struggling with her heavy load made him sad. He wondered, did she have no one to help her with this and all of the other burdens of her life? Is she all alone or, worse yet, married to some drunken brute?

He felt that he had to do something to help her. As he approached her he could sense her apprehension and was quick to assure her that he meant her no harm and only wished to be of assistance and to help lighten her burden. When their eyes met there was something she saw which gave her comfort; and that she could trust this young man with the sensitive, kind eyes. He carried her bundle to her apartment for her and accepted her invitation to come inside for some hot chocolate. He learned that her name was Emily; she was sixty-eight years old and lived alone since John, her husband of forty-five years, had past away six months earlier. It was said that he died of heart failure, even though he had no history of heart problems.

Emily confided that she knew that John had died of heart failure, but not in the way that the doctors meant. A few months before he died they had lost their daughter and son, and his entire family, in a terrible automobile accident that occurred as they were on their way to have Sunday dinner with them. They were the kind of children that every parent should have. Their son also had a wonderful wife and two small, beautiful children. They were the light, and central point, of their lives as they were a very close family and, all of a sudden, they were all gone and they were all alone. Their sadness was unbearable as they tried to console one another, but John could not be comforted. He could not eat or sleep and, most critically, he could not feel. He explained to Emily that he loved her deeply but he could not go on, that his heart was dead and he could not feel anything but extreme sadness. She knew exactly what he meant, even though she tried to encourage him to fight for his life, she knew that it was of no use because she, too, knew what it was to have a dead heart. A heart that functioned properly mechanically, but was no longer capable of feeling any joy. One which could only feel sadness, when it could feel anything at all. Indeed, John never smiled again and, two months later, he passed away while sitting in his chair looking at a family album. Emily was convinced that, at the moment of his death, she saw a faint smile come to his lips and a look of joy in his eyes that could have only been produced from seeing his lost family and then he passed from this earth.

Emily explained to B.A.D. that when they had lost their family she thought that they might be able to survive together, somehow. But in the six months that John, too, had been gone she existed in a world that could only be described as a living hell. They had been very close, had alternately leaned on, and supported one another for all of their adult lives. Now she was totally alone and had no one to be with, to lean on, in her time of grief, no one to take care of her as John had done. She didn't understand why she was still alive. What had she done to be required to remain here and suffer this pain so all alone? She now knew how completely John's heart had died and she longed to join him and the rest of her family. There comes a time when life is just too hard. The birds stop singing, the flowers stop smelling, and it is just time to stop living.

When B.A.D. had told her that he would come back again to help her with anything that she needed she looked at him and her eyes said that she never expected to see him again. He protested and assured her that he would be back the next day, right after school. She answered that she knew he would because he seemed to be a very kind and gentle young man, with an understanding of life beyond his years. When he left she kissed him on the cheek and she had a tear in her eye and a faint smile on her face, but her eyes still told him that she did not expect to see him again.

True to his word he returned to her apartment the next day. He arrived there just as they were removing Emily's body. When he asked what had happened, the EMT said that she had died in the middle of the night, probably of heart failure. He added that she seemed to have gone peacefully, he thought he detected the trace of a smile on her face. At first Bruno began to feel very sad, but he quickly realized that his sadness was for himself and not for her, for she was now where she wanted to be, with her family. He then felt very happy for her. When she had told him yesterday that she would not see him again he did not understand, but he did now. Unfortunately he now feels an even deeper sadness when he sees older, lonely looking, women who appear to be losing in their daily struggle with life. Does she have enough to eat? Will she be cold this winter? Does she have anyone to lean on, to share her burden, and lighten her load?

He seriously wondered if other people his age, or any age, had these same feelings. Was this just another example, like Harry Holt as a jewel thief or the 'Papal Incident', of the 'world according to Bruno.'

After having read an article of a young father, who took his own life to save his son from the same abusive hell he had suffered, he had decided that when situations presented themselves where people needed help that he would. That time had come now, when he observed that the light did not shine very brightly in Frankie's eyes. Not that he thought that he had been physically abused, but that he had been mentally abused could clearly be seen in his eyes. This was a mission worthy of his best efforts. A truly difficult one since he was also going to have to prove that Harry was a jewel thief and enlist the help of Frankie and Big Louie to help him with this, without them even being aware of it. He had to accomplish this to atone for the disgrace that he suffered in the infamous 'Papal Incident' and the resulting slippage on his mother's ladder of grace, for which he couldn't blame her. He had to justify the faith his father kept trying to show in his ability to judge people. He knew that his father's continued support was partially due to his trying to make up for giving him his name. He also knew that he got support from both of his parents simply because he was their child and they loved him, but he had his pride and he wanted the faith in his character judgment restored.

He was sure that what he was observing in Frankie was mental abuse, even if in a mild form. He could see what it had done to his self-esteem. Maybe B.A.D. got into trouble once in a while because of his over confidence, witness the infamous 'Papal Incident', but at least he liked himself and he still wasn't afraid to stick his neck out and take chances, as L. Terrence and Harry Holt would soon find out. He would redeem himself. He knew he could. He just needed another chance and this cruise, which he never wanted to go on, was going to provide him with his opportunity.

"Hey, B.A.D., I've found us another team member. Meet Rosebud and then let's get something to eat." Big Louie said as he approached the table with Rosebud in tow. Rosebud was an eighteen year old who was slightly built, even frail looking, at five feet six inches tall, and all of one hundred and thirty-five pounds, soaking wet, with small wire rimmed glasses, which added to the smallish look of his features. While not good looking, some, in an impish sort of way, considered him cute and he was as nervous as a cat.

"Rosebud! You've got to be shitting me! What friggin kind of name is Rosebud?" B.A.D. was almost choking on his words. First there is Jonathan Francis, then Louis and now Rosebud. What the Christ is next—Twinkle Toes!

"Rosebud is not my real name, it's just a nickname." A shaken and angry young man managed to get out.

"Nickname! What the hell kind of nickname is that?" B.A.D.'s response was automatic and out of his control. "Why didn't they just name you shit head and be done with it!"

"My mother gave me the nickname because, as a baby, my cheeks were as red and fresh as a new rosebud." As soon as he said it he knew he was digging his hole deeper. "Unfortunately she keeps calling me this and my friends have picked it up and won't let it go. Besides, what gives you the right to criticize my name anyway?"

"Believe me he has the right. I'll explain it to you later, after we get something to eat." Big Louie was getting very restless.

"Just out of curiosity, what is your real name?" B.A.D. asked.

"I'd rather just go by Rosebud."

"If you want to be part of the team I should know your real name," B.A.D. continued.

"Okay, my name is Doolittle," Rosebud replied.

"Now I suppose you're going to make me guess, is that your first name or your last name or just a commentary on your accomplishments?" B.A.D. said, very sarcastically.

"Of course it's my last name! My full name is Oliver Eldon Doolittle. There now you have it all and you know why, if the truth be told, I actually prefer Rosebud." He felt relief at having told them and was prepared to accept whatever abuse was going to come his way.

"You poor son-of-a-bitch, I can understand just how you feel, you must have been named after a close relative too. Who was it? One or both of your grandfathers or your father or both?" B.A.D was very sympathetic.

"No, I'm afraid not. I would probably feel a lot better if I could at least say I was carrying on the family name. Maybe even of some distinguished past relative but, I'm afraid, that's not the case. Unfortunately, my mother just has very bad taste in names. Weird taste is to be more exact."

"You've got to be kidding. She did that to you and it wasn't even because it was after someone in the family. Boy, she must have had one hell of a tough pregnancy to be that pissed off before she even got to know you."

"You would think so wouldn't you? You can probably guess that it has gotten my ass kicked more than once."

"Well, Rosie, now that you are part of our team, nobody is going to kick your ass anymore—at least not without having to kick ours, too." B.A.D. understood loyalty and knew how to motivate his team. Besides, in the 'young man's code of ethics' it was perfectly acceptable and natural to shit on one another, but something not to be tolerated by an outsider who might be doing it with malice in his heart. Such a breach in etiquette would be an attack on each member of the group and require appropriate retribution.

The team now consisted of four self-conscious young adult males who, on the surface, seemed to be a diverse but ordinary bunch, not capable of anything spectacular. But a closer look would reveal the potential of this group of young men: First, there was Frankie who, while totally devoid of self-confidence, had a sharp mind, a strong desire to succeed and a great arsenal of high tech equipment. Second, there was Louis Cochran alias Big Louie who had the size to deal with anyone that they might come up against and a jovial personality that made it comfortable and fun for his friends to be around him. Then there was Rosebud who, well it was somewhat difficult to elaborate on the assets that Rosie brought to the team but his need to belong to and be an important part of such a group could definitely work to his and the other members benefit. Beside he was a fourth person and he might also be able to gain some self-confidence from this experience.

Last, but not least, there was B.A.D., who was well equipped to lead the team. He was the bearer of a very sharp mind, capable of a high level of critical and strategic, as well as devious, thinking. He new how to motivate the other team members and was himself highly motivated by his need to clear his good name. He was also confident in their ability to succeed, not only because of his own self-confidence but because they were doing something good. And he believed, though he would not readily admit it, that those who were attempting to do good had the benefit of an extra force in their battle against evil, and, oh yes, he also was a brown belt in karate. While he was never a great athlete, lacking the skills and desire that his younger brother possessed, he did have the desire to keep himself physically fit and to possess the ability to take care of himself. He was a determined young man and not one to be under estimated.

"Okay, now that we have our fourth team member I have to get something to eat. Now, please!" Big Louie's patience had just about run out and his animal needs were beginning to take over, which could create a dangerous situation. "You promised B.A.D. and Frankie said you new the cook."

"That's true, I have met and made friends with one of the junior cooks."

Earlier in the day he had had the opportunity to meet one of the junior cooks while he was familiarizing himself with the ship's lay-out. It was something instinctive in him to always want to know his surroundings intimately. The junior cook, Pierre, initially began to chastise him for being in the kitchen area, which was restricted to crew only, but was quickly turned around by B.A.D.'s infectious smile, quick wit, and his willingness to help the cook with the heavy load that he was just about to lose control of and, for which, he would catch hell from his supervisor. Before they parted Pierre showed him where he could come down to the kitchen without being seen and help themselves to the snack food and other goodies whenever they wanted. This area was part of Pierre's responsibility and there was always more than enough food. Besides he would welcome some occasional company to break up the long, tedious days.

"Yes, and after we get something to eat maybe you could introduce us to the chorus girls. Big Louie told me that Frankie told him that you had already met one of them." Rosebud's voice was one of excited anticipation and he had a gleam in his eyes that B.A.D. knew only too well.

"Well, Big Louie I do have a friend in the kitchen and I can get us something to eat anytime we want, so let's go. I'm sorry Rosebud, but I haven't met any chorus girls yet, but I'm sure that I will before long and I promise to introduce you to them when I do." B.A.D. informed them as he led them towards the secret spot in the kitchen that Pierre had shown him.

After showing the rest of the group the way to the secluded stash of goodies, and eating his share along with everyone else, B.A.D led his team back out to the lounge and then left them for the night. It was eleven-thirty and, even though he had a twelve o'clock curfew, he was going back to the cabin to spend a little time with his family. He could use a little good-natured bantering with them. Mother would be up waiting for him, as always, and she would be ripe to exchange a few barbs with him. His father would normally be asleep, but tonight he would probably be playing Mario Bros. with B.J. because it was a vacation and B.J. would be relentless and Dad would be earning some of his 'Dad points'. As usual Mom would earn her 'Mom points' for continuing to be a great mother and would be the anchor and always be there to take care of them. It was her job and she was good at it. His father was required to be more physically active to earn his points and, as he had always done with him and Jennifer, he would be playing some sort of game, usually whatever it was that they wanted. He always used to lose too and it probably was on purpose, most of the time. However, when he was playing Mario Bros. with B.J. he was hopelessly outmatched and, as hard as he tried, he would undoubtedly go down to another in a long line of humiliating defeats.

CHAPTER 9

❀

"*H*i Mom, Dad! How are you doing?" B.A.D. felt like being friendlier than usual tonight.

"Hi, son, what have you been up to?" Mary was doing her job.

"Hi, B.A.D.! I'm not doing so well. How are you?" Al responded as B.J. continued to rack up the points.

"Oh, I'm okay. I see you are busy earning some more 'Dad points.'" B.A.D. responded.

"Yes, I'm earning them big time on the basis of the beating that I am taking." Al had learned long ago that a parent had to earn their 'points' with their children, the degree of difficulty determining how many 'points' you would acquire.

Al has had some occasions when he recorded some all time high scores; like the time when they took a family vacation to the White mountains of New Hampshire.

The trip started with his job of taking the family dog, Horace, to the kennel. Of course, this was not one of Horace's favorite times either. As soon as he is put into the car he begins to whine because he knows that he is either going to the kennel, which was hell, or the veterinarian, which was worse than death, making the kennel an attractive option. Jennifer had chosen to sit in the back to comfort Horace and was now paying the price.

"I told you not to do it." Al had tried to warn her that it was much better to sit up front and sternly reprimand him at the slightest sign of whimpering in order to keep him in check before he can build up steam. Instead, she had to play the motherly role and try to soothe Horace with soft talk while patting and stroking his head and back, like he was a little baby.

"Oh, poor boy. Don't worry, everything will be all right sweetie," Jennifer said as she hugged and kissed him.

With Horace, this was exactly the wrong thing to do. He feeds on it, like a fire feeds on oxygen, and works himself into a frenzied state, until he becomes uncontrollable. He was whining pathetically, jumping all over the back seat and Jennifer, and rapidly nearing the point of no return. Al realized that he was going to have to take control of the situation quickly or risk crashing the car when Horace decided to leap into the front seat and onto his lap. So, with lightning quick thinking, Al grabbed the newspaper lying on the seat next him and rolled it up loosely, so that it would make a 'soft club'.

"Horace quiet down or I'll slap your fat butt with the newspaper." Then Al slapped it down soundly on the seat beside him. This was something he had learned when Horace was just a puppy and he was learning to train him. The use of such a 'club' applied to the rump would create a very loud noise that would scare a dog without actually hurting. This was a lesson that both Horace and Al learned well and which had come in very handy ever since and was helpful now as it stemmed the tide of the frenzy that he was working himself into and they were able to get to the kennel safely, if not comfortably.

Once they were at the kennel Horace gladly jumped out the door, with Jennifer reluctantly in tow. She was barely able to hang on to the leash as she tried to control him before he escaped into the woods and made his break for home.

"Daddy help!" Jennifer pleaded as she was about to be dragged into the woods.

"Hold on baby, I'm coming." Fortunately she slowed him down enough for Al to catch up and get a hold of the leash himself. Horace was strong, but not strong enough to make any headway against Al's two hundred plus pounds. Once in control Al led, dragged is more like it, Horace into the waiting room of the kennel where a friendly young lady named Carol signed them in and said she would take Horace to his pen, which had access to an outside cage.

"We'll take him down there for you, if you would like?" Al said.

"Thanks, but that won't be necessary, I do this all the time."

"Are you sure? Horace can be a very determined dog." Jennifer hoped that she would reconsider.

"No really, I'll be just fine."

"Okay." They both replied as they looked at each other; they knew it was a big mistake.

Sure enough! No sooner had she forcefully led him down towards his cage than Horace came flying down the hall dragging the frightened young lady behind him like she was a rag doll.

"Someone help me! Please!"

"Jennifer, close the door," Al yelled as he leaped to grab Horace before he could make his great escape. Once again the fact that Al weighed twice as much allowed him to gain the upper hand, although not without a great deal of effort and only after having been dragged halfway across the room.

"Come on, Jennifer, let's get him into the cage." They were able to get Horace down the hall and in front of his cage before he finally managed to get some leverage, by digging his claws into the concrete floor, and was actually beginning to gain the advantage as he whimpered pathetically. Unfortunately, Al had left the newspaper in the car so that now the only chance they had was to physically overpower him.

It would not normally be a problem for Al to control Horace, especially with the help of Jennifer and Carol, but in this circumstance the effect was much different because he was a desperate dog!

His legs were going a mile a minute and his muscles were strained to their maximum as he tried to gain a foothold on the concrete but, with a great deal of effort, they managed to subdue him, sort of, in front of his cage. The difficulty now was to get him into it.

"I think that one of us is going to have to lead him in by pulling on the leash while the other two push him from behind," Carol said.

"That sounds like a good plan, but who gets to crawl in there with him?" Al said.

"We could draw straws," Jennifer suggested.

"Never mind, I'll do it."

"Are you sure? The opening looks kind of small, Dad."

"Be nice, Jennifer." However, as Al started to crawl through the open door he began to think how small it was. Of course he didn't have any trouble getting his head through but soon realized that his shoulders would not fit, at least not at the same time. Al had to snake his way into the cage by first putting one arm through and then the other. Having accomplished this he soon realized that there was no way in hell that his butt was going to fit through this opening. So, with the help of Carol and Jennifer, Al managed to back his way out and they decided that it would be best if Jennifer took his place and tried to lead Horace into the cage.

"Don't say a thing, Jennifer," Al said, and she could see that it was best to leave this alone.

It was much easier for Jennifer to fit through the opening and they managed to get Horace to follow her with surprising ease. Al thought that he got confused and might have thought that Jennifer was leading him on a new escape route. However, it wasn't long before he realized that this was exactly the spot where he did not want to be. Upon realizing this he made a mighty pull on the leash, yanking it out of Jennifer's hand and sending her sprawling backwards in the cage. He then turned and bolted for the door with a quickness that surprised Al and almost allowed him to get away. Fortunately, Al managed to grab the leash, before he got completely away, and held on for all he was worth. Horace was really panicking now and dragged him a good ten feet down the hall before he managed to gain control by grabbing one of the cage bars as he went sliding past. This stopped Horace dead in his tracks long enough for Carol and Jennifer to come to Al's aid.

"Are you all right?"

"Yea, I guess. At least as good as someone can be who has just been dragged ten feet down a concrete floor by a mad dog." They managed to get Horace off of his feet, and calmed down somewhat, while they re-thought their strategy. The only way that this was going to work was to get someone into the outside pen, tie a rope onto the leash and feed it through the swinging door to this person who would then wrap the rope around one of the poles to keep Horace from pulling free. They decided that it would be best if Carol went outside and entered the pen from there and Jennifer would once again lead Horace into the cage with Al pushing him from behind. They all agreed this plan had possibilities so Carol went and got a rope and Al attached it to the leash. Jennifer then took it into the cage and pushed it through the swinging door, where Carol was waiting for it and wrapped it around a steel pole for leverage. This accomplished, they were now ready to force Horace into the cage and then keep him there while Jennifer made her escape. So on the count of three Carol began to pull on the rope from her location in the pen, Jennifer pulled on the leash from inside the cage and Al had the pleasure of pushing his fat ass, while on his knees on the concrete floor, with his feet wedged against the bars of the opposite cage for leverage.

It wasn't easy but they did eventually get Horace halfway through the door where they were at a temporary standoff. They needed a brief rest to regain their strength and continue to wear him down. They could accomplish this because the rope was secured around the pole and he was continuing to struggle against it. They rested for a few minutes and then agreed that on the count of three that they would push and pull with all of their might. So on the count they gave it a Herculean effort and Horace flew through the opening leaving Al flat on his face on the concrete and Jennifer pinned between Horace and the wall to the outside pen. She finally managed to extricate herself from his 'grasp' and crawl out as Al propped himself up against the opposite cage. He managed to kick the cage door shut and yell to Carol that she could release the rope before it strangled Horace. Jennifer then reached through the cage to take off the leash and pat him gently. He responded to the patting and her soothing voice, but Al knew that this was not the best approach. Sure enough as soon as Jennifer stopped patting him and they started to leave he began to whine and beg as pathetically as any young child could ever manage. It was all Al could do to get Jennifer out of there before she broke down and started whining on him, too.

"Dad, how can we leave him, he's so pathetic."

"Don't worry, sweetheart, he will be just fine. A little time alone will do him good. Remember, absence makes the heart grow fonder." Al would say anything to get them out of there.

"Dad!"

When they finally got back to the house Mary who asked what took them so long and why they looked like hell. Fortunately for her neither of them had the strength to even answer her, never mind taking their revenge. They mumbled something about looking forward to the three and a half hour drive as they went past her. The quizzical look on Mary's face was precious because she knew how much they all hated driving in the car.

Their drive up was the typical family ride with the kids asking if they were there yet before they had even left the driveway and Mary asking before they were less than a third of the way there. This was Al's cue to state that if he were asked that question one more time he would turn around and they would go home. They were headed for Attitash, just the other side of North Conway, in the White Mountains of New Hampshire.

When they arrived at the resort, where they were renting a condominium, it was unusually hot. The temperature was approaching one hundred degrees and the air was as still as death. One doesn't expect to experience this type of extremely uncomfortable heat in the mountains.

They pulled into the office parking lot and immediately observed the one hundred and fifty foot, spring fed pool that was prominently advertised in the brochure. Al had made it very clear that he was looking forward to doing his laps in such a large, clear pool. Unfortunately, the pool looked more like a great green swamp.

"Hey, Dad! Take a look at the pool, I think you are going to have to share it with the swamp monster and other little critters," B.A.D said with a devilish little snicker.

"It doesn't look like it did in the brochure, does it?" Al was quite disappointed, as he really did want to do his laps in a pool that was twice as big as any he had ever been in. He wondered if it was just an obnoxious color but still safe for swimming. It did concern him that the Loch Ness monster could be hiding in it and no one would know it. What was just as concerning was that it would be just like B.A.D. to put a frog or a harmless snake in the pool as a practical joke.

Then they all thought that they saw something slither into the pool and when B.A.D. began to hum the theme from jaws, Al made up his mind to stay far away from it.

"Come on let's go inside and check in and hope that the rest of this place is better than the pool." Mary was a little testy.

When they finally got into the condo, the first thing they attempted to do was to turn on the air conditioning since it was hot and stuffy inside. They looked everywhere that they could think of, but could not find the controls to turn it on. After about a half an hour of this, they decided to call the front desk. When Al did, the desk clerk meekly informed him that the units did not have air conditioning as it was rarely, if ever, needed. When Mary heard this she was mad as hell, which was very uncharacteristic of her, and when

Mary is mad you had better get your ass out of the way. When she is hot and tired and mad you are really in deep shit.

Given the tension that was developing, they decided the best approach to the situation was to get out of there and go to the small, non-spring fed, fully chlorinated pool, which was definitely much more inviting than the green swamp. This was a good decision as a dip in the relatively cool water and then relaxing with a cold drink at the side of the pool had a very calming effect. The downside to this was that the kids met some friends who had been there for three or four days already and were filling them in on the things to do in the area. One of these was the attraction at the Attitash resort that was just up the road and had all kinds of great things for kids, including water slides, a water chute, and alpine slides.

Of course, the kids didn't waste any time at all in starting to work on Al to take them up to kiddie paradise. He made a half-hearted attempt to dissuade them from what appeared to have all of the makings of a parent's day from hell. Having failed at this Al was condemned to spend a long day at the mercy of his tireless children. As usual, Mary was quite adamant in her desire to let Al enjoy this moment with the children all by himself; she would just suffer by spending the day by the pool all alone. Al thanked her profusely for her thoughtfulness and reminded her that this was going to be worth a lot of Dad points and that she was going to owe him big time.

The kid's showed all of their usual patience and they were headed for their mountain adventure the very next day. At least Al figured that he would have the rest of the week to recover from his ordeal. As soon as they arrived Al knew that he was in deep shit; he could see three different rides, each one more sinister looking than the other.

He talked the kids into starting with the Aquaboggin, as it seemed the most tame; he could see that there was a fair number of other parents participating and surviving the ordeal. If he was not mistaken, some even seemed to be enjoying themselves. For the first ride they all walked up to the top together and Al concluded that he would at least be getting his exercise; especially since he wasn't going to do his laps in the green swamp.

As the four of them approached the top, they could see three different slides that you could take down to the bottom. The first one was intended for the smallest children and, surely, for the older adults. It wasn't as steep as the other two and appeared to have gentle, sloping curves. The second slide was about another fifty feet higher up and was definitely steeper, with more severe turns. Then there was the third one that was named 'the suicide slide'. One look at it and you could understand why they named it that. It was another hundred feet beyond the second slide and went straight down, without a single curve to slow you down in the least. Al decided right away that that was not for him.

Fortunately, B.J. was a little apprehensive so they chose the first slide to go down. Except for B.A.D. of course, his T-factor level would never allow him to go down the kiddie slide, as he called it, and he went on to the second slide. They sent Jennifer down first so that someone would be at the bottom when B.J. came down. She made it without any incident so it was B.J.'s turn and, after a slight hesitation, he was off and on his way. He, too, made it successfully and now it was Al's turn. He had been watching some of the other kids that looked like they knew what they were doing so he sat on the little rubber mat and pushed off as hard as he could. He then laid out straight, making himself missile-like, as he had seen the kids do. Well, he soon learned that these slides and this position was meant for people much lighter as he rocketed down the slide, gaining speed with every foot that he went. By the time that he hit the first curve, he must have been going fifty miles an hour and he went about as high up the side of the wall as you could without flying off and becoming airborne.

As he came whipping out of this turn, instead of being slowed down, he had actually gained speed and thought he could hear cheers from the crowd as he approached the next turn. This one twisted to the right as it went under a bridge and then took a sharp turn to the left as you came out from under the bridge. As soon as he hit this turn, he knew he was in trouble as he was once again too high and was slammed against the underside of the bridge and then ricochet off of the far wall as the slide turned back to the right. In a somewhat dazed state, he proceeded the rest of the way down the slide where he was then unceremoniously dumped into a small pool to the cheers, and/or jeers, of his children.

"Hey, Dad, that was great! Hurry up! Let's go again!" B.J. said very excited as he started back up for another ride.

"Ya, that was real cool, Dad," B.A.D. snickered and followed B.J...

"Are you okay, Dad? You came down the slide awfully fast and you kind of have a dazed look in your eyes." Jennifer was truly concerned as she helped him from the pool. Once again he was thankful that he had been blessed with a wonderful and sincere daughter.

"Yes, I think so." He managed to mumble as he crawled out of the pool with her help. He got out none to soon either, as another of the crazy little shits came flying off the end of the slide feet first and narrowly missed his butt.

"Maybe you should rest before going back up, or maybe you shouldn't go back up at all." Jennifer was very intelligent, too.

"No, that's okay. I really have to get up there to keep an eye on B.J. and, besides, I would never hear the end of it from your big brother."

They made it to the top just in time to see B.A.D. come flying by on the number two slide and B.J. perched at the top ready to follow his brother down this very steep slope. Al couldn't believe that he was on this one, considering that he was somewhat wary about going down the first slide and assumed that B.A.D. had talked him into it. Al raced to get to him, to save him from his eminent danger, he saw this gleam in his eyes that Al recognized all too well. It was the same look in his eyes that his brother gets when he is facing a big challenge and his adrenalin is pumping and the excitement is mounting as he prepares himself to meet it head on.

As Al got within the last twenty feet, and was just about to yell for the attendant to hold him back, B.J. bolted forward, gave a little war hoop, and went streaking down. Al fell to his knees as he watched B.J. fly past him and wondered how he would explain his broken bones to Mary. She would be bullshit that he didn't watch him more closely and think that this was because he was too busy having fun himself. It wouldn't even help that Jennifer was his witness; she would just say that she was sticking up for her beloved daddy. He'd be in the friggin dog house for months, maybe years. At this point, Al lost sight of him and could only kneel there and wait for him to go flying into the pool and hope for the best. It seemed like an eternity, his life flashed before his eyes and he wondered if he shouldn't have become a monk, before B.J. emerged at the bottom and appeared to be in one piece. Al held his breath to see when he came to the surface if he would be moving or just floating there like a drowned rat.

To Al's surprise, and everlasting relief, he bounded out of the pool, gave his brother a high five, and the two of them immediately began back up for another ride. Al managed to compose himself and get to his feet, with Jennifer's help, so that he could get into line for another ride down the first slide before they got up here to razz him and challenge him to go down the second one.

Unfortunately, the line didn't move fast enough and the little shits caught up with him before he could get away.

"Hey, Dad, you aren't going to go down that whooshes slide again are you?" B.J. said with a sneer learned from his brother.

"Yea, Dad, what's the matter? Can't handle anything more difficult?" It was B.A.D.'s turn to pipe in.

"Oh no, no, I was just waiting for the two of you so that I could go down the second slide with you. Let's go!" Al had to try to salvage some bit of respect from his kids.

So they got in line for the second slide and the boys were kind enough to let Al go first. When his turn came, he sprung into place to show them that he was anxious to have his turn; he didn't fool them at all by the look on their faces.

As he pushed off and started down he realized that this slide was even steeper than it looked and he was going twice as fast as he had gone on the first one. He thought he could hear the kids cheering when he almost flew out of the slide as he went around what was known as 'killer corner'. He knew that the kids at the bottom of the pool were quite impressed when he did a complete back flip as he came off of the end of the slide.

To add insult to injury, he was chastised by the young attendant on duty that such gymnastic stunts were not allowed and he would be asked to leave if he did that again. Al felt like telling her not to do him any favors and throw him out now.

Once again, Jennifer was there to help him out of the pool and back up the stairs toward the top of the slide. They were both checking out Al's extremities to see if everything was still there and working properly.

"Maybe you should stop and take a rest, Dad." She was very concerned.

"If I do, I will never live it down from your older brother." Al was resigned to meeting the challenge, no matter how stupid that might turn out to be.

"Where are your brothers anyway?" He managed to gasp as they continued to climb towards the summit.

"I think I see them going towards the 'Suicide Slide.'"

"Oh shit!" Al looked up and saw them nearing the top and felt a shooting pain go through his left arm. He was too far away and too tired to do anything about it. He could only hope that, when he brought B.J. back with whatever broken bones he had, and surely something would be broken after this slide, that Mary would take one look at him and show how merciful she could be by ending it quickly.

"You look, Jennifer, I can't," Al groaned as the boys reached the top and were preparing to take their turn.

"Well, there about ready to go." Jennifer was very matter of fact about it, which came from living with her older brother for all these years.

Al couldn't help himself and looked up just as B.J. pushed off and started down the slide. He was away in a flash and in an instant hit the pool at the bottom where his brother was already waiting for him. Al was relieved when he saw them both emerge from the pool in one piece.

Unfortunately, they were on their way back up in an instant and caught up to Al and Jennifer in no time.

"Hey, Dad, you have to go down the 'Suicide Slide' it's great!" B.J. was becoming intoxicated by the excitement.

"Yea, Dad, you should try it.,." Bruno said with a slight snicker.

"Yes, it does look like a lot of fun." Al was trapped; he would have to go down it now.

As they approached the top Al saw another father who was preparing to go down; his son too was prodding him. They had met earlier and had had the chance to commiserate with one another for a short time.

As he was about to push off they made eye contact and his look was that of a comrade in arms who was about to go on an extremely dangerous mission. A look that said, 'If I don't make it back tell my family that I love them and make sure that my wife knows that I died in the line of duty. Let my epitaph read 'Here lies a man who made the ultimate sacrifice in carrying out his fatherly duties.'

They exchanged thumbs up and then he pushed off, or was pushed, and then Al heard his blood curdling screams as he disappeared in a flash. In an instant he hit the pool with a thud and, although shaken, managed to stagger triumphantly from the pool with the help of several other men, who also looked a little battle scarred.

Before Al knew it, it was his turn to go down 'Suicide Slide'; better known as the 'S.S.', which, appropriately, was also the name of the dreaded Nazi secret police. Sitting there ready to go, he looked almost straight down and thought that this was designed by one really sadistic son-of-a-bitch. Then he was off, certain that he was pushed, and went down so far, so fast, that his breath was taken away and he hit the bottom so suddenly that he didn't even remember it. All he remembered was bobbing up for air to the cheers of the small group of fathers that had gathered around to help another 'comrade in arms'. As he got out, they all congratulated themselves for having survived the 'S.S.' Their empathy for one another created an immediate bond.

Mercifully, the time for this group had run out, which pleased all the fathers very much. That is until they heard those fateful words from their kids—'let's go on the Cannonball Express'.

"Oh shit," one man mumbled under his breath. Another said that he would like to get his hands on the bastard who put this hellhole together. It certainly wasn't a father. More likely it was a direct descendant of the Marquis De Sade. However, they all dutifully followed behind their children towards the second in this trilogy of horrors. From the looks on their faces and the swearing that was barely audible, you would think that they were on the 'Bataan Death March'.

As they approached the 'Cannonball Express' they just looked at one another and never said a word, but they all knew that they were in deep shit now. Once again they would have to hike up Mt. Everest for the pleasure of jumping into a tube that goes underground, twisting and turning, for one hundred and fifty feet before sweeping upward at the very end and then unceremoniously dumping you into a swimming pool. It is designed in such a way that the entire trip takes less than five seconds. A Ferrari can't accelerate that fast.

"C'mon, Dad, let's go!" The battle cry was sounded as the kids sprinted up the hill.

They just looked at each other and tried to pass it off as each other's kid calling them and not their own. But, in the end, they knew they were all doomed to take their turn of being shot out of a cannon. So they made their way up to the top as best they could, when one of them stumbled the others would help him go on.

As they were making their way towards the top they could see the kids coming flying out of the tube and landing into the pool. They certainly were having a good time; maybe this wouldn't be so bad after all. Then the first father arrived at the mouth of the tube and they all smiled and gave him the thumbs up while they secretly wished him well and hoped that they had a good emergency medical team ready, just in case.

They all held their breath as he positioned himself inside the tube and pushed off. They heard a distant scream as he was sucked into the devil's mouth and, in an instant, was shot out of the tube's anus. They were relieved to see that when he came to the surface he was still moving and able to make his way to the side of the pool and, eventually, got out and managed to make it to a lounge chair. He had an overwhelming look of relief on his face.

The rest of them were happy that he was setting a precedent that they would only be taking one ride through this hell hole. They were also discussing the fact that he went further out into the pool than any of the kids had gone before him and they wondered if there was something in the dynamics of the design that the heavier you were the farther you flew.

The next father to go down was somewhat heavier than the first and, sure enough, he went further out into the pool than did his predecessor. Then the next one to go down was the slightest built of them all and he definitely didn't go as far as any of the other father's had. As they continued to watch their comrades go through the trial by fire, one by one, it was clear that the heavier you were the further out into the pool you would go. The heaviest guy to go so far had gone a full twenty feet high in the air and landed three quarters of the way across the pool. This was compared to the average kid who went about ten feet into the air and only a third of the way across the pool.

At this point there were only three of them left to go down and, of course, they were the three biggest guys. There was Rocky, the Australian, who was the smallest of the three and weighed in at a about two hundred and ten pounds. Al was the next biggest and then—there was Moose. They weren't sure what the hell Moose weighed in at, but they were seriously questioning if he should go down or if he would even fit into the damn tube.

They decided to send the Aussie down next to see if he made it. What the hell he looked like a pretty tough guy and the Aussie's are a daring lot anyway so, with a mighty roar, off he went. There is no doubt that he emerged from the bottom of the tube more quickly than anyone else had; he was projected a full twenty-five feet into the air and came down with a splat almost ninety percent of the way across the pool.

"Oh shit!" Having seen this, Moose and Al just looked at each other and knew they were in big trouble. By now all of the kids had come back up to the top and were cheering them on. This is when Al learned how sadistic kids could really be. Unfortunately, there was no turning back. The testosterone was so heavy in the air that you could cut it with a knife and there would be no facing their sons if they were the only two fathers not to go down. So they just shook hands and wished each other well as Al took his place in the Devil's mouth. Taking a deep breath, Al closed his eyes and pushed off, swearing that one of these kids had greased the tube because he was going through it like a rocket. He was sure that he was going through it so fast that he was creating a vacuum behind him that would have sucked anyone smaller than Moose right in.

The good part is that you go through it so fast that you really don't have any time to think about it, but you also get shot out the other end before you have a chance to prepare yourself. Al came out of the end of that tube so friggin hard that he was catapulted at least thirty feet into the air with his arms and legs going a mile a minute trying to gain some kind of control over his flight. He was beginning to believe that this ride should have come complete with a parachute as he thought that he was about to go into orbit. Al continued to sail through the air while watching the far side of the pool approach rapidly. He wasn't at all sure if there was going to be enough pool area left for him to land in. At this point he let out a yell to warn people sunbathing on the side of the pool to run for their lives. The kids were certain that it was a yell of fear, but Al assured them that it showed that he was concerned for the safety of others even though he was in grave danger himself. But his warning was to no avail because the sight of a two hundred and twenty pound cannonball with flailing arms and legs hurtling at them at Mach II speed had them frozen in place, unable to move a muscle.

When he finally came down he had used up ninety-eight percent of the pool and hit with such force that he sent out a wall of water that engulfed everything in its path. He then continued rapidly to the bottom of the pool before regaining control and finally being able to push himself upwards toward the light. When his head broke the surface he could hear the cheers of the kids and the sighs of relief from his comrades. What he didn't realize at the time, but found out later, was that he had done two complete somersaults in the air before hitting the water.

As Jennifer and a couple of the other fathers helped Al from the pool he received very cold stares from several drenched mothers who had been at the side of the pool with their little ones. They were pissed and gave him that same look that Mary does. The one that says, 'I hope you had a good time acting like a big kid, you putz.'

Al thought about pleading his case to them, that he was just as much a victim as they were, when there was such a blood curdling roar that it could only be likened to what one might expect to hear if a huge grizzly bear managed to get his nuts caught in a hunters vicious trap.

Rocky and Al looked at each other, seeing the fright in the other's eyes, simultaneously realizing what it was as they yelled, "Moose" and then ran like hell. They gathered the woman and children and pushed them along in front of them as they attempted to get as far away from the pool as quickly as possible.

As the roar came closer, they turned just as Moose was projected a full fifty feet in the air, spinning backwards and totally out of control. They were all in awe of the spectacle because it is kind of hard to imagine a man that freak'n big, being hurled that freak'n high, and spinning that freak'n fast. Once they realized that they were clear, they were concerned that Moose might be in real danger of missing the entire pool and splattering on the deck, right before their eyes. They told the woman and children not to look.

Fortunately, the energy that had been generated by Moose sliding through the tube was primarily expended in launching him toward the moon and he managed to come down inside the pool, but only a hairs breath away from the edge. However, he still hit with such force that the air was audibly expelled from his lungs and the pool was almost emptied of its water.

Rocky and Al, along with the other fathers, rushed to see how he was, afraid of what they might see. When he came to the surface he was absolutely blue and gasping for air. They quickly got him out of the pool and laid him down on the grass. He was still struggling to breathe, and was turning a darker shade of blue.

"Do you think he needs CPR?" Rocky asked.

"I don't know, maybe," Al responded. "I don't know how to per-form it. Do you?"

"Yea, mate, but your friggin daft if you think I'm going to put my mouth on his. You'd better find someone else." He was adamant.

"Christ though, Rocky, I don't think I've ever seen anyone that blue before."

"Yea, he kind of looks like one of those friggin little cartoon characters. Don't he?"

"You mean a Smurf?"

"Yea, mate, that's it, he looks like a friggin Little Blue Smurf."

"He looks more like a big blue whale to me; or maybe like Nanuck of the north after taking a dip in the arctic. Maybe we should do something." Al was beginning to get a little worried.

"You're probably right, mate, but you're still full of shit if you think I'm giving him mouth to mouth. Maybe there is someone else who knows CPR." Rocky was not about to change his mind.

"I'll see. Is there anyone here who knows how to perform CPR?" Al addressed the crowd, which immediately began to mumble so much that you could hear a steady hum rise up from above the crowd. At the same time everyone looked down at the ground or up into the air, anything to avoid eye contact.

"C'mon people we have a serious situation developing here. This man could actually die or explode or some crazy shit like that." Al was trying to be as persuasive and serious as he could. Eventually it worked as a very petite, young mother timidly came forward with her little two-year-old girl in tow.

"I um, I um, know CPR, I guess."

"What do you mean, you think? You either know CPR or you don't. Which is it?" Al said, somewhat testier than he had intended to and, thereby, frightening her a little.

"Yes, yes, I know CPR. I can do it, I can!" The apparent challenge was exciting her.

"Hey, mate, maybe we had better think this over a little more. Christ, this young lady is so tiny that if Moose should suddenly inhale, as she is trying to resuscitate him, he could suck her breath right out. Hell, that beached whale could suck a lung right out of that tiny little thing. Although I would gladly perform CPR on her."

"You may be right, we probably shouldn't chance it. Thanks miss, but we don't think you should risk your own life. We'll have to think of something else." Al had no idea what.

"Well, if you think that is what's best." She said this as she got out of there as fast as she could, dragging her little girl behind her as she went, leaving them and the rest of the crowd standing there wondering what they were going to do when, all of a sudden, they heard a rumble coming from within Moose. Before they could get clear, a spout of water came out of Moose like it was coming out of the blow hole of Moby Dick and sprayed both of them. This drew a cheer from the crowd, but Al wasn't sure if it was because Moose was going to be okay or because Rocky and Al got soaked with his spray.

Moose let out a couple of more loud belches, spit up some more water, started coughing and managed to sit up. They went over and gave him a few pats on the back and helped him to his feet. No sooner was he up than the kids came over and said that they were ready to go on the Alpine slide now. They had had enough of this kid stuff and were ready for the ultimate thrill ride.

"Don't you think that we have done enough for one day," Al pleaded.

"Awe c'mon, Dad, it looks really great!" B.J. said excitedly as the other kids chimed in also.

"All right you guys, but let us have a rest first and something to drink," Rocky stated.

"Let's go now!" They all demanded.

"We'll go after we've had something to eat and drink, period!" Moose bellowed and ended all arguments as they headed for the restaurant.

As they sat on the deck overlooking the mountain they couldn't help but wonder what the hell lie in store for them next.

Al expressed what the rest were thinking, "I really think that the person who designed this playground from hell has to have been a direct descendant of the Marquis De Sade. No one else could be capable of inflicting such pain and suffering in one place and in such a short period of time."

"I'm telling you mates, this friggin 'Alpine Slide' looks a lot more challenging than anything that we have experienced so far."

"Yes, I think that we are in really deep shit here," Al added.

"I don't think that I can take any more of this bull shit. I just can't do it any more. It would be easier to go out and lie down on the mountain highway and let a log truck run over me," Charlie stated quite emphatically. He was one of the fathers with one of the most active sons and was near his breaking point.

"Oh c'mon, Charlie, you can do it if you just try." They all said in unison.

"No, I don't think that I can. I have to stop taking these vacations, they're killing me. I have to get back to work where I'm safe."

"What do you do for work, Charlie?" Al inquired.

"I'm a New York City police officer, in the narcotics squad," Charlie said, very matter of factly.

"Hell, Charlie, this ought to be a piece of cake for you." Moose was finally able to speak again.

"Did you see my son, the one with the shaved head and the pretty GD earring," Charlie said.

"Wasn't he the one that went down the slide standing up on the mat and then did a triple back flip into the pool? All of the kid's loved him and all of us fathers had our hearts in our mouths." Al would have shit his pants if that were one of his sons.

"Can you imagine what he is going to do on this 'Alpine Slide'? I'm afraid to!" Charlie was truly frightened by the thought.

"I'm with you mate. I've been attacked by sharks while snorkeling off of the coast of Australia and not been as stressed out as at this friggin place." Rocky was sympathetic, which was not helpful under the circumstances.

"Here, Charlie, have another beer. You've made it this far, you've got to pull it together and go on. It's all we can do. It's our lot in life as fathers to help our sons and daughters through the trials and tribulations of their formative years, even if it kills us. We certainly know that it ages us prematurely, causing us to lose our hair, get ulcers and then get Alzheimer's so that we can forget it all." Al had to try to spur him on; he had come too far and gone through too much to quit now.

"Yea, you can do it mate! Just suck it up and in no time you will be back safely on the streets and alleys of New York City playing with your drug cartel friends," Rocky added.

"Let's cut the shit men and pull ourselves together!" Moose bellowed, as he remembered his days as a green beret in Vietnam. "Lets get psyched up and take that lousy little hill."

"Moose, that's not a lousy little hill, that's a friggin mountain. And a big friggin mountain at that," they informed him.

"None the less men—we can do it! Remember we're fathers, fathers of teenagers. We're battle hardened from the shit that we have had to put up with—abusing our cars, drinking our beer, being brought home by the police, and listening to that friggin rap music." Moose was putting it into high gear now and he was doing a very good job of motivating them. The testosterone began to pump until the T-factor rose to the level where the brain hardens and all reasonable thought is temporarily suspended.

They jumped to their feet and shouted at the enemy that they were ready for them and to get their asses in gear and to get going. The children didn't quite know what to make of this, they probably thought that they had had one too many beers or gone down the water slide one too many times, or both. They hesitantly followed their fathers, not sure that they hadn't gone too far and pushed them over the edge. But then the testosterone began to flow in their sons and they too got that wild-eyed look in their eyes and were raring to get at it. Unfortunately, the daughters were caught in the middle without the benefit of a testosterone rush, poor Jennifer didn't know whether to shit or go blind.

They quickly made their way to the chair lift and prepared to attack the mountain. This was a challenge in itself in that you have to time the movement of the lift just right in order to get on or you will get your ass whacked and knocked flat on your face. There are all kinds of signs to keep the safety bar in place, while you are waiting at the bottom and all the way up to the top, and, just as you reach the most dangerous part, at its highest point, with the largest rocks below, and when you could crash into the side of the ramp they tell you to raise the stupid safety bar. Hell, Al would have been better off if he had fallen off earlier. Then, when you reach the top, to get off, you have to leap forward and run like hell before the chair hits you in the ass. This is one time you would have been better off to have frozen your ass off.

If you survive getting off of the chair lift safely, they give you this sled that is made of plastic and you are suppose to use it to go hurtling down a mere ribbon of concrete. As Al was perched on the top off the mountain waiting for his turn, looking down this long, really high friggin mountain, he couldn't help but wonder if his life insurance policy was up to date. By the time they finished their ninth run the time had mercifully run out. They all had harrowing runs down the mountain with a number of very near misses, constantly prodded and challenged by their sons. The fathers gathered at the bottom of the mountain to help each other back to the parking area so that they could finally get out of here. They were all stumbling about, helping one another, and checking their limbs to see if they were all in one piece.

"Are you okay, Rocky? You look like shit." Al couldn't help remarking as Moose was helping, no bodily carrying, him to his car.

Rocky spurted out in a high-pitched voice, "I hit that last bump so damn hard that I think my nuts are somewhere up into my left lung and I don't know if I'll ever see them again."

"I have to get back to New York and find Carlos, the leader of a Columbian hit squad, to help me come down from this," Charlie added, excitedly.

"How are you doing, Al? You don't look so good, either," Charlie asked.

"Charlie, your right! I feel like shit! In fact I feel so bad that if I were a dog, and I had a merciful owner, I'd be euthanised."

Al finally managed to drive them back to their condo before his legs froze up completely. Of course, the boys bolted into the condo well ahead of Jennifer and Al.

"Hi, Ma, we're back!" The two boys screeched out in unison as they rushed to get something to eat, again.

"Hi, guys, where is your father and Jennifer?" Mary asked, as they came stumbling through the door. "Oh there you are, did you have a good time playing with the kids, dear?"

"Ugh!"

"You didn't forget that you promised to take me to dinner and then dancing, did you?"

"Ugh!"

"Oh come on, Al, stop playing that fainting routine of yours. You've had your fun playing with the kids now get up and get cleaned up so that we can go out and dance up a storm." Mary was relentless, "Okay boys, your father wants to continue to play his games, drag him into the bathroom and throw him into the shower, clothes and all. That will get his lazy butt in gear."

For once she didn't have to tell the boys twice. They jumped to it with unusual enthusiasm. Each grabbed a foot and did double time dragging him toward the bathroom in the lower level.

"Oh, boys, do be careful. Bouncing his head down the stairs like that must hurt, even if he refuses to say anything besides ugh."

"I think you had better give it up Dad," B.A.D. brought him out of his daydreaming and back to his game with B.J.. "The kid is racking up an all time high score here."

He then went and gave his mother a good night kiss and Al the obligatory punch in the arm as he said good night. He was anxious to see what adventure the next day would bring.

CHAPTER 10

"**W**ell, here she is, finally. Nice that you could join us. What kept you?" Harry was a bit agitated. He was an impatient man and didn't like to be kept waiting. He also had to make sure that everyone knew who was in control.

"I had the strangest feeling that someone was following me. So I went around the deck a couple of more times before I felt it was safe to come in," Charlotte responded with a sincerity that gave Harry cause for concern.

"What do you mean following you?"

"I don't know. I can't put my finger on it, but I felt like someone was watching me."

"So what's new sweetheart? With a build like a brick shit house, and the way you flaunt that sweet ass of yours, you've always got men watching you and you love it. Why you've got the three of us right now with our eyes glued on you. And I bet you are just dieing for a real man," Brian 'Butch' Murphy said.

"In your dreams, jerk!" She shot back.

"You've got that right baby and believe me we do have a good time. Boy, what we did last night…" Murph let it die there for now, partly because of the look he got from Charlotte but mostly because he could see that he was irritating Harry and he knew that wasn't a smart thing to do. Brian Murphy was a pretty tough guy from South

Philly, and he didn't fear many men, but he feared Harry Holt. He knew from first hand experience that he was not only tough but he was also mean and smart, a lethal combination.

"Why do you think someone was watching you? Did you see anyone?" Harry asked as he gave Murphy a look that sent shivers up his spine. A lesser man might have had to answer nature's call right then and there.

"No, I didn't see anyone. I just feel like I'm being watched and not by the usual men's hungry eye's."

"Ah girl! I think you're just getting the jitters, what being so close to such a big score." He was relaxed now. If she had specifics that he could deal with, then he would. But he had been at this business for a long time and had seen plenty of pre-job jitters. Just the same he would be more observant himself.

"You're probably right! Why don't you introduce me to our new member?" Charlotte was calmer now; feeling safer in the company of her team members.

"Ya, right! This is Tom, Tom Stephens, our new safe and lock man."

Unlike Murphy, who was short and stocky, although powerfully built, Tom was tall and lean, with a build that was angular and well proportioned. A good looking and soft-spoken man, he was much different from Butch who was certainly not as good looking. The differences between these two had already caused some animosity that Harry had to keep under control.

"Well, it's a pleasure to finally meet you Tom. I think Harry has been trying to keep you from me." Charlotte was now totally over her jitters and back doing what she did best; flirting with just the right amount of coyishness, combined with just the right amount of slutty overtones, that the situation called for, or would allow. She was capable of going from looking and acting just a little trampy to that of a full fledged French whore and back again in an instant. Her job was to control and influence men with her sexuality and she was good at it, very good.

Besides being blessed with a certain raw beauty she was, as Murphy had so crassly pointed out, the bearer of the kind of body that not only turned men's heads but also made their T-factor levels rise and instantly excite their groins. It didn't help that she also dressed to maximize this effect, like what she was wearing now. A tight knit jersey with no bra brought attention to her ample, well-rounded, and very firm breasts. Her taut nipples, made hard by the too cold air conditioning, were straining against the thin layer of fabric for release from their confining prison. And the skimpy, tight shorts, worn over a pair of thong bikini panties, allowed her cheeks to protrude below the hem line; alternately tightening and relaxing as they peeked out and then retreated back as she walked. It was a joy to walk behind her, but a man had to be careful or he could become mesmerized and end up walking into a wall or right off the deck of the ship.

"It's a pleasure to meet you too, Charlotte. I've heard a lot about you." Tom was soft-spoken and very polite, but had the same hungry look in his eyes most men had when they met her.

"I hope you are not disappointed," she couldn't keep herself from flirting.

"Not yet anyway," he could play this game, too.

"Okay, let's cut the crap and get down to business," Harry had had enough of pleasantries and screwing around. "How are you doing with Sir Lawrence? Have you gotten the information that we need yet?"

"No, I haven't, because I can hardly get alone with him. Every time we plan to get together something spoils it. That kid of his and his friends always seem to be popping up just at the wrong time. I don't mind telling you that I'm getting pretty frustrated in more ways than one." Charlotte's exasperation was clearly showing.

"What's sa' matter baby not getting enough these days. Come on over here and I'll give you what you need and then some." Murphy was always trying.

"I can take care of myself better than you can." She was not about to take any crap from him.

"What do you mean they keep popping up? Do you think that they know anything about you two?" Harry's concern was back.

"I don't know. But it's like they know everything that we are doing, or about to do. Like they were following us or something."

"Murphy, get your arse out there and take a good long look around to see if you can see any wise arse kids nosing around," Harry ordered.

"Ah boss, she's just making excuses for not doing her job." Murphy was lazy and besides, he wanted to ogle Charlotte some more.

Harry didn't say another word, he just gave him a look that was as cold as death and took one step towards him. Murphy was up off of the bed he had been lying on and was out the door in a flash.

"Maybe you weren't imagining things after all, luv. But if anyone is following you we'll find out real soon, although I can't imagine his son Francis having the balls to do something like that. I've never seen such a placid young man as this kid is at our dinner table. You'd think he had been castrated or something. On the other hand that friend of his, the one they call Junior or B.A.D., is a different story. That young buck seems to have plenty of balls. He could be capable of trouble."

"You could be right, he is with Francis almost every time that they show up. All I really know is that I'm not getting very much time alone with his father."

"It's important that you do or our plan will be in trouble." Harry's mind was racing.

"Just what is this plan anyway? You said that you would let me know the details as soon as Charlotte got here," Tom asked quietly.

"Yes, yes it's time we filled you in on what we are planning to do and why we needed you along." Harry was back to the business at hand. "We have been working on this plan for over a year now, and it has all been geared towards this cruise. It was when we became aware of the reunion of two elderly sisters to celebrate the first time that they cruised to Bermuda, on their honeymoon, fifty years ago. You see, they are twins, had a double wedding, and took a joint honeymoon."

"That's very touching, I didn't realize that you were so sentimental. But what does that have to do with us?" Tom was now showing his impatience.

"Just give me a minute mate and you'll find out. As I was saying, these two old ladies and their husbands had a double ceremony and a double honeymoon cruise to Bermuda fifty bloody years ago this week. On their wedding day their grandmother presented them with matching necklaces that were laden with rubies and sapphires. Which, in their own right, are worth hundreds of thousands of dollars. But more importantly these necklaces are very rare and very old, dating back to the Czar of Russia in the 18th century; to the right people these necklaces are worth millions. The old ladies are filthy rich and would never sell them and, in fact, have actually willed them to the Smithsonian Institute upon their death, with the stipulation that they must remain there forever."

"What the hell, Harry, there can't be much of a market for the complete necklaces. They're too traceable!" Tom was emphatic.

"That is true, Tom, in most cases anyway; but these are such rare pieces that they attract the few collectors in the world that have to have them no matter what the cost. The fact that they can only show them to a few very close friends doesn't matter. These people are used to getting and possessing whatever they want. They are so filthy rich they can have anything that they want; at least they think they can and they are usually right."

"I see, but I still don't understand why you need me. If these ladies are going to be wearing the necklaces wouldn't it be easier to try to steal them at some point when they have them out of the ship's safe?" Tom asked.

"No, because they have hired two body guards to compliment the ships already heavy security and these are guys that you don't want to fool with. They are ex-green berets with combat experience in Vietnam, Panama, the Middle East and God knows where else and, even if we did overpower them, where would we go to get away. We can't exactly have a get away car waiting at the curb with its engine running," Harry informed him.

"That's a good point. When we break into the safe and steal the jewels how the hell are we going to get off of this ship?" Tom asked. "They will be searching the entire ship and everyone on it before they will let anyone off."

"That's where Charlotte comes in. The reason that Charlotte got involved with this dumb shit lawyer in the first place was because he is a big shot New York City lawyer with a lot of rich clients that he wasn't shy bragging about. He doesn't hold his liquor very well either; I learned a lot about him just by overhearing him one night in a restaurant where he was dining with his wife and some people that he was obviously trying to impress. I realized that a guy like this might be very useful in leading us to some big scores with his big mouth. So I decided that Charlotte should get to know him better and have an affair with him. That part wasn't very hard at all considering what a hot fox she is, his big ego, and the fact that this wasn't his first affair.

"From there it was just a matter of time before he would start to brag to her when he was going to be at some big function or dinner party with some big wig and what beautiful piece of jewelry the big wig's wife would be showing off. Our Lawrence is an admirer of fine jewelry and even thinks of himself as some sort of an expert on it. This helped us a great deal in being able to steal some of these.

Because of him we would know when to watch them. We would even be able to find out in what room and exactly where they hid their very expensive, supposedly impenetrable, safes. Then, while they were out at the party or the big function, we would break into their houses and install sophisticated monitoring devices, both video and audio, which would provide us with the exact location and, more importantly, the combination of the safe.

"From there it was just a matter of time to pick the right moment when they were out of the house and not wearing their best jewelry. This all started about two years ago and we have made about ten scores in that time. We think that Lawrence is beginning to suspect something or at least has decided to be more discrete with all of his clients getting ripped off. This will be our last job with him and then Charlotte will dump the jerk in a big way.

"Ever since he told her about the plans for this trip I have been working everything towards this big score. That includes starting to leave little bits of evidence that points the finger in his direction. Up to now they have been very subtle things, like committing the last two on the same evening that they were attending functions with Lawrence. But this time we will implicate him in a big way. We will plant some small pieces from the previous thefts, as well as some from this one, in his room to focus the investigation on him and away from us. Even if it doesn't hold up, it will direct attention away from us long enough for us to make our escape. Of course, poor Lawrence, the asshole that he is, will be ruined by the negative publicity no matter what the final outcome." Harry was pleased with his plan and was happy to show Tom how smart he was.

"That's a very good plan, Harry, my compliments. But when they don't find the major jewels on him, they still are going to search the ship from stem to stern and everyone on it. We'll never be able to get off the ship with them."

"Well, mate, you just leave that to me. I have that all worked out and you'll find out on a need to know basis." Harry said this with a

finality and a look that said there was no room for any further discussion.

Just then, Murphy came back into the cabin.

"Shit there ain't any kids out there except for some scrawny little
piss head hanging over the railing puking his guts out. The skinny
little candy ass is greener than anyone I've ever seen. The little prick
could pass for Kermit the friggin frog." Murphy was more than a little pissed off.

"Just the same, I want you two to keep your eyes out for Francis
and B.A.D., especially B.A.D. So, go up to the pool deck, have a couple of brews, and enjoy the bikinis. I'll meet you there in about an
hour or so." Again, there was no room for discussion, but that was
okay with Murphy, because drinking beer and ogling half naked girls
were two things he did well and enjoyed doing; so, he and Tom left
quickly.

"So sweetheart, I bet you've missed me, haven't you." Harry was
turning on the charm as he approached her.

"I can live with it," Charlotte answered coldly.

"What's the matter, Charlie girl. You really are up tight. If I didn't
know better I might think that you really missed Lawrence or something."

"Well you certainly haven't been lonely. How is your new friend,
what's her name, Sally is it?" Charlotte shot back.

"Ah! So, that's it, is it? My girl's a little jealous is she? I didn't think
you were the type. Besides, she is just a little distraction, something
to amuse myself with. Call it my goodwill gesture for the year. She
certainly needed the attention but, believe me, she can't compare
with you. That would be like comparing a pussy cat with a tigress."
Harry was cocky now.

He was also very cocky about his prowess as a lover. In this regard,
Charlotte would agree with him. They weren't in love but they were
lovers, good lovers. They had an animal attraction for one another.
An attraction that was a physical, hot, unbridled need to express

their very deepest desires. She knew that Harry really got off on using her to fulfill his aggressive animal instincts and his need for control. But, in her mind, she was using him.

"Come on now, Charlie girl, you know that what we have has nothing to do with monogamy and everything to do with being the hedonists that we are," he said as he reached out and took her shoulders in his powerful hands, pulled her to him, and kissed her.

Their kiss turned into immediate heat as their tongues began to probe the depths of each other's mouths, darting in and out, as they dueled with each other for domination. Harry then moved his hands from her shoulders and down the sides of her arms. Arms that remained by her sides letting him know that she was prepared to submit to him, but that he would have to work to illicit the response from her that he sought.

He made love to her with the wild abandon that turned both of them on so damn much. She was almost totally exhausted and her body tingled exquisitely from her head to the tip of her toes when he finally reached his orgasm. In near exhaustion, he collapsed on her and then rolled off and lay by her side, the both of them totally satiated. What a magnificent beast he could be, she thought.

"You know sweetheart, I think that you should get close to this kid, B.A.D., to see what the hell, if anything, he knows." Harry was immediately back to business. Charlotte was always amazed at how quickly men seemed to be interested in some subject, usually work, as soon as they had experienced there orgasm. It was as if there was a battle going on within them for control of the situation and the balance of power had just shifted dramatically with the onset of orgasm. She wanted to cuddle and savor the warmth that had been generated within her. This was always missing in her relationships with men. She wondered if, perhaps, this kind of tenderness was shared by two people who were in love and that's what made sex between them something deeper than the sheer physical pleasure that she had been able to experience. A feeling that was as much cerebral as it was physical, maybe she would know this some day. And then again, maybe not.

"Sure, I wouldn't mind coming on to him, he's kind of cute. How friendly do you want me to get with him?" Charlotte was now being coy.

"As close as it takes baby. He ought to be a piece of cake for you."

"It will be my pleasure, Harry. I'll start right away." She could also play this game, as she got out of bed and started to get dressed. She had learned that a woman could be just as seductive getting dressed as getting undressed.

"Maybe you could start a little bit later and come back to bed for a while longer." He was definitely excited by watching her movements as her naked body was becoming less and less so.

This was the moment she knew would come—she was back in control sexually. It always happened this way and was one of the reasons that allowed her the pleasure of totally abandoning herself to him while in the heat of sex. She would tease him further before she would stop and leave him wanting her even more for the next time.

"I really should be going to get our plan in action and before someone discovers us. Bye love." She gave him a deep, wet kiss as she left him wanting more of her. She loved it.

CHAPTER 11

❈

"*H*ey! What the hell happened to you two? We've been waiting for over a half-hour for you guys to report in; we were just about to go out and search for you." B.A.D.'s tone expressed both concern and irritation. "Christ, Rosie, you look like shit."

Big Louie and Rosie had finally made their way back to the rendezvous point with Louie all but carrying Rosie, who did look like he had been run over by a Mack truck and was sort of green.

"I ahh...I ahh..." that's all Rosie could manage to get out as he collapsed into a chair between B.A.D. and Frankie.

"He kind of got squished a little bit," Louie sheepishly informed them.

"What do you mean, 'squished'?" B.A.D. wanted to know.

"I sort of fell on him."

"What do you mean 'sort of'? You either did or you didn't," protested B.A.D..

"Well, I did, but I didn't mean to. He was just lying there when I turned to run and I tripped over him and sort of landed on him."

"There you go again with that sort of shit. You either fell on him or you didn't. Which is it?"

'Yeah, I fell on him. I'm afraid I fell square on him without any chance of deflecting some of my weight. But hell, he was just lying there and I had to get away or we would be discovered."

"Okay, first things first." B.A.D. had to get control of this situation. "Let's start with why you had to turn and run in the first place, shall we."

"Well, we were tailing Charlotte as you instructed us. And, by the way, we'd be happy to tail her anytime, day or night. What a woman!"

"Let's just stay with the story."

"We were following her when I thought she was getting a little suspicious so we had to stay further back and did just manage to watch her go into one of the state room cabins. You know the ones that have outside doors that open right onto the deck. So, we were outside of the stateroom waiting for her to come out. Quite a bit of time went by when, all of a sudden, a mean looking guy came out and started looking around like he expected to see someone. That's when I turned to run and hide, so that we wouldn't be seen, and Rosie was just lying there and I fell on him. I managed to get up and hide under the stairs, behind some tarpaulin, before he saw me."

"Did you just leave Rosie there to be found by him?" B.A.D. wanted to know.

"No! I wouldn't leave him. He had already made his way over to the railing and was hanging over the edge. He looked pretty green, like he was going to be seasick, or something. I figured this guy would just think that he was going to puke and be happy to leave him alone. Besides, if he didn't leave him alone I was right there and would have come out of hiding to help him." Big Louie was quite emphatic.

"Well, Big Louie, I am impressed—that's pretty good thinking." B.A.D. and Frankie both nodded their approval.

"But, Rosie, why were you lying down behind Big Louie?"

Rosie was hesitant "I don't know, really."

"Oh shit, here we go. First Big Louie sort of fell on you, and now you don't know why you were lying on the ground behind him. I give up! Were you just lying there to see if you could hear if there were any buffalo getting close or did you just want to put yourself in harms way? You have to have known that there are two things that you don't want to do around Big Louie: one you don't want to fall in front of him when he is in a panic situation and the other is that you don't ever want to look like anything edible."

"Like I said, I don't know exactly what happened. All that I know is that I was crouching down behind Louie and, all of a sudden, there was this terrible stench and I couldn't breathe. Then I started to get lightheaded and I think that I just passed out."

"What do you mean, a stench? What kind of stench?"

"I don't know how to describe it, B.A.D.. All I know is that there was a stink like I had never experienced before. I mean it was the foulest thing that I had ever experienced. And, shit, I come from New Jersey so that should tell you something. For a minute I thought that I was in Cleveland."

"Big Louie, did you smell this fowl stench, or do you know something about it?" B.A.D. wanted to know.

Big Louie said sheepishly, "Well, yes, I did smell it; and I do know something about it."

"Do you want to tell us about it. Or are you just going to keep us in the friggin dark?" B.A.D. was getting testy now.

"Okay, okay, I do know what it was that Rosie smelled."

"Let's not keep us in suspense any longer, just tell us about it."

"Well, you see I had some melted cheese on top of some re-fried beans." Big Louie said with a gleam in his eye.

"Ya, okay, so big deal. It's not real appealing to me, but it's not all that big of a deal." Now Frankie was getting impatient.

"You have to understand that when I eat cheese it does something to me, something really significant. And, when I eat melted cheese over re-fried beans, that something isn't very pleasant. You see I'm very sensitive to cheese and it gives me a tremendous amount of gas. And it is gas that does not make any noise when I have to release it, but the smell is absolutely deadly. One time, when my whole family had a large appetizer of Lindbergh cheese melted over fresh broccoli and Munster melted over re-fried beans, the neighbors called in the Environmental Protection Agency to investigate what they thought was some kind of extreme toxic spill. They had to quarantine the neighborhood for a week. Fortunately for us they never did find out the source of the stink"

"Are you trying to tell us that your 'Silent But Deadly' (S.B.D.'s) farts are so potent that they can actually knock a person out?"

"It's definitely been known to happen. In fact, once, during a cookout, I had an attack of the S.B.D.'s because of some cheese that I ate and they had to call the EMT's to give oxygen to some of our guests. Again, we didn't tell them where the smell came from and they never could figure it out. They attributed it to some kind of group hysteria." Big Louie was quite serious.

"Let me get this straight." B.A.D. was being quite sarcastic. "First you eat some cheese. Next noxious fumes seep from your ass. Then people faint. Is that about it, Louie?"

"That's about it. Except that they don't always just seep out, frequently they escape with a good deal of force totally against my will. You might even say that sometimes they just explode out of my ass." Big Louie continued quite seriously.

"I didn't realize that you could tell such a good story."

"I don't know B.A.D., that sounds just like what happened to me." Rosie was also quite serious.

"You guys are pulling our legs," Frankie agreed with B.A.D.

"Oh shit! I think you guys had better get out of here fast; I feel a big one coming on. Oh, no! Noooo...! It's too late! I'm really sorry!" Big Louie looked very embarrassed.

"What do you mean? I don't smell anything," Frankie said.

"Neither do I." B.A.D. added somewhat disgruntled because he didn't like to be on the receiving end of a prank. "And you can get up now Rosie, the joke's over. Come on Rosie get...get...agh...OH HOLY SHIT! What in God's name is THAT."

It took a few seconds, but it finally had reached B.A.D., then Frankie, and they both began to cough as they were gagging from the stench.

Frankie could barely speak; "My God Louie did this putrid smell really come from you."

"Yes, I'm afraid so," Louie sheepishly replied.

"I can't believe that this incredibly foul odor is just from eating cheese. I mean really—'what the hell crawled up your ass and died?" This last was said very slowly and with great emphasis, as B.A.D. struggled for a breath of fresh air. It was a losing battle.

"It's really true." Big Louie responded. "In fact, this is rather a mild case since I only had one kind of cheese and I only had a small amount, at that."

"You have to be kidding!" It was now Frankie's turn. "You mean it can be worse than this." He and B.A.D. attempted to revive Rosie by dragging him over towards the railing and, hopefully, some fresh air.

"Why do you think Rosie passed out and we didn't?" Frankie inquired of B.A.D..

"I don't know? It's probably because he is somewhat frail and is shorter than we are."

"What do you mean shorter? What the hell does that have to do with anything?"

"C'mon Frankie, get with it. Of course it makes a difference."

"I still don't see what being shorter has to do with it, but, all right, I'll play your silly little game. What does being shorter have to do with it, B.A.D.?'"

"It' really quite simple when you think about it Frankie. He's shorter and therefore he's closer to the source," B.A.D. happily informed him.

"I have to hand it to you B.A.D., that certainly DOES make perfect sense when you think about it."

This was said as they continued to try to revive him and think of how to get away from the stench themselves. That's when B.A.D. had an idea.

"Look, Louie, there is a slight breeze blowing from the bow towards the stern."

"Huh?"

"From the front of the ship to the back!"

"Oh, okay."

"You move over here on the other side of us and make sure that you stay on that side. If you have to fart again, you make sure that you fart towards the back of the ship. Of course it would be better still if you could just suppress them."

"I really can't stop them," Louie pleaded. "I could delay them but, when I do, they end up just coming out with more force and, I'm convinced, smelling even worse."

"He's probably right and, besides B.A.D., I think that anything that can fight its way out of that butt deserves to be free."

"Hey! That's good Frankie, I definitely agree with you," B.A.D. chuckled.

Rosie managed to state as forcefully as possible in a wheezing, coughing voice, "I think that it should be friggin illegal for you and anyone in your family to eat cheese, or to even be anywhere within fifty feet of it. It's a friggin crime against nature, that's what it is."

"Hey, Rosie, it's good to have you back with us. Are you okay?"

"I don't know? I guess so. At least as well as can be expected for a guy who has been gassed into a state of unconsciousness twice in the last twenty minutes." Rosie continued to cough and wheeze as he staggered to his feet with the help of B.A.D. and Frankie.

"I don't know, Rosie, I think that Big Louie could be a very important secret weapon on the battle field. Or even better, he could be used for crowd control in potential riot situations. There would even be a place for you in all of this." B.A.D. was enjoying himself.

"I can certainly agree with you on his ability to be a powerful force to disperse people or render them unconscious in a relatively harmless manner. At least I hope that there are no lasting side affects. But I don't understand how I could be of benefit?" Rosie responded.

"It's simple, you would be used as an early warning device. Somewhat the same way that they use canaries down in coal mines. Because they are more sensitive to gas fumes, they are affected before humans and can give them enough of a warning to save themselves. You seem to be more sensitive than the rest of us and you are closer to the source so you would provide us with an early warning so that we could try to get upwind of it or get gas masks or something," B.A.D. continued.

"Very funny, B.A.D.. But what I don't understand is that it doesn't seem to affect him at all."

"That's a good question Rosie. Why doesn't it affect you big Louie?"

"I don't know. But it doesn't seem to bother me or anybody in my family. In fact, we kind of like it." The minute he said this he regretted it as the others spoke almost in unison.

"You've got to be kidding."

"Oh that's gross."

"You're a sick puppy, Louie."

"Ya well you're going to be even sicker in a few seconds." Big Louie would get his revenge.

"Oh shit! Not again!"

"Quick let's get up wind of him. Don't breathe Rosie." B.A.D. barked out his orders as he herded the other two upwind of Big Louie and the coming stench.

"I pity the people who are down wind of you Louie. They won't even know what the hell hit them. Come on guys we have to get him to the back of the ship before someone gets really sick or it causes a panic." B.A.D. began to hustle all of them towards the stern.

As they were making their way to the back of the ship, they could hear a couple talk about the stench as they were coming out on deck.

"Oh my God, John, what is that smell."

"I don't know, Marilyn, but it certainly is the foulest odor I have ever smelled. I think we had better go back inside. It might be dangerous. Some kind of toxic spill or something."

"That's it, John! When we get back home, we are joining that environmental group that our kids have been asking us to. The planet is definitely getting more polluted than we wanted to believe. Please do get me out of here. I think that I am going to be sick."

Unfortunately, just as the boys passed by this couple, Big Louie let loose with another stink bomb. Rosie would have hit the deck again if it wasn't for B.A.D. and Frankie catching him and continuing to drag him towards the back as they both struggled for a breath of air. They hoped that no one would identify the source as they went past a woman in a lifeboat whose husband was pleading with her. She was precariously perched on the outer edge of the boat holding onto one of the support cables.

"I mean it, Madeline, you get your ass out of that lifeboat right now or this will be the last trip I ever go on with you. First there was that time in the islands when you tried to escape from the plane by climbing the fence and kicking me in the mouth, damn near breaking my jaw. Next you continuously screamed at the bus driver as we raced through the streets of New York, and then you tried to get into these very lifeboats when they were just going over the evacuation drill."

"I'm not coming out, Harold. I'm telling you this smell is unnatural. It has something to do with the Bermuda Triangle, I know that it does. This ship is doomed. We are in the land of the living dead."

"You're a Goddamn lunatic. Do you know that Madeline? You're crazy as a loon. No, you're mad, that's what you are. Just like that guy in the islands said, 'Mad' Madeline, that's what you are. Now you get out of there right now or I'm coming in to get you."

"You stay right where you are or I will jump. I mean it! I will! I would rather die than have to live with this stink in the land of the living dead." With this said she almost fainted as the smell was making her light headed.

"C'mon, Madeline, I don't think that we should stay out here any longer. It probably isn't safe and I can hardly breathe."

Just then a message came over the public address system—"This is the captain speaking. We are passing through some kind of unknown pollution, which is causing the foul smell that we have been experiencing. Until we can identify what it is and/or its source, I must request that all passengers and crew remain inside and not go out on deck."

"There do you hear that, Madeline. The captain is ordering all of us inside. That goes for you, too."

"Forget it, Harold, I'm not leaving this lifeboat. And that's final."

Then two crewmembers came by and forced Harold to leave Madeline and go inside.

"I'm sorry sir, but our orders are to get everyone inside."

"But what about my wife. She has panicked and won't come out of the boat?"

"We have some men coming with oxygen masks and they will be able to bring her in. Now please come with us."

"I love you 'Mad' Madeline. Regardless of being the crazy old bat that you are," Harold said as the crewmembers took him away.

They then went inside with Harold to wait for the crew to come that was prepared to deal with toxic spills.

"You let the kid have some cheese didn't you Bertha? Admit it! I know that it is true. I know the smell." Willy Cochran knew immediately upon coming on deck what had happened and that it could turn into a serious situation.

"Okay, yes I did! But I had to, the poor little thing was so hungry!" Bertha Cochran was ever the doting mother.

"But why cheese. You know what cheese does to him. How could you subject these poor people to that stench? They are a captive audience with no place to go but below deck, which may not help at all, or to jump into the Atlantic."

"Oh, it's not that bad. Besides there is a lot of open air out here and I thought it would get blown out to sea. How was I to know that this day would be the first one with little or no wind? Most of the time it is practically blowing at gale force."

"That's no excuse for taking such a risk. You know the near panic that he caused last time. And look at the woman over there in that lifeboat, if she takes the plunge it might touch off a wave of mass hysteria that could have them leaping overboard in droves. We could end up being responsible for the drowning of half the ship. Why did you do it?"

"He wanted it so bad that I couldn't deny him. Not after the embarrassment he suffered as a result of the incident on the bus and in the shower. I owed it to him."

"Ya, well, you won't have done him any favors if they ever discover where that stench is coming from. They'll probably put him out to sea in a small lifeboat and us with him."

"They wouldn't do that! Would they?" Bertha was definitely concerned.

"Don't be so sure. Do you see the look in some of these people's eyes? I think that we had better find Louis and get him down to our cabin." With that, Willy and Bertha went looking for their son.

By this time Big Louie and the gang had made their way to the ship's stern and managed to get behind some tarpaulin so that they could not be readily seen.

"Now point your butt against the railing and out to sea and keep it there." B.A.D. commanded Big Louie and none to soon as he let loose another stinker.

"I can't believe that you are still producing so much gas and with such a foul odor," Frankie added.

"I swear there was a green cloud produced with that last fart. You are really unbelievable. It should definitely be against the law for you to eat, smell, or even see cheese. Hell you shouldn't even be allowed to think about it." Rosie was still pissed off.

"I think that the seagulls following the ship are in big trouble." B.A.D. tried to lighten things up a little.

"Let's hope that there isn't an Albatross following us or we could be in big trouble," Frankie piped in.

B.A.D. was getting mischievous. "Ya know, I wonder if we could burn some of this gas off? Like they do with oil wells."

"I don't know about that, but I can tell you one thing—'I'm not going to cap it'." Frankie was emphatic.

"No, I mean it. The next time he farts we should light a match and see if it ignites."

Rosie wasn't buying any of this. "That can't really happen."

"Can you be so sure? I mean, after all, if anyone ever told you that a stench this bad could come out of a human being, or from anything for that matter, you would never have believed it." B.A.D. was applying his special brand of logic. "I think that we should experiment and see what happens."

"Well, I have some matches." Frankie was game for this. "But I'm sure as hell not going to light it. I'm not going to get that close to the source of the stink bomb factory. Besides, I think that you are right and may even be underestimating the potential firepower that exists here. I'm afraid that it could actually explode."

"Ya, well I'm not going to light it either." B.A.D. was in perfect agreement.

"Well don't look at me. I would probably faint before I could get it lit." Rosie was looking very worried.

"You guys are both right. I think that we should light something and place it on the railing so that we can all be a safe distance away.

Get that newspaper over there Rosie. We can use that as a torch," B.A.D. said.

So they got the newspaper and rolled it up, lit it and placed it on the railing.

"Now, Big Louie, when you feel one coming on I want you to bend over and aim your butt toward the torch so that we can see if it ignites." B.A.D. was very deliberate with his instructions. "And, Louie, you must be very careful to help force the gas out and not in."

"Why, B.A.D.?".

B.A.D. was going to love this, "Well, you want to be careful that you don't cause a back draft and have the flame shoot up your ass."

"Oh shit! I don't think that I want to do this!" Big Louie said.

But it was too late. Another one was about to be launched and there was no turning back now. So Big Louie made sure that he gave a mighty push as he farted.

"Holy shit, look at that friggin flame." Even B.A.D was shocked. He didn't really think that it would ignite, but ignite it did. When it lit there was a loud popping sound and then a continuing whooshing sound that was similar to that which accompanies the burning of a blowtorch.

"It must have shot out at least fifteen feet." Frankie was in awe.

Rosie now realized the full power of what he had been up against, "Shit, Louie, you could double as a flame thrower or maybe the Olympic torch."

"Hot damn, Louie, it's still burning. How long is this going to go on? Someone is sure to notice that the ship now looks like it is being powered by a flame throwing jet engine." B.A.D. was getting a little nervous that they would be discovered. "I think it's a damn good thing that we did burn the gas from this one off or anything within ten miles behind us would have been in deep shit. And I do mean that literally."

"Ah! Ooh! That does feel good." Big Louie had a big grin on his face. "That pushing definitely helped to get all the remaining gas out. I can tell when it's all over, usually."

"That's good because I think that we had better get our butt's out of here before we get discovered," B.A.D. instructed. "Besides I have to get going to find a way to get closer to Charlotte. There is something else going on with her."

"Fat chance of you getting closer to that fox."

"We'll see Rosie. We'll see."

CHAPTER 12

"Now that the Captain has signaled the all clear, let's go out to the pool and cool off. All this exertion has made me very hot and sweaty." Indeed Big Louie had sweat completely through his jersey.

"What the hell exertion did you do except to flap your fat butt cheeks. Hell, I'm the one that got knocked out and trampled on," Rosie complained.

"Ya! And I'm going to trample on you again if you keep talking about my fat butt."

With that exchange, Rosie was off and running with Big Louie in hot pursuit, well sort of. Frankie and B.A.D. followed them at a brisk walk, not wanting to appear to participate in the boyish antics of the other two. Unfortunately, Rosie and Big Louie had managed to get themselves in trouble again. As they had raced around the corner to the open pool area they ran smack into an older gentleman and sent his notebook and papers flying.

By the time that B.A.D. and Frankie arrived, the older man was cursing the two of them as he tried to gather his papers strewn around the deck.

"Why the hell don't you kids watch where you're going!"?

"We're sorry mister, really. We didn't mean it." Rosie and Big Louie spoke in unison as they stood there and watched the man try to gather his things.

"Are you guys in trouble again? You could at least help him pick his things up instead of just standing there." B.A.D. admonished them as he began to help pick up the papers.

"I think I would be better off just doing it myself," the man said.

"You three go ahead and I'll catch up with you."

"Okay, we'll meet you at the pool. Again we're sorry mister."

"If you're in charge of them you should keep them on a tighter leash."

"It was just an accident. They didn't really mean to do any harm. They're just a little young and rambunctious."

"Ya, okay kid, apology accepted. I guess I was being a little bit crabby."

"My name is Bruno DeGregorio. But my friends call me B.A.D.."

"My name is Walter Polaski and my friends call me 'The Pol'. Which is either short for Polaski or Polish, take your pick, both work."

"Nice to meet you, Mr. Polaski," B.A.D. said.

"Nice to meet you, B.A.D., and you may call me 'Pol' if you like."

"Okay, Pol."

They shook hands cautiously.

"I'm here with my family."

"I trust those weren't your family members that I just met?"

"No, they are some friends that I met on the cruise. I'm here with my mother, father, sister, and brother."

"That's nice."

"Are you here with your wife?"

There was a sudden look of sadness in his eyes and B.A.D. knew he had touched a raw nerve.

"No, I'm afraid my wife is dead."

"I'm sorry to hear that. Was it recent?" Shit another stupid question.

"It was three years ago, but it seems like yesterday." Walter Polaski could still not answer questions about his wife without a noticeable strain in his voice and a sadness, sometimes even a tear, in his eyes.

"I'm sorry, that was a stupid question," B.A.D. said.

"Ya it was, but it's okay. Everyone does it and you didn't mean any harm. But if people knew how much she meant to me and how much I miss her they really wouldn't bring up the subject."

"I really am sorry."

"Ya, me too kid…uh B.A.D.. I didn't mean to lay that one on you. I don't know why I did. I never have before to anyone, never mind to a complete stranger. There's something about you that I like, that I trust. And my profession for forty-five years has trained me to be a very good judge of people."

"Oh, what do you do?"

"What I did was to be a Chicago cop. I was a Sergeant Detective in the homicide division before I was forced out last year because of the stupid mandatory retirement age rules."

"That's pretty impressive, Pol. I bet you have seen a lot in that time; you must have been pretty good to have been that successful."

"Ya, kid, I was damn good at it. Sorry if that sounds like bragging, but you just ask any cop in Chicago about 'The Pol' and they will tell you about me, and they'll do it with respect because I earned it. But that doesn't make any difference when they say its time to retire. No matter how good you are, when it's your time, you're out on your ass."

"Please don't call me kid. I prefer B.A.D., Bruno if you must, but not kid."

"Sorry, it's an old habit and not a good one, B.A.D. it is kid. Hey, I'll try anyway. Besides that's not so bad, 'Kid B.A.D.' the next middleweight champ. Sounds pretty good. How did you get a nickname like B.A.D. anyway? Are you a trouble maker?"

"No, I'm not a trouble maker. They're my initials for Bruno Alphonso DeGregorio. Enough said?"

"Ya, enough said, B.A.D.."

"Okay, Pol, give it a try anyway. But I don't understand what's so bad about retirement. The way I hear most people talk they are looking forward to it."

"When my wife was alive we talked a lot about our retirement and, if she were still here, we would probably be really enjoying ourselves right now. We got along very well and loved being together. My life was my wife, my kids, and my job. With some of the hours and dedication that I put into my job some people might have questioned that, but my priorities were always in that order, and Mary knew it. But when she died my world collapsed. I lost my wife, my lover, and, most important of all, my best friend, all at once. The kids had already grown up, moved out, and started families of their own. They are still very important to me but there wasn't much time in their busy lives for me, then or now, and I understand this.

"They're great kids and I love them dearly but, once they grew up, Mary and my job were my everyday life. When I lost her that everyday life was shattered. Many times I have thought about joining her, but I couldn't do that to the kids and, besides, Mary would be very disappointed in me. So I buried myself in my work and went from a good, dedicated cop to a fanatical, great cop. They would sometimes call me the bulldog because when I got on a case I just wouldn't let go until it was solved. I would sometimes spend eighteen hours a day, seven days a week to break a case. So when I had to retire I was forced to give up the thing in my life that was keeping me going.

"Now I am just irrelevant. I am irrelevant to the Chicago police department, to a lesser extent I am irrelevant to my children, but most of all I am irrelevant to myself."

"I can understand now why retirement has been so difficult on you." B.A.D. spoke softly and carefully considered what to say next.

"By the way Mary is a nice name, it's my mothers name. I like it because it reminds me of kindness, warmth, and love."

"It reminds me of those things, too. Now I know why I liked you right away."

"Thanks".

"You're a very sensitive young man. Aren't you?"

"No, not really." B.A.D. was a little embarrassed. "It's just that my mother is sweet and I love her."

"Have it your way, but remember that I know people and can size them up immediately. And, agree or not, you really are."

"What is this you are writing?" B.A.D. was quick to change the subject and he began to flip through some of the papers he had helped pick up.

"Give me those!" Pol snapped as he grabbed the papers from B.A.D.. "No one has ever seen these and they're garbage anyway."

"I'm sorry, Pol, I didn't mean to pry into your personal papers. I was just interested in what you were doing, that's all."

"I know. I'm sorry. It's just that these are some personal thoughts and I don't know if my writing is any good."

"How will you ever know if no one but you ever reads them?"

"True, but these are kind of sensitive things and I wouldn't like to have someone laugh at me."

"I wouldn't laugh, I promise. I'm sensitive, remember." B.A.D. could be persuasive.

"Okay, you can look at them if you really want too." Pol said this as he turned and looked out to sea. He couldn't bear to look at B.A.D.'s' face as he read them.

B.A.D. picked up the notebook and started at the most recent entry. From the number of revisions it was obvious that he had spent a lot of time on this:

Once I was a young boy.
I played young boy's games

and dreamed young boy's dreams.
I had a young boy's mind and body,
that responded to my every desire.
Yes, once I was a young boy.
Once I was a teenage boy.
I played teenage boy's games
and dreamed teenage boy's dreams.
My mind and body were powerful
and I was invincible.
Yes, once I was a teenage boy.

Once I was a young man.
The games were fewer now, but I
still dreamed young men's dreams.
I was young and strong and
I could make a difference.
Yes, once I was a young man.

Once I was a young husband.
The games were gone, but now I
had a wonderful wife to share my dreams.
We were young and in love
and our life was ahead of us.
Yes, once I was a young husband.

Once I was a young father.
There were new games to play
and new dreams to dream.
We grew older without noticing

as the children consumed our lives.
Yes, once I was 'Daddy'!

Once I was a middle-aged man.
The games were gone forever,
the children had grown and moved away.
The dreams were fewer but more focused
as my wife and I grew closer still.
Yes, once I was a middle-aged man.

Once I was a happy man.
Then the game of life turned sour and
claimed my wife, my lover, my best friend.
Now the dreams were gone forever
and all that remained was work.
Yes, once I was a happy man.

Once I was a workingman.
The game now was one of survival
and work was all encompassing.
There were no dreams only small victories
as difficult cases were solved.
Yes, once I was a workingman.

Once I was........
Once my body restricted me, but
now I am free to travel at will,
from sea to sea and hill to hill,

at peace as my soul floats with thee.
Yes, once I was.....but now are we.

When B.A.D. got through reading this he had to wait a moment before he could speak. "This is very good, Pol. I'm not sure whether it would be described as poetry or prose or what. I do know that it is good and has a lot of meaning."

"I don't know what you would call it either. But do you really like it?"

"Yes, I really do."

"Thanks."

"Your welcome."

"The last part was especially interesting. Do you really believe in another world, an after life where you will be reunited with your wife?" B.A.D. asked taking a chance. Walter Polaski looked at the serious young man and hoped the tear would not escape his eye as he answered, "Yes. I have to."

"Who are you on the cruise with?" B.A.D. knew that this could be another dangerous question, but he had to ask.

"I'm here with my younger brother, George, and his wife, Janet. It was my kids idea."

"You sound thrilled about it."

"It's not that. I love my brother and his wife; she's a doll and he's a good brother. If Mary were alive this is exactly what we would be doing. But she's not and I just feel like a third wheel. Who are you here with?"

"My family, as I said."

"Oh yes, that's right you did, sorry. I bet you have a nice family."

"Yes, I think I do. No, I know I do. You should meet my parents, I think you would like them."

"Yes, well maybe I will."

"I'll see to it, I know they would like you. But right now I had better get going or else I will miss dinner. We have the early seating."

"Yes, I do too, so I had better get going."

"I'll see you again tomorrow." B.A.D.'s tone of voice made it almost as much of a question as a statement.

"Sure kid, I mean 'Kid B.A.D.', I'll be easy to find since I'm at the same spot everyday, all day." The Pol liked B.A.D. but figured he probably wouldn't see him again. After all, what would a young man like him want to do with an old man?

They shook hands like old friends and B.A.D. turned and began to leave.

"Hey, B.A.D., I like you and if there is anything that you need you just come to the 'Old Pol.'"

"I like you too, 'Old Pol', and I'll remember that if you really mean it."

"Yes, I really mean it." For the first time Pol smiled.

B.A.D. smiled back and left. As he was leaving, he turned back and asked, "Pol, do you hear the birds sing?"

"Well, yes." A perplexed Walter Polaski answered.

"Good." B.A.D. smiled again and continued on his way. When he arrived at dinner there where the usual faces with one new addition, an addition that sent a slight chill threw him.

"Well hello, Bruno, I was beginning to think you were going to miss dinner." His mother was always worried that he would not eat properly.

"Hi, Mom, Dad, everybody, sorry I'm late." B.A.D. mumbled, a step up from the usual grunt, as he kissed his mother and gave his dad a slight shot in the arm as he took his place between his brother and sister.

"Bruno, I would like you to meet Father Anthony Demarco. He is a new member of our dinner party since his previous table was over crowded and he so graciously offered to move."

"Hello, Father Demarco." B.A.D. was polite, but cool towards him. He had not been at all comfortable around priests since the infamous Papal incident.

"Hello, Bruno. And, please, Father Tony is fine."

"Bonjour. And how is everyone this evening?" Jean Paul, the Maitre'd, inquired in as pleasant a tone as anyone ever could.

There was a mixed chorus of hello's and bonjour's in reply. The females always seemed to be particularly responsive.

"I hope that you will all enjoy your dinner tonight."

Again he got a good response from the females as he continued to exchange compliments with each of them before moving on to the next table.

"Your timing was good, mate. I was just about to mention that the cruise director is attempting to organize a basketball tournament, if she can get enough teams together. I would think that you, Francis, and your other mates would be interested. It would help keep all of you occupied and out of trouble." The tone of this statement seemed good natured and innocent enough, but when Harry said it he looked straight into B.A.D.'s eyes and then into Frankie's. B.A.D.'s flinch was barely perceptible and only he and Harry noticed it, but Frankie couldn't help himself and his eye's quickly locked onto the plate in front of him as he slid lower in his chair.

What was this all about, B.A.D.'s mind was racing to process the possibilities. Was there nothing more to it than just an obvious assumption that they would be interested in a basketball competition. But why the cold stare directly into their eyes? If he was searching for something, Frankie's response would certainly give him reason to continue. The only thing that they were involved in, out of the ordinary, was the following of L.T. and Charlotte and what the hell would that have to do with him. Then it hit him, could it have something to do with that goon that the guys saw her with today.

"Well, I certainly hope the boys aren't getting into any trouble. But that does sound like fun for them and it is best to keep them occupied," Mary said very motherly as Margaret nodded in agreement.

"Which of our friends did you have in mind?" B.A.D. was searching to find out if Big Louie had been spotted along with Rosie and that they didn't buy the fact that Rosie was just sick. If this were the case then he was definitely tied into Charlotte and the goon. And, if this was so, what did it mean.

Harry's eyes darted back and forth from B.A.D. to Frankie as he spoke. "Oh, just friends. I assume that you have made some other friends on the cruise. Besides, this is a coed event and you must have met some girls by now. I bet that Jennifer and Alison would love to play, after all, I assume that there will be a lot of cute young boys playing."

He didn't mention Louie or Rosie, but he was still searching for something.

"Oh can we, please guys?" The two girls both pleaded with their older brothers.

"I don't know, I'm not that much into basketball." This was true, but B.A.D. was also very leery of Horseshit Harry's motives.

"Neither am I, in fact I've only played when they made us in gym class." This was also true but, more importantly, Frankie didn't want anything to do with Harry. He scared the living shit out of him.

"I even bet that your little brother would like to play. Wouldn't you B.J.?" Harry asked.

'No shit', B.A.D. thought. That's like asking if a cat has an ass or if a bear shits in the friggin woods, the kid lives for basketball. He even wanted to bring his own ball on the cruise, but mother wouldn't let him. B.A.D. knew that he deflated it and packed it with his underwear.

"Ya, c'mon Bru, it will be fun." B.J. was excited.

"Ya, you'd love that, Ace." B.A.D. used the nickname that B.J. had received from him and his Dad, because of his basketball skills. Even though he was only ten, he could out shoot and out ball handle the both of them, easily.

"I bet you guys could probably even talk your Dads into playing with you." Harry said. He would like nothing better than to add to his macho image, at these guys expense, through a physical game.

Lawrence answered with obvious disdain, "I'm afraid I never had much interest in that sort of game, I prefer the more gentlemanly games of golf and tennis."

B.A.D. could feel Frankie cringe as he watched him sink lower in his seat, pretty soon he was going to be completely under the table.

"Well, my Dad loves to play with me. You'd like to play wouldn't you Dad?" B.J. was putting on the pressure.

"Well, maybe, it depends on who is playing and if it's just a friendly game I suppose it would be all right." Al liked to see his kids enjoy themselves and he didn't much care for the snobbish slight from Lawrence or the poorly concealed challenge from Harry.

"How many people will be on each team?" B.A.D. asked.

"I don't know mate, probably seven or eight. It's a single elimination tournament, I think, but you can check with the cruise director if you think ya can get a team together that has a chance at all." Harry couldn't help becoming more aggressive.

"We'll put together a team that will beat yours if we get to play you." B.A.D. couldn't let this challenge to him and his family go unanswered; Frankie now almost disappeared from view.

"Great, mate, we'll be looking forward to it. By the way Sally how would you like to join our team, we already have one female and we need one more."

"I really don't know how to play," Sally answered.

"That's all right, we'll do all the work. You just have to stand there and look pretty."

"Sure, why not." Sally didn't particularly like the male chauvinist remark but she didn't have anything better to do.

"Great."

"Well, this looks like it is going to be such a big event maybe I can even get the Van Goff sisters to wear their famous matching necklaces at the finals." Lawrence added sarcastically, taking the opportunity to stroke his own ego by letting everyone know that he knew them well.

"Sounds great mate, but what necklaces are you talking about?" Harry was immediately concerned that he may have acted too ignorant about them.

"What necklaces! They are two of the most well known pieces of jewelry in the world. I've talked about them several times at dinner." Lawrence became somewhat agitated, he couldn't believe he had been placed with such cretins. He should not have listened to Margaret and the kids and insisted on sitting with the sisters, even if they didn't want to.

"Oh ya, those necklaces, I remember now. Sorry but I don't pay much attention to such things. I suppose it would liven up the show," Harry said.

"I was only kidding, I really don't think that they would risk taking out such expensive jewelry for a basketball game. You won't see those fabulous pieces of jewelry until their anniversary celebration on the first night after we leave Bermuda." This was supposed to be a secret for security reasons, but he just couldn't help showing that he possessed insider knowledge.

"Well, that's too bad because I'm sure that the ladies would love to have a chance to see them up close. By the way, Father Tony, would you like to play on our team, we could use another player."

Harry couldn't believe that this jerk just told him all that he needed to know. He changed the subject quickly so that it would appear that he had absolutely no interest in the jewelry at all.

"Sure, why not, I could use the exercise," Father Tony said. "I've played a little bit of round ball with the young kids in my parish in Brooklyn."

"Is that where you are assigned?" Mary asked.

"Yes, I have been a parish priest there for the last five years and now I'm about to be reassigned. That's why I'm on this trip. My family felt I needed a little rest before starting a new assignment."

"Coming from a parish in Brooklyn you deserve a little rest and relaxation. That's a really tough crowd down there," Lawrence said very sarcastically.

"Yes, they can be very tough, but there are many very good people there that have very difficult lives." Father Tony answered very sincerely and with an angry overtone.

"I think that most of those people are responsible for their own circumstances and can improve their situations if they wanted to work for it," Lawrence said, obviously convinced of the rightness of his position.

"Do you think that these people would choose to live in poverty if they had a choice?" Mary had to interject as she beat Father Tony in response.

"Yes, I do. They are lazy and are content to live off of the system and I don't believe that they have it as bad as people like you would have us think. And I don't want my money going to help any of these people who just want to live off of the system." Lawrence was begging for an argument.

"Please, Lawrence, let's not have one of those discussions on our vacation." Margaret was unusually firm with her husband.

"It always amazes me that people, who have never had to face what these people have to, can come to such a conclusion. Besides, sometimes we have to help those who we think may not deserve it in order to get to those that do." Father Tony was choosing his words carefully.

Mary loved the response, but she wasn't going to be as nice as Father Tony had been. This time it was Al's turn to shoot her a look that said 'please not here and now'. Although he agreed with her position fully, she could be very passionate about it at times.

"I would just like to say one thing and then I think we should turn our conversation to something a little lighter but still important, like what wine we will have with dinner. We should remember that, after we all have had a chance to philosophize on the merits of who should or shouldn't get our help, and when it is all said and done the fact remains that, no matter the reason, a hungry child is a hungry child," Al said calmly, but convincingly.

Then, fortunately, the wine steward showed up, "Buono signore della sera, signora e signorina, how is everyone this evening?" Eduardo Zabelli was as cheerful as ever.

There were 'hellos' and 'how are you' all around. Except for Jennifer, of course, who wouldn't let the opportunity go by so easily.

"Buona sera, Eduardo, come e Lei questa sera? (Good evening Eduardo how are you this evening?)" Jennifer was happy to be able to practice her Italian.

"Buono signorina della sera Jennifer, guarda stasera bello. E il Suo Italiano viene insieme con completamente allora, pari sebbene non ho avuto un caso dargli qualchi lezioni. (Good evening Ms. Jennifer, you look lovely tonight. And your Italian is coming along quite well, even though I have not had a chance to give you any lessons.)" Eduardo was quite friendly.

"Grazie. Amerei perche darmi alcune lezioni. (Thank you. I would love for you to give me some lessons.)" Jennifer responded.

Before this went any further, Al had to show Eduardo, and remind Jennifer, that he knew some Italian, too.

"Sarei molto felice partecipare nelle lezioni anche. In fatto insisterei come penso che posso dimostrazione Lei una cosa o due di mio proprio. (I would be very happy to participate in the lessons. In fact I would insist, as I think that I can show you a thing or two of my own.)

"Ma di signore del corso che sarebbe piu piacevole ha la Sua assistenza. (But of course, sir, it would be most pleasant to have your assistance.)" Eduardo replied as he struggled to keep his composure.

Jennifer just pouted and gave him a dirty look as she finally deciphered the general meaning of what he had said. Except for this little exchange, the rest of dinner went in the typical fashion.

CHAPTER 13

*F*rankie was as nervous as a cat as they made their way to the lounge, where they were going to meet the rest of the team. "I know that he was directing his comments towards us. Didn't you see the way he was staring at us? I wanted to crawl under the table. What the hell was that all about?"

"I don't know what it was all about. Probably nothing. I think that Harry Holt just likes to antagonize people, he certainly enjoyed doing that to our fathers," B.A.D. said. "I can't figure out what he would be searching for. Unless he is connected to Charlotte and that goon that Louie and Rosie saw her with today. But I can't figure what the hell that's all about."

"I don't know, either. But I do know that he scared the shit out of me." Frankie was very nervous. "I think he could be a very dangerous man."

"I think that you're right. We are going to have to be alert and very careful, until we find out what the hell is going on," B.A.D. continued as they arrived at the table that Big Louie and Rosie had commandeered.

"Hi, guys," Frankie and B.A.D. said.

"Hi, what kept you?" Rosie replied.

"You wouldn't believe it," Frankie blurted out to B.A.D.'s dismay. B.A.D. didn't want to spook these guys anymore than they already were after this afternoon's incident.

"Ya we have a priest at our table and I thought our parents would never stop talking so that we could eat," B.A.D. said quickly as he shot a look at Frankie that said 'shut up stupid'. Fortunately, Frankie was pretty quick himself and had already recognized his error.

"What a dull conversation it was, too," Frankie added.

"Ugh! That sounds terrible. I would hate to have a priest at our table. It's tough enough having to watch your language around your parents," Big Louie said.

"Let's get down to business. My father will be saying good night to my mother soon and telling her that he is going for a walk and then to do a little gambling in the casino. Of course we all know where he will really be headed." Frankie was back to his somber mood.

"I don't mind telling you that I am more than a little nervous about this after the near run in with that guy this afternoon," Rosie said.

"A little nervous, hell your scared shitless. C'mon admit it." Big Louie loved to pick on Rosie.

"I didn't see you coming out to take care of that guy. You stayed hidden under the stairs," Rosie shot back.

"I told you that I would have if you needed me." Big Louie was getting very serious now.

"Okay guys, let's forget about that and not argue among our-selves." B.A.D. was taking over now. "Just remember the escape routes that we discussed earlier and be on the lookout for anything that looks strange and we will be all right."

"Ya, I guess so, but I sure would like to know what that guy has to do with Charlotte and why he should care if anyone was following her," Rosie added.

"Well, let's keep our eyes open and maybe we will find out. But now it is time to swing into action. Rosie you and Big Louie go and find Frankie's father and stay with him. He will be in the forward lounge with Mrs. Carr having a drink before he takes her back to their room and tucks her in. Frankie and I will go stake out Charlotte," B.A.D. instructed.

"Why do we always have to get stuck with following L.T. and you guys get Charlotte?" Big Louie complained.

"Ya, how come?" Rosie added.

"I've explained this before. When we have to follow the both of them you get L.T. because he will recognize us if he spots us, and he won't know who the hell you two are." B.A.D. was a little exasperated.

Frankie was getting a little tired of their whining, "Oh hell, B.A.D., let them have Charlotte, we're getting pretty good at this following routine and my father is oblivious to it anyway."

"Okay, have it your way, but be on the lookout for that goon." B.A.D. gave them an extra little scare as he and Frankie left for the forward lounge to find Frankie's father.

"Make sure you check in every fifteen minutes on the quarter hour unless there is an emergency." B.A.D. gave him final instructions as they turned the corner and were out of sight. They had set up a routine to check in every fifteen minutes exactly on the quarter hour so that there would not be any transmissions during a critical time. If either party were in danger of being discovered they would turn off their radio and maintain silence until it was safe to make contact.

B.A.D. and Frankie were quickly into position on the deck outside of the forward lounge. From this spot they could see if Frankie's parents came out of the lounge and headed directly to the cabin or if they decided to come out onto the deck for a more leisurely stroll to the cabin. It wasn't necessary for them to try to conceal themselves at this point because it was perfectly natural for them to be there and L.T. wouldn't yet be trying to be secretive.

Rosie and Big Louie had positioned themselves in a little alcove under the stairs at the opposite end of the hallway from Charlotte's cabin, a distance of about twenty yards. They were sure that she was in there, as she always came back to her cabin after dinner to wait for L.T. and then, eventually, to go out when he didn't show.

It was now ten o'clock and time to check in. Big Louie was the radio operator for the Ravens, their team code name.

"Eagle, Eagle this is Raven One do you read me. Over." Big Louie loved this part of the stake out.

"This is Eagle One. We read you, go ahead Big Bird. Over." B.A.D. answered for the Eagle team and couldn't help using the nickname that he and Frankie had given Big Louie.

"All is quiet here. Request permission for Tweetie Bird to go out and take a look around. Over." If they were going to use his nickname then he would use the one that he had come up with for Rosie.

"Roger, Big Bird. Permission granted for Tweetie Bird to reconnoiter, but be careful." B.A.D. knew that it was safer to stay in hiding, but he also knew that it could be very boring and that they needed relief.

That was just what Murphy had been waiting for as he hid in the utility closet. He had been in there for two hours waiting for something to happen, and he was about to give up when he heard the sound of the radio static and then a faint voice. Although he couldn't make out what was being said he knew that it had to be the young men that Harry had told him to be on the lookout for. He wanted to spring out from his hiding spot and strangle the little bastards, but Harry had told him to be patient and just observe what was happening. He couldn't believe his eyes when he saw the little green kid he had seen earlier in the day. Brian Murphy wanted him, the hell with Harry.

When he had been given the okay to leave his hiding spot, to see what was happening, he had been relieved to be able to get out of that cramped, boring place. But, now that he was out of the protection of the hiding place and of Big Louie, he was having second thoughts and wasn't sure he wanted to be out there exposed in this way. He moved very slowly, being cautious not to make any noise, as he left his spot and proceeded down the hall towards Charlotte's cabin.

He felt both exposed and excited by the danger that he imagined. While he moved slowly forward he was on the alert for anyone who might come by, particularly that guy who they almost ran into earlier. He was so intent on looking up the hallway in front of him that he failed to see that the door to the utility closet he had just past was open slightly.

As he passed by, it opened further and was enough to be noticed by Big Louie. But, before he could sound a warning, a man leaped out and grabbed Rosie from behind. It was the same man they had seen earlier in the day and, with one hand over his mouth and the other around his waist, he picked Rosie up and began to carry him down the hall towards Charlotte's cabin.

With a hand clasped over his mouth, Rosie's screams for help were just muffled little noises and his attempts to kick and wiggle free were to no avail. He was in the vice-like grip of this powerful man and he was not about to get away without help.

Big Louie was temporarily stunned by what he saw, but he quickly gained his composure and called on the radio to B.A.D..

"May Day! May Day! Eagle One this is Big Bird. Come in, over."

"Big Bird, this is Eagle One, what's happening?" B.A.D. responded.

"The guy that we saw this afternoon has just grabbed Rosie and is taking him down the hall. I'm on my way to help him."

"Okay, Louie, we're on our way! If you can free him use escape plan B and let us know. Good luck!"

Before B.A.D. had finished his sentence Big Louie was charging down the hall with all the speed and ferocity that he could muster. He wanted to prove that he would have come out of hiding the first time, if that was what had been called for. As he was half the way to them, he let out a roar to get the abductors attention so that he would stop and turn. He didn't want to slam Rosie into the wall.

His roar had the desired affect, as Murphy turned and was stunned to see such a large young man charging him with such surprising speed. The affect was not lost on Rosie, either. Big Louie had already flattened him once today and that was one too many times. He was aware of the fact that Murphy was temporarily frozen by what he saw and had relaxed the grip that he had on his mouth. As soon as he did, Rosie took advantage of the situation and bit down hard on his hand.

Murphy dropped Rosie as he grabbed his hand and howled in pain. But Rosie wasn't through yet, the man had scared him more than hurt him but both had made him very mad so he managed to slam his heel down very hard on Murphy's toes causing him to lift his foot up in agony. This happened a split second before Big Louie came crashing into him with his full force. The fact that Murphy was balancing on only one leg when he was struck, and that Big Louie exerted his full force on impact, sent him crashing backwards to the floor so hard that he did a complete somersault and landed up against the wall in a daze.

During this action Rosie had managed to leap out of harm's way just before impact and was safely lying on the floor next to the man who had attacked him.

The adrenalin was really pumping through Louie at this point and, before Murphy had even come to rest against the wall, he had turned, reached down and, grabbing him by the collar, lifted Rosie off of the floor and began running down the hall to execute escape plan B. He went a full five steps before Rosie's feet ever touched the floor. Still on the move he turned on the radio and informed B.A.D. that—"I've freed Rosie and we are executing plan B, over."

"Good work, Big Louie. Is there anyone in pursuit?"

He looked back over his shoulder and was surprised to see the guy was already on his feet and coming after them. "Yes, he's after us."

"Well, continue your escape and I will continue on my way to support you," B.A.D. replied. "Frankie you go back and find your father before he leaves your mother and get him to go gambling with you."

"He will never go gambling with me when he can be with Charlotte."

"Yes he will if you ask him in front of your mother. He won't have any choice. I'll continue on to help Rosie and Big Louie as best I can."

"Okay, good luck," Frankie said as he left to find his parents.

B.A.D. moved rapidly to try to intercept them. He knew what route they were taking so he had a chance to get there before them if he moved quickly.

Both Louie and Rosie were running just as hard as they could in an effort to reach the concealed stairway before their pursuer could get too close to them. They wouldn't be able to use this escape plan if he was close enough to see them duck under the stairwell and, through the partially concealed door, to the hidden stairway that would bring them to the back storeroom where they would meet Pierre, the assistant cook. They had to be sure not to let this man find their special hiding place. There was no way that Big Louie was going to let this happen, since it came so well stocked with food.

Unfortunately they were losing ground to him. After recovering from his initial daze, Murphy was using every ounce of energy he had to catch these little bastards. His nose was bloody, his pride was injured, and he was really pissed off. He would get them or bust a gut trying.

While Rosie was just beginning to find his stride, Big Louie was fading fast and there was no way he was going to be able to keep up this pace. They were going to need help, and fast.

"Eagle One, this is Big Bird, come in, over," Big Louie panted.

"This is Eagle One come in, over," B.A.D. answered.

"We're in trouble, he is gaining on us and we are almost at the hidden stairway, but we are not going to be able to use it because he will be able to see us," Big Louie said, breathing very heavily.

"It's okay, I'm ahead of you and hidden in the hall just before you turn to get to the hall that has the hidden stairway. When you get to the end of that hall just make sure he is not there and then quickly slip into it. I will meet you in the back room of the kitchen later." B.A.D. was hoping that they could make it to him before they were caught. He had positioned himself in a broom closet halfway down the hall and was ready.

Then he saw them come around the corner with Rosie in the lead and Big Louie a few steps behind. Unfortunately, their pursuer was only a few steps behind Big Louie and gaining rapidly; if he caught him before he got to B.A.D. they would be in big trouble. As they reached his position the man lunged forward, about to grab Louie's collar, when B.A.D. sprung the trap. He would have waited a split second longer to insure that he didn't catch Louie by mistake but he had no choice.

Just as he was about to grasp the kid who had flattened him, his foot caught the rope that B.A.D. had secured across the hall and had yanked tightly. Again he went down hard and landed flat on his face and, once again, was dazed. As he lay there temporarily out of it, Rosie and Louie were able to get to the hidden stairway and B.A.D. was able to go back down the hall the way they had just come. By the time Murphy got the cobwebs out of his head the little bastards had escaped and there was no way he was going to find them, but if he ever did he would fix their asses good.

They took the stairs two at a time and didn't relax until they were within the safety of the storeroom and relating their close call to Pierre. They were barely through telling their story when B.A.D. arrived.

"Hi Pierre, how are you?"

"Bonjour Messier B.A.D., I'm fine and how are you?"

"I'm good, thanks. How are you two guys doing?"

"We're fine now," Big Louie announced, as he stuffed another éclair into his mouth.

"Speak for yourself Louie. As long as you are feeding your face you're happy, but I damn near got killed by that creep." Rosie was still obviously shaken from the experience.

"Hey! I took care of you didn't I? Just like I said that I would." Big Louie was proud of himself and happy for the opportunity to have proved himself.

"Yeah, you sure did. You should have seen him B.A.D., he was awesome! He nailed that guy like a run away freight train and sent him flying head over heels and he ended up against the wall. But if I hadn't moved quickly myself I would have ended up against the wall with him."

"What do you mean?" B.A.D. asked.

"When Big Louie let out his roar the guy turned to see what the hell was coming his way and, when he did, he relaxed his grip on my mouth and I was able to bite his hand and cause him to drop me," Rosie explained.

"Yeah then he slammed his toe with his foot so that the guy was hopping on one leg. He set him up really good for me," Big Louie said.

Rosie shook his head, "I hate to think what would have happened if he hadn't dropped me."

"No need to worry about that Rosie I was prepared to go low and cut his legs out from under him if he was still holding onto you. I would have hit him right at the knees and knocked him right on his ass without harming you in the least. Believe me Rosie I know what I'm saying, just like I told you that I knew what I was doing this afternoon." Big Louie was getting a little fat headed at this point.

"Okay guys, you both handled yourself very well, but we now have a problem that we have to deal with. I think that you two should stay here for awhile until that guy is sure to have tired of looking for you

and has given up and gone somewhere to get a drink or something,"
B.A.D. instructed.

"That's fine with me since there certainly is enough good things to
eat to keep me around here for as long as you want," Louie
announced as he devoured a cream puff.

"But what are we supposed to do when we want to leave?" Rosie
was ever the practical one and not nearly as hungry as Big Louie.

"Well, if you have to leave before Frankie and I come back to get
you, make sure that you move only where there are other people
around so that you don't give him or them a chance to get you alone.
In the meantime you two can eat to your hearts content and teach
Pierre some more English," B.A.D. instructed.

"Where are you going?" Rosie asked.

"I'm going to check in with Frankie to make sure that everything
is under control there and then I'm going to find Charlotte and see if
I can make contact," B.A.D. answered.

"Nice work if you can get it." Big Louie added.

"Ya, but how are you going to be able to meet her? I know you are
pretty talented but this is a tall order, even for you."

"Well, Rosie, since Frankie is keeping L.T. busy she is going to be
left alone again. And we know that when he is an hour late she often
leaves and goes to the lounge for a drink, usually by herself, so that
will give me the opportunity I need."

"Well, good luck pal," Big Louie added as he downed another can-
oli.

❋   ❋   ❋

After checking in with Frankie at the gambling casino, and con-
firming that he did, indeed, have his father occupied, B.A.D. made
his way to the lounge in search of Charlotte. As he walked in, he
spotted her immediately. Incredibly, she was sitting by herself in an
out of the way dimly lit booth. He couldn't imagine her sitting all by
herself, but there weren't many single men, other than the crew, on

the cruise. She looked like she should be waiting for someone and she probably hadn't been there very long. Since he knew that she wasn't waiting for anyone who was going to show up soon, he steeled himself and headed for the table.

"Hello! My name is Bruno," Bruno said cheerfully, once again thinking that he had to do something about that friggin name and soon.

"Hello. My name is Charlotte." She responded pleasantly enough so as not to scare him away, but not so pleasant as to seem too eager to get too know him. She was happy that he was going to make this even easier than she thought and was also somewhat surprised that he had enough brass for someone his age to so boldly come over to her.

"May I sit with you for a moment or are you waiting for someone?" Immediately he was pissed at himself for using such a stupid line. He had given her two ways to shoot him down.

"Well, I'm sort of waiting for someone, but I doubt that he is going to show. Please have a seat." He was nice and direct without being pushy, she liked that.

"I've seen you by the pool and thought I would just say hello. I can't believe that anyone would keep you waiting for even a moment." Ah that was a little better he thought.

"Well, thank you. I've seen you, too, and I'm happy that you came by." That would help make it easier for him. He seemed like a nice enough young man; maybe this wouldn't be as unpleasant as her usual tasks. "I didn't feel like being alone tonight."

"A woman as beautiful as you should never be alone." That was kind of thick but he couldn't help himself; she was gorgeous and she stirred all kinds of pleasant emotions within him. He almost forgot the main reason for getting to know her. "Who are you waiting for?"

"Actually, now that I think about it, no one important at all."

Charlotte was beginning to realize just how much she meant that. For, even though she was involved with him because of Harry, she had become used to her life with L.T.. It had developed into one of the better relationships of her life. She thought about how ridiculous that was since she was nothing more than his mistress and he used her whenever it suited him. Yet he was not mean or cruel to her, not even unkind really, just unthinking. She was one of his possessions and he treated her like it without even knowing what he was doing, as cold as that could be it was better than what she was used to.

"Surely you must know some other people on the ship." B.A.D. thought that was a rather natural question.

"No, actually I don't. Not until now, anyway." She had to wonder if he was searching for something. This was going to be more intriguing than she thought.

Of course B.A.D. knew that was a lie. But why should she lie to him, she didn't know him or did she? Was she really tied into Harry? But how and why? She seemed too nice to be involved with a jerk like him. He liked her and he was going to have to be careful.

"I'm very happy that you came over to say hello, I was getting very lonely." She was beginning to turn it on now.

"Believe me it is my pleasure, I would be most happy to be able to take away your loneliness." She had the smile of an angel, he thought. Actually it glowed like an angel, but it was more sensuous than angelic, with her full, red, moist lips inviting him to taste them, to caress them, to penetrate them....

"Is there something on my mouth?" Charlotte asked as B.A.D stared at her.

"I'm sorry for staring, but I really couldn't help myself, you are very beautiful." B.A.D. was apologetic but not sorry; it had given him an opportunity to tell her how beautiful he found her to be.

"Apology accepted, but not needed, I'm flattered. Most men con-centrate on other parts of my body than my face." Charlotte was really beginning to like this young man.

"I must admit that I have noticed that, too, and, as nice as your figure is, your face is what really attracted me to you." B.A.D. was letting his guard down but didn't care.

"So you are attracted to me?" Charlotte was getting coy and enjoying it.

"Yes, I must admit that I am." B.A.D. was abandoning all pretenses now.

'Careful young man you could be getting in over your head.' B.A.D.'s conservative conscience was trying to rear its ugly head again.

'Oh, Mr. Brain, will you cool it.' B.A.D.'s libido was not about to sit idly by and let his conscience ruin a good thing.

"Well, I must admit that I am flattered. Such a handsome young man like yourself has a lot of possibilities on this ship." Charlotte thought that might be laying it on a bit thick, but it was not without truth and, besides, they were both having fun stroking each other. This was more enjoyable than the usual situation where she always had to be so careful about her male companions large, but fragile, egos.

"You are much too kind. But if I did have my choice of being with anyone on this ship that I chose, you would, without a seconds hesitation, be my first choice. So, you see, I am indeed the fortunate one." He was beginning to get a strong sense that there was a lot more to this woman than what was so obvious to the eye.

"Oh please, Bruno, you are going to make me blush." She was beginning to feel what she had always imagined a young, innocent, schoolgirl would feel like when she was being pursued by her young prince charming. It was a good feeling, even though she knew that she could not escape the reality of her situation for long; perhaps she would for this one night and to hell with Harry Holt.

"I'm glad, because blushing certainly becomes you." B.A.D. said very sincerely, he was in love. She said Bruno in such a sweet tone that, for the first time in his life, he wanted to hear it again, at least from her lips.

'Mr. Bruno Alphonso DeGregorio get a hold of yourself right now!' Mr. Brain was attempting to rest control from Mr. Heart while he still had a chance and certainly before Mr. Dick got any further involved.

"I do think that, perhaps, it is getting a little warm and stuffy in here," Charlotte said.

"Would you like to take a walk out on deck, the air is much cooler and there is a lovely moon tonight." He was praying that she would say yes.

'Bruno, you may run into your mother out there.' Mr. Brain had to start to use the heavy artillery now; he knew that a walk in the moonlight with a beautiful woman would bring Mr. Dick into the act and put him at a severe disadvantage.

'Oh, give us a break will you Mr. Brain. An opportunity like this doesn't come around very often.' Mr. Dick was now definitely involved.

Charlotte gave him a big warm smile, "I would love to."

Out on deck it was a beautiful night with a warm breeze and a full moon illuminating the ocean. For a while they just walked and enjoyed the atmosphere and each other without saying a word. Somewhere along the way, almost without knowing it, they joined hands.

Charlotte was the first to speak, "You were right, the moon is beautiful tonight."

"Yes, it is, and it is now more beautiful with you here." B.A.D. was so sincere that it didn't come across as corny to either of them.

When they reached the stern they stopped to view the wake of the ship as the white caps glimmered in the moonlight. As they stood there, they slowly put their arms around each other; again it seemed so natural that they almost didn't realize that they were doing it.

"This is wonderful, Bruno, but I think that I'm getting a little cold and I would like to get warmed up. Maybe we could go inside for a nightcap." To Charlotte this was the ultimate in invitations.

"Of course we can. Shall we go back to the lounge then?" B.A.D. knew that he was going to have to be careful, as he was not old enough to be served himself and he didn't want this to be under-scored to her. Once again, the way she emphasized the r and the o when she said his name made him begin to love the name of Bruno.

"Oh no, let's go down to my cabin, I have something to drink there and it is much more private." Charlotte knew this would excite him.

"That sounds fine to me." Fine hell, that would be wonderful, he couldn't wait.

'You shouldn't be going to her cabin B.A.D., you are asking for trouble. What would your mother say?' Mr. Brain was beginning to play hardball.

'Lighten up a little, will you Brainy. This is all very innocent and we are just going to her cabin for a little drink.' Mr. Heart responded.

'It won't stop at that, and you know it Sweet Heart.' Mr. Brain was trying to be forceful and sarcastic.

It didn't take them very long to get to Charlotte's cabin and they went in immediately.

"Would you care for some scotch or brandy or something?" Char-lotte asked him.

"No, I don't think I want anything more than to just sit here and enjoy talking to and looking at you," Bruno said, as he took a seat in the only chair in the cabin.

"That's sweet of you, I think that I'll just have something cold like a coke. Would you care to join me?"

"Yes, that sounds good."

She poured them both a coke, handed Bruno his, and then sat on the bed opposite him as she dimmed the lights. As it was her second nature to do, she leaned back seductively emphasizing her breasts, which needed little help, and her long, fabulous legs. She was wearing a red summer dress, with spaghetti straps, that buttoned up the front from the v-neck to the hemline, which was two or three inches above the knee. It had a loose fitting flared skirt that clung to her and made him wonder if she was wearing any underwear, she was obviously not wearing a bra. On her, the dress was at once wonderfully simple and amazingly erotic.

'Mr. Heart you are losing control. I'm getting increased testosterone level readings and you know what that means. Don't you? So let's get back into control here.'

'Yes, Mr. Brain, I know it means Mr. Dick is beginning to assert himself and will be in control if it gets out of hand, so to speak. But I'm sorry I can't help myself anymore, I'm in love.'

'You're hopeless, I knew that this would happen if I let you have your way. At least try to stop pumping the damn blood so fast, it circulates the testosterone more quickly and will accelerate the time when we will approach the critical T-factor.'

'I'm afraid I can't. Did you see that smile she just gave us?'

'Oh hell you're further gone than I thought. Mr. Eyes, this is your captain speaking, look away from her right now. Mr. Eyes, that is a direct order. Do it now!' Mr. Brain knew that he had to act quickly, and forcefully, if he was going to regain control of the situation.

'Yes sir.' Damn that Mr. Brain can be a pain in the ass, he thought, and, with a mighty effort, forced Bruno to look down at the floor and away from this astounding vision.

"Is something the matter?" Charlotte asked as she saw Bruno look away and also thought she could detect the slight trace of a blush. Again she felt that sensation of being a young schoolgirl and yet she knew she was more of the teacher than the student. She liked the feelings that this young man stirred in her and decided that she would, indeed, be the teacher; she would take total control of the situation and do what she knew how to do best.

"No, nothing is wrong. It's just that you are so beautiful; I know I was starring and I didn't mean to. I'm sorry, but I can't help myself." For the first time that he could remember he was totally out of control of the situation. He was not only unable to analyze anything, he couldn't think straight, he wasn't even sure of his own name, and was getting very lightheaded. He was becoming totally consumed by the beauty of the woman before him.

'Frontal Lobe, please report the T-factor levels in the gray matter.'

'Yes sir, we are reading fifty mega-T's and rising.'

'That's impossible, less than a minute ago we were only at ten mega-T's. Check it again, please.' Mr. Brain had never seen it rise that fast before.

'Instantly, the report came back—seventy-five mega-T's, sir.'

'What the hell is going on out there? Mr. Eyes, I ordered you to look away and never rescinded that.'

"Please don't apologize, Bruno, I am very flattered." Charlotte responded in the softest, sexiest voice in her repertoire.

He had never heard his name said more enticingly, it would never sound the same to him again. He watched helplessly as she began to slowly, teasingly, unbutton her dress. As she did so she looked at him in a way that made him almost melt and when she lightly moistened her lips with her tongue he thought he was going to faint.

'Mr. Eyes, I told you to look away and that's an order.'

'Do you see what I see? Those are the most wonderful breasts I have ever seen and they are not more than four feet from me.'

Charlotte had finished with the last button and then leaned back against the pillow and, as she did so, the dress opened further and fell away, fully exposing her breasts to his view. He was mesmerized, he couldn't move, he couldn't speak, all he could do was to stare and breathe heavily.

'I repeat, Mr. Eyes that is an order.' There still was no response. 'I need a current reading. Damn it, Frontal Lobe, I need a current reading and I need it now!'

'Yes, yes sir. We are at two hundred and fifty mega-T's and rising at the rate of ten thousand T's per nano second.'

'HOLY SHIT! Are you sure F.L.?' If this were true they were on their way to some kind of record and this was not a record that Mr. Brain wanted to attain.

'Yes, Brainy, I checked it three times.' F.L. knew that they had entered into unchartered territory and were still accelerating.

'Mr. Heart, will you turn that damn pump of yours down before we explode. Mr. Heart, Mr. Heart answer me! Bridge to Central Processing Control I'm getting no response from Mr. Heart.'

'Captain this is Central Processing, normal communications are functioning properly, but Mr. Heart is not responding, he is totally pre-occupied. In fact he is racing at a rate that has us very concerned and he is not responding to our usual stimuli.'

'Then have Nerve Endings deliver a real jolt, I want that son-of-a-bitch to think he's having a friggin heart attack.'

As she lay there, his eyes finally moved from her breasts and down her body, noticing her flat stomach and then he got the answer to his question—she wasn't wearing any underwear. The sight of her lying there almost totally naked, tracing her hand up her thigh, slowly across her vagina, then up to her stomach, until she reached her breast and stroked the nipple, ever so slowly, sent a chill through his entire body. Then he felt a stabbing shock to his heart that had the odd effect of increasing his excitement and all other sensations were inconsequential compared to that which was welling up in his groin. This was the point at which the transformation was complete and 'Little Dickie' became 'King Richard' and fully prepared for battle.

'Mr. Brain, the jolt was delivered as ordered, but it appears to have had the affect of increasing the heart rate and the pleasure that Mr. Dick is feeling.' Central Processing reported.

'No shit you guys, his damn T-factor rate doubled to twenty-thousand T's per nano second with that shock. Another pisser move like that, you shit heads, and this whole body will just be one big friggin dick.' F.L blurted out in a near panic state, ignoring all normal protocol.

'All right F.L., control yourself, we get the picture. Please give me a current reading.' Mr. Brain knew the seriousness of the situation and attempted to be as calm as possible to avoid a complete panic.

'Captain we are at five hundred and fifty mega-T's and still accelerating. And sir, I'm not sure, but I think, no I'm quite certain now, that gray matter is actually starting to turn pink.'

'Mr. Eyes, this is my final order, look away immediately! Now!'

'You have to be shitting me, Mr. Brain, have you taken a good look at what I'm seeing? I'd rather risk going blind than to stop looking at this woman. It doesn't get any better than this, so get lost! Sir.'

'Mr. Eyes, you'll pay for this along with Mr. Heart and especially Mr. Dick.' Mr. Brain was running out of options. The jolt to the heart had been a calculated risk that backfired. He knew that it was possible that such a jolt would just cause a surge of adrenalin to be released and further stimulate the flow of testosterone throughout the body. He couldn't risk a second jolt. He would have to resort to guilt and call in Mr. Conscience again.

'Okay, Mr. Conscience, it's time for you to get back into the action.'

'It's about time, Mr. Brain.' Mr. Conscience knew that he should have been allowed to continue what he had started at the beginning. He could only hope that it was not too late. 'Okay, Mr. Dick, get control of yourself now. What would your mother think if she knew you were in here with a naked woman?'

'Ouch that hurts, Connie, but I think that she would understand that I am just a weak male and that I couldn't be expected to be able to control myself under these circumstances.'

'C'mon, Dickie, picture the look on her face if she could see you in this condition.'

'Your a dirty player, but I think it is already too late.'

Ah yes he was weakening, guilt was great. 'What is the T-factor reading now F.L.?' Mr. Brain asked.

'It has reached six hundred mega-T's but, unbelievably, the acceleration rate has slowed dramatically. What did you do?'

'Just remember that I have a lot of weapons. Now for the finishing blow.' Mr. Brain felt that he was back in control.

At that moment Charlotte rose from the bed and let her dress slide slowly, teasingly, down her fantastic body and left it lying on the floor as she approached Bruno. He couldn't take his eyes off her. He was so mesmerized by the luscious vision coming towards him that he couldn't even breathe. She stopped so close to him that her legs touched his, sending a lightning bolt through him, as he remained seated. She then reached down and took each of his hands in hers and placed them on her breasts. He thought he had died and gone to heaven. She beckoned him to stand and, as he did, she leaned forward to kiss him. But just before she did, she whispered 'I want you very badly' and then proceeded to give him the hottest, wettest kiss he had ever had and, at precisely the same time, she put her hand on his crotch and gently squeezed.

That's when all hell broke loose and all kinds of alarms sounded.

'May Day, May Day, Mr. Brain, we have just rocketed past the seven hundred and fifty mega-T mark and are fast approaching a giga-T. So much for your friggin powers. Do you know what could happen if we hit a giga-T?'

'Don't be insubordinate, F.L., I can still make you pay for it. And I'm well aware that at a giga-T level of testosterone we will be in serious danger of becoming a permanent Dickhead!' Mr. Brain couldn't believe that he was so close to regaining control and then to lose it so quickly and totally, she indeed was a remarkable creature.

'All cerebral systems are commanded to go to condition red immediately and to remain that way until the crisis has passed. That means that we must shut down all of our functions to the lowest possible level to allow only minimal blood and, therefore, testosterone to flow to the head. This will force us to revert to our most primitive state, something just this side of Cro-Magnon man, and to temporarily relinquish all control to Mr. Dick. But make no mistake about it, I shall return and, when I do, it will be with a vengeance—DICKIE!!!'

As they lay back and rested in each other's arms, it was Charlotte who spoke first, "Well, Bruno, that was some performance. I mean three times in an hour without barely missing a beat between them." Charlotte was more than just being kind, she was impressed and pleased. But she could see that he was already beginning to get that far away look in his eyes that all men had as soon as they were satisfied.

'Central Processing, get ready to sound the all clear. I think that this time it might be the real thing.' Mr. Brain was proceeding cautiously.

'That's what you said the other two times, we're beginning to think that we might be in a perpetual state of arousal.'

'Well, I think that this one is for real. F.L., I need a T-factor reading.'

'We are at seventy-five mega-T's and dropping, sir.'

'Good the crises is past; Mr. Dick is now just a mere wisp of himself. Mr. Conscience, front and center.'

'Yes sir.'

'Mr. Conscience, he is all yours and I want you to give it to him good,' Mr. Brain said in no uncertain terms.

'So Bruno, shit head, did you enjoy yourself? Was it worth it? How will you feel when you see your mother and she asks you what you've been up to? And did you have a good time?'

"Well thank you, but you had a great deal to do with it. I've never been quite like that before." Bruno felt great that he had been able to please her, even if he now had those nagging doubts about what he had just done. Damn he hated guilt.

'Damn right you've never been like that before, you were totally out of control-you animal. How would you feel if you met this girl's parents? And how about your friends who were in danger tonight? How would they feel if they knew you haven't done anything to try to find out who the hell almost killed them? I think you had better get back to business, you've used this woman and ignored your duties long enough!'

'Damn good job, Mr. Conscience, Mr. Dick is more like Mr. Worm at this point.' Mr. Brain was pleased.

For a long while they just lay there holding one another, even though he seemed somewhat distant he continued to caress her with his hand. She liked it. Most of the men she knew rolled over and no longer touched her when they were through-their conquest completed. Then the spell was broken and she was jerked back to reality.

"Who was that short stocky guy you were with today?" Ah shit that was a damn clumsy way to try to find out who she knows. I'm not thinking straight. What the hell is the matter with me?

"How do you know I was with anyone and why do you care? Have you been following me?" Charlotte was getting upset; she felt that she had been the one who was used. So much for the girlish feelings and Prince Charming. What a fool. "You have, haven't you? Well, haven't you?"

Her sudden shift in attitude caught him by surprise and he answered before he thought. "Yes, we have."

"What do you mean—'we'? Who else is involved and why?" She was really upset now and wondering what the hell she would tell Harry. She knew how dangerous he could be and she feared for Bruno; she was mad at him but she still liked him.

"Please don't be upset, we were just trying to help Frankie. And, besides, I didn't know you then."

"Again, who the hell is 'we' and who the hell is Frankie."? Charlotte repeated.

"You know Francis Carr, I know you know his father, Lawrence." B.A.D. was actually happy that this was going to be out in the open, he thought anyway.

"What do you know about Lawrence Carr and me?" She was relieved to hear that this had to do with Francis' father and not Harry and the jewels.

"I know that you are seeing him and have been for some time now. And I know that it has upset Frankie a lot." B.A.D. was hopeful that maybe now they could change things. "Why would someone as beautiful as you get involved with a married man, especially a man like Lawrence Carr?"

"What right do you have to question me on my private life? You don't know anything about me accept that I turn you on physically. You don't know anything about me, who I am, where I come from or what I've been through in my life." Charlotte was visibly upset.

"No I don't, but I would like to." B.A.D. meant this very much.

'Well, I don't want to talk about it. Actually, I would like you to leave now." She couldn't handle the flood of emotions that she felt, as all the bad history flashed back.

"I'm sorry, Charlotte, I didn't mean to hurt you." He was surprised and touched by the intensity of her reaction.

"Please go, I don't want to discuss it right now."

"Yes, I'll go, but I hope you will see me again," B.A.D said sincerely as he kissed her on the cheek and, reluctantly, left.

CHAPTER 14

"*I* don't know what it is about him, but I just can't get him out of my mind, no matter how hard I try." Sally was again explaining her feelings to Mary, as if she were her sister or best friend, as they sipped coffee on the pool deck.

"Well, Sally, I don't know how much I can help you with this one. I mean I understood when you had that little fling with Harry Holt. After all he is rather handsome, certainly charming, and definitely intriguing so, since you both are unattached, why not enjoy yourself. But I have a hard time with this one, after all he is a priest." Mary was trying to be sympathetic, but having difficulty with it.

"You don't have to tell me about it. I went to catholic school, too, and know all about guilt, believe me. There is just something about him that attracts me, more than a little bit. In fact, I have to admit that he turns me on in a big way." Sally just had to talk to someone about this.

"Please, Sally, I don't know if I can talk about a priest like this. Besides, you are bound to be disappointed, remember he has taken a vow of celibacy." Mary struggled to maintain her composure.

"I know it. But he has an interest in me. I know that he feels the same way that I do. Don't ask me why I am so sure, but I am. And, believe me, it's not because I am so self-confident, or have a big ego or an over active imagination."

"Now that you mention it, I have noticed that he does look at you in a way that a priest shouldn't. And I haven't seen him look at any other woman that way. But I just can't get involved in anymore controversy with the church." Mary continued to be distressed by what they were discussing.

"Excuse me, I'm sorry, I don't understand."

"I'm afraid that it is a long story and not a very pleasant one. It has to do with the time that I was to meet the Pope with my church group and my oldest son Bruno caused a disaster, an absolute disaster. Please, I can't talk about it anymore." Mary's worst nightmare was flashing back and it caused shivers to run through her entire body.

"Don't worry I don't plan on letting this go anywhere. That's why I am asking for your help. I'm not sure that I can handle it all by myself and I already feel like a fallen woman, after having gone to bed with Harry the first night that I met him. I had never done anything like that before." Sally was embarrassed.

"I certainly can believe that, Sally. I'm not exactly sure what I can do, but it might help me get back on the good side of the church." Mary was buoyed by the prospect.

"Just being there for moral support and for you to feel free to step in if you think that I am weakening." Sally felt better now that she had confided in Mary.

"Well, I will certainly be happy to do whatever I can."

"Hi, hon. Good morning, Sally, are you ladies ready to go into Hamilton to do some shopping today. We will be docking in Bermuda very soon," Al said, as he sat down next to Mary and gave her a little kiss.

"I know that I am looking forward to it. I'm also looking forward to standing on firm ground," Mary said.

"Yes, me too. On both counts. I'm also looking forward to going to one of the fabulous beaches I have heard about." Sally was a little excited.

"Hello, how is everyone this morning." Father Tony was very cheerful as he came over to the table.

"We're fine, Father Demarco, and how are you." Mary quickly responded, politely, but somewhat formally, as she emphasized the word father and intentionally used his last name.

"I'm quite good thank—you. Who wouldn't be on such a beautiful day to visit Bermuda and Horseshoe beach?" Father Tony said with his eyes glued to Sally, but in an adoring, not lecherous, way.

"Oh, are you going there, too. I am so looking forward to it, I have heard that it is one of the world's most beautiful beaches," Sally answered. She, too, had an adoring look in her eye.

"That's what I have heard. If you are going there, perhaps we could share a cab. Such a beautiful place needs to be shared to be fully appreciated," Father Tony added.

"Yes, you are so right. Maybe we can all go together since we had planned taking the kids there, too. We can get one of those van taxis to hold all of us." Mary could see that Sally was definitely right about the Father's interest in her. She was determined to help her resist him, and it was obvious that she needed a lot of help.

Al thought that they had been undecided about just what they were going to do, but he could sense there was some underlying reason for Mary's actions, so he left it alone.

"We would like to do some shopping first and then go to the beach. Perhaps you would like to join us and keep Al company while Sally and I shop?" If he wanted to go to the beach with Sally so badly Mary would make him suffer first.

"Well, thank you, that would be nice, I'd love too." Father Tony was very sincere.

"That would be wonderful, I would like that, too." Sally answered before she thought and then looked at Mary rather sheepishly.

Mary was beginning to realize just how bad Father Tony had it for Sally, and she for him. This might prove to be tougher than she thought.

"Excuse me, but I have to go down to the cabin to get my book," Al said.

"Would you get mine for me, too?" Mary asked, she did not want to leave the two of them alone.

"Okay, I'll be back shortly."

❋   ❋   ❋

"Hi Pol, how are you today?" B.A.D. had gone looking for him and knew just where to find him.

"Oh, hi there, Kid B.A.D., I'm fine. How are you?" The Pol was pleased to see him again. He didn't think he would.

"I'm fine, too. Well sort of, I think." B.A.D. had a lot on his mind.

"What's troubling you kid? Come on lets have it, maybe I can help." The Pol was excited by the possibility that he might be needed by B.A.D. and be able to help him. He would give anything to have something to get involved in rather than just sit there and look out at the ocean.

"Well something happened last night that I don't really understand and has me worried," B.A.D. said.

"Why don't you sit down and tell me about it?" The Pol was calm, but forceful.

So B.A.D. sat down and proceeded to tell 'The Pol' the entire story. He told him all about Charlotte and L.T. and how they have been following them. Then he told him about the two incidents with the goon and how upset Charlotte had gotten when he mentioned L.T. to her.

"I can understand why the girl got upset and I don't know if that is anything to worry about or not. But this man that attacked your friends, and then chased them down the hall, is something to be concerned about. Have you told your parents or anyone about it?"

"No, I haven't told anyone. I can't."

"I don't understand, why can't you tell anyone? I thought that you had nice parents?"

"I do, but I made a terrible mistake once under somewhat similar circumstances. If I brought this up to my mother she would go mental on me. My mother is a very mild mannered and pleasant woman, but, believe me, when she is reminded of 'the incident' she goes absolutely mental."

"I'm sorry to hear that B.A.D., but you have to confide in me or else I can't help you. Why don't you just tell me the basics of this 'incident' and then I will decide how much, if any, additional details I need." The Pol was confident as he was in his element now.

"Well, I'll do my best, but it is a very difficult subject for me to talk about."

"Give it a shot kid."

"About four years ago, when I was fifteen years old, the Pope was coming to Boston for a big ceremony. My mother was on our church council and, since our church had been one of the leaders in establishing a special fund for the Pope's favorite project, they were scheduled to have a private audience with him. I can't tell you how excited she was about meeting him."

"I can certainly imagine it. I would be pretty excited myself."

"The day of the big event everything was going along fine. We were all dressed to the hilt and my normally very calm mother was as nervous as a cat. She had already warned us kids that we had better be on our best behavior or we were dead meat. We had received the message loud and clear and were actually being quite good, to all of our amazement. I was just hanging around behind the stage, waiting for my mother's turn to meet the Pope, when I thought I overheard a couple of men plotting something."

"Why do you think that they were plotting something?" The Pol couldn't help but to start asking questions.

"It had a lot to do with the way they were whispering to each other and trying to conceal themselves from view. Then I noticed that one of the men was changing his clothes and was trying to look like the Bishop. The other man then started to talk about the security for the Pope in great detail. When he pointed out where he thought the weaknesses were I began to get very curious. But when he said that the biggest weakness was from someone who had access to the stage, because he looked like he was suppose to be there, I really began to take notice. He also indicated that this would be much easier than normal to accomplish, because of all of the robes and hats that they wore. He also pointed out that these robes would make it very easy to conceal a weapon," B.A.D. said.

"I admit that this does sound interesting, and even somewhat suspicious, but certainly could be a normal conversation of individuals who are concerned with the safety of the Pope," Pol interjected.

"Yes, I suppose that it is true, but you have to remember that I was only fifteen and that I had a very active imagination. However, it was the fact that the man, who looked like the Bishop, was so nervous and the other man, who was dressed like a priest, kept trying to calm him down. He would say things like 'no one will notice' and that 'the confusion will cover things up'. Then the supposed priest handed the 'Bishop' something very secretly and he put it under his robe. That was all I needed to see and hear."

"What did you do then?" Pol asked.

"I went looking for help, for someone to tell. The first security officer that I found just laughed at me and told me to go find my parents and stop trying to create trouble. I gave up on him and tried to find another guard to listen to me. Again I was unsuccessful and was getting very frustrated. So I went looking for my parents, who happened to be looking for me also. It was time for us to take our place at the bottom of the stage where we would wait until it was time for my mother and the others to have their audience with the Pope. Unfortunately, my parents were far too occupied with the ceremony to even let me talk."

"As we were waiting there, I thought that I was going to bust a gut because no one would listen to me and I watched the Pope descending the stage and being approached by the 'Bishop'. They weren't more than twenty feet from me when I saw the 'Bishop', who was trembling with fear, start to reach under his robe as he continued to move towards the Pope. I couldn't just stand there and watch the Pope get gunned down right in front of us, so I leapt over a small barrier and threw myself on the alleged 'Bishop'. To the horror of everyone, especially my mother, the two of us went tumbling to the ground in a heap, right in front of the Pope."

"That took some guts, kid." Pol was impressed.

"Ya, but no brains. As my mother told me many times that day and for a long time afterward. Especially since it took all of that day and most of the night to convince the police that I really thought that I was saving the Pope and not trying to hurt the Bishop. Of course it was the real Bishop and what he had under his robe was a special plaque to present to the Pope."

"That is too bad kid, but I can certainly see how you could have made such a mistake. And better safe than sorry, right." Pol was trying to be polite.

"Not if you are my mother. Needless to say, neither she nor anyone from our church got to meet the Pope. The other members of the church council could never quite forgive her. Oh they tried to be polite, but it was never the same and she finally had to resign in disgrace. So you see I can't go to my parents at this stage. I don't even know why that guy is after us. I will have to have proof positive before I will discuss it with anyone but you and my friends." B.A.D. was finished and somewhat exhausted by having to relive that horribly embarrassing incident.

"Yes, I can understand that now," Pol said.

"Will you help us?" B.A.D. asked for his help for his own benefit as well as for Pol's.

"Yes, I will help you, because you certainly are not imagining the attack on your friends. For the time being you and your friends should be very careful and stay together as much as possible. I will keep my eye on you and lookout for the man who made the attack. I should be able to recognize him by what you have told me. I will also see if I can find out if there is any connection between him and this Harry character. The treatment that he gave you and Frankie at dinner could be related or just his being a jerk." Pol was very comfortable in giving instructions; it was just like old times.

"Thanks, we will do whatever you say."

"For now just be careful and continue to let me know what your plans are so that I can keep tabs on you."

"Will do, Pol, see you later."

"Okay kid, be careful."

CHAPTER 15

"Hi, Dad, I'm glad I found you here." B.A.D. had come back to the cabin hoping that he would find his father alone, because he needed to talk about his problem with Charlotte. It was not often that he would open up for this type of conversation, but he needed help in dealing with this situation.

"Hi, son, I'm glad to see you, too. What can I do for you?" Al knew that there must be something serious on his mind; he didn't get approached this way very often anymore and, when he did, it usually meant there was something important on his son's mind.

"I was wondering if we could have one of those 'special rules' talks we sometimes have?"

"You mean when you can ask questions or my advice and I'm not allowed to counter with any questions of my own?" Al said.

"Yes, and where we can't interrupt each other and we talk to each other as man to man and not father to son," B.A.D. answered.

"Okay, Bruno, you've got it. Go ahead, let's have it."

"The first thing that I wanted to discuss was how someone like Mr. Carr can be the way that he is."

"What do you mean?" Al asked.

"For starters, how can he have such a negative attitude about so many people? I mean, how can he feel that so many people are living in poverty because they like it or are too lazy to do anything about it?

And at the same time, people like him are deserving of, no entitled to, all the riches that they have, and more."

"I see. Well, that doesn't always have such a clear-cut answer. In some cases I think that it is because certain people, like Lawrence Carr, are born into circumstances that make it difficult not to be 'successful', at least from a monetary and status point of view. And, because they often do work hard, they believe they have been able to make something of themselves and that everyone else ought to be able to also. They don't seem to be able to make the connection between their having been able to attend the best schools and that their family connections and money may have helped them more than a little bit. They don't realize or want to acknowledge that they were already a long way up the ladder before they ever had to start their climb and that this is not true for the majority of people. I really believe this type of person, for the most part, does not have the capability of comprehending just how far down some people have to start out in life.

"Then there are those people who really did start at the bottom and have worked their way up to the top. Sometimes these people forget just what lucky breaks they may have had along the way. Also, I think, these people don't want to acknowledge the poor because it reminds them too much of themselves and they are embarrassed and scared that they could possibly be there again."

"Okay, I guess I can buy that. But why are some men so mean to people. Even to people in their own family. Again, for example, Mr. Carr cheats on his wife and, except for when it comes to his future career, he doesn't give his son, Frankie, the time of day. He seems to be a very selfish person to me. He treats his family like crap and it doesn't seem to bother him a bit. And, judging from the number of marriages that end in divorce, his relationship with his family doesn't seem to be in the minority. If you treat your own family like that it's no wonder that you would treat other people so callously."

"Well, Bruno, I'm afraid that some people can be very insensitive, at the least, and even downright bastards," Al replied.

"Sometimes I envy them because it seems easier for them than for people who care. They can shrug off people who are poor, homeless, and in pain and it doesn't bother them in the least. They have already justified that these people deserve their lot in life and they resent sharing what they have, even though they have much more than they need. Perhaps it might be good to be like that. Life certainly would be easier," Bruno said half seriously. "I have even heard Mr. Carr make the comment that 'nice guys finish last.'"

"Yes, Bruno, I have heard that phrase before, but it all depends on who you think is keeping score. It can be hard to care, it hurts sometimes, it hurts often. But you are what you are, a sensitive young man, and you can never change that. At least you can't change it for long, or by very much and still be happy with yourself. You know that whenever you do something that is even a little unkind, and we all do sometimes, that you feel bad about it and you don't like yourself very much. Even if you try not to, you can't help but feel bad and that is because you are sensitive. And because you know that there really is never any justification for being unkind," Al answered.

"It would be a lot easier if you could," Bruno said.

"I agree that it would be, but it is this same sensitivity that can result in a level of joy that those bastards can never know. Remember, it only hurts when you can feel it. And, even more importantly, these joys can come about as the result of much smaller incidents. Things they could never get even the slightest bit of pleasure out of people like yourself can experience tremendous joy from. Think about it. They can never experience the joy that a parent gets from the small accomplishments and victories that their children experience each day. Also remember that, what it takes to be really strong, to be really tough, is to be gentle—*ALWAYS.*"

"I'm not sure what you mean?" Bruno said.

"Well, remember the other night at dinner when Father Tony said that 'sometimes you have to help those that you may think don't deserve it in order to get to those that do', well that is gentle strength."

"I think that I understand. But it still seems to me that being sensitive carries a lot of weight with it. For example, I met a girl, her name is Charlotte, and she is not like anyone I've ever met before. I don't know how to explain it, but there is an underlying sadness about her. She is involved with a married man and I don't understand this, because she is so beautiful and doesn't need to do this."

"Are you in love with her?" Al asked.

"At first I thought I was. We did make love and I do like her a lot. But, no, I don't love her in the way that you love mother, although I do care for her a great deal and I want to be her friend. I think that she is being used now and I have this feeling that she probably has been for most of her life. I may have used her or she me, I am not sure. I am very confused."

"Have you told her any of this?"

"No, I don't know how to talk to her or what to say. She got mad the last time I tried to really talk to her. I don't know if she will even talk to me now."

"One of the best ways to break the ice is to give her flowers."

"Yes, that's good, I can probably get some roses at the ship's store."

"That would be nice, but you might want to consider something less formal, less conventional. Certainly roses are beautiful, and are the only flower that is appropriate for certain occasions, but they are not always the best choice. Often the giving of roses is done simply to demonstrate the amount of money that you have spent on them. And, too, they are often given with the expectation of something in return, especially if they are not in celebration of a special occasion. Sometimes it is nice to give someone whom you care about a simple bouquet of cut flowers. Everyone should have someone to give them flowers for no other reason than just because they care. It really is the thought and not the cost that counts. There are times when simple daisies are more appropriate than elegant roses, because they are for friends as well as lovers. With daisies you are saying—'I hope that you have a nice day and if you do, then I will, too, and that is all that I want.'"

"I think I can really get into that. I can understand what you mean, but the problem is that I never know what to say. I'm always afraid that I am going to say the wrong thing."

"It can often be difficult to know what to say, but remember it is the thought and not the words that counts. If there is sincerity in your heart, kindness in your eyes, gentleness in your voice, and tenderness in your touch, then the thought will survive the words."

"I think I can do that. I still can't understand how some people can have such a cold and distant relationship like the Carr's, but there seems to be a lot of them based upon my limited observations and the high divorce rate. How is it that you and Mary can have such a close relationship for so long? You seem to get along so well together and I know that it is not just on the surface." Bruno used his mother's name to try to maintain the man-to-man atmosphere.

"Are you sure that you really want to hear this? You may be sorry that you got me started."

"Yes, I do."

"Well, it's not so easy to explain. It would be too simple just to say that we are in love. That is certainly true, but it goes much, much deeper than that. You see, I believe that ours is a truly unique love story. Oh, it will never be famous like Romeo and Juliet or anything like that, in fact few people, if any at all, will ever know its true depth.

"Many people can be physically attracted to one another and make love but not be in love. Physical love is probably the easiest and most common form of love and, while it can be very pleasant and satisfying in its own right, it is the least meaningful form of love. It is fine when both parties understand that that is all it is and enjoy each other for the moment, but it can be the most destructive and cause the most damage when it is mistaken by one or both parties for something more than it is.

"When two people make this mistake and marry, it most often turns into sadness and doesn't usually work; although sometimes a closer relationship will evolve over time. It is possible, and even probable, that this could account for the high rate of unhappily divorced couples that exist. People should spend time together and suffer hardships together before they bond for life. It is only the passage of time with one another, as friends as well as lovers, which can give birth to a great love relationship.

"For example, sometimes we will be sitting in a restaurant having dinner, it may be a special place or a just an ordinary one, and it will suddenly become very romantic for me as the wine causes her to blush and the candle light flickers on her lovely face, giving it a special glow. Then I will see the same twinkle in her eye that I enjoyed so much when she was just a young girl of fifteen. One that I still enjoy, even after all these years, and that produces a warm glow throughout my body. It is wonderful to have a wife who still has a sparkle in her eyes. It's particularly wonderful, maybe only possible to fully appreciate and recognize it, if you've known her and been in love with her since she was just a young girl. This is when I feel an inner glow and an indescribable contentment, experiencing an overwhelming calm, because I have had a glimpse of what heaven must be like. Sometimes I feel like we are still just a boy and girl in love, but who can now love in a way that can only have developed over these many years so that we truly are as one. She can still make me weak in the knees and give me butterflies in my stomach and it is almost impossible for me to go by her, or anywhere near her, without touching her in some way. Even if it is just to brush her shoulder or touch the tip of her finger.

"Sometimes the most confusing thing to me is that I am just a common man who has been blessed with such an uncommon love. She makes me happy, she excites me, she makes me laugh, she can make me cry, she can make me feel like a boy in love, she can make me feel like a man, she can make me feel blessed, she can soothe my troubled times, she can make me feel a joy that is not of this world, but most wonderful of all she can warm my very soul. I am sure that twenty, thirty or forty years from now we will still be having romantic dinners and we will look at each other with the same love. I'll see that same look in her eye and get that same warm feeling all over again, no matter how old my bones are. She has, and always will, give me a warm fuzzy feeling all over.

"That is because we not only love each other as husband and wife, or as man and woman, which is primarily physical, but we love each other as the very best of friends. But now I realize that it goes far beyond that. In our way, in our world and, most importantly, in our minds, ours is a great love story because our souls are in love. It is not a love story merely for this lifetime, but a love story for eternity, because we are soul mates and our souls have been in love for a long time. Once you have found your soul mate you will never separate. No matter how difficult the circumstances may be, you don't, you wouldn't, you couldn't, leave your soul mate.

"I know that when we are apart I never feel like a complete person. There is always the feeling that a part of me is missing. I believe that it is because my soul is lonely and there is no other person in the world that can cure this. My children come close, being with them always makes me feel good, but this loneliness in my soul still persists. Without her my soul is lonely, no matter how many people are around me. It took me a long time to understand this loneliness. At first I thought I was just some kind of weird person, an introvert. One day I realized the magnitude of my loneliness and then I knew that it was beyond my control. It was this realization that was so wonderful yet so hard, even painful, to understand, that it took a long time to fully comprehend that we were blessed as soul mates and that this was part of the price that we had to pay. We are soul mates but we didn't know this right away, which would be too easy.

Of course we immediately had a strong attraction for each other and were always comfortable with each other. Our love constantly grew stronger as we went through life's experiences together.

"I think one of the good things about growing old is that sometimes life is revealed to you in ways that you could never have understood when younger and relatively unscarred by it. We were probably married fifteen years before we really understood and believed that we were soul mates. I think that when time has taken its terrible, relentless toll, and has done its irreparable damage, fully depleting our bodies, our souls will still be young and full of joy. I can close my eyes and see a vision—a vision of the two of us soaring through the heavens no longer restrained by these crippled, used up bodies, that were only temporary houses for our souls anyway."

"Do you really believe in souls and an after life Dad, I mean Al?" Bruno asked.

"Yes, I do, because I have seen it. Once, when I was going through a very difficult period, I was mentally exhausted to the point that my fatigue went beyond anything normal, to the point that I think my soul was tired and needed relief. I went to bed to get some much needed sleep and, as my head reached the pillow, I exhaled more deeply than I ever have and immediately felt a great relief. It was as if my spirit had escaped my body and I slept instantly and I dreamed that I was dying, I dreamed that I was flying. My spirit soared through the sky and I felt a great exhilaration and joy as I experienced flight. It was as if I was floating on a cloud one moment and then racing towards the earth or up towards the heavens the next. When I awoke I knew I had to face the same problems, but I was able to do so with a renewed ability to deal with it because I had experienced a glimpse of what was to come one day.

"When the time comes for us to leave this earthly plane, we will laugh and play together without the daily worries, pains, and struggles of this world. No longer bound or restricted by these frail bodies, that fail us ever more frequently as we grow older and the years ravage us, we will soar into the heavens and dance the 'Dance of Angels'. As we first attempt to come together to kiss we fly right through one another, but, in the process, we release Angel Dust that falls to the earth, bringing a little joy to those it touches. It wouldn't take us long to master the Angels Kiss as we would love practicing. Eventually we would perfect our ability to come together and perform this feat. Then we would soar into the heavens separating into different directions and then turn and streak back towards each other until our souls would come crashing together and, in a burst of energy which would send a shower of Angel Dust falling to earth, we would join as one. A rare merging of two souls into one with a childish squeal of joy that would echo through the heavens and make God and the angels smile, like the smile of loving parents upon the joy of a new birth. And if you have never experienced the birth of your own child then you have missed one of life's great experiences. With the union of our souls complete we would fly through the skies and, for the first time, see heaven and earth through the same eyes, feel the same winds, and hear the same sounds at exactly the same instant and in exactly the same way. This rare fusion of souls would create the greatest of all Angel Kisses and generate an electric charge that would make the silver clouds rain Angel Dust upon the earth like a blanket of snowflakes, spreading warmth and joy upon whomever they fell. Then we would do three loop de loops and soar straight up to the highest point in the heavens to spend all of eternity together.

"Then someday when you are feeling lost and alone and you feel a warm breeze caress your entire body, causing you to have an unknown inner warmth, a warm fuzzy feeling, but there is no wind and you cannot explain it, do not fear for it is only our Angel Dust caressing your body. If you concentrate intensely and you are very, very quiet, so quiet that you can hear the wings of a butterfly and you think that you hear the sound of the wind gently rustling through the trees, but, again, there is no wind, fear not because, in the stillness of your mind you will know it is not the sound of some distant siren's song, attempting to lure you to an unknown danger, but it is only us singing our love songs to you. Then you can go and enjoy your day, enjoy your life, knowing that you are always loved and watched over. And that someday you, too, will sing the Song of the Angels with us, as we dance the 'Dance of Angels forever more."

"Whew!" Was all that Bruno could manage?

"Yes, I know." Al gently replied.

"What are you two up to?" Mary asked as she came into the cabin. She had wondered what had taken him so long to get their books and had come looking for him.

Neither could answer, as Bruno got up, kissed his mother and gave Al the obligatory shot in the arm, but without the usual sting, as he quickly left the room.

CHAPTER 16

"Well, I don't know what that was all about, but I don't have time to find out now! I have a mission and you are going to be able to help me with it!" Mary said with enthusiasm.

"Oh! And what, may I ask, is this all about? Or don't I want to know?" Al could tell by the determination in Mary's voice that something big was up.

"We are going to go do a little shopping before we go to the beach," Mary said.

"Yes, I know."

"You don't understand! Father Tony is interested in Sally," Mary said.

"What do you mean interested? Are you telling me that he has the hots for her?" Al responded.

"To put it rather bluntly, yes. And this is my opportunity to make amends with the church for that fiasco with the Pope and my church group."

"Mary, you know that it is not good to interfere in other people's business like this. I'm surprised at you since you are usually the first one to point it out."

"I'm not interfering because Sally asked for my help. She has found herself attracted to him also and doesn't want anything to happen. So she has asked for, and I have consented to give her, my help. That's why we are going shopping first; he has to earn his time at the beach with her and maybe he'll give up and go away. At the least we will reduce the beach exposure."

"I don't know, Mary, this kind of thing usually doesn't work out the way it is supposed to. What will be, will be." Al's feeble attempt at philosophy had little affect on her.

"It's going to work this time, because it's the right thing and because I need it! So remember that this shopping spree is meant to be very unpleasant for him. That should be easy for you."

"Don't get nasty now, I'll be happy to bitch and moan while we are shopping. I'll start right now by telling you that I don't at all like the use of the words shopping and spree in the same sentence. In fact, it scares the shit out of me!"

"That's good sweetheart, but please remember not to use foul language in front of the father."

"Wait a minute! You're afraid that the good father wants to introduce lovely Sally to Big Jim and the twins and I can't say 'shit' in front of him. I think that something is out of whack here."

"Don't get sarcastic now and, besides, you don't know that he also calls his Jim and that it is big, too," Mary said with a little gleam in her eye, showing that she hadn't lost her sense of humor.

"Okay, I'll try to be a good boy and do my part, but, if we fail, maybe we'll at least get lucky and he calls his Wee Willy."

"You're hopeless, Al. Let's get going," Mary said as she laughed and tossed a small pillow at his head.

Al was happy that he had managed to lighten the mood a little as they left to go on deck and meet the others.

"Hi there Sally, Father Anthony, I'm glad that you are both here because we have to get going." Mary, once again, emphasized the word father as she assumed control of the group. "Al, get B.J. and let's go, Bruno and Jennifer are going to meet us at the beach later."

The five of them then made their way out of the ship and onto Front Street, which was bordered by the harbor on one side and lined with shops on the other. The two men and the boy followed the two women as they made their way towards the shops. This was intended by Mary to keep Sally and Father Anthony apart and, in that way, was working fine. The problem was that Sally had chosen to wear a pair of white shorts that, while not too tight, displayed her attractive derriere very well. It was also obvious that she had chosen to wear her bathing suit under her shorts, and it was also obvious that it was rather briefly cut. This was not lost on the good father, as he almost walked into a streetlight and Al thought that he should have worn his robes to cover his growing emotions. As soon as they went into the first store to look at some sweaters and jerseys, Al managed to get Mary aside while Father Anthony and Sally looked things over.

"What is it Al? I was trying to keep them apart as much as possible and now you've allowed them to get together." Mary was a little flustered.

"Well, believe me, you would be better off with them side by side than with us trailing the two of you." Al was remaining calm.

"What do you mean?"

"I mean that those white shorts, with the bikini bathing suit underneath, has the good Father's eyeballs in sync with the rhythmic movement of Sally's buns. I don't think that your attractive backside has been lost on him either. I know that I have certainly enjoyed following the both of you."

"You men are incorrigible. You two walk in front of us from now on and I'll just direct you to where I want you to go. Now I've got to get back and take control of Sally and you take care of Father Anthony." Mary was not going to give up easily.

As Mary reached them, Sally was preparing to try on some jerseys that they had selected.

"Yes, those would look good on you. Let's go back to the fitting rooms so that you can try them on. While we do that, Father, why don't you go look at the sweaters with Al." Mary said this as she whisked Sally away, leaving the good Father standing there with his mouth open.

"Hey, Father Tony, I think that this one would look good on you," Al said as he approached him. He was just trying to do his job.

"Oh, yes, that does look pretty good, I think that I'll go back there and try it on." Father Tony was heading towards the dressing room before Al could stop him.

It was just as the two of them almost reached Mary that Sally came out to look in the mirror and ask Mary what she thought. Instantly, Mary knew that this was a big mistake. Sally had been wearing the top to her bathing suit under a rather loose fitting lightweight sweater, but had to remove it in order to try on the jersey. Unfortunately, or fortunately, depending on your point of view, the jersey that Sally was trying on was a bit too small for her and very favorably revealed her ample breasts. It was obvious that Sally exercised and kept herself in good shape. It was also obvious that the air conditioning in the store was too cold, causing her nipples to harden and visibly strain against the fabric of her shirt, as if they were fighting for release from their prison.

There was a faintly audible gasp as she stepped out into the room. Al couldn't quite tell if it came from Father Tony or his ten-year-old son. Then again it could have come from him or from any one of the other dozen men in the store whose eyes were bugging out. Mary's chin almost hit the floor before she could compose herself and hurry Sally back into the fitting room. But, before she did so, she couldn't help but notice the look on Father Tony's face and, with some admiration and not a little guilt, the large bulge in his pants told her that it wasn't a 'Wee Willy'.

"Ah, Sally, I don't think that is quite the look that you want for today. How about if we go to the shop next store and look for that black dress you want for the ship's party tomorrow night," Mary sputtered, as she pushed a stunned Sally back into the dressing room.

"I think maybe we should go wait outside for them," Al said as he took the good father and B.J. each by the arm and led them away.

As the five of them, with the men in the lead this time, approached the next store Mary couldn't help but realize that this was not going as she had originally planned. She would have to try to work harder to get the situation under control and back on track. As they entered the store, Mary made sure that Al took Father Anthony to look at some of the men's clothing as she took Sally to the back of the store to look at the dresses. Despite the fact that Mary had had to tactfully discourage Sally from a couple of dresses that she had deemed to be too revealing under the circumstances, they were making good progress and had found two or three dresses for Sally to try on before Father Tony had managed to work his way back to them, despite the best efforts of Al to keep him away.

"How are you ladies doing?" Father Tony asked as he approached them.

"Oh, I think that we are doing pretty good. I have found these three dresses that I am going to try on. It's good that the two of you have come back here just now so that you can give me your opinion on how they look, Mary didn't like the other two that I tried on." Sally was filled with enthusiasm.

"Well, they just weren't her." Mary was somewhat defensive as she gave Al a cold stare for having failed to keep Father Tony away.

Al just shrugged his shoulders and accepted the fact he was destined to lose in this endeavor and was prepared to accept his fate and the consequences, whatever that might be.

"Well, I think that she should try these on, especially this one, and we can all have a chance to see how they look." Father Tony smiled as he held up a rather simple black dress.

Mary was actually pleased with the one that he had chosen, it was a very simple and conservative looking dress. She then led Sally away to the dressing room before there could be any more discussion.

They all waited outside by the three-way mirror when Sally nervously came out to get their reaction. It didn't take long for her to find out what they thought.

"Well, Sally, that looks really good on you." Al was the first to respond.

"Do you really think so? What do you think Father Tony?" Sally couldn't help the fact that she was enjoying the attention.

"I think that you look like an angel," Father Tony said in a reasonably appropriate tone of voice, but his eyes, and the smile on his face, said much more.

While the dress was a simple one, it also turned out to be an extremely provocative one. In its very simplicity it took nothing away from Sally's natural beauty and, in fact, enhanced it. That she was still not wearing a bra was not concealed by it, either. The hardness of her nipples contrasted with the softness of her breast, which was largely visible as a result of the scooped neckline of the dress. The generous amount of thigh that was revealed was not lost on the men, either.

Mary took one look at her and one look at all of the men, whose eyes were feasting on her, and she knew that she had to end this and get her out of here as quickly as possible.

"Yes, that does look wonderful on you and a little jewelry will dress it up nicely. I think that you should take it and then I think that we should be getting to the beach; Bruno and Jennifer will be expecting us there shortly," Mary said this as she took Sally by the arm and led her back to the dressing room.

"Yes, I think you are right, it does look great on her and I think that she should take it," Father Tony added.

"Well, if everyone feels the same way, who am I to argue, I'll take it!" Sally was enthusiastic.

"Good then let's get going," Mary said. Then she hustled her into the dressing room before the men got any more excited and followed them in.

"She looks fantastic, doesn't she?" Father Tony said as Al led him away from the dressing rooms and towards the front of the store to wait for the ladies.

"Yes, she does." Al answered sincerely, as he now knew for sure that Mary was correct, the good father definitely had the hots for Sally.

As soon as Mary came to the front of the store, with Sally in tow, she directed Al and Father Tony to go outside and get a cab for them while they paid for the dress.

Dutifully Al, B.J., and Father Tony went outside and had managed to get one by the time that the women came out of the store. They made a quick stop at the ship to drop off the purchases and then went on in the same cab to Horseshoe Beach, where they arrived at about noontime and planned on spending the better part of the afternoon there. As they left the cab and walked towards the beach its beauty awed them.

"Wow, it really is beautiful! Isn't it?" Sally was very impressed.

"Yes, it certainly is," Mary agreed. "Here is the women's dressing room. We'll meet you guys out on the beach in five minutes."

"Okay, we'll get a good spot. See you in five minutes or a half hour, whatever," Al replied.

Since Al, B.J. and Father Tony had their swimsuits on under their clothes, they went on to the beach to select a spot for the blanket, Mary and Sally went to the dressing rooms to put on their tops as they, too, were already wearing the bottoms of their suits.

It didn't take them long to get out of their clothes and put their tops on and then their cover-ups. They then met outside of the individual dressing rooms to walk down to the beach together.

Sally was both a little nervous and a little excited. "I hope that this suit isn't too daring. My friends talked me into it. They said that I shouldn't be so modest. I don't usually wear a two piece suit."

"I don't blame you, if this wasn't a family vacation I might have been a little more daring myself. Besides you have kept yourself in good shape and are single so you should show off your assets. How were you to know that you would be pursued by a horny priest?" Mary couldn't help the last comment about Father Tony. "I'm sure it will be fine and you always have your cover-up, anyway."

"Thanks, you make me feel a lot better. There they are; right over there."

"Hello ladies, that didn't take very long," Al said.

"Well, we didn't have that much to put on," Mary said, wishing she hadn't.

"I must say that you men managed to pick a beautiful spot," Sally said.

"It wasn't very difficult considering that this beach is so big and there are so many beautiful spots," Father Tony replied.

As the women removed their cover-ups Mary revealed an attractive figure that was modestly displayed in her conservative one-piece suit and, while certainly attracting the men's attention, did not evoke an unusually strong sexual response because it was so conservative. However, when Sally dropped her cover-up the men dropped their jaws, because she was wearing a very brief, white two-piece suit. The top of her suit was very low cut and the cups were filled to overflowing with her soft, firm breasts. The bottom was quite skimpy and cut very high on her hips and, while everything was covered, it enticingly revealed her shapely, tight buns, and drew attention to the convergence of her thighs.

When Mary saw this she knew that her job was going to be much more difficult than she thought, if not damn near impossible, and there wasn't anything that she could do about it. After all, this suit was not anymore revealing than at least half of the others on the beach and she even admired her for letting her hair down and allowing herself to display her womanhood. If only they were not there with a priest who was obviously no alter boy.

"Shall we go down to the water for a dip before we relax and work on our suntans?" Al said.

Everyone agreed that was a good idea and they made their way to the edge of the water with Sally, B.J., and the good father about ten feet in front of Mary and Al.

"Are you enjoying the view?" Mary said to Al as she gently poked him with her elbow.

"Yes, I have to admit that I am. And I'm sure that Father Tony is also. I think that you are fighting a losing battle."

"I think that you may be right, but I'm going to keep trying anyway."

As they reached the water they couldn't believe how warm and clear it was. They could easily see the bottom through the turquoise blue water even fifty feet away. They all immediately went in and enjoyed frolicking in the water. However, this was when Mary realized that she would probably have very little effect on what would or would not happen, as she saw the results of getting Sally's suit wet. Once wet the suit clung to and molded itself around her body and appeared to become somewhat transparent. Although it was not certain that you could actually see through the suit, or were just seeing the darker lining, it was obvious that this was a tremendous stimulus to the imagination.

They spent the next three hours sunning and swimming, with Jennifer and Bruno checking in and then going off with their friends. As Mary sat helplessly by, Sally and Father Tony continued to enjoy each other's company with the process of rubbing suntan lotion on their bodies producing a particularly electrifying affect. Mary could see that Sally constantly kept catching herself and would shy away from Father Tony, only to forget again and fall back to enjoying her interaction with him. She was beginning to realize that she was up against some pretty stiff odds, so to speak.

"Hello there everyone. Mary and Al, are you two ready to go for our underwater excursion?" Bertha Cochran said as she, her husband Willy, and Madeline and Harold, approached their blanket.

Immediately, Mary was in a panic as she remembered that they had agreed to go on a diving expedition with them this afternoon. She tried to think of some excuse not to go so that she wouldn't have to leave Sally with the horny Father.

"Oh yes, we were just about to get ourselves together and get going. We're looking forward to it." Al answered, before Mary could come up with an excuse not to go.

"Good! Maybe we can get one of those taxi vans and all go together?" Mad Madeline said.

"Yes, that would be nice," Big Bertha added.

"Well, I'm not so sure that we can go," Mary said.

"What do you mean? We have reservations for all of us and we were looking forward to this." Big Bertha sounded like she was ready to pounce if the answer was the wrong one.

"We are here with Sally and Father Tony and we can't just leave. Maybe they would like to come with us?" Mary said.

"Oh, Mary, please don't worry about us, we will be just fine here," Sally said.

"Yes, Mary, we will be perfectly all right. Don't worry, I will look after Sally and I promise that I will take good care of her," Father Tony said, sincerely.

This was just what Mary feared most as she was now going to lose any possibility to control the situation. If only she could get out of this.

"I'm sorry, but I know that the boat is all booked up so it would be impossible to invite Sally and Father Tony along. I really am sorry," Big Bertha said.

"Oh please, don't give it another thought. I really don't want to move from this beach, it is so beautiful. But thanks anyway," Sally said.

"Maybe you should go along without us." Mary would give it a try.

"Hey, mom, I want to go. You promised that we could go diving when we got here," B.J. pleaded.

"Yes, Mary, come on it will be fun," Mad Madeline added.

"Let's go, Mary, Sally and Father Tony will be just fine and we did promise B.J. that we would participate in his great underwater adventure," Al said, as he got up and started to gather their things.

"Yes, all right I'm coming. It's not that I don't want to go with all of you it's just that, well I agree with Sally, this is such a beautiful beach that I didn't want to leave," Mary said, resigned to her fate.

"Well, enjoy yourselves. We'll see you back on the ship for dinner," Sally said.

As they began to leave, Mary was sure that she saw the hint of a smile on the good father's face that said he couldn't have been happier with the turn of events. But it was too late for her to do anything about it as she was herded toward the taxi stand by Big Bertha and Mad Madeline, after she had checked in quickly with Bruno and Jennifer to make sure they were all right and knew what time to be back at the ship. They didn't have to wait very long for a van type taxi to come along, but there was some concern as to whether or not they could all fit in. The van was suppose to be able to carry at least nine people and there were only eight of them, counting the driver, but, as soon as Big Bertha got in, it was a tight fit getting the rest in and they almost had to leave Al behind.

After a cozy forty-five minute ride on the narrow, twisting roads they arrived at the harbor just outside of Hamilton. As they pried themselves out of the van, they all agreed that the beauty of this spot rivaled the beach they had just come from. Looking out over the bay the sun glistened off of the turquoise blue water, which invited the boats to ride her.

"This certainly is a beautiful spot, look at that view," Al said. Everyone agreed that it was a gorgeous view, including Mary.

"I think that is our boat over there." Harold said as he pointed to a thirty-two foot cabin cruiser with a lot of diving gear in the back. The boat was named the 'Daisy Mae' and the captain's name was Bob. Harold had made the reservations from the ship before they even docked in Hamilton and had come over the first thing in the morning to check everything out, making sure that the booking had not been screwed up. He knew from firsthand experience how upset Madeline could get when things did not go right and she was already nervous about the idea of going under water, with just an air helmet on her head, to swim with the fishes.

"Hello, Captain Bob, is it okay to come on board?" Harold asked, as they reached the boat and stood alongside.

"Hello, Harold, you are right on time. That's good, I like that, and you certainly can come on board mate," Captain Bob said with a big smile on his face. He was a slightly built, wiry Englishman in his fifties whose weathered skin spoke for the many years that he had been making his living on the water.

As they all took the one step over the side of the boat and then down onto its deck it was obvious that Big Bertha was going to have difficulty with this maneuver. That's when Captain Bob and his first mate John, who was a large, muscular man in his thirties, rushed to help Willy who was trying to assist her. They managed to get her over the side, but then were almost knocked to the deck as her weight shifted towards them. If it were not for Al and Harold coming to their aid just in time they could have been crushed under her weight.

"Thanks guys, I have difficulty getting over those kinds of things," Big Bertha said, as she sat down and tried to catch her breath. Her husband Willy also took a seat hoping to get some color back into his face after turning ashen when he thought that he was about to be crushed like he had almost been on the bus ride. Either he was going to have to gain some serious weight or she was going to have to lose a ton or one of these days he was going to be crushed, literally.

"Welcome aboard everyone, I'm Captain Bob, this is my first mate John and my deck hand Joshua. We hope that you will enjoy the excursion that we have planned for you today. If there is anything that we can help you with just speak up and we will see what we can do," Captain Bob said.

"If everyone will just take a seat we will get underway. Once we have cleared the harbor area you are welcome to move around a bit and help yourself to cold drinks that are in the cooler. It will take us about thirty minutes to get to the spot that we think is some of the best shallow water diving on the island," Captain Bob continued, as Joshua cast off the lines and John maneuvered the boat away from the dock.

As they made their way out of the harbor, they all were quiet as they took in the beauty of the water outlined by the strips of land that enclosed it, making it a beautiful bay, and was home to some fantastic houses. The sun was warm, the water was calm, there were beautiful homes, and beautiful boats to look at so everyone was in a good mood and looking forward to their coming adventure. Even Mary had put Sally and Father Tony out of her mind and was trying to absorb all of the beauty around her and the pleasure of being with her husband and son.

"Are you sure that this is a safe thing to be doing?" Madeline asked no one in particular. She was obviously more than a little nervous. Her husband Harold had talked her into it and was beginning to have second thoughts himself on the wisdom of getting her to do it.

"Oh, I'm sure that it is or there wouldn't be so many of these offered on the island," Al said.

"Ya, Madeline, I wouldn't be concerned, there aren't many sharks in these waters. And I don't think that there are any man-eater species at all," Willy added, thinking that he was helping to soothe Madeline.

"What the hell do you mean "sharks"! I'm not going into any water where there might be sharks! Nobody said anything about any friggin sharks! Harold you shit, you didn't tell me about any friggin sharks!" Mad Madeline was working herself into a frenzy.

"I'm with Madeline, I'm sure as hell not going into any water with any sharks. You can turn this boat around right now if you think that I am," Big Bertha added.

"Captain will you tell these ladies that there are no sharks in these waters?" Harold asked, actually it was more like pleading.

"He is right ladies, we never see any sharks in these waters and there has never been a shark attack reported in all the years that I have been here." The Captain had no difficulty saying this because it was only a little white lie. There were small sand sharks and gray sharks that frequented these waters, but both of these species were harmless and it was true that he had never heard of a shark attack in this area. If there was any danger at all it would be from barracudas and not sharks, but he thought better about mentioning this.

"See I told you two that there was nothing to worry about."

"You had better hope so, Harold, or you're going to be in deep shit with me," Mad Madeline said.

"Yes and you will be in deep shit with me too!" Big Bertha added.

"Yea, yea, you ladies have made your point and I'll take my chances, thank you very much."

"Okay everyone we're at the spot that we want, so we can start to get ready to dive," Captain Bob announced.

"Good, but how does this gear work?" Al asked as he fumbled with the heavy helmets.

"It is really quite simple," Captain Bob said as he approached Al with a weight belt in one hand and a helmet in the other.

"First you have to put one of these weight belts on so that you will easily be able to walk on the bottom of the ocean. Then we put on the helmets, which are heavy enough to just sit on your shoulders without being fastened to anything. Once you are under water, the weight of the helmets will not bother you at all and we will then loop this safety rope through the ring on the side of the belt and we will do this to all of the other divers so that we will be able keep everyone together and keep the air hoses from getting tangled with one another. We will have two separate groups, one led by my first mate John and the other led by Joshua. I will stay up top on the boat to make sure that everything is okay. So why don't we get started with this," Captain Bob concluded, as he put the helmet on Al and gave him a chance to get used to breathing in it.

"That seems pretty easy," Al said.

So everyone got up and put on their weight belts and then their helmets. They then took their places near the rear of the boat and got ready to jump into the sea. Everyone that is except for Big Bertha who was having more than a little trouble getting the belt around her waist. In fact, it only made it about halfway around her.

"This must be a belt for a very small person, it doesn't come close to getting around my waist. Maybe you have an adult size one for me?" Big Bertha understood that she was a large woman, but she had great difficulty in admitting that she was an extremely large woman.

"Well, you might be right, but they are the only size that we have. Maybe if we attach two of them together they will make it all the way around you." Captain Bob had never had this happen to him before; the belts have extra long straps and have been able to get around any waist that he had previously come across. But he had never had a customer as 'BIG' as Big Bertha and he wasn't sure that even a doubled up belt would be big enough. When the two belts were attached to one another they just did make it around her, attaching at the last hole.

"There we are, they are attached now so we should be able to get going," Harold said.

"Yes, let's do it before the belts explode," Willy spoke up.

"Don't be a wise ass, Willy," Big Bertha said.

"It is time for us to get into the water now anyway." Captain Bob wanted to get things going before he had a brawl on his hands.

"So let's get up and over the side. We'll start with you Harold, next will be Madeline, then Willy, and Big Bertha. Joshua will anchor this group and you will be on the left side of the boat. Then we will have Al, Mary, and B.J, who will be anchored by John, go to the right side of the boat. Both groups will be able to see one another, because you will actually be quite close, and we just divide the boat by left and right so that we can make sure that the lines will not get crossed. So let's get started shall we." Captain Bob was taking control.

So Harold put on his helmet and walked down the short stairs at the back of the boat and into the ocean. Everyone watched with anticipation to see just what would happen as he descended beneath the turquoise water. It was a comfort to be able to see Harold walking so casually on the bottom of the sea and everyone seemed to relax, including Madeline and Bertha.

"That doesn't look so bad. I can do that, too," Madeline announced, as she put on her helmet and followed her husband to the bottom of the ocean. The two of them greeted each other with big smiles and high fives, they were proud of themselves.

"Okay, Willy, you are up next," Captain Bob said.

He didn't hesitate, as he picked up his helmet, put it on and went over the side with a wave of his hand and joined Madeline and Harold under the ocean.

"Now it is your turn Bertha. Let me help you with your helmet and over the side." Captain Bob wanted to get her overboard while everything was positive and before she had too much time to think about it.

"All right I am ready to do this, but I am warning you that there better not be any sharks down there or I'll be back on this boat and on your ass like a horsefly on shit," Big Bertha pronounced, as she put on her helmet and accepted the help from both Captain Bob and John as she descended the stairs and walked into the ocean. Well, she almost walked into the ocean; the problem was that as she entered the water she didn't sink at all. She initially went under, but bobbed back to the top like a cork and then just floated on the surface, the weight belts seeming to have very little affect on her natural buoyancy. The crew couldn't believe what they were seeing. The use of one belt, and the weight of the helmet, had always been more than sufficient to bring anyone that they had previously had to the floor of the ocean.

Big Bertha was just floating there, bobbing up and down, waving her hands in the air as if to say 'what the hell is going on here'. In the meantime, the crew was standing there trying to think what to do.

"Christ, Cap'n, I've never seen anyone float on the top like that and she has two bloody belts on," John expressed what all three crewmembers were thinking.

"What the hell are we going to do to sink her?" Joshua said.

"I don't know because she is floating like a giant cork, even with the two belts on." Captain Bob said, as he thought hard about what to do.

"I think that what we may be able to do is to tie additional weight belts to the rings on the belts that she already has around her waist and just let them hang down from her sides. This way we can use as many belts as needed, provided that the belt around her waist is secure enough to hold them all."

"That sounds like a good idea, Cap'n, but we better hope that the belt around her waist doesn't come off or she will shoot to the surface like a rocket. I think that we should attach another double belt around her waist so that we can attach the safety line to this one, separate from the multiple weight belts," John said, only half kidding.

"Let's give it a shot. You two get into the water and tug her over here near the stairs and I will hand you the belts and you just keep putting them on until she sinks. When she does I will hand your helmet to you, Joshua, and you go down and tie the safety rope through the loops and then to yourself. You will be the lead for this group," Captain Bob instructed.

They proceeded to put their plan into action and it worked. But not before they had to attach six additional weight belts, for a total of eight, and then she still went down very slowly. As soon as Big Bertha was on the bottom, Joshua attached the safety rope to her belt and then to the belts of Willy, Madeline, and Harold, in that order, and finally to himself.

"Okay, we can now get the rest of you into the water so you can start to enjoy the beauty that abounds down there," the Captain said, a little out of breath.

"Let's start with you first, Al. I hope that you are going to just take one belt, because we have just enough left," Captain Bob said with a smile. However, the look from Al told him he hadn't made any points with him, although he noticed the little smiles on Mary and B.J.'s faces.

"I think that one should do it just fine," Al replied, as he fastened the belt around him and made his way to the stairs at the back of the boat, where the Captain helped him with the helmet and into the water. Al was much relieved when, after just a short pause, he began to sink and made it all the way to the bottom.

Then B.J. and Mary followed Al into the water and were soon together on the bottom of the sea. In no time, John had the three of them securely fastened to his safety line and they began to relax and enjoy the feeling of walking on the bottom of the ocean with schools of beautifully colored fish swimming and darting around them. They could look over and see the other group about thirty feet away. They, too, seemed to be enjoying themselves now that they had finally settled in on the bottom. However, it soon became apparent that the group could only move if Big Bertha wanted to move and only in the direction that she wanted to go.

They were on the bottom for about a half an hour when some bigger fish swam by, coming quite close to the group led by Joshua. It was immediately apparent that this made the group nervous, as Joshua was busily waving and moving his hands in motions obviously aimed at calming the group's nerves. It was at this point that a large shadow crossed over Al and headed directly towards Big Bertha. When Al looked up he damn near shit; he saw a twelve foot shark swimming overhead and he quickly looked at John who signaled that it was okay.

But, as the shadow crossed over Big Bertha, it turned and started to circle over the group and the panic on their faces could be seen from thirty feet away. Again Joshua signaled that everything was okay and was having some success convincing them until the shark dove towards Big Bertha; coming within two feet of her. That was it, she had had enough of this bullshit, and Joshua could signal until his friggin arms fell off, she was out of here. With a lightning fast movement, that Joshua was at a loss to prevent, she unbuckled her weight belt. The same belt that had the eight weight belts attached to it but, unfortunately, she left on the second belt with the safety line attached.

As soon as she began to undo the major weight belt Joshua knew they were in deep shit and he was right. The instant that the weights fell away from her, she shot to the surface like a rocket and pulled the rest of them with her like they were puppets on a string. They were sucked up so fast that they would have been in danger of getting the bends if they had been deeper. They went up so damn fast they scared the shit out of the shark, which quickly swam away. From below the surface all they could see was Bertha swimming like hell for the boat with Willy, Madeline—who was flapping and kicking wildly-, Harold, and Joshua helplessly in tow.

At this point, John decided that he should bring his group to the surface, too. Perhaps he could be of help. Besides, he wasn't sure that Bertha wouldn't be so panicked that she would take over the boat and speed to shore with them in tow, under water.

When they got onto the boat, it was John who spoke first, "Is everyone all right? I've never seen anyone go to the surface that fast, never mind a string of five people all at once." He looked around and saw that everyone looked okay, that is if you ignored Willies bloody nose and the fact that Mad Madeline was sobbing hysterically and clutching so hard at her husband Harold's arm that she was drawing blood and bringing a tear to his eyes.

His comment went unanswered, if not unnoticed, as Bertha and Madeline continued to lay into the Captain. "You friggin little shit, you said that there were no fucking sharks in these fucking waters. I told you that I wasn't going to go into any water with sharks. I'm scared shitless of sharks ever since I saw 'Jaws'. You have me so pissed off that I could squash you like a bug," Bertha said, as she moved menacingly towards Captain Bob.

"Yea, you little piss ant, who the hell do you think you are to lie to us like that. You think that, just because you are a man, and a Captain, that you can lie to a couple of stupid little woman, don't you. Well, I have a good mind to show you that you have messed with the wrong two women. How would you like it if we cut your balls off and fed them to that shark?" Once again, Mad Madeline was on the verge of being out of control.

"Now, Madeline, I think that you may be over exaggerating the seriousness of the offense," Al said, trying to relieve some of the tension.

"Back off, Al, and don't give me any of your horseshit about 'shit happens', or you can join the Captain and see what kind of real shit can happen." Madeline was not about to be calmed by Al.

"I'm with the two of you, but I think that my son has heard and seen quite enough of adult reasoning for now, so I suggest that we all relax and have a drink on our way back to shore," Mary said in a low-key voice that quieted everyone down, and brought the situation under control and also protected the family jewels.

"You're right, Mary, I need a drink and then I just want to get back to the ship and get cleaned up," Bertha said.

"Yes, me too, and I think you guys had better get those drinks quickly," Madeline added.

"That was very good, Mary, you may have saved the Captain's life or, at least, his manhood," Al whispered to Mary.

"It was no big deal and, besides, I am anxious to get back to the ship to see about Sally and Father Tony," Mary replied.

The rum punch drinks were brought out quickly; the rum having been poured quite liberally. The crew knew that just one of these, sitting under the strong Bermuda sun, would quickly mellow out anyone, and they made sure that Bertha and Madeline were the first to be served. The Captain was very sincere in his apologies to Bertha and Madeline and everyone else, but he emphasized that it was a harmless variety of shark and even they are rarely seen in these waters. The rest of the trip back was pleasant, and everyone was in a good mood when they reached the dock. They said their good-byes and were quickly into two cabs and on their way back to the ship, but they would be a little late for dinner.

"Let's get showered and changed quickly, so that we can get down to the dining room as soon as possible. I want to find out what happened with Sally and Father Tony," Mary commanded Al and B.J.. They accomplished this in record time, only to find out that Sally and Father Tony were not there and had not been seen since they had left for the beach earlier in the day.

"I don't understand why they aren't here yet. They have had plenty of time to get here," Mary was distraught. "Jennifer, Bruno, have you seen them?"

"They were still on the beach when we left at six o'clock," Jennifer said.

"Well, they should be here by now, DAMN IT."

Mary bit her lip as she felt her chance to redeem herself slip away.

CHAPTER 17

"I'm glad that you talked me into having dinner here, instead of going back to the ship." Sally said to Father Tony, as she sipped on her second, or was it her third, glass of wine. When they had finally decided to leave the beach, Sally had wanted to hurry back to the ship because they were going to be late for dinner, and she knew that Mary was going to be quite worried. But Father Tony had been very convincing in suggesting that they shower, get back into their casual clothes, relax, and have dinner in the restaurant on the beach. Sally was concerned, since she would now not only be braless under her jersey but she would also be pantyless under her white shorts. But somehow it was an easy decision to make, given the situation of being nearly naked all day long on the beach with a handsome, also nearly naked, man and the sultry weather conditions that existed. Besides, she wasn't dressed anymore seductively than anyone else in the restaurant. After all, it was a very casual, outdoor location and many of the patrons were still in their bathing suits, some with cover ups on and some with very little on.

"Yes, it is beautiful here, isn't it? The bright red/orange sun, sinking into the blue ocean on the horizon, is one of life's beautiful pictures. One that is made even more wonderful by viewing it with such a beautiful, vibrant woman as you." Father Tony said.

"It is gorgeous, isn't it?" Sally responded. As she looked at him with stars in her eyes. She understood that she was in deep trouble, knowing that Mary would be concerned, but she couldn't help herself. She still hadn't done anything that she had to be ashamed of. "I have never had dinner in a place like this, practically on the beach and overlooking a beautiful blue lagoon, I hate the thought of leaving."

"We don't have to leave yet. It is still early and we should have another glass of wine and watch the sunset," Tony said, as he poured more wine for the both of them.

"I really shouldn't have anymore, I'm beginning to feel what I've already had. Besides, we have already missed dinner and people will be getting worried about us." Sally's attempt to stop things here, before they went any further, was only half-hearted, at best. A fact not lost on Father Tony.

"Sally, have you ever seen a bright red/orange sun sink into a blue ocean on the horizon?" Tony asked in a tone of voice that was soft and non-threatening, almost seductive.

"No, Tony, I haven't. It does sound beautiful," Sally responded, not realizing that she used only his first name for the first time today; this was not lost on Tony.

"Trust me, it truly is beautiful and you just shouldn't miss it. It is one of those rare moments that you will cherish for a lifetime." Tony was very sincere and very convincing. It was obvious that he had made his point, when Sally took another sip of her wine and looked out with awe, as the sun descended towards its rendezvous with the ocean. They had another glass of wine and stayed this way for the next hour; watching the sun become more brilliant and finally, in a blaze of red, orange, and yellow colors, melt into the sea.

"Oh yes, Tony, you were absolutely right, it is the most magnificent sight that I have ever seen," Sally said enthusiastically. "But, now that it is over, we probably should be getting back."

"There's no need to rush out, the moon shining on the water is as enchanting, in its own way, as the sun setting into the sea. Let's finish our wine and take a walk along the beach before we go back," Tony said this as he finished his wine and got up to leave. He wasn't going to give Sally an opportunity to say no.

"I don't know, we probably should be getting back. It does look beautiful though, doesn't it? And the night is pleasantly warm and the moon is so full and bright." Sally was talking herself into it and Tony knew he didn't have to say anything more. He just took her by the hand and led her out of the restaurant and down to the beach. "I have to admit that the beach is even more beautiful in the moon-light." She caught herself, just in time, before she added that it was the most romantic atmosphere that she could ever imagine. The combination of the wine and going around half naked all day was having its affect on her.

"It is unbelievable how beautiful it is and the fact that we have it all to ourselves. At least this part of it," Tony said. It was true that they were all alone, as he had led them to a secluded little cove that could not be seen from the main portion of the beach. Indeed, from the main beach, it was impossible to determine that such a place could even exist. "Shall we just sit for a moment and watch the moonbeams dance on the water?" Once again, he gave her no chance to answer, as he led her to a flat rock that invited them to spread their blanket on it and use it as a bench. Had he spread the blanket on the ground she would have resisted, but the rock seemed safe enough.

"This beach continues to reveal its beauty, just when you think that you have seen it all. I wonder what it has next?" Sally's senses were becoming overwhelmed.

"It can't reveal anything more beautiful than your lovely face, with the moon shining on it," Tony said, with a sincerity that made it sound very believable and not just a come on.

"Thank you, Tony, I'm flattered, but I don't think that we should stay here any longer," Sally said, but she made no attempt to move.

"I mean it! You are beautiful and I've thought so from the very first time that I saw you," Tony whispered to her, as he put his hand on her back and began to rub it gently.

"Please, Father, you shouldn't be talking like this. You are a priest and we can't do this." Sally was trying to appeal to his sense of duty; she knew that she would not be able to fight off her desire to be made love to by this man that she hardly knew, but had strong feelings for from the first time that she met him. As strange as it was, she was afraid that she had fallen in love with this man, with this priest.

"Please understand that it is something that I will have to deal with. You must trust me when I say that you shouldn't concern yourself with it." Tony was calm, soothing and quite convincing. And he was telling her what she wanted to hear. "I think that I am in love with you. I know that we haven't known each other for very long, but I have felt very close to you from the very first time that we met."

"I know what you mean, I felt the same way, but we still shou..." before she could finish, Tony pulled her close to him and kissed her passionately. A kiss that made her entirely forget who he was, and that they had only met a few days ago, and she returned his kiss with equal passion. This served to heighten his desire for her and he pulled her even closer to him, to increase the passion of his kiss. The depth of his lust for her was transmitted through the intensity of his kiss and inflamed her craving for him to a level she had never experienced before. He wanted her, and she wanted him, like she had never wanted anyone, and she would gladly submit to his desires, and to her own.

"You are the most beautiful woman I have ever met. I want you like I have never wanted anyone or anything in my life," Tony whispered to her as he stood the two of them up and held her close to him. All the time he was rubbing her back ever more aggressively, his hands finding their way under her shirt.

"God help me, I want you, too. Like I've never wanted anyone before." Sally could barely speak as she kissed him with a wetter, hotter kiss than she thought she was capable of. She pressed her breast into him and felt the hardness of his groin grind against her pelvis. After a long time, she allowed him to step away from her and to slowly lift her jersey up over her stomach, then over her breasts and finally over her head, until it was completely off and tossed to the ground. As she stood there topless, he moved the tips of his fingers from her waist along her full breasts and to the tips of her nipples, which became even harder, and he continued to lightly manipulate them, for what seemed the longest and most glorious time. Then he held a breast in each hand and massaged them firmly, as he moved back to her and they kissed again. Once again, he stepped back and admired her beauty and she could see the look in his eyes as they engulfed her body. But, instead of being embarrassed or offended by it, his eyes said that she was beautiful, like a goddess, and that he loved her.

Then Tony stood, picked Sally up in his arms and carried her to the blanket and placed her upon it. Sometime during their love making Tony had removed all his clothes, or maybe she did it, and then spread the blanket on the sand. She had no idea when this took place, she was floating between reality and a semi-conscious celestial state, as he lay upon her and she watched the stars dance in the heavens above. Sally could not believe how blissful she felt as she prepared to receive him, a man that she felt love for and believed felt love for her, although she did not know if they were in love. All that she knew was that she was eager to surrender herself to the passion, to the fire, to her desires and to him.

CHAPTER 18

"I can't imagine where they could be at this time of night," Mary said as she and Al sat in their cabin. "They should have been here for dinner."

"I hate to tell you this, but we happen to be on a very romantic island and they are two people who are obviously attracted to one another," Al answered her. "I don't think that you should blame yourself, you did everything that you could. You can't overcome the very natural human response when two people are sexually attracted to each other. I am sorry to say but, my guess is, King Richard has already been introduced to Lady Jane."

"Thanks Al, that doesn't help at all. Besides, you don't know that anything like that has happened. They probably just lost track of time and decided to grab something to eat somewhere and talk about the joys of living a spiritual life."

"If you say so, dear," Al said, as there was a knock on the door. He was happy for the intrusion; he could tell that Mary had not appreciated his condescending tone. "Yes, come on in."

"Hi, Mom, Dad, we are going to go out for awhile, okay," B.A.D. announced.

"Who is 'we' and where are 'we' going?" Mary immediately responded with the questions that she had been asking for a lifetime.

"'We' is the guys and me and 'where' is out and about on front street." B.A.D. was also quick with the answers that he had been giving for a lifetime.

"Okay, but don't be late." Mary added the usual response.

"No, I won't be too late mom." Again the standard response, as he was off to meet his friends. They had spotted the man who had chased them the other night and were now keeping him under surveillance and planned on continuing to do so to try to find out more about him and his companions. At the moment, Frankie and Rosie were watching him and they were to be joined by Big Louie and B.A.D. at any minute.

"Hi guys! How is it going?" B.A.D. whispered, as he and Big Louie came up to Frankie and Rosie where they were hiding to keep an eye on their quarry.

"Another guy came up just a minute ago and they have been standing at the railing talking and looking around," Frankie said. "Look they are starting to leave. We had better get ready to follow them."

"Yes, but we had better be careful so that they won't see us. They already act like they are looking for someone," B.A.D. said, as they began to follow them.

The two men quickly made their way to the stairs leading down to the dock, out to the street, and into a car parked a short distance away. The group of four was not far behind, but well hidden, as they hit the street and managed to get a cab right away.

"Follow that car!" Frankie demanded, obviously caught up in the moment.

The taxi driver was a little surprised. "Say what, mon?"

"The guys in that car are our friends and we have a little contest going to see if we can follow them without them knowing about it," B.A.D. added quickly to head off any suspicion or reluctance by the cabbie.

"Okay, I see mon, I can get with that. You'll see that Jamal can follow them without them ever knowing it." The cab driver was obviously happy to have something to liven up his day and break up the monotony of driving people around all day. "You see, mon."

"It looks like we were lucky to get into your cab," B.A.D. said as they were following at a safe distance but keeping them in sight all the while.

"It looks to me like they are headed for the warehouse district, mon. I don't know what anyone would want to come down here for at this time of night," Jamal said. "It looks like they are stopping at that building over there." The car that they were following had pulled up to a large warehouse building and the occupants got out and went into a door marked office.

"Can you pull over there and wait until we see what happens?" B.A.D. asked.

"I really can't just sit here, mon. I've got to get going ya know," Jamal said.

"Of course we know that we will have to pay, and we will be glad to pay you extra," Frankie said.

"Ah mon, I know that, but you see I'm scheduled to get off duty in a few minutes and I have a lady waiting for me and I can't disappoint her now can I, mon," Jamal answered with a big smile on his face. "I also don't want to disappoint myself, either. Do ya get my drift, mon."?

"Yes, we get your drift, mon. You can let us off here and we will find another ride back," B.A.D. answered.

"Are you sure, mon? There aren't very many rough places on Bermuda, but this area can be a little tough," Jamal said. "I don't know if you want to be just let off down here without a car."

"It's all right, we will be fine and good luck with your lady," B.A.D. said, as he handed Jamal the money for the fare, and the others got out of the car and he followed them.

"Okay, mon, good luck to you, too," Jamal answered as, he accepted the money and then drove off.

"Let's be real careful not to let them see us, since we have no way out of here but on foot," B.A.D. cautioned, as they hid in the bushes across the street from the office door that the two men had disappeared into. "Frankie, you and Big Louie go over and look in that window and Rosie and I will go around the side to look into the window there. Remember everyone, be careful."

"Okay, B.A.D., that sounds good. Let's get going Big Louie." Frankie responded as he led the way for the two of them towards the window B.A.D. had indicated. At the same time, B.A.D. and Rosie started for the other window. As they got into position, they then started to look through the windows, but they couldn't see anyone. They kept looking for about ten minutes when there was a shout from the direction of the Frankie/Big Louie team.

"What the hell are you kids doing here."? A deep voice bellowed, as he put a gun into Big Louie's face and his companion grabbed Frankie around the neck.

"Did you hear that B.A.D.?" Rosie whispered in a quivering voice.

"Yes, I did Rosie. Come on let's get out of here and hide behind those bushes over there before they see us," B.A.D. said, as he led him to the cover of the bushes before the two men, with Frankie and Big Louie in front of them, came around the corner.

"Okay, we know that there are two more of you out there. You had better get your asses out here or your friends are going to sleep with the fishes!" Murphy demanded. "And you had better do it damned fast or it's going to be too late for your friends."

"What are we going to do?" Rosie asked B.A.D.

"I'm afraid that we are going to have to surrender," B.A.D. responded, as he prepared to reveal himself.

"But they might kill us or something else bad like that," Rosie said in a near panic state.

"I'm telling you kids that you only have a minute left before I start shooting," Murphy said fiercely. Then he put the gun to big Louie's head and cocked the hammer. That was all that B.A.D. could take, he was the leader and he could not let one of his men suffer while he stayed in hiding.

"Come on, Rosie, we can't let them be alone or be hurt while we stay hidden," B.A.D. said to Rosie, as he stepped out from behind the bushes. "We are over here."

"Get over here, right now!" Murphy demanded, as he pointed the gun at them. "Who the hell are you kids and why the fuck are you following us?"

"We aren't following you, we are just out looking for some action," B.A.D. said, trying to act as if this was all some big misunderstanding.

"Get over here and get in there and be quick about it," Murphy demanded as he waved in the direction of the door with his gun hand, as Tom pushed Frankie and Big Louie along in front of him. The four of them went through the door ahead of Murphy and Tom.

"Okay, what are you wise asses doing here? What the hell kind of action do you expect to find looking in the windows of an old warehouse office?" Murphy really didn't expect any answers from them, but he enjoyed scaring the shit out of them as the first installment of payback time for the grief and humiliation that they had caused him. "You know that you little bastards are trespassing in here, don't you?"

"We aren't trespassing, you told us to come in here," B.A.D. boldly responded. He was nervous, but he instinctively knew that it was best not to show it.

"Well, after I shoot you little pricks, there won't be anyone but us who will know that. We'll just explain to the cops that we came here and surprised you in the middle of a robbery and had to shoot you before you shot us. Those guns that we are going to plant on you will be mighty convincing," Murphy growled, as he raised his gun and aimed it at B.A.D.'s head, ready to pull the trigger.

"Wait for Christ sakes!" Tom said, as he grabbed Murphy's arm, just in time to cause the shot to whistle over the boy's heads. "We had better talk to the boss before we do anything like that."

Murphy had fire in his eyes as he faced Tom. "I don't give a shit what Harry says, I'm going to kill these little bastards." His look said that he would just as soon kill him, too, if he got in the way.

"If you piss the boss off you will be joining them and you know it. I'm sure you will get your chance to get revenge on these little punks, but you know that you had better wait for orders before you do anything. I'm not going to get in your way, but you know what I'm saying is for your own good." Tom knew it was best not to challenge him directly; not if he wanted him to think at all rationally.

"Yea, okay, but don't ever grab my hand like that again." Murphy was particularly dangerous because he was ruled by his machismo. "Okay you little bastards, pick up your friend and get in that other room."

When the shot was fired, they all jumped and turned white as a ghost, then Rosie fell to the ground. At first B.A.D. thought that he was shot, but then realized that he had just fainted. On the orders from Murphy, B.A.D. and Frankie helped Rosie to his feet and followed Big Louie through the door that they had been directed to.

"What the hell one of you guys stinks so bad? Where the hell have you been? In a sewer or something?" Murphy gagged, as he helped them along with a hard push to B.A.D.'s back, causing the boys to go stumbling in to the next room and land in a heap on the floor, as the door was slammed shut and locked behind them. They found themselves in a fairly large room, about thirty feet by fifty feet, which had a few boxes in it and another smaller room with some linen supplies and a janitors sink.

"Are you okay Rosie?" B.A.D. asked.

"Yea, I'm okay, I guess. I don't know what happened," Rosie answered.

"You fainted, that's what happened. But don't feel bad, I damn near fainted, too," Frankie said.

"We were all scared and with good reason. I think that stupid son-of-a-bitch would have shot us if the other guy hadn't stopped him," B.A.D. said. "Did you hear that guy use the name 'Harry'? Now I know for sure that these guys are connected to Harry Holt. But I have a feeling it wasn't a good thing that he used his name in front of us."

"Yes, I think that you are right on both counts," Frankie agreed. "And that guy was right when he said someone smells like a sewer. Phew! What a smell. What is it?"

"I don't know, but it smells like it is you Big Louie. What is it?" B.A.D. said, as he and Frankie turned to face Big Louie.

Big Louie slouched his shoulders and starred at the ground, shifting his weight from one foot to the other, "I'm sorry guys, I couldn't help it. Hell, that asshole put his gun right in my face and he scared the shit out of me."

"Couldn't help what, Louie?" Frankie asked.

"I told you that he scared the shit out of me!" Louie repeated.

"You mean literally?" B.A.D. asked.

"Yes, I shit my pants," Louie answered sheepishly.

"You're kidding! You mean you actually shit your pants?" Frankie said.

"Yes, and you might, too, if you had a gun thrust in your face like that." Big Louie was managing to get a little more defensive.

"You really are very anal, aren't you?" B.A.D. said.

"Yea, but I wish he was a little more retentive," Frankie said as he and B.A.D. both laughed a little.

"I think that he just took my Dad's philosophy of life a little too literally," B.A.D. said.

"And what philosophy is that?" Frankie asked, still laughing a little.

"Shit Happens!" B.A.D. responded. They both laughed a little harder.

"I really don't think that's so funny," Rosie said.

"Thanks Rosie, I'm glad that someone understands," Big Louie said.

"Yes, you are being very understanding considering that we have to smell it now." Frankie said.

"Yea, what's the story, Rosie?" B.A.D. asked.

"It's just that I can understand how it happens. That's all," Rosie answered.

"What are you saying? How well do you understand?" B.A.D. asked.

"I just understand. That's all," Rosie answered, getting more defensive now.

B.A.D. pressured him, "Rosie, what's the story?"

"Well, if you must know, I shit my pants, too," Rosie confessed. "I think that it happened when I fainted. I'm not sure."

"Oh that's great. We're stuck in here with two guys with a load of shit in their pants and we've got two guys out there who want to shoot us. What else is going to go wrong?" Frankie said.

"I think we had better stop worrying about the mess in here and start figuring out how we are going to get out," B.A.D. said, as he slowly approached the door. As he peered through the keyhole he could see the two men and he could hear them talking very loudly.

"I'm going to go get Harry now. Remember, Murphy, he is going to want to make the decision on what to do with these kids," Tom said, without trying to sound authoritative, not wanting Murphy to get going again and do something stupid.

"Don't worry your ass about it, Tom. I won't do anything until he gets here, unless they give me some trouble," Murphy sneered back, as Tom went out the door. He grabbed a beer and sat at a table, with his gun in front of him.

B.A.D. moved quietly away from the door and into the farthest corner, behind some boxes, and motioned for the others to follow him. "The guy who saved us from getting shot, his name is Tom, has left to go get Harry. The other guy, Murphy, is the only one out there but he still has his gun," B.A.D. informed them. "Now is the time to make a break for it, before the other two get back."

"I don't think that we should mess with this guy. He would just love an excuse to shoot us," Frankie said.

"Yea, Frankie's right B.A.D.." Rosie and Louie responded.

"I know he would, but now is our best chance. When there are three of them it will be impossible and, remember, we now know Harry's name and have seen the other two so they can't let us leave. At least we can't take that chance. I know that you are scared, I am too, but we have to do it now." B.A.D. was calm and showed the confidence that helped the others settle down and listen to him.

"Okay, but how do you plan on getting out of here? There are no windows and there is just the one door, with that thug out there, who would just love to shoot us." Frankie was a little calmer now.

"We'll have to distract him and get him to open the door and come in," B.A.D. said.

"Just like in the movies, except that this is not the movies and that is a real gun," Big Louie said.

"And, even if you could distract him and get him to come in here, what the hell would we do then?" Rosie added.

"Take it easy guys, we are going to get out of here. I already have an idea, but we have to work fast." B.A.D. was responding to the challenge the way that he hoped he would if ever he was in a threatening situation. "The first thing that we have to do is to get you two out of those clothes and cleaned up."

"I'm all for that. You guys are beginning to smell even worse," Frankie said.

"Yea, well you should have to find out what it feels like," Rosie said.

"There's a sink over in that corner and there are some towels there. You can go over and wash yourselves but, first, take off your pants and underwear over near the door," B.A.D. instructed.

"I'm not going to take my pants off in here. I'll be bare assed," Big Louie said.

"Yea, I'm not walking around here bare assed, either," Rosie added.

"If you two putz's would rather walk around with a load of shit in your pants be my guest. We are not particularly looking forward to the sight of you two, either," B.A.D. said. "But, if you are not going to do it, get over in that corner as far away from us as you can, because we can't stand the smell any longer."

"Okay, I'll do it, don't get pissed off," Big Louie said. "But why over there by the door?"

"Because I have plans for your shit filled underwear," B.A.D. said. "I want you to put your underwear on the floor and cover them with this newspaper, right about there. And, Rosie, I want you to take yours and tie the end of this rope to them. Then we are going to throw the other end of the rope over that steel girder and run it over to the back wall, where we are going to be."

"I get it, you are hoping that he will step in the shit on the floor and fall, giving us enough time to get out of here," Frankie said.

"That's about it. It's pretty simple I know, but, sometimes, simple things work the best. Besides, we don't have any time to come up with something better."

"But why tie up Rosie's shit filled pants?" Frankie asked.

"It's a back up system. If he doesn't step in the shit on the floor maybe we can drop the shit on him from above," B.A.D. said.

"Ugh! Your a cruel guy, B.A.D.. But I love it," Frankie said.

"We had better stop talking and start doing or we are going to run out of time." B.A.D. said. So, without any further discussion, they methodically went about putting their plan into action. When every-thing was done, and Rosie and Louie had cleaned up and put towels around themselves, they were ready to spring their trap.

"Everything is in place, so now we have to start to make a lot of noise to make him come in here. I think that we should call him names to get him really pissed off so that he won't be thinking clearly and notice our traps," B.A.D. said, as he led them to the far wall, away from the door, and behind some boxes.

"Okay, now!" B.A.D. instructed and they all began to shout at once.

"Hey, you idiot, come in here." Frankie attempted somewhat fee-bly.

"Yea, you creep, come in here so that we can kick the shit out of you." Rosie's attempt was somewhat better.

"Yea, asshole, come in here so that I can sit on you again," Big Louie added.

They continued this yelling for a good five minutes before they had finally got a reaction. They knew that he was moving because they could hear him, as he threw his chair against the wall. Then, shortly after this, the door opened and he stood there, red faced from anger, with the gun in his hand.

"You little bastards have made a big mistake, because I'm going to fix your friggin asses for good now," Murphy bellowed, as he raised his gun and came storming into the room. Just as B.A.D. had hoped, he was too mad and too intent on hurting them to see the trap that had been set. On his second step into the room his foot came down on the newspaper, which slid on the shit underneath like it was grease, and his legs went out from beneath him, the gun went flying in the air, and he landed hard on his back, which knocked the wind out of him.

At this moment B.A.D. couldn't help himself and let the rope holding the bag go for good measure. The drop was perfect, the underwear opening as it fell releasing its contents directly on Murphy's face. "C'mon let's go before he regains his senses. He'll kill us for sure now," B.A.D. commanded. The four of them bolted for the door, making sure to avoid the reach of their fallen foe. They almost crushed each other, as they all tried to go through the door at the same time.

As they went through the second door, and were outside, they didn't know which way to go so they just followed B.A.D. as he turned left and began running as fast as he could. Both Louie and Rosie had lost their towels before they had even made it through the second door, but they weren't about to stop to retrieve them. It was this sight, four young men running down the street, two of whom were naked and looked like a runaway bull and a plucked chicken, that was caught in the headlights of the car as it approached. Just like deer, they were mesmerized by the bright lights and just stood there watching the car pull up within ten feet of them. They had resigned themselves to the fact that they had not escaped quickly enough and now were caught.

"Hey, Kid B.A.D., do you guys need a lift?" Came a familiar voice from the car's open window.

"Pol, is that you?" B.A.D. asked in relief and amazement.

"Yea, it's me and I think that you had better get in quickly," Pol said very calmly.

"C'mon guys let's get in, he is a friend of mine," B.A.D. said.

"Thank God, I thought that we were dead!" Big Louie said as B.A.D. jumped into the passenger's seat and the other three fought to get into the back seat. As soon as they were in, and even before the doors were closed, Pol put the gas pedal to the floor and the wheels squealed as they shot forward. As they spun around the corner on two wheels they were sure that they heard gunshots.

What they couldn't see was that Murphy had just emerged from the warehouse and was firing at them, even though he was half blinded by the shit on his face. At the same moment a car driven by

Tom, with Harry in it, pulled up and Murphy jumped in and ordered them to chase the get away car as he explained what happened.

"What are you doing out here anyway, Pol?" B.A.D. asked.

"I was following you guys from the time that you left the ship. Unfortunately I lost you when I had to stop for some people crossing the street and you went out of my view. So I just kept circling around hoping to find you and, finally, I did."

"And none too soon, either," B.A.D. said. "But where did you get a car?"

"Hey kid the word around my old precinct was that 'The Pol could pull a rabbit out of a duck's ass, if he needed too, to solve a case'," Pol said with a chuckle, as he continued to speed away, having already noticed the headlights of the car in chase. "By the way, why are your two friends running around bare ass, anyway?"

"It's a long story. I'll tell you about it when we get back to the ship, but don't you think you had better slow down?" B.A.D. said.

"Not unless we want the car that's chasing us to catch up," Pol said.

"Chasing us, what do you mean chasing us?"

"Don't get excited now Louie. You know what happens when you do, and that could be very unpleasant in these circumstances," B.A.D. said.

"Yea, hell it is bad enough having to sit between two naked guys, but if either of you friggin guys shits again I am going to open the door and throw you out," Frankie said in no uncertain terms.

"You guys had better quit bitching and hang on because these guys are gaining on us," Pol said, as he took another corner on two wheels. "I'm afraid that I didn't have much of a choice in the cars that I had to borrow from and this one is not very fast. I don't think that we can out run them so we will have to out maneuver them."

The car was careening down the road; going from side to side to keep the other car from coming up beside them. In an effort to out maneuver them, Pol took a very sharp turn down a one-way street, which caused the chase car to have to slam on its brakes, back up, and then come after them. This gave them a little breathing room, but not for long. The two cars continued to race through the warehouse area, with the Pol demonstrating his superior driving ability and the chase car managing to stay close with it's greater horsepower. The Pol was looking for his opportunity to lose them, or at least put enough distance between them to allow him to make a break for Front Street and the ship so that he could let the boys' off and then ditch the car.

Finally, he determined that he would have to create his own opportunity so, on the next little straight away, he put the car into a power turn, which sent Big Louie tumbling on top of Frankie and Rosie. This put them face to face with their pursuers, who were less than fifty yards away and closing fast. "Hang on guys we are going to see who has the biggest balls," Pol said as he floored the gas pedal and sped directly toward the oncoming car.

"Big balls shit! I think that mine have receded up into my throat and I'm going to choke on them," Frankie gasped, as the cars hurtled toward each other.

"Holy shit! What the hell are you doing, Mr. Pol? I don't think that I am going to be able to contain myself," Big Louie shouted.

Rosie just turned ashen as he tried to speak, but nothing would come out.

"Do you think that they will chicken out?" B.A.D. asked calmly.

"I'm counting on it, kid. My experience says that they will. In any event, we are going to find out very soon," Pol explained, as he aimed directly for them. Within seconds they would collide head on, if one of them didn't veer off, and it was obvious that the Pol had the courage of his convictions. Finally, at the last moment, the chase car turned sharply to avoid a collision and, in doing so, went over the curbing, onto the lawn and crashed into some bushes.

"That will keep them occupied for a little while. At least long enough for me to drop you off at the ship and then go and ditch the car," Pol said.

"Is everyone okay back there?" B.A.D. asked as he turned to see how they were. He was greeted with the look of three ghostly white faces. "Hey guys, lighten up we made it just fine, Pol was terrific."

"Well, we didn't make it totally fine," Big Louie answered.

"Oh no! Not again?" B.A.D. asked.

"Yes, I'm afraid so. I really couldn't help it," Big Louie said.

"Neither could I," added Rosie.

"It really did scare the shit out of us, B.A.D.!" Frankie said.

"Et tu, Frankie?" B.A.D. couldn't believe what he was hearing. Not only had the dynamic duo repeated themselves, by soiling the back seat of the borrowed car, but Frankie had joined them in this shameless display of anal expression.

"My God what is that foul smell?" Pol asked.

"I'm afraid that, when our compatriots get overly excited, they aren't very anally retentive," B.A.D. answered.

"Are you trying to tell me that they shit their pants, kid?" Pol asked.

"Well, Frankie shit his pants. The other two didn't have any pants on to shit in, since they had already done this once before, so they just shit in the back seat, I guess." B.A.D. was a little embarrassed with his team in front of the Pol.

"Ah, don't let it bother you boys. I have known many a rookie cop, and some veterans too, that have reacted in a similar manner when faced with such danger. But I am going to have to leave a few extra bucks so that the owner can get this car cleaned up properly. It really does stink in here, I can't wait to drop you boys off so that I can ditch this car and get out of here."

"How are we going to get back onto the boat with no clothes on?" Rosie asked.

"I don't know kid. That's not really my problem. Kid B.A.D. will have to take care of that. I've done my part for tonight," Pol responded.

"You are right Pol. Just let us off over there in the shadows near those bushes and we will take it from there," B.A.D. said.

"You've got it, kid," Pol said, as he pulled into a dark spot near the stern of the ship and next to a row of hedges that extended the length of the ship, all the way to the stairs.

"Thanks a lot Pol. You were a lifesaver. See you tomorrow," B.A.D. said.

"No sweat kid. Happy to do it, and we'll talk later. Now get out of here before those guys catch up with us," Pol said, as he put the car into gear and took off, leaving the four of them hiding in the bushes.

"What are we going to do now B.A.D.?" Rosie asked.

"Yea, how are we going to get on board with no clothes on?" Big Louie asked.

"I don't know, but, whatever it is, I am going to do it fast so that I can get out of these pants and the load that is in them," Frankie added.

"You guys make your way down behind these bushes to the stairs. In the meantime, I'll go out to the sidewalk and make my way to the stairs that way. I will go up first to clear the way and, if I can, turn off the lights focused on the stairs. Then you guys go as quickly as possible up the stairs and to the secret passage down to the storeroom, where we can get some chef's clothing and then make our way back to our rooms," B.A.D. instructed.

"But someone is sure to see us," Rosie said.

"Maybe not. It's very late and I will make sure no one is around when I signal you. Besides, I don't have any other ideas, so let's get going."

So B.A.D. walked down the sidewalk, while the other three made their way behind the bushes. Then B.A.D. went up the stairway and took his time looking to see who was there. Fortunately, no one was around and, after a short time looking, he found the main switch to the lights for the stairway and the immediately surrounding area. B.A.D. then signaled the team to get ready and went back and threw the switch, sending the area into total darkness. The three of them practically killed each other trying to be the first to get up the stairs. Needless to say, Big Louie won the battle and led the way up. Frankie and Rosie followed him, but not too closely because neither of them was going to get directly behind and somewhat under that huge bare butt. Especially a butt with such a propensity for expressing itself in so unpleasant a manner when excited. Driven by the fear of being caught buck naked, or with a smelly load in his pants, they moved swiftly to the hidden stairway and the safety of the storeroom.

CHAPTER 19

"It is quite an awesome sight, isn't it?" The unseen voice said.

B.A.D. was startled, as he turned from the railing, where he had been gazing out over the ocean, to see the stranger who appeared to be in the shadows. But there were no shadows.

"Excuse me?" B.A.D. said.

"The ocean, its size and power, is awesome isn't it?" the stranger repeated.

"Yes, it certainly is," B.A.D. replied. "Who are you? And please come out from the shadows so that I can see you better."

"I'm a friend, a special friend, and I will come closer, but you will not see me any better," the stranger answered as he approached B.A.D..

"What friend? I don't know you. What is your name and why won't I see you any better?" B.A.D. was confused and his senses were alert to danger, but, strangely, he did not feel threatened, even though the stranger didn't get any clearer as he approached. Despite the fact that there was a bright moon shining, the figure that approached was still blurred, as if B.A.D. were looking through a camera that was out of focus.

"No, you don't know me. But I know you. I know you very well," the stranger said. His voice was firm and authoritative, but, at the same time, very calming, almost hypnotic. "And, even though I stand directly before you, you will not see me any better. You should consider yourself extremely fortunate to see me at all, very few people ever do."

"I don't understand this at all. Why can't I see you? Who are you? What are you?" B.A.D. said excitedly, as the urge to cut and run swept over him, but he didn't move. He wasn't sure why he didn't run, he wasn't even sure if he could run. It was as if there was a force field, emanating from this figure, which had engulfed him. All of his instincts told him that he should consider this to be a dangerous situation that called for action, but he was immobilized, and the panic that he felt for a split second was quickly replaced by an overwhelming sense of calm. A calm that he knew was caused by what stood before him. "Who are you? What is your name? How do you know me?"

"Slow down, I understand your need to know these things, but, before I tell you, you must relax and go with your instincts. You have good ones and they will not fail you. The sense that I will not harm you is correct. Indeed, I am not here to harm you, but to help you, to protect you. I'm here to teach you to learn to concentrate deeply and use your senses completely, and, when you do, you will hear the wings of the butterfly," the apparition stated.

"How do you know about the wings of the butterfly."? B.A.D. said, even as he was struggling to overcome the shock of hearing these words.

"We know everything about you, about your family, about everything," the apparition replied calmly, but matter of factly.

"What do you mean we? Again, who are you? Who is we? What the hell is going on here? What have I done?" B.A.D. was excited, even though he was trying hard not to be.

"Ha! Ha! Ha! Excuse me, I am sorry, but it is amazing how the whole world lives with such a guilt complex." The apparition was definitely amused.

"Are you, are you God?" B.A.D. asked, not quite believing what he was saying.

"No! No! I'm not God, or Allah, or Buddha, or whatever you choose to call your maker. But I am a messenger of the 'Maker'," the apparition responded.

"Is that what you call Him, the Maker?" B.A.D. asked.

"Sometimes, but not often. Actually, I don't see the Maker very much, since I report to the Director of Earth. And it is not a he or a she, but is gender neutral. It is probably best if you just refer to the Maker as THE," the apparition said.

"Just simply the?" B.A.D. asked.

"No, not just simply 'the' but very much capital THE," the apparition responded.

"What does THE want with me? What have I done?" B.A.D. asked.

"There you go again, what is it with this guilt complex. I certainly knew all about guilt during my many lives, but I never realized how out of control it had gotten until I was finally released from my earthly bonds and assigned this new duty. Those who should feel guilty most often do not and others, like yourself, feel guilty for no apparent reason or, more likely, for the wrong reason. I can bet that what first came to your mind is the little affair that you had with the young lady. I believe Charlotte is her name. Isn't that right?"

"Somehow I don't think it would do me any good to deny it."

"You've got that right, but then you're not a liar anyway. But why do you feel guilty, I know it is not because you had sex with someone that you just met, or because your mother and the church would be disappointed in you. No it is not that and you and I both know it, and we know what it is."

"We do?"

"Yes, we do. Think about it. Doesn't it have something to do with the fact that you used her, without concern for her feelings? You can tell that she is a troubled young woman and that your affair with her has confused her even more, heightening her internal pain."

"Yes, I suppose so. I can't argue with that," B.A.D. admitted.

"I thought that you would understand. That is why we chose you, because you are sensitive and have a good understanding of human nature, even if you do not fully realize it yet. I think that you will understand when I say that there are not 'sins of the flesh', but only sins of the mind, sins against the spirit. There is no guilt, no sin from experiencing pleasure unless that pleasure results in someone else's pain. Damage to the spirit cannot so easily be repaired as damage to the body, and, unfortunately, damage to the spirit can often transcend lifetimes before it is cured."

"I think that I understand."

"We thought that you would, since we know that you were given an unusually gifted mind. But you have also shown a high level of kindness and tenderness, qualities that we can never be sure about until they have been tested, so we have determined that you could be of help to us."

"I wish that I knew your name, and does this mean that I will get to meet THE?" B.A.D. asked.

"No, you will not get to meet THE, that only happens when you reach Level 2. What you will be is a messenger of good for me and, therefore, the Great One, and I will be your only contact. I report directly to the Director of Earth and rarely get to see THE myself," the apparition replied.

B.A.D. said with a puzzled look, "Well, could I at least know your name and how I am suppose to help you. I mean, you guys have all this power and I am suppose to help you!"

"Okay, I understand your need to have a name to refer to, but you should understand that on Level 2 we have no need for names. But, among my many bodied lifetimes on Level 1, I think that the name I liked the most was Zachary. So you may call me Zachary." The apparition, Zachary, replied. "And, yes, you will be able to help us because, you see, we must work through people like yourselves to accomplish good deeds. That is the way that THE has decreed that it must be."

"Zachary, that's an interesting name, a strong name. I wish I had one like that," B.A.D. answered.

"But you do! Bruno is certainly a strong name and I find it very interesting. Especially since you would never expect someone with such a name to be so intelligent and so sensitive. So, you see, it is a name that has a certain mystique to it. I think that you should wear it proudly," Zachary responded.

"I never thought of it that way, perhaps you are right. I will have to think about it. But what do you mean by Level 2?" B.A.D. asked.

"Well, I really hadn't planned on getting into all of that at this time, but I will give you a brief overview for now," Zachary replied. "Their are two different planes that exist simultaneously. That is two planes that co-exist in the same place and time. One is this Earthly plane, that you live on, and the other is the Spiritual plane, the one I occupy."

"And how does one transcend from this Earthly plane to the Spiritual plane?" B.A.D. asked.

Zachary smiled, but his patience was being tested. "You are very inquisitive, aren't you Bruno. Well, on the Earthly plane there are Zones, seven of them to be exact. Everyone begins at Zone 1 and then must develop upward from there. It can sometimes take many lives to move upward by even one Zone, depending on how a person develops."

"What do you mean by Zones?" B.A.D. asked.

"These Zones represent uses of one's brain power, but must be combined with spiritual healing to reach and pass through Zone 7," Zachary said.

"I'm still not sure I understand what you mean?"

Zachary thought for a moment, "For one thing, Zones are a state of mind. You might best understand this if you think about athletics. For example, have you ever heard the comment about a basketball player that is hitting every shot in sight, playing like he is unconscious? This refers to the players mental state and the fact that he or she is in an unreal state of mind, and that they have achieved some higher level, even if only for a short period of time. This is a very small example of how the mind can work, but the higher uses of the mind must be combined with a life of goodness and kindness, a high state of spiritual being. For instance, Albert Einstein has attained at least Zone 6, I believe, and Mother Theresa is in Zone 7, I am sure."

"I think I understand now, except that you said that we all start at Zone 1 and certainly some people are born into vastly different circumstances."

"Yes, that is certainly true, but the first thing is that not everyone is in the same Zone now and, therefore, they live in different circumstances. The second reason is that the more wealth and power that one has been given on Earth the more that is expected of them. We know that you have a strong sense of fairness and, because of this, you might think that life is grossly unfair, because of the discrepancies between people. And it would be true if everyone got the same credit for accomplishing the same goal, but it is much more complicated than that. You have been given a fine mind and a strong sensitivity and you are expected to use them. Use that mind now. If you were creating the world, would you be satisfied designing a system where everyone starts at the same spot, proceeds through only one life at the same rate and ends at the same finish line, at the same time?" Zachary said and then paused for a long moment before he continued. "No, I doubt that you would. So how do you think that THE would approach it?"

Bruno's eyes lit up like a light going on, "Yes, since you put it in that way, I understand much better now.

"Good, I thought that you would be able to grasp it."

Then his eyes became dark again as they focused, "But still, when I see some people with such tremendous physical and mental handicaps, or people who experience so much tragedy and misery in their lives, I have a hard time believing that these could be God's, excuse me, THE's design."

"Did you ever think that THE wants to see how they deal with these handicaps."

"Yes, that is the usual explanation, but it seems so cruel and so unfair," B.A.D. replied.

"I suppose it would to you. Again your strong sense of fairness comes through; not only do you think that it is unfair, you feel as if you should be doing something about it."

"I do?" B.A.D. responded.

"Hey, don't play coy with me. Remember this is 'Zach the App' you are talking to, not one of your buddies. I am fully aware of your sensitive nature," Zachary said. "Did you ever stop to think that, besides testing them, that THE is testing those of you who appear to be more fortunate. How you respond to these individuals and their 'needs' says a great deal about you and what zone that you have attained, and if you are ready or not to move into the next zone. Make no mistake about it, these individuals are most often in very advanced zones and will be waiting many years, and lifetimes, for you normal people to join them on the 'Spiritual Plane.'"

"So, are you saying that everything that happens has a reason and is controlled by THE?" B.A.D. asked.

"Well, not everything. We view the big picture here, and are concerned with arriving at our ultimate goal. Sometimes, things happen along the way that we rather they hadn't, but that we were either to busy or otherwise pre-occupied to prevent. As long as they don't throw us off schedule too much from attaining our goal, we allow them to happen. Then again, as your Dad says, sometimes it is just that 'Shit Happens.'" Zachary said with a smile.

"Are you kidding me!"? B.A.D. said.

"No, I'm not kidding you. Sometimes things just happen with little or no rationale to it." Zachary said. "Again, as long as they don't throw us off of our major goal."

B.A.D.'s eyes lit up again, "No shit, so my Dad was right about things sometimes happening for no apparent reason."

"Yes, that is correct. Now let's get to what I am really here for. Your mission, should you choose to accept it, is to work with me for the forces of good against the forces of evil. Because, make no mistake about it, there are forces of evil out there that must be defeated, and, in order to defeat them, it is necessary to combine as many forces of good as possible. You see, I am your apparition, or angel, and, therefore, you will never be alone again. However, it is often necessary to bring many apparitions into the picture to win in certain situations. If you are willing to take on evil, in any situation that you find it, you will be able to marshal additional forces of good to assist you. Only when the forces of evil are defeated and eliminated can the will of THE be satisfied, and allow Paradise to exist. And, I've got to tell you that THE is getting awfully tired of some of these dickheads, who are running things, and, if it doesn't change soon, THE may have to take more serious steps."

"Like what?" B.A.D. asked cautiously.

"Like mass Bobbitization!" Zachary said with a little grin, his sense of humor getting the better of him.

"Whoa that is drastic!" Bruno said, "May I ask a question?"

"If it is a short one," Zachary said.

"Well then, briefly, what would your advice to us be? In twenty-five words or less." Bruno couldn't let this opportunity go by.

"I'll give it to you very simply, in two words, Bruno," Zachary said, very sincerely and forcefully—"**BE NICE.**"

"That seems simple enough," Bruno said. "But it doesn't always seem to be that way."

"You would think that it would be, but many, too damn many, of you are not nice. You are just *not nice* people." Zachary said. "Unfortunately, it can be easier, in the short run, not to care. It can be easier to be self-centered now, but they *will* pay for it."

Bruno smiled and said, "Can I ask one more question before I answer you?"

Zachary's patience was near the end as he replied, "Yes, I guess so, go ahead."

"Can you tell me who, 'They', are?"

"You really do have quite a sense of humor, too, don't you! I like that, but it has come down to the time to tell me. Are you with us or not? Are you? Well are you?" Zachary challenged.

"Yes! Yes! Yes! I am!" Bruno shouted.

"Hey, B.A.D., wake up! C'mon wake up your scaring me!" B.J. pleaded, as he shook his brother by the shoulders.

"What! What! B.J., what are you doing here?"

"What do you mean, stupid, this is my room, too."

B.A.D. sat up trying to get his bearings, 'Yea, yea, right."

"Are you all right? You don't look so good." B.J. was actually concerned.

"Yes, I am okay, I just had a very vivid dream I guess, that's all."

"Well, it's time for us to go down to breakfast anyway, so you had better get up."

"I don't think that I can. Just tell Mom that I am still sleeping, okay?" B.A.D. said.

"No, I won't, because you promised that you would be there today. You haven't been there for one breakfast on this cruise and we only have two mornings left, so you have to make this one. So get your fat ass up and get down to breakfast," B.J. said, as he boldly ripped the covers off of his brother.

The two boys were wrestling playfully, although aggressively, when they heard the bang on the door.

"You boys cut it out and get your butts down to the breakfast table and fast, if you know what is good for you." Their mother was giving them orders in the tone of voice that said—'you can joke about it, but you had better do what I say in the end.'

"Yea. Okay, Mom, we'll be there right away." They said in unison as they continued to wrestle. But they knew that they had better stop soon and get down to the table before too long, or they would disappoint their mother and they didn't want to do that. So they stopped, with one last little punch to one another, and got cleaned up to go to breakfast, although this process still took them twenty minutes or more.

"Well, it is about time that you two got here," was the greeting they received from their mother, as the two of them entered the dining room and approached the table.

"It is good to see the two of you down here for breakfast. I really didn't think that we would," their father said.

"Yea, mates, it is good to see you two together again," Harry said.

B.A.D. stiffened, as his guard immediately went up. He had hoped Horseshit Harry would not be there. "What do you mean by that?"

"Oh, nothing mate. I just thought that you two were going to sleep the rest of the voyage away."

"No, we are still here and we will continue to be," B.A.D. answered rather pointedly, as the two of them took their seats.

"Well, that's good, because I was talking to the ships entertainment director just this morning and she would still like to have the basketball championships later this morning. As sort of a highlight before tonight's Grand Ball."

"But I thought that the championship was cancelled because there wasn't enough interest to get teams together," B.J. said.

"Well, that is sort of true. In fact, the only teams that we can get together are yours and ours. We have been fortunate enough to attract two new players." Harry informed them. "But I think that your team is probably one or two people short."

"We kind of thought that the tournament was cancelled, so we didn't really pursue it any further," B.A.D. responded.

"Well, we have our team together and are ready to go, but I can see that we have frightened away all of the competition. Too bad, I thought that you guys had the guts to at least give it a try," Harry added sarcastically.

"We'll play you and we'll kick your ass!" B.J.'s competitive spirit was aroused, as he started to rise from his chair and go towards Harry just as his brother grabbed him and pulled him back down.

"Hey, it is good to see that at least one member of your group has a competitive spirit, even if he is just a little kid," Harry sneered.

"If we can't get a team together I will kick your butt one on one, if you've got the balls." B.J. was furious; he was a gutsy little kid and could never let such a challenge go by. Besides, he had supreme confidence in his basketball abilities.

"Watch your mouth young man. I don't want that kind of talk coming from you," Mary reprimanded him sternly.

"Sorry, Ma, but I am not afraid of him or any of his team and I will play them by myself if I have to." B.J. said this with such sincerity, and with such an air of willing sacrifice to uphold his and his families, honor, that it caused a quiet to come over the entire table for a very long moment.

"We'll play you, Harry. What time is tap-off?" Al said in a very controlled, monotone voice that said his young son was not the only one who was not afraid of him and would defend the family honor, if need be. At the same time he gave Mary a quick glance that said that this was his domain, that he was very serious about it, and that it was more than just a game. She would have to have trust in him and her boys, and they would expect her unwavering support. A support that had proven to provide them with great strength and determination in the past.

Harry stared as he answered, "Are you sure that you have enough players and that you guys are up to it?"

"My boys are up to it! Just tell us the game time." Mary's cold and matter of fact statement emphasized the fact that this had already risen above a mere basketball game and that she was prepared to play her role and give her unwavering support to her family.

"We will play your team even if we are short handed," Frankie added.

"Whatever it takes," B.J. added.

"I think that you guys are going to need all the help you can get, because we are going to run you into the ground," Harry said smugly.

Then the words that came from Lawrence stunned everyone, not the least of which was his son. "If they don't have enough players, then I will join their team. If they'll have me."

"Well, Lawrence, you surprise me. Are you sure that you want to do this, it appears that it is going to be quite a competitive game," Harry said, obviously enjoying himself.

"I said, 'If they don't have enough players I will join their team.'" Lawrence said, feeling good that he was involved in something with his son and he had supported him, as AL had supported his son. He wasn't sure, but maybe that is why he did it. It certainly wasn't because he really wanted to play basketball and get his ass kicked by these thugs.

Al's eyes never wavered from Harry's, "Again I'll ask you. What time is tap off?"

"How about eleven this morning. I think that everything can be arranged by then," Harry said.

"Good, we will be there," Al answered.

"Good, my team will be there at ten forty-five for warm-ups. We'll see you boys there," Harry said, as he got up and started to leave.

"Fine, we'll be there," Al responded, as Harry left. "Well guys, I think that we had better get going, maybe we can get a little practice in before the game. I have a feeling that we are going to need it."

"Are you sure that you want to do this Lawrence?" Margaret was surprised and concerned.

"Ya, Dad, you don't have to do this if you don't want to." Frankie was happy that his father had spoken up for him and his team, but he would let him off of the hook gently if he wanted out.

Lawrence looked at his son and spoke softly, "Francis, you do need another player and I said that I would help and I will. Unless you don't want me to?"

"Oh no! It would be great to have you on the team," Frankie answered, his eyes bright.

"Do you even have any basketball sneakers?" Margaret asked.

"I have athletic shoes that I use to play squash, they will do fine," Lawrence said.

"We are glad to have you with us, but I do think that we should get changed and get down to the court to get some practice in. I have a strong feeling that we are going to need it," Al said as he started towards his cabin.

"I believe that you are right, Al. We will meet you there in fifteen minutes." Lawrence responded, as he took his wife gently by the arm and proceeded towards their cabin. It was a very simple gesture, certainly imperceptible to the unobservant eye, but one that transported her back thirty years to a point in time when they were very young and very, very much in love. A time before they were 'successful' and trying to be members of New York's society. The suddenness of this change in him confused her, but she was enjoying it and would do so as long as it lasted, however short that may be.

"I don't know Al. Are you sure that you want to do this. Remember your back problems, you may end up bedridden for the rest of the cruise. You know how bad it was just a few years ago." Mary was trying her best to protect her ageing warrior, even though she was proud of him for coming to his young sons defense and standing up to the stupid, boyish challenges of Harry Holt.

"Don't worry, I will be careful, I don't plan on doing anything stupid, besides I feel pretty good. I haven't had any real back pain in a long time," Al responded.

"Shut your mouth, that is exactly the kind of talk that I don't want to hear," Mary quickly answered, squeezing his hand, as they reached their cabin and entered it.

CHAPTER 20

❀

$\mathscr{A}$s the rag tag team of players was practicing shooting, the last two, Frankie and his father, L. Terrence, came onto the court.

"Hey guys come on over and loosen up and take some shots before we talk about our strategy," Al said as he looked at his team. He had to admit that it certainly was a sorry looking group of players. First, there was the kid that they called Rosie who was about five foot six and one hundred and twenty pounds soaking wet, if he was lucky.

"Hey, Rosie, let's see your outside shot," Al barked, as he saw him get the ball about twenty feet from the basket.

"Sure, coach, anything you say," Rosie answered as he let the ball fly. As the ball left his hands it had good arc and sailed straight towards the basket. It would have been a perfect shot if the basket had only been nineteen feet away. Unfortunately the ball fell at least a foot short of its target and was a perfect air ball. "Sorry coach."

"No problem, Rosie, we will just have to get you in a little closer. Maybe you should play center," Al said jokingly, although the look on Rosie's face questioned if he was serious. "Don't worry son I was only kidding." A look of instant relief came over Rosebud's face.

Then there was Frankie. He would not make the same mistake with Frankie, because it was painfully obvious that he could not shoot a set shot to save his life, but maybe he was a good driver.

"Hey, Frankie, let me see you take the ball and drive to the basket for a lay-up," Al instructed.

"Yes sir, I will try," Frankie said, he was uncomfortable calling Mr. DeGregorio coach, as he was not use to having a coach. He was also very nervous about doing this.

As he started to drive to the basket, he fumbled with the ball for two or three steps and then kicked it out of bounds.

"That's O.K., Frankie, try it again, only this time start a little closer to the basket," Al encouraged him.

So Frankie started about one dribble from the basket, which he was able to successfully complete, only to awkwardly leap towards the basket off of his wrong foot and have the basketball slam up against the rim and come flying back to hit him in the face and almost knock him down.

"Are you all right, Frankie?" Al asked. He thought that perhaps Mary was right, maybe they shouldn't be doing this.

"Yes, I'm fine," answered an embarrassed Frankie, as he wiped the blood from his nose and made his way out of the line of fire.

Then Al kept his eye on Big Louie for a while. He noticed that he barely moved from the spot that he had chosen to occupy, but that, when a ball did come to him, he was able to shoot it up at close range with a fair degree of accuracy. This could be a little promising as it was obvious that Louie certainly could occupy a significant amount of space and it looked like it would be difficult to move him from it. With a little bit of leaping ability and some effort he should be a good rebounder.

"Hey, Louis, let's see you go up to get some of those rebounds," Al said.

"Okay coach." Big Louie answered as he took one step to grab the next ball and then two full steps to get another. But at no time did he leave his feet.

"That's good, Louie, but how about showing us how high you can jump to pull one down," Al said. He didn't understand the inquisitive look that he received back from Louie.

"Dad, I don't think that you quite understand. That *is* how high Big Louie can jump," B.A.D. said as he came up beside his father.

"You're kidding?" Al said.

"No. I'm not," B.A.D. responded.

"But he didn't leave his feet at all. I mean you couldn't have slipped a sheet of paper under his sneaker, even if you moved at the speed of light," Al answered.

"Watch him very closely Dad. You have to focus on the heel of his left foot as he reaches for the ball," B.A.D. said. "There do you see it?"

"I think so? I mean I think I saw his left heel lift off of the floor a little bit. Maybe."

"That's it."

"That's it?" Al said. "You mean that is as high as he can jump?"

"That's it, that's all there is," B.A.D. responded.

"Well, Bruno, I think that we could be in even more trouble than I thought. Outside of your brother and your sister Jennifer's ability to shoot, you and I could be the best that we have, and we both know that our basketball abilities are quite limited."

"Yea that's true, Dad, but we can play defense and you have always said that it is defense that wins games. Besides, we do have B.J. for offense and you know how good he can be," B.A.D. said, as they both turned to watch him warm up. Even though he was only ten, he had all the form and grace of a much older, talented athlete. He had a pure shooting stroke that came from many hours of practice and even more hours of studying players as he watched them on television. He didn't just watch a game to see them play; he watched a game to study the form and technique of the most talented players.

"You are right there. He is certainly going to surprise them and we may be able to take advantage of it early, but I'm afraid that these guys might play a little rough and he is only ten," Al said as they watched him drive to the basket, dribbling the ball between his legs as he went, and performing a double pump fake before releasing the ball to the backboard, were it bounced true and through the net.

"You're right, but the refs are going to be a part of the ships crew, so maybe we can keep the game from getting too rough. But we had better get the rest of the team together to go over our strategy, which should include protecting B.J.," B.A.D. said, as they both moved towards the rest of the team.

It was at this point that some of the blue team came in. Among them were the two thugs from the night before. Immediately Big Louie, Rosie, and Frankie came running up to B.A.D..

"Did you see who just came in?" Rosie almost shouted.

"Yes, I did. Now get a hold of yourself and quiet down."

"What are we going to do?" Big Louie asked nervously.

"Yea, what?" Rosie was even more nervous.

"It is a good question," Frankie added. He remained relatively calm in an attempt to support and emulate Bruno.

"The first thing is not to panic. There is nothing that they can do to us with all of these people around."

"Yes, but what about after the game?" Rosie said.

"There is 'the Pol' over there. Let's go and see what advice he has for us."

"Hi, B.A.D.! Boys! How are all of you after your little adventure last night?" The 'Pol' asked, with a little smile on his face.

"We're fine, thanks to you," B.A.D. said.

"Believe me, it was my pleasure."

"Do you see those two guys standing over there giving us those dirty looks?" B.A.D. asked.

"Yes."

"They are the ones who captured us last night."

"Are you sure?"

"We're positive!" The four of them repeated in unison.

"Well, I am kind of surprised that they would show themselves so publicly," Pol said.

"It certainly removes any doubt about them being connected to Harry Holt. It is definite now," B.A.D. said.

"Yes, I would say that it is. It also makes me wonder what they are up to. They are either very bold or very stupid," Pol said.

"I don't know about the two who captured us, but I don't think that Harry Holt is stupid," B.A.D. said.

"No, I don't think he is, either. That's what worries me."

"What should we do?" The other three boys said.

"Just be calm, there is nothing they can do in such a public place. Make sure that you stay in the public eye, in large groups, after the game. Especially until I figure out what they are up to."

"Okay Pol, that sounds good. Come on guys we have to get back to the team."

"I'll see you boys later."

"Ya, see you later. Thanks Pol."

"Ya, thanks!" Big Louie, Frankie and Rosie repeated as they all left to join their team.

       ❧   ❧   ❧

"Hi! You're going to play in the game aren't you?" Bertha asked as she sat down beside Charlotte, who was watching Bruno and the rest of his team practice.

"Hi! Yes I am." Charlotte responded. "Do I know you?"

"No, we don't know each other, but I have seen you around and my son mentioned you were on the other team. My name is Bertha. Yours is Charlotte isn't it?"

"Yes, it is. You are well informed aren't you? But I don't believe I know him either."

"He is the extra large one standing over there under the basket and, like every other male on the ship, he certainly has noticed you."

"Of course, why should he be any different.?" Charlotte said a little dejectedly.

"Are you telling me that you don't like the attention?" Bertha asked.

A serious, almost sad, look came across Charlotte's face, "Well, I thought I did, I guess. At least it is something that I have going for me, but sometimes I would like someone to like me just for myself. Even just once."

"Haven't you ever had a serious relationship?" Bertha asked.

"No. At least not in the way I would like it to be, or the way I imagine some people have it when I see them together with their families. You know what I mean. The kind of relationships that go on for a long time, that survive the bad times as well as the good times, a relationship that goes well beyond sex. I think I got a little glimpse of how it would be like to be with someone like that, someone who cared how you felt and not just themselves, but I'm not really sure. Even you probably have one of those good kind of relationships," Charlotte said, not meaning to be unkind, but she knew that it sounded that way.

"Yes, even me," Bertha said, feeling that she may have been wrong to try to be friendly to her.

"I'm very sorry, Bertha. I didn't mean it to sound that way. I really didn't!" Charlotte said, more sincerely than she thought that she was capable of.

"No problem, Charlotte, apology accepted. I should probably apologize to you as well," Bertha said.

"To me! For what?" Charlotte responded.

"Because, as much as I hate to admit it, I have been as guilty as everyone else of just looking at you as this great body, and assuming that you were very shallow, in order to make myself feel better," Bertha announced. "And I should know better, because we really have a lot in common."

"Don't feel bad, I know that is how most woman view me. In fact, sometimes it is all I hold on to. As you can imagine, I don't have very many female friends. More precisely, I don't have any female friends," Charlotte said. "But I don't really see what we have in common?"

"Well, believe it or not, we have our bodies in common," Bertha said with a little grin on her face.

"Excuse me if I don't quite understand that."

"It's true! People look at us and immediately make decisions about us, based solely on our looks, before they ever get to know us. Of course the conclusions that they draw about each of us are radically different, but the fact remains that they are judging us on our appearances instead of upon who we really are."

"I'm still not sure if I fully understand."

"Well, they look at you and they see this gorgeous body and beautiful face and never get to know the warm, intelligent, and very vulnerable person behind it all."

"You're very kind Bertha. Thank you." Charlotte was definitely touched by the sincerity of this woman she had just met. A woman, she had to painfully admit, that she had first just looked down upon as a terribly overweight, fat slob. How could she be so judgmental when she hated others for doing the same thing to her? She felt awful. A feeling that, at first, she couldn't describe and then she knew exactly how she felt. She felt like shit!

"Oh, I am not so kind, believe me. My initial reaction was the very same thing. But then I thought of it and I watched you and I could see the sadness in your eyes. I asked myself—'why should such a beautiful woman be so sad. If only I looked like her then all of my pain would be gone'. And then I understood that, inside, you were no different than me. Our hearts, our minds and, most of all, our souls need the same recognition, the same love and tenderness, regardless of our outer appearance. When we don't get this we do whatever it is that makes us feel better, if only for a little while. Even though we know it is only fool's gold and that our initial euphoria will soon be replaced by an even deeper depression that only serves to perpetuate the self-destroying cycle," Bertha said. "In your case, you use your beautiful looks and fantastically exciting body to try to get the attention and recognition that you crave, only to dislike yourself further when it is all over and you are alone with only your thoughts. Thoughts that demand to know why you are such a failure and why the mere act of living is so fucking hard."

"You have been there haven't you? You do understand," Charlotte said, barely able to hold back the tears that wanted to come crashing forward in an uncontrollable torrent.

"Yes, I have been there. More times than I care to remember," Bertha said. "Only with me it's binging on food that is my escape. When something happens, like catcalls calling me a fat pig, that hurts me and I turn to food, just as you turn to sex, to ease the pain. And, of course, this only makes things worse. But I have come to understand that, just like you could never be ugly, I can never be thin and physically attractive by our society's standards. It is interesting that if I lived on the island of Tonga, in the South Pacific, I would be considered a thing of beauty. Because of this shallowness in our society, there are very, very few people outside of my immediate family and circle of friends that know me. That know that I am an intelligent woman, with a doctorate in psychology, and that I am sensitive and loving and need to be recognized for my accomplishments and loved and cared for. I am a human being and, like all human beings, I need to be loved and nurtured and respected, for no other reason than I am human."

"I never realized that pain and humiliation could take so many different forms. I'm sorry for my initial thoughts about you Bertha. I would like to be your friend, if you would let me," Charlotte said.

"Well, Charlotte, dear I am sorry for my initial thoughts also and I would very much like to be your friend," Bertha said, as she gave her a little hug that only woman had the privilege of getting away with.

"I think that I had better find a way to sneak out of here before the game starts," Charlotte said.

"Sneak out? Why I thought that you were going to play in the game?" Bertha asked.

"I was, but I feel very uncomfortable about doing it now. I mean, this uniform is at least one and maybe two sizes too small for me and, after our talk, I don't feel like being on display today. See!" Charlotte said, as she stood up and took off her cover up to reveal a uniform that looked as if it had been painted on. The jersey was molded to her round, firm breasts and it was obvious that she wasn't wearing a bra, since the affect of the air conditioning had caused her nipples to harden to the point that they threatened to pierce the constraining material and make their escape to freedom. The shorts that she was wearing were not only skin tight, but would have made short shorts look like Bermuda shorts.

The affect of Charlotte's suddenly standing, causing her breasts to bounce as they did, did not go unnoticed by the boys on the basketball court. The pass that Frankie had just made to Rosie hit him in the head, as he turned to see her. Then Big Louie almost crushed Frankie, who had been moving towards the basket for one of his patented lay-ups before he was distracted. Big Al and Lawrence both had to sit before their emotions became too obvious. Even B.J. missed a shot without noticing or caring. The only male in the gym that was not affected in this way was B.A.D.. It wasn't that he didn't find her attractive, but more that he knew there was much more to this woman than just a hard on and that he had to talk with her, today.

"Yes, I see what you mean Charlie girl. I think that you had better sit down before someone hurts themselves down there," Bertha said as she gestured toward the court. As soon as Charlotte saw the chaos that she was causing, she sat down quickly. Just a few minutes ago she would have been pleased with this, but no longer.

"Mr. Shipley! Mr. Shipley could you come over here for a moment please?" Bertha said as she saw the ship's first mate come into the gym and begin to walk by them.

"Yes. Bertha Cochran isn't it? What can I do for you?" Bruce Shipley said. He was a pleasant man, who had been the first mate on this ship for the past five years, and prided himself on his ability to remember the passenger's names.

"That's very good, Mr. Shipley. I am very impressed that you remembered my name, since we only met once, very briefly," Bertha said.

"Thank you! And yours is Charlotte, isn't it?" Bruce Shipley said.

"Why yes, it is. But I don't believe that we have met," Charlotte responded.

"Excuse me, but I am a lot less impressed with that Mr. Shipley. In fact, that is what I wanted to talk to you about. I suggest that you find the social activities director and have her find a more suitable uniform for this young lady, and quickly. The game is about to start and she can't, and won't, go on the court in this uniform. I am sure that no one intentionally was looking for her to be on display in this way," Bertha said. She noticed a little look of disappointment on Mr. Shipley's face. "If there is some problem with that, then I would be happy to take it up with the Captain."

"Well, now that you mention it, the uniform does appear to be just a little tight. I'm sure that we can find something that will fit a little better," Mr. Shipley said.

"I'm sure that you can find something that will fit a lot better and find a sports bra while you are at it," Bertha said.

"Yes, of course Bertha. If you will please come with me Miss, I will find the social director and I am sure that she will be able to find an appropriate uniform, bra and all," Mr. Shipley said, as he began to lead the way across the court to the social director's office. This, in itself, almost caused a minor catastrophe, as all heads turned to watch Charlotte walk across the floor, causing some players to crash into one another and others to sit down quickly.

Within about ten minutes of Charlotte's leaving the gym, things were back to normal and both teams were now warming up. The referees were going to be Paul Jones, the assistant social director, and the ship's first mate Bruce Shipley, who was beginning to wonder if this game was such a good idea now, since it certainly was not going to be as enjoyable to the eyes.

The players on the red team would be Al ('Big Al') DeGregorio, also the coach, L. Terrence ('L.T.') Carr, Jennifer ('Jenny') DeGregorio, Alison Marie ('Alie') Carr, Bruno ('B.A.D.') DeGregorio, B.J. ('Ace') DeGregorio, Louis ('Big Louie') Cochran, Francis ('Frankie') Carr and Oliver Elden ('Rosebud') Doolittle.

The players on the blue team would be Harry Holt, Tom Stephens, Brian Murphy, Sally Roberts, Charlotte Johnson, Father Tony Demarco, Hans and Brock, the two Van Goff sister's guards, who didn't seem to have last names, and, last but not least, Harold ('Happy Harold') Wilson, who was a last minute addition to even off the sides.

As Charlotte was about to come back into the gym, wearing a much more modest uniform, she was approached by Lawrence Carr.

"May I speak with you briefly, Charlotte?" He asked.

"Yes, I suppose so," Charlotte answered. "I know that we haven't seen much of each other on this cruise, but it is not my fault."

"No we haven't and I know that it is not your fault. It almost seems as if something or someone was trying to keep us apart. But that isn't what I really wanted to talk to you about."

"Oh! Then what is it?" Charlotte was confused.

Terrence began, "I don't quite know how to tell you this."

"Are you trying to tell me that you are dumping me?" Charlotte asked.

"I wouldn't put it quite like that. I just don't think that we should see each other as lovers anymore," Terrence said, uncharacteristically nervous.

"I don't understand when you say we shouldn't see each other as lovers any more. What other way is there for us? Are you dumping me or what?" Charlotte was a little more than confused.

"I have to admit that I don't really understand it myself, either. But something unusual has happened to me on this very strange cruise."

"What do you mean?"

"Well, for one thing, I have been observing the family that is sharing our table and, even though they have very little in common with me, I have found myself envying their very close family relationship. I have also had the opportunity, albeit somewhat forced, to spend some time with Margaret and I have enjoyed it. Now this basketball game has given me the chance to participate in something with my son and daughter, something of their choosing. I know that it sounds really strange, but it is like there is a cloud of goodness engulfing this ship at times."

"Funny, but I think I kind of know what you mean."

"Well, whatever the reason, I am suddenly feeling very guilty, both for how I have treated my family and also for how I have treated you. So, if it is not too late, I am going to try to correct the situation."

"I don't really know if it is too late or not Terrence, but I do think that you should try," Charlotte said with surprisingly mixed emotions.

"Thank you, Charlotte, that helps. It helps a lot and I would like to help you, also."

"Again, I don't know what you mean."

"I mean that I would like to help you change your life, too. I would like to help you get some training. Perhaps I could help you go to college."

"Me go to college?" Charlotte almost fell over.

"Yes. I think that you are very intelligent and, with a little help, you could make it." Terrence was very sincere.

"I don't know what to say. You would really do that for me? Why?"

"Yes I would, because I realize I do care for you, as a person and not just as a lover. I think that you deserve it and are capable of a lot. I guess that I would like to be your friend and make up for some of what I have done in the past."

"I really don't know what to say. Are you telling me that you would help me with money to go to school and not want anything in return?" Charlotte said. "You'll excuse me if I have a hard time with this, but no one has ever offered me anything like this before. Let alone...." She didn't finish her sentence.

"You can finish it—'Let alone someone like me.' I understand your feelings perfectly well. I have a hard time understanding it as well, but that is exactly what I mean. We can't be lovers anymore, but I hope we can be friends and I hope that you will take advantage of this opportunity, for your sake and for mine."

"You will have to give me a little time to sort this out. I'm very confused."

"Of course. We can talk about it some more, later. But, for now, I think that we had better get back in there before we are missed."

"Yes, you go ahead in and I will be in in a minute," Charlotte said, her head still reeling from this unexpected turn of events.

So Terrence returned to the gym, leaving Charlotte to contemplate this potentially significant change in her life. As she was standing there, trying to comprehend what had just happened, she was approached by Bruno.

"Hi, Charlotte, how are you?" Bruno said as he came and stood next to her.

"I'm okay, I guess." Was the best that she could do in her confused state.

"Are you all right? You look a little pale."

"Yes, I'm okay. Thanks for asking."

"May I see you after the game is over? I would like to talk with you, and to get to know you better."

"Yes, I suppose so. You know where my cabin is," Charlotte said instinctively.

"Yes, but I think that it would be better if we didn't meet there. I do want to talk with you. Could we meet on the main deck—say a half hour after the game is over? That would give us a chance to get cleaned up," Bruno said.

"Yes, that would be fine," Charlotte said, more confused now than ever. She had said yes because she liked him, as well as because Harry had instructed her to, but his desire to meet in public, rather than in the privacy of her cabin, not only confused her, but made her want to see him more for herself than for Harry.

They both then went back into the gym, where Charlotte still turned heads, but more for her beauty than her body.

CHAPTER 21

❀

$\mathcal{F}$inally, after another fifteen minutes of warming up, it had come time to start the game. The announcer indicated that it was two minutes to tap off so the teams came off the floor and grouped at their respective benches.

"From the looks of the other team, I think that we could be in a little trouble here," Al said. "We should keep in mind that this is just for fun."

"I don't want to have to listen to 'Horseshit' Harry for the next two days if these guys beat us, especially if they beat us in a big way," B.A.D. said.

"We won't lose, just give me the ball." The words that came from B.J. were strangely distant, like they came from a computer that was disassociated with his body.

"I want you to stay very clear of these guys Ace. You are only ten years old and, at five feet and ninety-five pounds, you are no match for them. While we might have the two tallest players on the court in Big Louie and myself, they definitely have the overall physical team strength and I don't want anyone getting hurt, especially you. I have to admit that I don't like the looks of this 'Butch' Murphy and I certainly don't like the looks of Hans and Brock, and I don't have to tell any of you about Mr. Harry Holt," Al said. He was worried about the look in his young sons eyes.

"We will not lose," B.J. repeated.

"Don't worry about him Dad, he will be fine. Besides, it is already too late. Look at his eyes, he is already in zone two and we haven't even started the game yet," B.A.D. said quietly to his father.

"That's what worries me, Bruno. I have seen 'Ace' play as if he were unconscious before. I mean hitting every shot in sight, but that was always after the games had been in process for a while. I have never seen him this intense before the game even had begun."

"Okay, Red team, you have to get your starting team on the floor so that we can get going some time today." The first mate Bruce Shipley said.

The Blue team had already put its starting line up on the court and it consisted of Hans at center, Harry Holt and Tom Stephens at forward, and Father Tony and Charlotte at guard.

Al had decided to take Bruno's advice and started Big Louie at center, Bruno and Frankie at forwards and Jennifer and Ace at guards. Everyone had agreed that it made sense to start off with the three DeGregorio siblings on the floor at the same time; they had played many hours together and this would give them a distinct advantage in the early going.

"Okay guys and girls let's line up here for the tap off. The Red team is going this way and the Blue team that. Is everybody clear on that? Let's have a good clean game now. Everyone please remember that this is just for fun," Bruce Shipley said as he stepped forward to throw the ball up.

As the ball went up in the air so did Hans, but not Big Louie. The tap was clearly the Blue team's for the taking but for the fact that Hans had expected more of a challenge and, therefore, sent the ball flying out of bounds.

Harry Holt immediately began to chastise Hans for this and, while he was doing so, Ace quickly retrieved the ball and sent a pass flying to Bruno who, knowing his brother's hustling play, had already broken for the basket as everyone else was standing around. This resulted in a quick two points for the Red team.

The Blue team began to re-group as Father Tony brought the ball up the court. Still thinking that this was to be a friendly, low intensity game, the good Father threw a lazy pass to Charlotte. A pass that never reached it's intended target as, the ever alert, Ace cut in front of her, picked it off and raced up court for an uncontested lay up. The Blue team was stunned and the crowd, obviously partial to the Red team, cheered wildly.

The Blue team again took the ball up the court, but Father Tony was a lot more alert this time. He had appreciated the effort of this young man, but he did not want to be embarrassed again. This time he spotted Harry open in the right corner and threw him a pass with the necessary zip on it this time. The ball was caught cleanly by Harry who immediately turned and sent a very good looking shot towards the basket, which was true to its mark and gave the Blue team their first two points.

The teams went back and forth for the rest of the first half. The Blue team relied on its inside strength and the outside shooting of Father Tony, who was a good basketball player. The Red team continued to rely on the outside shooting of Ace, Jenny and Rosie, who turned out to be a good player and was the lead guard when Ace was rested. At the end of the first half, the Red team, to the delight of the crowd, managed to maintain a five—point lead as each team went to a corner of the gym to rest and re-group for the second half.

The Red team was in good spirits as they got drinks of water and ate oranges. "Hey we are doing pretty good. We need to keep up our defense and improve our rebounding," Big Al said.

Over on the Blue team bench, Harry said calmly, "I think that we should get out there and warm up before the second half starts." However, he grabbed Butch's arm to keep him back as the others went out onto the court. "Butch, I want you to get this young kid out of the game before it is too late and he beats us. But you have to make it look like an accident or this crowd will string us up."

"No problem boss, I will be happy to take care of the little creep. I would be happy to take care of the rest of these kids, too," Butch said.

"Keep yourself under control for now, you'll get your chance. And, for Christ sakes, don't make it too obvious or you'll have the crowd ready to lynch us," Harry said.

Then the buzzer went off to signal the start of the second half.

'Butch' Murphy wasted no time in accomplishing his mission. The next time that the Red team came down the court he looked to cover Ace. In doing so he made sure that he gave him enough room so they would give him the ball for him to take his shot. This worked as Rosie passed him the ball and Ace immediately began to take his shot. Butch, anticipating this, leaped into the air as if to block the shot, which he didn't do, and came down, as if he were off balance, crashing his forearm into B.J.'s nose as he reached out with his other hand and appeared to try to keep B.J. from falling too hard to the floor. As he lay there on the floor with his hands covering his face, you could see the blood start to trickle out between his fingers.

The game stopped immediately as Butch stood over him and asked if he was okay while the crowd held its breath. Big Al was there in a hurry and he knelt down to look at his son, who was fighting back the tears. Mary was about to go out onto the floor to see to her son when Bertha stopped her and suggested that she wait to see if he was really hurt, as young warriors are not fond of having their mothers come out to wipe their noses and kiss their booboo's.

Being the competitor that he was, B.J. was already on his feet and making a move towards his intimidator saying that he would stay in the game and kick his ass, even as the blood ran from his nose all over his shirt. But Al caught him and led him over to the bench where the ship's doctor could take a look at him. All the time Butch was very apologetic and so sincere that he was almost believable. Al sent Big Louie and Bruno in for the two of them so that the game could go on.

"I'm going to kick your ass for that, you friggin jerk," Bruno said, as he walked up to Butch and looked him in the face with a cold, calculating stare that even had the short hairs on this hardened criminal standing on end.

"Ya, sure kid, and just who the fuck do you think you are," Butch answered in a tone that was strangely hesitant for this hard ass.

"I'm Bruno Alphonso DeGregorio and, like I said stupid, I am the guy who is going to kick your friggin ass. Now tell me what word you didn't understand you dumb shit and I will spell it for you." Bruno spoke in a tone that was calm and matter of fact. Butch was taken by surprise and was fumbling for an answer.

"All right you two, cut it out, and let's just play basketball," Bruce Shipley said in an attempt to control what looked like was going to become an ugly situation.

As the game went on, the Blue team was able to close the gap. Then the crowd began to call for Ace, a chant started by Mad Madeline. They all wanted the Red team to win, particularly since the brutal foul by Butch on Ace, who was the obvious crowd favorite.

"You have to give Al the okay to put B.J. back into the game. None of you are going to be happy, especially B.J., if you lose this game like this," Bertha said to Mary.

"But I don't want my young son to get hurt any further playing with these rough men over a stupid basketball game," Mary responded.

"I know how you feel. But you don't know that he is going to get hurt and you also know that it is more than just this stupid game, it has to do with how he and the rest of your children will respond to adversity in the rest of their lives. Believe me, I know, it is true," Bertha was very sincere.

"Heaven help me Bertha I'm going to agree with you," Mary said as she gave the nod to Al.

"Dad you have to let him back into the game. Just look at him, I think that he is already in zone four. Besides we will look out for him. Won't we guys?" Bruno pleaded.

"Yea we won't let them get near him," Big Louie said.

"Yea coach, come on." The rest of the team pleaded with Al who, at the same time, caught the nod from Mary that it was a go.

"All right. It will be Big Louie, Bruno, Rosie, me and Ace down the stretch. We have to rebound like hell and set a lot of hard picks for Ace and Rosie. Let's go and kick some ass," Al said with an enthusiasm that caught high fives all around as they ran onto the court. That is except for Ace, who just slowly walked onto the court and stared directly at Butch and then intently at the basket.

The game went back and forth with great intensity and the Blue team had a two-point lead with less than a minute to go. The Red team decided not to take their last time out and, instead, pushed the ball at the basket as quickly as possible. They felt that they could score with a high percentage of accuracy and so they just needed as many scoring opportunities as possible.

Rosie passed the ball into Big Al who then pushed it back out to Bruno. Al and Big Louie then set a double screen for Ace, who faked left and then cut around the screens to catch the pass and launch a fall away jump shot that again hit for three points and gave the red team the lead by a point with thirty-five seconds remaining. The noise was deafening as the crowd roared with delight.

The Blue team immediately called for a time out to regroup and determine their best strategy. Both teams went to their respective benches and Butch and Bruno exchanged dirty looks as they passed.

"Your ass is mine kid," Butch snarled.

"In your dreams, jerk." Bruno couldn't help but respond as the adrenalin was pumping.

"Okay guys, let's knock it off," Ref Jones said as he came between them.

"I think that we should take some time off of the clock and move the ball around. Our best opportunities would be to get the ball in to Brock who has a distinct height advantage over that kid Bruno or for me to take the shot over that little jerk. Whoever shoots, I want to make damn sure that we are all going to the boards for any rebound. I am going to be really pissed off if they beat us," Harry said.

"We have to play tough defense, but don't foul anyone, we don't want to lose this thing at the foul line. If they should score we need to call a time out right away," Al said and everyone on the Red team agreed.

As the two teams took the court the Red team packed it in down low, not wanting to give up any easy baskets. The Blue team moved the ball around very cautiously, not wanting to make any mistakes. Tom had the ball and was looking for Brock, but he was being fronted very effectively by Bruno so he didn't want to risk the pass. Instead, he passed the ball to Hans, who was temporarily open. However, Big Al was on him quickly and kept him out further from the basket than he was comfortable with so he didn't take it. Instead, he passed the ball back to Tom who saw Harry breaking for the basket and hit him at the foul line with a perfect pass.

He had a clear path to the basket, as Ace could do nothing to prevent it, if he didn't put the ball to the floor. Unfortunately for the red team, Harry was going to play this right by taking it straight to the basket and not giving Ace an opportunity to steal the ball. Ace knew there was only one thing that he could do. So he gritted his teeth and stepped in front of the hard charging Harry. To the horror of Al and the entire crowd, Mary not the least, B.J. was very successful in getting tangled up in Harry's legs and brought him crashing to the ground. Unfortunately for B.J. he ended up between Harry and the ground and had the wind knocked out of him as the referee blew the whistle to stop play.

"Are you all right Ace?" Al said, as he raced to his son who was lying on the floor gasping for air.

Needless to say that Mary was already on her feet, and starting towards her son, when Bertha caught her arm to hold her back for the second time.

"I don't think that you want to go down there right now. He probably is fine and, in any event, he will never forgive you if you go down there and embarrass him. I know how badly you want to hold him and comfort him, but, believe me, it is better this way," Bertha said as she eased Mary back down into her seat.

"I suppose you are right, but he had better get up pretty soon or I am going down there anyway," Mary said.

In the meantime, the ships doctor arrived at B.J.'s side in a matter of just a few seconds and began to examine him.

"Please step back so that he can get some air and I can examine him," Dr. John Crawford said as he knelt down to examine B.J.. "Are you all right young man?"

All B.J. could do was nod slightly, trying to indicate that he was all right, but no words would come out, no matter how hard he tried. He also tried to get up, but the doctor wouldn't let him.

"You just lay there for a moment young man until I can determine if there is anything seriously wrong with you or if you just need to catch your breath and nurse your bruises," Dr. Crawford said, as he had to physically restrain B.J. from getting up.

Everyone held their breath awaiting the doctor's report and would have been outright hostile to Harry if it had not been so obviously a kamikaze attack by young Ace, and totally out of Harry's control.

As Al and Bruno stood close by and watched intently, the doctor decided that Ace could get up and go to the bench, where he would examine him further. So he had Al and Bruno help him over to the side of the court. Of course, Al had all he could do to keep from picking him up and carrying him over to the bench like the little boy that he was. It was obvious that Bruno had similar feelings. By the time that they got him to the bench, and sat him down, he was able to speak again, just barely.

"I'm okay. I can go back in." Once again he tried to get up.

"You sit and forget about going back in. You are lucky that you didn't break your neck," Al said in a tone that was out of fear rather than anger.

"Yeah, but you sure are one tough little dude," Bruno said, giving his brother a little pat on the back.

"Thanks, B.A.D.," Ace said with a gleam in his eye. His big brother was not one to throw compliments around very freely; he knew that one such as this came from his heart and that is why it meant everything to him. With this his adrenalin was really flowing and he was determined to get back in and win the game.

"Don't encourage him, Bruno," Al said, with a smile returning to his face; he was also clearly impressed and proud of his son. Of both his sons.

"Come on, Dad, we have to win this game," Ace pleaded. "He has a one and one and, if he hits the first one, he can tie the game and the second one can then put them ahead. Then you will need me to score."

"Don't worry, Ace, we are not going to lose this game. You have my word on it." Bruno said, as he looked into the stands and caught the eye of Bertha Cochran. As their eyes met, he signaled, with a nod of his head, that it was time to put their contingency plan into action. Immediately, she was up and making her way down to the bench, carrying a rather large handbag with her.

The referees announced that they had awarded Harry a one and one situation and were receiving some flak from the Blue team for their call.

"That was a deliberate foul and we should be getting two shots and the ball back," Harry was complaining to Bruce Shipley, the head referee.

"You were fouled on the floor, before you were in the act of shooting, and therefore you are getting a one on one shooting situation. It was not a breakaway foul and you are not getting two shots and the ball back." Shipley remained firm.

"You're full of shit, that was a deliberate foul and we should be getting two shots and the ball back," Harry said.

"You are lucky that you are not getting strung up for running the kid over. He is definitely the crowd favorite and you could be in deep shit if we award you the two shots and the ball. Besides, you don't deserve it, so quit bitching and get to the line for your foul shots," referee Shipley directed. "Come on guys lets get out onto the court so that we can finish this game."

"All right guys lets get out there, Frankie you replace B.J.," Al said. "If they score, at all, then we have to call a time out right away."

Everyone took their place around and along the foul line to await the shot, or shots, from Harry. Taking his place on the foul line Harry was determined that he had to concentrate deeply on his foul shots, because, if he could hit both of them, he could put them ahead and most probably win the game since the Red teams best scorer was on the bench.

So Harry took his time and concentrated hard, before launching his first shot that was true to its mark and was good for a point. As he prepared for his second shot everyone held their breath. The Blue team knowing that they would probably win the game with the one point advantage, only ten seconds left and the kid on the bench. The Red team hoped for a miss so that they would at least have a tie and hope that Ace could come back for the overtime period. Then Harry put his shot up, which was slightly off of target, and rolled around the rim, for what seemed like an eternity, before it fell through the net and gave the Blue team the lead by one.

"Time out!" Al called to the referee as soon as the shot was good.

As the Red team approached the bench, Ace was already up and pleading with his father to let him go back into the game. For an instant he thought about it, the desire to win temporarily getting the better of him, but the black eye that was welling up on his sons face, the ships doctor advising against it and, not the least, the stern look on Mary's face brought him back to his senses.

"I'm sorry, Ace, but it is out of the question. Now help us develop our strategy to win this game," Al said, as he gave his dejected son the obligatory shot on the arm.

As the rest of the Red team gathered around Al and Ace, it went unnoticed that Bruno met Bertha at the end of the bench and received a zip lock baggy.

"Are you sure this is going to work fast enough? We only have a matter of a few seconds," Bruno asked.

"You'll wish that you had that much time. This is a particularly good, but deadly potent mixture. It is a secret family blend. But are you sure that this is absolutely the only way? I am afraid that we might cause a panic." Bertha was quite serious.

"Yes, with Ace out of the game, I am afraid it is the only way. Now please get my mother, Mrs. Carr and 'Mad' Madeline out of the stands and by that exit door over there. That's the same one that we will be using," Bruno said, once again feeling that calmness that always seemed to come over him when he was putting a plan into action and he felt that he was in control of the situation.

"Of course. And good luck to you and the rest of the team. Tell Louis that we are proud of the way that he has played and that we approve of this," Bertha said, as she went to get Mary and 'Mad' Madeline and locate them to a safer spot.

"Okay guys! Listen up! This is going to be the plan," Bruno said, interrupting the huddle where they were trying to come up with their own plan.

"We have already decided to get the ball to Rosie for a good shot and then crash the boards," Al said.

"Well, Rosie is our best remaining scorer, but I have a little insurance to help make this succeed. Especially since they will be expecting it to go to Rosie," Bruno said, as he looked at Big Louie and handed him the zip lock bag. "Big Louie, your mother told me to tell you that they are proud of the way that you have played today and that it is okay to do this."

"That's nice, Bruno, and he has played well, but don't you think it is a little early for plaudits?" L.T. said.

"Yes, it is. But, believe me, it is important to our winning."

"Are you sure she wants me to do this?" Big Louie asked, as he took the bag, knowing what it was without even looking.

"I'm sure," Bruno said.

"What the hell are you two talking about?" Big Al asked.

"Yes, what is going on? We have a game to win here," L.T. said.

"Trust me, Dad, L.T.. This is the most potent weapon we could have. It is even better than having Ace back in the game. But it can only be used once. And then only at the end of the game," Bruno said.

"I don't understand," Big Al said.

"Neither do I," L.T. added.

"If that is what I think it is, then we should listen to B.A.D.'s plan," Frankie said.

"Okay. If you say so son." L.T. agreed to the delight of his son.

"If that is what I think it is, I'm getting the hell out of here!" Rosie said, as he turned to run, only to be caught by Big Louie and pulled back to the huddle.

"Sorry, Rosie, but we need you as the decoy," Bruno said.

"But, B.A.D., you know how badly this affected me last time," Rosie pleaded.

"Just hold your breath and you will be all right."

"Besides, we will make sure that you get out into the fresh air in enough time," Frankie assured him.

"Well, okay. But my life is in your hands," Rosie said.

"Would you guys mind telling us what the hell you are talking about," Big Al said.

"This is the plan. You should take the ball out of bounds, Dad, and look as if you want to get it to Rosie, who will be moving around between the half court and the foul line. Frankie and I will be looking like we are trying to set picks for Rosie and Big Louie will be down under the basket just outside the three second area," Bruno explained.

"So what is different from our plan?" Big Al asked.

"Yes, that is what we had planned," L.T. added.

"But the difference comes when we fake the ball to Rosie and I set a pick for Frankie, who will cut off of the pick, receive the ball from my Dad and drive to the basket for an uncontested lay up. With Big Louie there to make sure that it is uncontested." B.A.D. said this with extreme confidence in his voice.

"But what makes you think that it will be uncontested. They will probably leave two guys down low with Big Louie and let you and Frankie run free on the outside. Let's face it, they will most likely take their chances that neither of you will take the outside shot," Big Al added.

"You're right that they will leave two guys down low, but that plays right into our hands. They will be at ground zero and be incapacitated almost instantly. That will leave the four of us to cut-off the remaining three of them should any of them find the strength and the desire to try to stop Frankie," B.A.D. said.

"I don't understand how they are going to be incapacitated. And if they are, why isn't Big Louie going to be?" Al asked.

"That's a good question, Al." L.T. added.

"Just trust me. When Big Louie yells out 'ignition' I will set the pick for Rosie and you get the ball to Frankie. Then, Rosie, if you are able, you and I will look to cut off anyone who tries to pick up Frankie," B.A.D. said.

"Aren't you forgetting that I suck as a basketball player? I probably won't even get the ball in the basket without anyone covering me," Frankie said, obviously nervous with so much responsibility riding on his shoulders.

"Don't think that way Frankie. You can do it if you just concentrate and believe in yourself. I believe in you," B.A.D. said in a calm voice.

"Yes, I believe in you, too. And you should believe in yourself, you can do it." L.T. told his son as he gave him a shot in the arm.

"Okay, I'll do it!" Frankie said. He was sky high, nothing could stop him now.

"Good, now there is just one more thing. As soon as Frankie is clearly free towards the basket, Dad, you have to make sure that you get Jenny and, L.T., you have to get Alie and get out that exit over there. Don't worry about us. We have been through this before and I have already taken care of mom and Mrs. Carr," B.A.D. said.

"All right, son, we are in your hands," Al said, as they broke the huddle just as the ref, Bruce Shipley, was coming over to get them started.

The Red team had already taken their positions, with Hans and Brock set up down low, under the basket. Harry, Tom and Butch prepared to challenge the pass in and definitely cover Rosie.

"Okay, Big Louie, it's time," B.A.D. said, as everyone else was taking their positions on the floor.

"Are you sure that this is okay with my mother?" Louie asked, before removing the contents of the bag.

"Yes, I am. Just look over there if you have any doubts," B.A.D. said. He was looking in the direction of their mothers, who had taken a position next to an exit at Bertha's insistence.

As Big Louie looked over, he caught his mother's eye and they locked onto one another for a short but very intense moment. Then his mother nodded her head and blew him a kiss. That was all that Big Louie needed. He would go out and do the family proud. So he reached into the bag and took out a big handful of the family's special cheese blend and put it to his nose so that he could enjoy the pungent odor; it was like a fragrance from the God's to the Cochran family. He then devoured it, and the remaining contents of the bag, before running out to take his position on the court.

If anyone had looked closely, they would have seen a gleam come into his eyes, as if he had just seen the woman of his dreams, and an ecstasy come across his face, as if he had just climaxed with this vision. Then, as his eyes rolled back into his head, he managed to shout out the final battle cry—

"IGNITION! BLAST OFF! HALLELUJAH!" Louie had gotten a little carried away.

The players, as well as the crowd, were temporarily stunned by this sudden outburst coming from the largest person on the floor. But this would be nothing to the shock that they were about to experience. Those who were watching Hans and Brock got a view of the impending cataclysm. Since these two were at ground zero, they were instantaneously engulfed in the stench that emanated from deep within the bowels of Big Louie and immediately surrounded him, and everything within ten feet of him, simultaneously with his war cry. In seconds the entire gym would be penetrated, as the large circulating fans were blowing from directly behind him.

With both Hans and Brock gasping for air and stumbling toward the nearest exit, mumbling something about poison gas warfare, the basket was left unprotected. The Red team quickly recovered from the affects of Big Louie's war cry and swung into action with Bruno setting a hard pick against Harry for Frankie. Then Rosie did his part by fainting in front of Tom Stephens and Frankie cut off of Bruno's pick and headed for the basket. By this time the stench was reaching the others in the gym and Big Al had all he could do to get the ball into Frankie. The plan was working perfectly, as both Frankie and Bruno knew enough to hold their breath—avoiding the nausea and light headed feelings that came from breathing the noxious fumes.

Unfortunately the stink did not seem to affect Butch Murphy as he made his move toward Frankie. In fact, he seemed to be exhilarated by the stench, like a happy little pig in shit, and was closing in on Frankie. A wild look was in his eyes. This could spell disaster; Frankie had enough trouble putting the ball in the basket when he was uncontested. He would have no chance of scoring while being attacked by the wild eyed Butch.

There was nothing anyone could do but watch this scene unfold. No one was close enough to help. No one except Big Louie, that is. And he was more than up to the task as he, too, was energized by the smell, which was like lilacs and roses to him. So he moved with an uncharacteristic quickness; shifting all of his weight forward and slamming full force into Butch Murphy just as he was reaching for Frankie. He hit Murphy with such force that he flew at least ten feet sideways, before hitting the floor and sliding another fifteen feet into the wall. It was a moving pick and a foul for sure, but both of the referees were gasping for breath and could not have blown their whistles if they had wanted to, which they didn't.

So, left all alone, Frankie soared toward the basket and put his shot up off of the backboard and through the net for the win. The crowd roared and then gasped fighting for air. The Captain announced that the Red team had won the trophy and that B.J. DeGregorio won the most valuable player trophy. Then he called for an emergency evacuation and for everyone to return to their cabins, as they seemed to be passing through the same green cloud of stench that they had experienced on the way to Bermuda.

As everyone was scrambling for the exits, Bruno looked to make sure that their mothers were safely out and then he checked that their fathers had successfully helped their sisters out. He also saw that Charlotte and Sally were being escorted safely from the gym by Father Tony. Satisfied that they were all safe, he turned to pick up Rosie and escape with Frankie and Big Louie.

CHAPTER 22

T he all clear had been sounded about a half hour after the evacuation of the gymnasium. Bruno was pleased, he would not have to fight his mother to let him go to his meeting with Charlotte.

"Hi! Have you been waiting long?" Bruno asked as he approached Charlotte, who was leaning on the rail and looking out over the ocean.

"No, just a few minutes. It is so very pleasant out here that I didn't mind," Charlotte answered.

"I brought you these," Bruno said, handing her a small bouquet of artificial daises.

"Well, thank you, Bruno," Charlotte said pleasantly, but with a somewhat quizzical look on her face.

"I know they don't look like much, but I wanted to give you these because daisies are for friends. Unfortunately, there were no real ones available in Bermuda or in the ship's flower shop so I had to settle for artificial ones," Bruno said, responding to her look. He left out the fact that, even to get these, he had had to 'borrow' them. But it was an ugly hat anyway and he felt that Mad Madeline would be better off without it. He certainly knew that Happy Harold would be pleased.

"The thought is wonderful, Bruno. But are we friends? I know that we have made love together, but I don't know if that makes us friends," Charlotte said candidly. She was not going to play games and lead him on, the hell with Harry.

"No, I don't think that that makes us friends and, in fact, that may even get in the way of our being friends. If that happens, then I will truly be sorry that we did it. Because, as unbelievable as it was, I would rather be your friend," Bruno said.

"That's what I don't understand. I mean I understand perfectly well when men want to be 'friendly' and get to know me. They are looking for sex. But I don't understand you. I mean you could have accepted my invitation to my cabin and expected to make love to me again," Charlotte said.

"Yes, I know. But the last time I felt like you were looking for something more, if only for an instant, and I didn't give it to you because I was possessed by my desire. I would like to get to know you better," Bruno said.

"I don't really understand, but I did feel something a little different, something that I had never felt before, and I would like to be your friend, too." By now she was more than just a little confused. She had never had a male friend before; now she had two in one day. Maybe Terrence was right, maybe there was something unusual about this boat.

"Good, then let's take a little walk. I know a place were we can sit in some lounge chairs and view the ocean, but still have a little privacy." He led her to a semi-private spot on the top deck that had just two deck chairs and a clear view of the ocean.

"Oh, this is a beautiful spot; without the normal flow of people. How did you find it?" Charlotte asked.

"I like to explore and know my environment." He offered her a deck chair and took the other one for himself.

At first, their conversation was the typical surface small talk, but, as they continued, Charlotte became more and more comfortable; it helped that Bruno was a good listener. Eventually, with his encouragement, she began to tell him about her background and her early life. It was not a pleasant story. First, there was her father, who all but ignored her no matter how hard she tried to get his attention and affection. This neglect only worsened with her parents divorce and was, eventually, replaced by an abusive and overly affectionate step-father. She had run away from home at the age of sixteen and had been on her own ever since.

"Didn't you miss your family?"

"There wasn't much to miss."

"Didn't you miss their love.?"

"I don't think that they loved me." Charlotte said. "I know my father didn't. My mother was too worried about losing my stepfather, and he wanted to love me in the wrong way."

"That's impossible." Bruno said. "They're your parents. They have to love you."

"My dear Bruno, you are so sweet and so lucky. You don't have any idea that parents don't always love their children and children don't always love their parents."

"No. I don't understand." Bruno said. "How can you say that your father didn't love you."?

"He never showed it. He never said it."

"He never told you that he loved you?" Bruno was amazed. "He never told you that you were his special little girl?"

"No."

"Never? Not even once."

"No. Never. Not even once."

"I'm sorry for you."

"I know. Thank you. But I don't think you really understand."

"Maybe not. But I understand more than you think."

"How could you?"

"Because I've watched my father. Not only with my mother, but also with my sister. He shows his love for her all the time and often tells her that she is special."

"She is very lucky."

"I never really appreciated it until now. But, yes, I think that it is very important to her."

This went on for more than two hours. Charlotte had never before spoken of these things to anyone and would have stopped long before this, if not for Bruno's encouragement. As she spoke, they held hands until there was nothing more to say and then they just sat quietly, mesmerized by the beauty of the ocean.

The only break in their silence came when Bruno asked her if she cared to join him and his family for the evening's celebration. She had indicated that she wasn't sure if she would be able to, but she would if she could.

They continued to sit close to each other expressing their feelings for one other through their clasped hands, without saying another word. As they sat this way, totally absorbed by the electricity between them and the immense ocean around them, they observed what looked like, from a distance, a small bird coming straight out of the sun directly toward them. As this figure came closer they realized that it was not a bird but was, instead, a large butterfly. It was the largest butterfly that either of them had ever seen and it landed on the railing directly in front of them. It amazed both of them that a butterfly could contend with the strong sea breezes and fly this far from land to arrive here on the ship. It was the most beautiful butterfly that they had ever seen, a combination of golden yellow and burnt orange, with touches of cobalt blue, and crimson red. The butterfly appeared to look directly at Bruno and then flapped its wings for a few seconds. When it received no response from Bruno, it flapped its' wings more vigorously and for twice as long.

This was initially lost on Bruno, until he started to feel a pounding in his chest. A pounding that stopped as soon as the wings of the giant butterfly stopped flapping. At this point Bruno was somewhat surprised and didn't know what to make of it. Then the butterfly flapped its wings vigorously again and, this time, Bruno could feel the vibration deep within his chest. It was a vibration that did not hurt or give him any discomfort. Indeed, it brought a soothing calmness that overwhelmed his entire body. It was as if he was feeling an all possessing warmth that was generated from somewhere deeper within him than he thought humanly possible. A warmth that gave him the sensation that his entire body was aglow with an ethereal light that originated from another plane. A plane that was not occupied by those of us who are human. He closed his eyes to see if the vibration would go away, but it would not.

At this point, he had to fight the panic that was about to overwhelm him and force him to flee from this illusory experience. Then, overcoming his temporary fright, he allowed himself to relax and remember the words that his father had said to him—'son if you concentrate very, very hard, I believe that you have the rare ability to hear the wings of the butterfly'.

Comforted by these words, he opened his eyes and stared directly at the butterfly, which seemed to be staring back at him. The butterfly now stopped flapping its' wings and the vibration within him immediately stopped. Then the butterfly flapped its' wings twice and stopped. This time Bruno experienced something more than just the vibration; he thought that he did hear something. But he was confused for he did not seem hear it with his ears. So he concentrated even harder, as the butterfly again flapped its' wings a half dozen times and then Bruno knew that he heard it this time, but he was certain that he did not hear it with his ears. Indeed not, but he did 'hear it' deep within himself and then he knew that he had 'heard' it with his soul. He could never explain how he knew this. He just knew it.

This knowledge gave him a feeling of inner peace that he could never have imagined. He looked into the eyes of the butterfly and smiled. He felt as if he could also see the butterfly smile, as it flapped its wings twice more before it lifted off and flew directly into the sun.

Both of them watched in wonder, as the butterfly was able to fly straight towards the sun, unaffected by the strong breeze that was blowing. It seemed to grow larger, as it got further away, until they could no longer look into the sun. They both felt as if they had experienced some magical moment as they bathed in the after glow of what had just taken place, only Bruno realizing the full extent of it, and reflected on the wonderful afternoon they had spent together.

For his part, Bruno had learned that, not only does every child need a loving mother and father, but little girls need the love and attention of their fathers in a special way. They need to be made to feel special by their fathers. At a young age they need to be shown love and tenderness and to be taught that they have special value—simply because they are female. And they should not only hope, but should expect, to find this same treatment as an adult. All too often they are still searching for this love and tenderness, a sense of self and acceptance that they can never find.

For her part, Charlotte would never forget Bruno, for he was not only her first real male friend, but he taught her something that she had never experienced before. Indeed, she had not even imagined that such feelings, such a relationship, could have existed between a man and a woman. For that day, they had both discovered the wonderful gift of giving love, and of receiving love, without the need for making love.

CHAPTER 23

"Do I really have to wear this crap?" B.J. complained, as his mother was fixing his bow tie.

"Watch your mouth young man. I don't care if you are the most valuable player you'll still act like a little gentleman, especially tonight in front of the Captain and the entire ship. Besides, you look so handsome. Just like a little Ken doll," Mary said, giving him a big hug and kiss on the cheek, much to his dismay.

"Ya Ace, just think, this crap may even help you find Barbie," Bruno said automatically, unable to control himself.

"Never mind you and watch your mouth, too. I can come over there and give you a big kiss and, besides, you look like a big Ken doll, too. Come over here so that I can give you a big hug," Mary said with a laugh.

"Come on, Ma, that's enough of this crap."

"Al, will you talk to your boys?" Mary instructed.

"Okay boys, let's cut the crap and finish getting dressed." Al dutifully instructed them, as he wrestled with his own bow tie.

"Gee, thanks a lot Al, that was a big help."

"No problem hon., anytime," Al responded, as he gave up in his effort to tie his bow tie and mumbled something about who the hell wanted to wear this crap anyway.

"Honestly, Al, sometimes I think that I have three boys to take care of," Mary said as she came to his aid and took over the task of tying his bow tie.

"Ya, Dad, watch your language," Bruno added with a chuckle.

"Ya, Dad." B.J. had to put his two cents in.

"Never mind you two. Watch out or I'll take my belt off."

Of course, this really got a good laugh out of the whole family since none of them could ever remember receiving the slightest bit of physical force from him, never mind using a belt. In fact, the one time that he had actually taken his belt off to see their reaction his pants fell down.

"Watch out, Dad, or your pants will fall down and, frankly, that is not a site that I would care to see again. Once is more than enough." Jennifer decided that it was her turn to speak up.

"Ya, Dad, please spare us," Bruno chuckled.

"Watch out you guys I have suspenders on now to hold them up."

"Ya, and that means you don't have a belt to take off." B.J. was not to be left out.

"Okay kids! That's enough now or we will never be ready in time," Mary said sternly enough to get everyone moving.

Eventually everyone got themselves together and they made their way to the main dining room, where the evening's festivities would begin by meeting the Captain and his wife. As they waited in line to be greeted by the Captain, B.J. was very fidgety and had to be reminded twice by Mary that he was to act like a little gentleman tonight. There was to be no burping at dinner and, of course, farting was absolutely out of the question.

"Ma!" B.J. said complaining about being accused of farting in public.

"Well, you do have a propensity toward it," Mary said, again letting her sense of humor out.

"A what?" B.J. said.

"It means that you fart a lot." Bruno was just trying to be helpful.

"I do not!" B.J. was getting indignant.

"No? Well if you don't watch out you'll end up like Big Louie."

"Like you never fart, jerk," B.J. said. Admittedly a weak response, but it was the best he could come up with.

"Come on guys, cut the crap," Al said, stepping in between them.

"I give up," Mary said.

After another twenty minutes of waiting in line, they finally got their turn to meet the Captain and exchange pleasantries. A process that took less than two minutes.

"You mean that's it! That's what we were afraid of being late for!" B.J. was incredulous as they moved on.

"I am afraid that you are going to learn that older adults have a lot of ways of wasting their time and punishing themselves, apparently for no good reason at all," Bruno said.

"Hush you two or someone will hear you," Mary said.

"So what? If it is true!" B.J. said very innocently.

"Okay, cool it guys!" Al spoke up and meant it this time.

The DeGregorio's then proceeded to their normal table to take the seats they had been occupying for the better part of a week. They didn't know if they would be sitting with the Carr's or not; L. Terrence had been trying all week to get his seat changed for this special event. He desperately wanted to sit with the Captain and the Van Goff sisters, a place of honor that he felt he deserved so very much. So, when they arrived at the table, they were quite surprised to see the Carr's already there.

"Hello, Margaret, Terrence. How are you?" Mary and Al said. Well, Mary actually said it and Al just grunted it.

"I'm doing fine, but I don't know about Larry Bird here." Margaret joked as she nodded at L. Terrence.

"Very funny, Maggie, but I am doing fine, too, at least mentally if not physically," L. Terrence said.

"I know what you mean L.T., my butt is dragging, too," Al said. Getting a dirty look from Mary.

"If I stood up mine would be dragging on the ground," L.T. said, as Mary and Margaret looked at each other and just shook their heads.

"Well, it was worth it. The kids really enjoyed themselves and I think that we will enjoy ourselves better this evening, too," Al said.

"I'm sure of it," L.T. added.

"I will have to agree with that, also," Margaret said.

"Yes, I guess that I do, too. Even though I thought that I was going to lose my youngest son to those brutes," Mary said.

"How is young Master Ace?" Margaret asked.

"I have to admit that he is fine. A little bruised but the MVP award, and the praise that he received from his father and brother, more than compensated for it."

"Well, he certainly deserved it," L.T. said.

The young adults were busy congratulating themselves on the day's victory and exchanging high fives all around. Then everyone took their seats in the same configuration as they had all week. When Father Tony and Sally arrived, they graciously added their congratulations. Noticeably absent at this point was Harry Holt.

Just then the ship's first mate came over to their table.

"Hello. Congratulations on a fine victory today. Unfortunately I didn't get a chance to congratulate you earlier because of that odor. A very strange experience indeed. In twenty years at sea I have never encountered anything like it. How is everyone this evening?" Bruce Shipley said.

"Thank you. We are fine," Mary said and Al grunted his concurrence.

"Yes, we are fine, Mr. Shipley. And how are you?" Margaret said.

"I'm fine thank you."

"What can we do for you this evening?" L. Terrence said.

"You had asked earlier if you and your family could sit at the Captain's table with the Van Goff sisters, since you knew them well," Bruce Shipley said.

"Yes that's true, I did."

"I am happy to tell you that we have an opening at a table next to the Captain's," Bruce Shipley proudly announced.

"Thank you very much for your effort, but I think that we will remain here."

Bruce Shipley was somewhat perturbed, "But you have been after us all week to accommodate you."

"Yes, I know, and I am sorry for putting you through the trouble, but I believe that we would enjoy ourselves more if we remained here. And I am sure that you have other people that were trying to get closer to the Captain's table. You can give it to them," L. Terrence said.

"Please don't stay on our account," Mary said.

"Yes, please don't. We certainly would understand and not be offended," Al added.

"Thank you for your thoughtfulness, but I really do believe that we will enjoy ourselves more here. That is, if it is all right with you Margaret?" L. Terrence said.

"I couldn't be more pleased. I know that I will be happier here than up there, but I am surprised that you don't want to go. Although I am not unhappy about it, believe me," Margaret said.

"Well, Mr. Shipley, I guess that settles it. Thank you for your efforts. I will come by later to give my best to the sisters," L. Terrence said.

"Very well, sir. Ladies. Gentlemen. Enjoy your evening." Bruce Shipley said, taking his leave.

The atmosphere around the table was decidedly pleasant; everyone was very friendly and in a partying mood.

❧   ❧   ❧

"It is time to start to put our plan into operation," Harry said.

"But, boss, I don't understand why we are breaking into the safe now, when the necklaces are out being worn by the sisters at the party," Butch said.

"I hate to admit that I agree with him. Why are we breaking in now and not early in the morning, after the jewels had been returned?" Tom said.

"I told you two that I would reveal the plan to you on a need to know basis and, right now, the only thing that you need to know is that we are going to break into the safe now. The safe is not guarded because the main jewels are out. There are currently only some smaller jewels in the safe and we need some of these to plant on Mr. L. Terrence Carr. Are either of you questioning me on this?" Harry said, the hint of a threat in his voice.

"No, boss, not me. I was just wondering, that's all," Butch said.

"Ya, me too," Tom added.

"Do we have to plant these on Terrence? I mean, is it worth the risk?" Charlotte said.

"Why, Charlotte, do I detect a little softness in your voice for the good jerk, Mr. L. Terrence Carr?" Harry said, sending cold chills up her spine.

"No, of course not. It is just that I wonder if it is worth the risk. That's all," Charlotte said, hoping that she was convincing.

"Oh, I see. Well don't you worry your pretty little head about it. I don't think that Murphy or Stephens are worried about it. You just get that pretty little ass of yours up on deck so that you will not be missed. Then I will follow you in a few minutes. If either one of us are not visible when this takes place we may become suspects and that would upset my plans," Harry said.

"Whatever you say, Harry, your the boss."

"You've got that right sweetheart and you had better not forget it, either," Harry said strongly.

"Of course not, Harry." Charlotte gave him a little kiss on the cheek and left.

"Okay, you guys know what has to be done. Get to it while I go to the party and make myself visible. Believe me, after today's humiliation, I would rather be doing what you are doing than what I have to do."

"Don't worry, boss, we know what to do," Butch said.

"Good, you had better." Harry then left for the ballroom.

"Let's get our stuff together; we don't have very much time," Butch said. Then he started to gather the things that they would need to accomplish their mission.

"I still don't understand why we are breaking in now," Tom said.

"Shit, you heard me, I don't know either. But I do know that we had better get our friggin asses in gear or we will have to answer to Harry for it. And, believe me, we don't want to have to do that." Butch said as he went about gathering his things.

"Hell, I don't really give a shit, as long as I get what I have coming to me out of this," Tom said.

"I don't know exactly what you are expecting, but I do know what we will get if we don't get our asses in gear and get our task accomplished as planned." Butch said.

"Don't worry about it, I'm ready. Let's go!" Tom said as he opened the door and left.

❧   ❧   ❧

"Hello, Charlotte. I'm happy that you could join us tonight." Bruno rose to greet her. "You look beautiful."

"Thank you, Bruno," Charlotte said nervously.

"Mom and Dad, this is Charlotte. Charlotte, this is my mother and father."

"Hello, Charlotte."

"Hello, Mr. and Mrs. DeGregorio."

"And this is Mr. and Mrs. Carr," Bruno said.

"Hello, Charlotte, how are you?" L. Terrence said.

"How are you my dear?" Margaret said warmly.

"I'm fine, thank you Mrs. Carr." Charlotte was more than a little shocked at the very friendly reception that she received from everyone; particularly from L. Terrence and his wife, Margaret.

"Please, my name is Margaret."

"It is nice to meet you, Margaret."

"Please join us, we have enough room. We've just finished dinner. Have you eaten yet?" Bruno said.

"Yes, please do," Mary said as she made room for her.

So Charlotte nervously took a seat next to Bruno. She still could not believe the wonderfully friendly treatment that she was receiving.

Then it was Harry Holt's turn to make his appearance and he did so with the usual bravado and swagger in his step.

"How is everyone this evening?"

"We're fine, Harry, and how are you?" Al was the first to speak.

"I'm fine, too. Thank you. Congratulations on your victory today. Of course it was fortunate for you that the ship encountered that stink cloud or the results of the game certainly would be different."

"Perhaps, Harry. But I'm sure that no one can accuse you of being a good loser," L. Terrence said.

"That's because I'm not a loser," Harry said defensively.

"No, of course not," L. Terrence said.

"If you will excuse me, I think that I will go and pay my respects to the Captain and the lovely sisters," Harry said.

"Yes, we certainly understand, and we would be happy to excuse you," Al said, pleased to be rid of him.

As he left, he gave Charlotte a knowing look that told her that the plan was underway. The thought of this gave her an ache in the pit of her stomach. When the plan had first been developed she had no problem with it. It was just another job and L. Terrence Carr had used her and deserved what he was going to get, but the events of the day had changed everything. He had changed miraculously in the way he treated his family, and her, and she could no longer go through with it.

"May I speak with you alone for a moment, Bruno?" Charlotte asked.

"Yes, of course. Let's go out on deck," Bruno answered as he led the way out. They easily found a place with privacy as everyone was inside. "What is it?"

"I don't really know how to tell you this," Charlotte said, obviously very nervous.

"Don't worry. You can tell me."

"I don't know where to begin."

He calmly answered, "Just start anywhere and I'll ask questions as needed."

"I've been having an affair with L. Terrence Carr," Charlotte managed to blurt out.

"Yes, I know," Bruno responded softly.

"You know?" Charlotte was surprised.

"Yes, I do."

"How long have you known?"

"Since the beginning of the cruise, when I met his son Frankie."

"So Francis has known all this time. I am sorry for that. Now I understand how you two always seemed to show up when we tried to get together."

"Yes, you are right, it wasn't just coincidence."

"And that is why you wanted to get to know me."

"Yes, it is why I wanted to get to know you, but it is not why I wanted to be your friend."

"I am glad on both counts. That we got a chance to become friends and that you interfered with Terrence and I getting together. It gave him the chance to spend some time with his wife and family and rediscover the love that he had for them."

"What are you telling me?"

"I'm telling you, that, it is all over between Terrence and me, and it was his decision. Believe me, it was a surprise to me when he told me it was over, but it was an even bigger surprise by how nice he was about it." Then she went on to tell Bruno everything. About how she came to be involved with him, her involvement with Harry Holt, and what was happening as they spoke.

❦   ❦   ❦

"I still don't understand why we are breaking into this fucking safe now, when we know the necklaces we want, and any other valuable jewelry, are out being worn at the banquet," Murphy complained.

"Quiet for Christ sakes or someone will hear you," Tom Stephens replied. "I don't understand, either, but the boss has told us that this is his plan and so we have to do it. You have to admit that it is a lot easier than we had expected."

"That's true, they no longer have the guards that have been here night and day. And, for us anyway, the alarms are the easy part, it is the guards that can get messy," Murphy acknowledged.

"I assume that they took the guards away to work the banquet and protect the necklaces while they are out of the safe. But let's cut the chatter and get this over with before the banquet is over and the guards come back," Tom said.

"Ya sure, let's do it."

Then they proceeded to easily break into the purser's office where the safe was kept. It was an easy task, as they had been video taping the activities in the room for the past several days. This was accomplished by the miniature video cameras and audio sensing devices that recorded everything that happened in the two rooms. This included the recording of all of the security devices, the combination to the doors of both rooms and the safe, but most of all the location and combination of the hidden panel that controlled all of the movement and heat sensory equipment.

It was an impressive list of equipment and took a while to install. But, this too, was relatively easy as it was done at the very beginning of the cruise, while the ship was docked and in between unloading one group of passengers and preparing the ship to receive the next group. During this time, everyone, including the Captain, was totally consumed with cleaning and re-stocking the ship. These rooms were unimportant, as quests were not allowed in here, and there was nothing in the safe to protect. It was an easy task to dress as two of the many service people, who came on board for the four hour window that existed, and sneak in and plant the devices. Then all that remained was to turn on the transmitter located in Harry Holt's cabin and record everything on tape.

"I also don't understand why we are leaving the cameras and audio equipment behind. We never have left them before," Murphy said.

"Again, I don't know, but I am sure that Harry has a good reason. Now let's get this stuff and get out of here before someone comes back," Tom said, having a difficult time controlling himself when dealing with Butch's stupidity.

It took them no time at all to gain entrance to the inner office, open the safe and remove the small amount of jewelry that remained. Jewelry that had not been good enough to be worn to the celebration. Having done this they left, leaving the safe and inner office door open. Harry wanted the theft of the jewels to be discovered before the celebration was over, and he knew that the security was checked at eleven each night.

The two of them then quickly, but carefully, made their way to the Carr's cabin, where gaining access was a simple task. They then hid the jewels in one of the empty suitcases and left.

CHAPTER 24

"I can't believe that an actual jewel theft is going to take place so close to me and that my friend's father is going to be implicated," Bruno said.

"Believe me, it is going to happen. Unfortunately, I know only too well," Charlotte answered.

"You have taken a big risk telling me all of this."

"I know, but I just can't go through with it. Not after meeting you with the remarkable change in Terrace. I'm certainly no angel, but before meeting Harry I had never done anything that was seriously illegal."

"I'm sure that your cooperation, and Mr. Carr's influence, will go a long way towards your defense. But first we have to stop this theft."

"I don't think we can just go and tell someone now. We have no way to prove what I have said. It would be my word against Harry's and, I am afraid, we would lose that argument."

"I suppose you are right. I know someone who can advise us on what to do, but first we have to remove the jewels from Mr. Carr's cabin, before they spring the trap on him. You had better get back to the table. We don't want Harry to get suspicious. I have to get Frankie to help me."

So they both went back into the dining room, as the floorshow was about to begin. While Charlotte took a seat near Mary, Bruno grabbed Frankie and told their families that they would be back shortly.

"Where are you going Bruno?" Mary asked.

"We are going below for just a few minutes. We will be right back," Bruno responded.

"I want you to be right back, you promised to spend this last evening with the family."

"Yes, Mom."

"Al! Al! Earth to Al!" Mary said, having to raise her voice to awaken Al from his deep thought. "Are you with us Al?"

"Ah, excuse me, but I was just reflecting on the trip. What is it?" Al said.

"Tell Bruno to make sure that he and Frankie come back shortly."

"Bruno, come back shortly."

"Sure, Dad," Bruno said, as he and Frankie quickly left.

"Thanks a lot Al," Mary said sarcastically.

"No problem," Al replied. "So how are you enjoying that beer, Ace?"

As Bruno led Frankie towards his parents cabin, he quickly related what Charlotte had told him.

"So what are we going to do? We can't let my Dad get into this kind of trouble."

"Of course we can't. What we are going to do is to go to your parent's cabin, find the jewels that they hid and get them out of there."

"Then what are we going to do with them?"

"Then we are going to plant them in Harry Holt's cabin."

"I have a key to my parents cabin, but how are we going to get into Holt's cabin?"

"No problem, I got a key from Charlotte," Bruno said as they reached the Carr's cabin and Frankie unlocked the door and let them in.

"I wonder where they hid them?" Frankie said.

"I don't know, but you look under the beds and the mattresses and I will look in the closet."

It took them about ten minutes, but they finally found them in the luggage.

"Look at this Frankie," Bruno said, as he removed the small bundle of jewels to show to him.

"It doesn't look like much."

"It's enough to get your father into a lot of trouble."

"Right! Let's get them the hell out of here."

So they took the jewels and quickly made their way to Harry Holt's cabin. As they approached it, they looked carefully about and continued to walk past it in order to make sure that there was no one in the area. When they had satisfied themselves that it was all clear, Bruno opened the door while Frankie kept watch. Having gained access to the room they were very anxious to hide the jewels and get out of there.

"I would hate to get caught in here by Holt or his henchmen," Frankie said.

"Ya, I know what you mean."

"Where the hell should we hide them?"

"Well, if the suitcase was a good place for them, it should be a good place for us."

So they located the luggage, also in the closet, put the jewels inside and prepared to leave.

"Be careful to only open the door a small way, so that we can check the corridor, before we step out into it," Bruno warned.

"I'll be careful," Frankie said, as he slowly opened the door just a hair.

He looked up and down the corridor and didn't see anyone, so he opened the door all the way and they both quickly went out into the corridor. Once they were clear of the room they felt a great relief and congratulated each other on their success.

"Boy am I glad that's over with."

"I have to admit that I am, too."

"Thanks a lot, Bruno. This has helped my father a lot and I couldn't have done it without you."

"Don't give it another thought, Frankie, I'm glad that I could help."

They were both quite pleased with themselves and a great deal more relaxed, as they reached the end of the corridor to take the stairs back up to the main deck and the celebration. Unfortunately, as they rounded the corner, their joy was turned to instant panic: they came face to face with Butch Murphy and Tom Stephens.

"Oh shit!!!" Bruno and Frankie exclaimed.

"It's you! You little bastards!" Murphy shouted.

"Whoa! Move it, Frankie!" Bruno ordered as he grabbed his arm and pulled him in the opposite direction.

"You fucking little assholes are dead meat!" Murphy shouted, as he took off after them.

"No, Murphy! Let them go! Harry will be bullshit!" Tom demanded, as he took off after Murphy.

"I am going to kill these little bastards and you'd better not get in my way or I'll kill you, too!" Murphy yelled, his eyes wild, as he continued to chase Bruno and Frankie.

The two of them ran like there lives depended on it, which they did. Unfortunately their superior speed was negated by the elderly couple that was making their way down the corridor. Their presence forced the two of them to slow down to go around them; they didn't want to hurt them. Fortunately, for the couple, they were able to get out of the way before Murphy came through. He could have cared less if he hurt them or not.

"Frankie, we are going to have to split up if we are to have any chance at all. You take the secret staircase and go for help," Bruno managed to spit out, as they continued to run down the corridor.

"No, you take it B.A.D. and get the help."

"Don't give me any shit, Frankie, this asshole wants me and is not going to let me get away. You go for the stairs and I will lead them away. Now go for it!" Bruno ordered.

So Frankie broke to the right and headed for the secret staircase, while Bruno broke to the left. It came as no surprise that Murphy followed Bruno to the left and told Tom to go after Frankie.

"I am going to kick your ass, you little bastard," Murphy screamed, as he followed after Bruno.

The chase was intense, as Bruno made his way down the stairs and deeper into the bowels of the ship. This wasn't the direction he would have chosen, but there was no other way, if he was going to give Frankie a chance to get away. He could hear Murphy close behind him, so close that he could almost feel his hot breath on the back of his neck. But he did not dare turn around to see just how close; he was afraid that would slow him down just enough for Murphy to catch him. He hoped that he could out run him because he was younger and in better shape, but the desire for revenge within Butch Murphy would not let him quit until he had captured his prey.

In the meantime, Frankie was opening up the distance between him and Tom Stephens and was almost at the secret staircase. By the time that he reached the staircase he had left his pursuer far behind, almost as if he had not really wanted to catch him. This allowed Frankie to quickly use the secret stairs, race through the kitchen, and begin his ascent up the main stairs towards the ballroom.

Since the boys had taken much longer than they had agreed, Mary was getting upset and suggesting that Al go look for them.

"They have been gone for almost forty-five minutes and they promised that they would only be gone for fifteen or twenty minutes."

"You know how kids can be, they probably met some of their friends and lost track of time."

"I want them here with us for the last night of the cruise."

"All right, I'll go look for them," Al said, resigned to the fact that he really had no choice.

So Al left the ballroom and began to descend the main stairs heading for their cabin first, but, before he was halfway down, he ran into Frankie, who was breathing very heavily.

"Mr. DeGregorio, thank God you're here!" Frankie managed to blurt out between breaths.

"Easy Frankie, what's the matter? Why are you out of breath? Where is Bruno?"

"They are after Bruno. We have to help him."

"Who is after him? Where are they?"

"When I last saw him he was heading down the back stairs. Who it is, is a long story that we don't have time for now, but they are two of the guys that played against us in the game today and they are dangerous."

"Okay, you go get your father and have him get the Captain for help, while I go and look for Bruno," Al commanded.

"Yes sir," Frankie said, then raced up the stairs.

Al felt a deep sense of panic, as he quickly made his way downward and back towards the stern of the ship. As he went, he thought that the run in that Bruno had with the guy called Murphy was too intense to have resulted from just a basketball game, Bruno would not have become that upset over a game. He had to find him before this Murphy did.

Unfortunately, Al would not get there before Murphy could catch Bruno. The narrowness and lack of any lengthy halls worked to Bruno's disadvantage, as he was unable to use his superior speed. The final obstacle was a steward carrying a tray; Bruno had to slow down to keep from knocking him over. His pursuer had no such compunction as he bulled him over and tackled Bruno, dragging him to the ground. He hit Bruno once, dazing him, and raised his fist to hit him again. But, before he could land the second blow, his arm was grabbed by the steward who had regained his senses.

Butch was forced to temporarily abandon Bruno and concentrate on the steward. This was a break for Bruno, but a disaster for the steward, as Butch was all over him with a barrage of punches that had him pinned against the wall and unconscious. The only reason the steward hadn't fallen was because he was being held up by the blows that Butch was landing to his midsection.

When Bruno came out of his daze, and saw what was happening, he got to his feet as quickly as he could and grabbed Butch, pulling him off of the steward and spinning him around. Butch instinctively lashed out with his right hand, but missed as Bruno ducked under it and counter attacked with a hard punch to the stomach, followed by a blow to Butch's face—rocking him back on his heels. However, Butch was the survivor of many fights, some of them very vicious, and he was capable of absorbing a great amount of punishment, more than Bruno was capable of delivering. With almost no hesitation, Butch was lunging toward him. It was only Bruno's superior agility that allowed him to avoid being crushed by his more powerful assailant. As he dodged the oncoming Murphy, he was able to land a karate chop to the back of his neck. While this was a sharp blow, and obviously caused him some pain, it didn't slow him down. He wheeled around and lunged at Bruno once again. Again, Bruno was able to avoid him and this time landed a kick to the back of Butch's knee, which succeeded in bringing him to the floor.

Then, almost before he even hit the floor and more quickly than Bruno thought possible, Butch grabbed a plate that had been dropped by the steward and, with a flick of his wrist, sent it hurtling towards Bruno's head. This time his agility only allowed him to avoid a direct hit, but did not save him from receiving a glancing blow that was sufficient to daze him and make him drop to one knee. Then, like a wild animal smelling a chance for the kill, Butch was on his feet and delivered a crushing blow to Bruno's head before he had any chance of recovering from his dazed state. The severe blow sent him crashing to the floor. He lay there limp and totally vulnerable to his would be killer.

"Now I'm going to kill you, but I'm going to make you suffer first, you little bastard," Murphy shouted. In a blind rage he brought his leg back and prepared to deliver a vicious kick to Bruno's ribs. As he began to swing his foot forward, he was only vaguely aware of the presence of someone else. The shout that rang in his ears caused him to hesitate and turn towards the noise.

"NO!!!" Al shouted, as he roared down the hall, lowering his head, and smashing his shoulder, with the full force of all of his considerable weight, into the chest of his son's attacker. To say that Al was enraged was to say that Attila the Hun was a pacifist. As the blow to his chest knocked the wind out of him, Al continued driving his legs forward, picking him up and slamming him into the far wall—head first.

As Murphy slumped to the floor, with blood gushing from his noise and a gash on the back of his head, he appeared to be unconscious. If Al had been like his son's attacker, he would have made sure that he had finished him off, but he was nothing like this man, who lay before him, indeed not, he was a father and the image of his son laying there bleeding tormented him. So he made a fatal mistake and turned to see to his son, who was coming out of his daze.

"Are you all right son?"

"Yeah, I think so. Thanks to you or I would be dead," Bruno managed to say, as he was helped to his feet by his father.

"You are dead kid!" Murphy growled as he lay there bleeding and pointing his gun at them; preparing to shoot.

For an instant, the two of them froze and then Al made a move to step in front of his son, but it was too late as they heard the shot ring out. Then Al looked in horror at his son, expecting to see him mortally wounded, he knew the shot had not hit him, although he expected a second one meant for him. However, there was no wound on Bruno and there was no second shot. As Al turned to see what had happened, he saw their attacker holding his right shoulder and writhing in pain with his gun lying by his side. Then he looked down the hall and saw Tom Stephens standing there holding a gun. He didn't know why he had shot Murphy. Had it been an accident, had he intended to shoot them and missed? Would he shoot them now? This thought caused him to move to get the gun that lay beside Murphy.

"Don't do it, Al! I'm not going to hurt you. If I were going to do that I would have let him shoot you both," Tom said. He rapidly approached them and kicked the gun away from both Murphy and Al.

"Hold it right there." Came a shout from the other end of the corridor. It was 'The Pol' and he was aiming a gun at Tom Stephens' head.

"Go easy, Polaski, we are both on the same side."

"I don't know what side you are on, but you had better put that gun down. Now! Then I'll listen to what you have to say," 'the Pol' demanded.

"I'm telling you, Polaski, I know that you are a cop and we are on the same side," Stephens said.

"Since you know who I am, I think it would be best if you put down your weapon until we can determine just who you are." 'The Pol' was adamant.

"All right damn it, but be careful there may be others around." Tom handed his gun to Al.

Then Al went and picked up Murphy's gun, so that he could be sure there would not be any more close calls.

Bruno steadied himself against the wall, still a bit woozy "He did save our lives Pol."

"Maybe so, but it is better to be safe until we get some confirmation of exactly who he is," Pol said, then approached Tom. "By the way, who the hell are you anyway?"

"I guess it doesn't matter anymore now, my cover is blown to hell now anyway."

Before Tom could tell them who he was the corridor began to fill with people. The Captain led the way, followed by two of the ship's security officers. Close behind them came Frankie and his father.

"What is going on here?" The Captain demanded.

"We have it under control now, Captain. It appears that the jerk lying over there, bleeding, and moaning like a little wimp, tried to kill young master Bruno and his father. This gentleman here, Tom Stephens, apparently saved their lives, which we are all very grateful for, but I don't know what kind of relationship he had with the jerk," Pol said.

"Is that what happened, Mr. DeGregorio?" The Captain asked.

"Yes, it is."

"Let's get this guy to the infirmary, where the doctor can look after him. Then we can talk to Mr. Stephens and find out what is going on," the Captain ordered.

The security officers followed the Captain's orders and helped Murphy up and led him away to the infirmary. They were followed by Tom Stephens under the watchful eye, and gun, of 'The Pol', who was followed by Bruno, Al, Frankie, and Terrence.

Once they were in the infirmary, the doctor began to work on Murphy. Captain Swenson left two armed guards to watch him and led the others into the next room to determine what had happened.

"Who is going to tell me what the hell this is all about?" The Captain demanded.

"That jerk in there was beating up on my son, and yelling that he was going to kill him, when I came into the corridor and was able to stop him. Then he pulled out a gun and would have shot us if Stephens hadn't come by and shot him first."

"Is that true Mr. Stephens?" The Captain asked.

"Yes, it is. I came around the corner and saw Murphy about to shoot Mr. DeGregorio and, since I couldn't let that happen, I was forced to shoot him," Tom Stephens responded.

"Then you know him?" the Captain asked.

"Yes, I do," Tom said.

"How do you know him? Why are you carrying a gun? And why was he beating this young man and why was he about to shoot him and his father?" Captain Swenson impatiently asked his questions in rapid-fire succession, the last one directed at Bruno and Al, as much as at Tom Stephens.

Tom looked angrily at 'Pol' and then at Bruno. "Well, I suppose I will have to tell you now that these meddling idiots have screwed everything up."

"Yes, I suppose that you will and I would appreciate it if you would be concise, but complete. I strongly suggest that you don't leave out any important details. I do not take kindly to people carrying guns on my ship, to say nothing of them firing them at other passengers." The Captain was a very straight forward man who thought that he was in complete control of his ship and did not like it one bit when he wasn't.

"My real name is Tom Jarrad and I am a Detective Lieutenant with Interpol. For those of you who are not familiar with Interpol, it is an international police organization and I have been undercover in an attempt to catch a ring of international jewel thieves," Tom said, obviously very proud of who he was and just as obviously very disgusted at the turn of events.

"Then am I correct in assuming that this has something to do with the Van Goff sisters' necklaces?" The Captain asked.

"You can assume that, yes," Tom responded.

"And this Murphy is part of a gang of thieves that has invaded my ship?" The Captain was furious that his ship had been violated.

"Yes, he is, along with Harry Holt and Charlotte Johnson. And, of course, they thought that I was a part of their team, also. Their plan is to steal the necklaces and to put the blame on Mr. Carr in order to create a diversion to let them get away."

"Me! What the hell does this have to do with me?" Terrence Carr demanded.

"Perhaps we should continue this in private," Tom suggested, as he glanced at Frankie and looked at Terrence.

"That's not necessary, we know all about their plan," Frankie answered, before his father had a chance.

"Just what do you know?" Tom asked, beginning to take control of the situation from the Captain.

"We know that they have stolen some minor jewels from the safe and planted them in Mr. Carr's cabin, to try to implicate him," Bruno spoke up.

"They have already broken into the safe?" Captain Swenson said indignantly. With a nod of his head he sent a one of his crewmen to see if this were true.

"Yes, we did already break in and steal a few insignificant pieces and plant them in Mr. Carr's cabin."

"You bastards! Why me?"

"I don't really need to answer that, do I? Obviously your involvement with Charlotte was all intended to set you up to take the fall for this heist. They have been planning it for two years."

"My, my involvement...." Terrence couldn't finish the sentence because of the embarrassment that he felt at being exposed, as not only a cheat but as having been duped so badly, in front of his son.

"We know all about that, but Charlotte doesn't want to be a part of this anymore and has helped us by telling us what was happening and allowed us to remove the jewels and plant them in Horseshit Harry's cabin instead," Bruno said. He was trying to establish that Charlotte was now reformed.

"You did what?" Tom asked.

"We took the jewels out of Mr. Carr's cabin and hid them in Harry Holt's cabin, so that the blame would be shifted away from Mr. Carr and to him," Bruno said, somewhat proud of himself.

"That's just great, now Holt will know that someone is on to him and he will be even more careful. He may even call the whole thing off. Great work kid, you screwed things up really well." Tom was disgusted.

"I'm sorry if we screwed things up, but we couldn't let Mr. Carr get caught up in this situation."

"Thank you, Bruno, and thank you, Frankie. Just how much do you know about this situation?" Terrence asked, the pain in his voice obvious.

"We know everything, Dad," Frankie said softly.

"Everything?" Terrence asked.

"Yes, everything. Including the fact that you have ended it and have offered to help Charlotte," Bruno said.

"This is all very nice gentleman, but I am only interested in getting Harry Holt. He is the mastermind of the gang and everyone else is incidental to me. However, because of your interference, I am probably going to lose my chance to get him. Right now all I have him for is conspiracy to commit a crime and that's not good enough."

"Not necessarily, Stephens, we might be able to salvage the situation." 'The Pol' said. He did not like Tom Stephen's abruptness.

"What do you have in mind, Polaski?" Tom said.

"If we keep this guy, Murphy, under wraps and don't let anyone talk to him and remove the jewels from Holt's room and place them back in Carr's cabin, then Holt won't be any the wiser for it," 'The Pol' said.

"And how will we explain what happened to Murphy?" Tom asked.

"We can tell him exactly what happened, but just leave out the part of your seeing the boys coming out of his cabin and say that I shot him instead of you," 'The Pol' said.

"It might make Holt change his plans, somewhat, but I don't think it will make him give up altogether." Tom's enthusiasm was coming back.

"That leads me to ask just what the hell is his plan? Why did you break into the safe to steal a few minor jewels when you knew that the necklaces were already out and with the sisters and their body guards?" 'The Pol' asked.

"He wanted to get some jewels to plant on Carr to take the pressure off of him," Tom said.

"Ya, but he would have had the same jewels to plant if he had waited and got the necklaces, too. Now the security will be tripled and he won't have a chance. There's something not right here," 'The Pol' said.

"If I knew his plan I would tell you, but I don't. We will just have to let it unfold and be ready for whatever happens."

"I'm not sure that I want this to continue," The Captain said.

"Without my testimony you really have no reason to arrest Holt and, if you do, he could sue you big time," Tom said.

"Is it really necessary to plant the jewels back in my cabin? My wife doesn't know anything about this," Terrence said.

"You should have thought about that before you got involved with your little girl friend," Tom said without any sympathy.

"The deal is that Terrence Carr is going to have to be kept out of this, or it is off," 'The Pol' said without leaving room for negotiation. He knew how important it was to Bruno and Frankie.

"All right, I don't care, he is just a semi-innocent bystander anyway."

"And you have to go to bat for Charlotte to get her leniency for her part in this," Bruno said.

"Listen kid, you are not in any position to dictate terms to me."

"I think that he is, because if you don't agree we will call this whole thing off," Al said in support of his son.

"Even if I agree I'm not sure what I can do to help her." Tom was trying to short-circuit this discussion.

"If you recommend leniency for her cooperation, and with the help that I can give her from the people I know, she will be in good shape," Terrence said.

"I'll do what I can. Okay."

'Pol' knew to get a commitment. "That's not good enough. I want your word that you will do everything that you possibly can to help her."

"All right, you've got my word, Polaski. Actually I don't mind anyway, because I think that she is just a tough luck kid that deserves a little help. So is it settled? Can we get this show on the road?" Tom said in a much more cooperative tone.

"Okay, let's do it then."

"Just a minute gentlemen, I need your assurances that there will be no further gun play and that the safety of my passengers will not be jeopardized," Captain Swenson said.

"We will do the best that we can. We have no interest in having any gun firing either," Tom answered.

"All right, I am not sure that we should do this, but let's go. We will put this Murphy into the brig, under close guard, after the doctor is through with him. Mr. Stephens you will keep me informed of everything that is happening and I will assist you with my security forces as needed," Captain Swenson advised him.

"Thank you Captain Swenson. I will keep you informed as I learn of anything significant. It is my expectation that, once he has taken the jewels, I will just remain with him, keeping him under surveillance, until we arrive in New York and can then have the New York police assist us with all the help that we need," Tom said.

Pol scratched his head, "I still think that there is something very wrong about this."

"Let me worry about that. You and the kids just keep out of this before someone other than Murphy gets hurt," Tom responded sarcastically.

"Don't worry, we are not planning on getting involved any further. Are we boys?" Al said, turning to Bruno and Frankie.

"No, Dad," Bruno said.

"No, sir," Frankie said.

"Come on, Frankie, we have some things that we need to discuss," Terrence said warmly to his son, as he put his arm around him and they left.

"Yes, Bruno, we had better get back to your mother. We are very late and she is going to be very worried." Al then lead Bruno and 'The Pol' back to the party.

As they approached the table, they could see by the look on the faces of Mary and Margaret, who were sitting with the rest of their children, Father Demarco and Sally, that they were really ticked off.

"Where have you guys been? You have been gone for over an hour," Mary said and Margaret nodded her agreement.

"Believe me it is a long story; a very long story. It is getting very late, and we all agreed to meet for a sunrise breakfast to celebrate our last day at sea, so I suggest that we all go back to our cabins and we can fill you ladies in then." Al spoke as calmly as he could, and gave Mary that look that said 'don't argue with me now, but wait until you here the whole story first'.

"Okay, you are probably right. It is late and we have to get up early," Mary said. She couldn't wait to hear what story he had this time.

CHAPTER 25

It was a beautiful morning as they made their way towards the bow of the ship where there was a special sunrise breakfast available on the pool deck. The main group, including the DeGregorio's, except for Bruno, the Carr's, the Wilson's, the Cochran's and Sally Roberts, were already up on deck at the railing having coffee and juice while enjoying the warmth of the sun as it rose out of the ocean and into the sky. Three of the four boys, Frankie, Rosie, and Big Louie, were there with their parents. As a result of the occurrences of the night before, the boys had gladly agreed that they would stay with the adults until the cruise was over. As they looked to their right, towards the ship's stern and at the deck below, they could see Bruno, with 'The Pol' and Father Demarco, coming to join them. The three of them had wanted to take a walk before breakfast.

"I still don't understand why they broke into the safe before the necklaces were put back. And then nothing else happened last night," 'The Pol' said. Although they had all agreed not to talk to anyone about what happened the night before for, fear of it getting back to Holt, they both felt very comfortable with telling Father Tony, especially since it looked like nothing was going to happen anyway.

"It certainly doesn't seem to make very much sense," Father Tony agreed. "Maybe he has decided to call it off."

"Yes, that's possible, I suppose. But I don't think so," 'The Pol' said.

"I don't think so either. Holt is too smart and has too much of an ego to let the jewels go," Bruno agreed.

As they continued to walk, they saw a door open about fifty feet in front of them. Harry Holt stepped through the door and was quickly followed by the Van Goff sister's bodyguards, Hans and Brock. Harry was looking back at Hans, who was handing him a small leather bag. It was this activity that kept them from immediately seeing the group coming towards them.

"That's it! That's why they broke into the safe early. They never wanted the necklaces to be put back into it," 'The Pol' said as he began to reach for his gun.

"No shit! You're right!" Father Tony said.

"Look Harry!" Brock shouted, as he was the first to see them.

As Harry looked up, he was surprised to see anyone on deck so early in the morning; he could immediately see in 'The Pol's eyes and his sudden movement that he understood what they were up to. Because he and Hans were pre-occupied with the bag, it was Brock who had kept at the ready for just such a situation.

"Take him out Brock," Harry ordered. They both knew that he meant 'The Pol', because they knew he was an ex-cop and was probably carrying a gun. Then Harry and Hans would take care of the pain and the ass kid, Bruno, and the priest. Unfortunately 'The Pol' didn't move as fast as he used to and was also slowed down as he moved to push Bruno down and out of the line of fire. Brock responded to Harry's command with lightning speed, since his 9mm pistol was at the ready, concealed just under his coat, and fired off two shots in rapid succession at 'The Pol's heart.

The confrontation was being watched by the shocked group at the sunrise breakfast. They looked on in horror as they saw Brock fire his pistol at their friends and family members.

Fortunately for 'The Pol', Father Tony seemed to have anticipated exactly what was going to happen and stepped in front of him just in time to receive the two bullets square in the chest. Everyone was stunned and Sally screamed in horror, as they saw the bullets rip through the fathers cloak and he staggered backward, but then it was like everything was suspended in time; Father Tony did not fall and was not bleeding. As if in slow motion, he threw his magic robe open, raised his own 9mm Beretta and fired off two shots of his own that hit Brock in the right shoulder and the right leg, effectively disabling him. Both Harry and Hans recovered in time to escape back through the door they had purposely left open.

"Quick, after them!" Father Tony commanded as he crashed through the door, just opposite them in pursuit of Harry and Hans. 'The Pol' and Bruno were right behind him as they entered the inside corridor and were faced with two choices, they could go up or they could go down. They knew that their enemy had the same two choices as they had.

"Is it up or down Pol?" Father Tony asked.

"Definitely up! For them to go down would mean entrapment and Holt is too smart for that. In fact, I'm sure that they were in the process of making their escape when we ran into them and screwed it up," 'The Pol' answered. "And by the way, who the hell are you?"

"You're right, up it is. And who I am can wait until later. Let's go. You stay here Bruno," Father Tony ordered.

"No way, guys, I'm in this thing all the way."

"He's right, Bruno. You had better stay here," 'The Pol' said as he followed the good father up the staircase and toward the main deck.

"Yeah, just like my father would say gentlemen, 'in a pigs ass I will'." Bruno followed close behind them.

In the meantime, the group was recovering from the stunning surprise of the events that just took place.

"I don't understand. Why didn't Tony get hurt from the bullets that hit him?" Sally had more relief than question in her voice.

"I don't know. Maybe we have just seen a case of divine intervention," Mary said as she recovered from her shock.

"Or maybe we have seen the benefits of modern technology in the form of a bullet proof vest," Terrence said.

Al was already on the move, "You're probably right, but whatever, I'm getting over to make sure that Bruno gets the hell out of there."

"I'll go with you Al! You stay here Frankie. You kids stay here, too!" Terrence ordered as he followed Al.

"Be careful you guys," Mary said.

"Yes, please be careful," Margaret repeated.

Al and Terrence then left on the run to go to the aid of Bruno.

A determined look came over Mary's face, "I have to do something, I can't just stand here while my son and my husband are in danger."

"I'm with you Mary. But what?" Margaret said.

"Follow me, if you really want to do something," Mad Madeline said.

"C'mon Madeline, this is no time to go 'Mad' on us again," Bertha said to her knew friend.

"No shit, Bertha, but this is no time for any friggin cheese either. If you ladies really want to do something then you will follow me. And if you don't, then shut up." Madeline said vehemently as she led the way down the forward staircase. Although somewhat surprised by her demeanor, the others followed.

As Father Tony, 'The Pol', and Bruno emerged onto the top deck they immediately took cover behind a rolled up tarpaulin that was close to the door. It was a good thing that they did, because Harry saw them as they came through the door and let go with a burst from his semi-automatic machine pistol and tattooed the lifeboat suspended just behind them. The effect of the power of this gun was not lost on Bruno who noticed that Father Tony's 9mm Berretta and 'The Pol's standard police revolver were badly over matched.

Both Father Tony and 'The Pol' then rose to return the fire in an attempt to pin Holt and Hans down. As they did so, they didn't get more than two shots off before they both ducked back down quickly, very quickly. And, almost instantly, Bruno found out why as he heard the awesome sounds of the extremely rapid fire and saw the bullets rip through the boat behind them. He was in shock as it looked like at least a hundred bullets tore through the boat.

"Holy shit! What the hell was that?" Bruno said.

"That was a friggin Israeli Uzi, Bruno. And I told you to stay below damn it!" 'The Pol' said.

"We are badly overmatched in terms of fire power," Father Tony said. This was said as another round of bullets ripped into the tarpaulin in front of them and the boat behind them. The gunfire was to provide cover as Harry and Hans made their way to the far side of the ship and towards the stern. As they did so, two of the ship's security guards came bursting through a door opposite them. Unfortunately for them, they were spotted immediately by Harry and Hans who opened fire before the guards knew what the hell was happening to them. Fortunately, they both managed to duck back through the door before they were ripped apart.

Hearing this shooting, and realizing that it wasn't aimed at them, both Father Tony and 'The Pol' moved to their left and right, respectively, and popped up firing in Holt's and Han's direction. While their shots were not on target they were timely enough to provide enough of a diversion to allow the security guards to escape with their lives. Then they quickly ducked back behind the tarp as the firepower was leveled at them. After firing a burst at their pursuers, Harry and Hans then continued their journey towards the stern of the ship.

"They definitely want to get to the back of the ship, but I can't see why. When they get there they will be facing a large open deck with very little cover for safety," 'The Pol' said.

"You're right, I don't know why they are heading there either. We can make our way back there by going down this side of the ship and attempt to pin them down when they get to the open deck area," Father Tony said.

"Okay, let's go. And you stay here this time Bruno!" 'The Pol' ordered as he followed Father Tony's lead.

They quickly made their way to the stern deck, exchanging gunfire with Harry and Hans as they went. While they made their way as quickly as they could towards the stern they were also careful to make sure that neither one of their enemies circled back on them and hoped that they would soon get some help from the ships security force, such as it was, to help even out the fire power.

"Where the hell is he, Harry?" Hans said.

"He is not due for another three minutes, Hans. It wouldn't be a problem if it weren't for that stupid cop and their early morning walk," Harry said.

"And what the hell is with this friggin priest?" Hans said.

"I don't know, but I don't think that there are very many priests that wear bullet proof vests," Harry said. "Fortunately, for now, we have the fire power advantage but, if he doesn't get here soon, I am afraid that the ships security will eventually change that."

"I'm afraid you're right. We are going to have to split up and spread out a little more to take full advantage of our firepower and to handle the next group of security guards they throw at us. I'll go back towards the middle of the ship to protect our rear and double our fire zone," Hans said, his military background showing.

"Okay, let me know when you're ready and I'll lay down some cover fire, but move quickly because we are running out of ammunition," Harry said.

"Get ready, NOW!" Hans said as he fired a frightening burst from his Uzi and raced for a spot of cover about twenty yards away, trying to stay as low as possible. As he ran, Harry continued his firing; keeping the priest and the cop pinned down.

"What's happening?" Father Tony asked, as they kept as low as they could to avoid the barrage leveled at them.

"I'm not sure, but my guess is that they have spread out to reduce themselves as a target and to take advantage of their fire power. If that's so, the next time we stick our heads up they have a better chance of blowing them off. Especially since there is at least one of them that we are not exactly sure where he is," 'The Pol' answered.

"That was my guess, too. Unfortunately, if we are right, that means one of them could be circling around on us and we will end up in a cross fire as well as being out gunned," Father Tony said, moving into a crouch position getting ready to take a chance and rise up and fire at them.

"What the hell do you think that you are doing?" 'The Pol' said.

"We've got to get some shots off at them to keep them from moving on us anymore or we're dead," Father Tony responded.

"Do that and they'll blow your head off. That bulletproof vest won't do you any good against a headshot; and you can bet that they will be aiming for your head," the Pol' said. "What we need is a diversion so that we can find out where they are before they can turn their fire back on us. Then, at least, we will be able to fire in their general direction and keep them off balance and under cover."

As 'The Pol' said this they looked back at Bruno and saw him pointing in the direction of Harry and Hans. Apparently he had seen their movement and was now trying to tell them where they were, but this wasn't working because his motions were not precise enough to be of much good. Then they saw 'the kid' point to his own chest and then straight up in the air. To their terror they both understood that he was going to expose himself so that they could get a fix on their enemy. They both were about to shout no when they saw Bruno turn and get ready to move; they realized it was too late, and the best thing they could do for him was to be ready to shoot.

Bruno counted to himself and on three took a deep breath and stood up. He was immediately spotted by both Harry and Hans; they turned in his direction and fired. The fact that they had to turn slightly and refocus on him gave Bruno the split second that he needed to duck back down and narrowly escape being hit as a fusillade of bullets rained just over his head. He lay there crouched down and had the mixed emotions of so much fear that he damn near shit his pants and the adrenalin high that prepared him for whatever he needed to do next.

As soon as Bruno had stood up, Father Tony and 'The Pol' moved in position to fire, the good father focused on where Harry and Hans had been and 'The Pol' took on the job of locating the new position. They were good at their work and were quick to fire on their enemy with Father Tony shooting off half a dozen shots in rapid succession to force Harry to take cover. 'The Pol' took a different approach since he had never taken to the new 9mm, as many of his police brethren had, but preferred to stick with his standard .38 caliber police revolver. He preferred to rely on fewer, but more accurate shots and he always found the .38 to be more accurate, and more powerful, than the 9mm and, since he invariably rated as a sharpshooter, it was hard to argue with him. So he took his time, which took ice water in his veins since he was facing a man who was about to aim an Uzi at him, and popped off one shot that tore through Han's shoulder and knocked him to the deck, but Harry was then able to return the fire in time to allow Hans to crawl back to cover with his Uzi.

"Nice shot Pol, but I wish the hell that the ship's security force would show itself again," Father Tony said.

"Yea, me too. They are obviously not professionals, but we could use any firepower they could provide. Especially since I have a bad feeling about this," 'The Pol' said.

"What are you thinking?" Father Tony asked.

"I don't know, Tony, but I do know that they weren't just out for a morning stroll and they wanted to get to the stern deck very badly; which makes me want to get off of here," 'The Pol' said.

It was at this point that Al, Terrence, and Frankie burst through the door behind Bruno and dove to his side just as the door was riddle with bullets. Then Father Tony and 'The Pol' returned the fire taking the pressure off of the others only to have it redirected at them again.

Finally, there was the sound of semi-automatic rifle fire coming from the tower at the bow of the ship directed at Harry and Hans. It was a good vantage point that offered excellent protection for Captain Swenson and one of his security officers. This forced Harry and Hans to return their fire; taking the pressure off of Father Tony and 'The Pol'. It also had the effect of forcing them to use up all of their ammunition. Under intense pressure from the semi-automatic rifle fire coming from the tower and the fire coming from Tony and 'The Pol', Harry and Hans signaled that they were prepared to give up.

"Hold your fire we are ready to surrender," Harry shouted.

"Hold your fire, hold your fire," 'The Pol' shouted. "Okay, both of you come out and leave your guns behind."

As both of them came out from behind their cover, Father Tony proceeded towards Hans and 'The Pol' stepped out onto the open stern deck and walked towards Harry. That's when it happened. That's when they first heard the unmistakable 'thup, thup, thup' of the helicopter that suddenly rose from the stern of the ship and descended upon them without warning, and with bullets blazing from the AK47 being fired by the man sitting in the passenger seat. 'The Pol' was the first one in its path and just managed to dive out of the way as the bullets tore up the deck where he had been standing. Unfortunately, in escaping certain death, he hit his head and lay there stunned.

The chopper continued flying directly towards the tower; firing on them before they could overcome their initial shock and fire back. They barely managed to scramble inside and jump down the small stairway as the tower was riddled with bullets that ripped through the thin metal. The chopper then turned to head back to the stern of the ship, where it could land and pick up Holt and the others, and would kill anyone who was in the way.

As it was turning to come back, 'The Pol' was on one knee, struggling to get up. He was going to be caught in the open and would be dead meat. Seeing this, Bruno was already moving to help him. As the helicopter was coming back it managed to keep Father Tony pinned down, after he had empty his clip at them. He was now forced to stay under cover while he was searching for his last clip. Harry was moving into position to run for the chopper as soon as it set down; he knew it would have to take off before it actually even touched down or they risked being caught on the deck and would be an easy target. He could see that Hans had been hit in the leg as well as the shoulder, probably by the shooters on the tower, and was not going to be able to make it to the rendezvous point. That was too bad, but there was no way that he could help him and still get away.

"Bruno no! Don't go out there!" Al shouted as he followed him. If he couldn't stop him he wouldn't let him go out there alone.

Just as the two of them reached 'The Pol' the chopper was above them, but the gunner was on the wrong side and the pilot was just about to swing the craft around when he saw something that he had never seen before. Fluttering right in front of him was a giant butterfly. For a moment he was mesmerized because this was impossible, not even a large bird could withstand the turbulence created by the chopper blades, but here was this butterfly staring him in the face, seemingly unaffected. Then the pilot was brought out of his trance by the gunner and continued his turn while the butterfly flew away. The delay had given them added time to begin to drag 'The Pol' to cover, but it was not enough. The gunner now had the three of them directly in his sights.

"Turn this friggin thing around so I can get a shot at them. That's it I have them in my sights now," the gunner shouted.

BAM! BAM! BAM! BAM! BAM! BAM! BAM! BAM! BAM! BAM! BAM! BAM! BAM! BAM! BAM! BAM! BAM! BAM! BAM! BAM! BAM! BAM! BAM! BAM!

"What the hell was that?" The pilot said as the gunner reeled in pain, dropping his gun, and pulling back in his seat. The pilot could see that his arm and shoulder were peppered with small holes that were oozing blood as the hammers of hell were exploding all around him.

This gave Bruno and his father the chance they needed to get 'The Pol' to cover. Then they looked back to see what was happening. All they could tell was that the shooting was coming from the very stern of the ship.

What they didn't know was who was doing the shooting, but they sure as hell would be surprised when they found out. The awesome barrage of gunfire was being generated by 'Mad' Madeline and her band of angry mothers.

They had gone below deck and worked their way to the stern, where the skeet shooting had taken place earlier in the week. They convinced the ship's officer in charge, threatened him is more like it, to unlock the cabinet containing the shotguns and ammunition used for the skeet shooting. Having loaded a dozen guns, they prepared themselves for action. It was Mary, Big Bertha, and 'Mad' Madeline that did the shooting and Margaret and Sally handed them new, fully loaded, shotguns as they needed them.

Both Mary and Big Bertha took the more is better approach and fired off as many shots in as short a time as possible. This was somewhat difficult for Mary as she had never shot a gun before, and the recoil was hard for her to handle, but her son and her husband were out their and she was doing a credible job under the circumstances. The story was different with Big Bertha, she was no more accurate than Mary, but she was a lot more productive. Given the strength and the bulk that she had going for her she was able to fire off shots in such rapid succession that it almost looked like she had an automatic weapon. Both Sally and Margaret had a hard time keeping her supplied with freshly loaded shotguns. This barrage, though very inaccurate, was effective; for the noise and sheer volume of shot leveled at or near the chopper was frightening.

However, the most effective shooting came from 'Mad' Madeline who took the rifle rather than the shotgun approach. She took careful aim and squeezed off her shots with the precision she had learned as a girl hunting in the mountains of Montana with her father. It was her shots that hit the gunner and caused him to drop his weapon. It was also her shots that hit the hydraulic line and caused the chopper to start to smoke and behave erratically.

The pilot was struggling with all his skill to keep his craft from plunging and slamming into the deck, while the gunner was fighting to remain conscious. They had to abandon all thoughts of landing and picking up Harry and instead pulled the helicopter up and headed back for home base, leaving a trail of smoke behind.

Suddenly, Harry found himself in the open with no weapon and nowhere to hide. Then he saw the AK47 that had fallen from the chopper and he raced to pick it up. As he did, he felt the cold steel of the pistol pressed against his temple.

"Go ahead Harry, if you think you are quick enough or if you just want to end it all right here. I would be happy to accommodate you," Father Tony said.

He knew that he had no chance to turn this situation to his advantage; he decided to surrender and live to fight another day. So Harry dropped the gun and put his hands behind his back in order not to give his captor any excuses to shoot him.

"Oh that's too bad, Harry. I would have loved to end it all now." Father Tony picked up the AK47 and directed Harry towards the others.

"Thank you Bruno, Al. I'm okay now." 'The Pol' gained his feet and was able to stand on his own.

While Father Tony approached the others, with Harry under guard, the ship's security guards and the ship's doctor carried Hans away on a stretcher and under tight security.

"I'll take that Mr. Holt," Captain Swenson said as he took the bag containing the jewels.

Then Mary, Margaret, Sally, Big Bertha and 'Mad' Madeline came running up to them. Both Mary and Margaret gave their husbands and sons a big hug and Sally ran up to Father Tony and gave him a big hug and kiss.

"I'm so glad that you are all right and that you are not a priest. Your not are you? I mean priests don't wear bulletproof vests and carry guns. Do they?" Sally was excited and relieved so she was babbling somewhat.

"Not that I know of. And no, I am not a priest. I am an FBI agent and I was here under cover to try to catch this jewel theft gang that has been working out of New York City," Tony said as he gave Sally another big hug and kiss.

Everyone was in such a celebrating mood they didn't see Brock, who had managed to crawl up the stairs and now was just inside the door to the stairway, and was about to burst through. After being wounded by Tony, no one paid any attention to him as they chased the others.

Suddenly, the door burst open and Brock stumbled through, bleeding from his leg and his shoulder, but with his gun held in his left hand and pointed at them, ready to fire. Everyone was stunned, as they were caught flat footed, and they knew that someone was going to die.

"BAM"

The explosion of the gun caused everyone to winch, but the only one that felt the searing pain was Brock. Everyone was shocked to see him writhing in pain as the blood spurted from his left shoulder. Then they saw Tom Stephens standing behind him holding a smoking gun. Harry had knocked him unconscious, because the chopper would be at capacity with himself, Hans, and Brock; there was no room for Tom. Fortunately, Tom had come to and was able to get up on deck just in time to save them from Brock.

Unfortunately, while everyone was concentrating on Brock, Harry grabbed Bruno and had him hanging over the rail, holding him by the feet.

"Bring him back in, Holt!" Captain Swenson ordered.

"Yeah right, Captain. And you can kiss my arse, too," Harry said.

"He is right, Harry. If you let that kid go, you will be up for murder as well as grand theft," Tony said.

"I don't give a shit. I would just as soon die as spend time in prison," Harry answered.

"If you hurt him I will make you pay dearly," Al said as he swung his leg over the railing in an effort to be in position to help his son.

Then 'The Pol' calmly walked up to Harry, stuck his revolver into his crotch, and cocked the hammer.

"I know that you are not afraid to die, Harry, but I do think that you are afraid of spending the next thirty years in prison as a friggin eunuch." 'The Pol' was dead serious.

"You wouldn't do it," Harry said looking down into the water, as if he were searching for something.

"I wouldn't hesitate for a second," 'The Pol' said.

Again Harry searched the water below and then it appeared that he spotted something.

"Okay, Pol, I'll bring the kid in—just give me a little space," Harry said as he began to pull Bruno back up. As he got him all the way over the railing he then pushed him onto 'The Pol' and jumped up and over the railing and sixty feet down into the sea. No one could believe their eyes, as they had just witnessed Harry Holt jumping to his death. They all looked down over the railing, but they could not see any trace of Harry as the ship continued to quickly slip away.

"I don't think that he could have survived that, and, if he did, he will most likely drown before we can find him, if we ever do. We will immediately put a boat over the side to look for him but, by the time that we do, we will already be two to three miles away from the spot," Captain Swenson said.

"Shouldn't we stop the ship and look for him right away?" Mary asked.

"I'm sorry, Mrs. DeGregorio, but, even if I did stop the engines now, it would be another twenty-five miles before we came to a stop. We will also radio the Coast Guard and get them to send a helicopter and a cutter to look for him," Captain Swenson said.

With everyone emotionally exhausted there was nothing left to do, but to go back to their cabins and finish getting their things together for the departure at mid-day.

What no one on the ship could see was the two-man mini-sub that had picked up Harry. There was never any question that Harry was a very smart man, and he was also a man that believed in having more than one option available at all times. He didn't get his jewels, but he would live to get another chance. He vowed that he would get another chance at that kid, too.

※   ※   ※

As they were waiting in the terminal, in yet another line to get their luggage delivered, they reflected on how happy they were to be returning home and its relative peace and quite.

"I am really glad that, between Tony and Tom Stephens representing the police, and Terrence handling the legal portion, we were able to give our depositions on the ship and they are letting us go straight home," Mary said.

"Yeah, but I'm glad that we are all going to have to come back in a month or so to testify against Hans and Brock. That will give us a chance to meet with our friends again," Bruno said.

"Yes, well all I want to do now is get home where I can relax and recover from this vacation from hell," Al said.

"Oh, come on Al, it wasn't that bad," Mary said.

"All I know is that I hope that our driver is a middle aged guy with thirty years of experience, who refuses to go over fifty-five miles per hour, and knows where the hell he is going," Al said as they emerged from the terminal. Immediately he knew he spoke too soon.

"Hey, Mr. Al! Mr. Al! It's me, Nadine! They let me out of jail and gave me my license back just in time for me to drive you all back to Boston. Isn't that great!" Nadine came bouncing up to them with a huge smile on her face.

Upon hearing this, 'Mad' Madeline streaked across the terminal and, with an effort worthy of the Olympics, leaped up and over the railing and into the harbor. This time 'Happy' Harold didn't try to stop her; instead he followed close behind. 'Big' Louie made a dash for the nearest nachos and cheese stand. Bertha said that she had better go to the bathroom now; much to Willy's delight. Another woman decided to skip the preliminaries and, recognizing the inevitable, wet her pants. Next to her, a man began to strangle his wife for no apparent reason. As the port authority police were dragging him away, he was mumbling incoherently about having some kind of flashback that his wife was whining and moaning uncontrollably and it was driving him crazy.

"Oh God! Why me? Why me?" As soon as he said this, Al knew that he was in trouble. He could see from the look in their eyes, and the big grin on their faces, that he was going to get their answer in no uncertain terms as he uttered these fateful words-

'Et Tu Brute'.

"That's right, Al, because—

"SHIT HAPPENS!!!"